DETECTION UNLIMITED

GEORGETTE HEYER

An Owl Book

HOLT, RINEHART AND WINSTON
New York

Library of Congress Cataloging in Publication Data
Heyer, Georgette, 1902–1974.
Detection unlimited.
I. Title.
PR6015.E795D4   1985   823′.912   84-19739
ISBN: 0-03-003298-9 (An Owl bk.) (pbk.)

First published in hardcover by
E.P. Dutton, Inc., in 1969.

First Owl Book Edition—1985

Printed in the United States of America
10 9 8 7 6 5 4 3 2 1

ISBN 0-03-003298-9

Author's Note
To all such persons as may imagine that they recognize themselves in it, with the author's assurance that they are mistaken

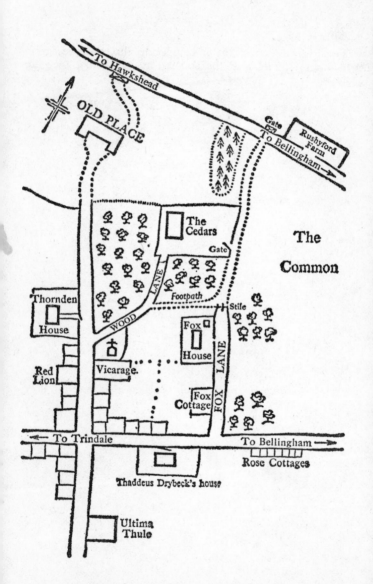

CHAPTER ONE

MR. THADDEUS DRYBECK, stepping from the neat gravel drive leading from his house on to the road, found his further progress challenged, and, indeed, impeded, by the sudden onrush of several Pekinese dogs, who bounced and barked asthmatically about his feet. Repressing a desire to sweep them from his path with the tennis-racquet he was carrying, he used this instead to guard his ankles, for one of Mrs. Midgeholme's Pekes was known to bite.

"Shoo!" said Mr. Drybeck testily. "Get away!"

The Pekes, maddened to frenzy by this form of address, bounced and barked more than ever; and one of them made a dart at Mr. Drybeck's racquet.

"Peekies, Peekies!" trilled a new voice, in loving reproach. "Naughty! Come to Mother at once! It's only their play, Mr. Drybeck."

Three of the Pekes, feeling that the possibilities of the situation had been exhausted, abandoned their prey; the fourth, standing four-square before Mr. Drybeck, continued to bark and growl at him until snatched up into the arms of her owner, who dealt her a fond slap, and said: "Isn't she a pet? This is Mother's eldest little girl, aren't you, my treasure? Now, say you're sorry to poor Mr. Drybeck!"

Mr. Drybeck, perceiving that the animal was being thrust towards him, recoiled.

"Oh, you've hurt her feelings!" said Mrs. Midgeholme, kissing the top of the Peke's head. "Wouldn't he shake hands with you, Ursula? Never mind!"

The expression in Ursula's indignantly bulging eyes appeared to be one of loathing rather than of hurt, but this reflection Mr. Drybeck kept to himself, merely saying in his precise way: "I fear I am not fond of dogs."

"I'm sure you are *really,*" said Mrs. Midgeholme, unwilling to think ill of a fellow-creature. Her eyes, which, from their slight protuberance, bore a resemblance to those of her dogs, ran over him appraisingly. "I expect you're off to the Haswells'," she said sapiently. "You're a great tennis-player, aren't you?"

Mr. Drybeck disclaimed, but felt the description to be just. In his youth he had spent his every summer holiday competing in tournaments, and to his frequent success the row of trophies upon the mantleshelf in his dining-room bore testimony. His style of play was oldfashioned, like everything else about him, but the young men who considered him a desiccated exponent of pat-ball nevertheless found him a difficult adversary to beat. He was by profession a solicitor, the last surviving member of a firm long-established in the neighbouring town of Bellingham. He had never married, was extremely precise in all his ways, and disliked nearly every form of modern progress: a circumstance which possibly accounted for the sadly diminishing numbers of his clients. The older members of the community amongst which he had lived all his life remained faithful to him, but the younger men seemed to prefer the methods employed by his rival and *bête noire*, Mr. Sampson Warrenby, an upstart of no more than fifteen years standing in the district. Sampson Warrenby's rapidly expanding business, at first a small thorn in Mr. Drybeck's flesh, was fast assuming the proportions of a menace; and since the day, just after the War ended, when he had had the bad taste to move his private residence from Bellingham to the hitherto select village of Thornden, it had become impossible for the indignant Mr. Drybeck to continue to be socially unaware of his existence. He had bought a house in the lane which debouched on to the main Bellingham road at a point almost opposite Mr. Drybeck's small but ancestral home.

"Alas, *my* tennis days are over!" proclaimed Mrs. Midgeholme. "But you'll meet my Lion."

Mr. Drybeck was unalarmed. Major Midgeholme, who had been given the name of Lionel by optimistic parents, was a shy man of retiring habits, quite cast into the shade by his kind-hearted but somewhat overpowering wife.

"I'll walk with you as far as the corner," pursued Mrs. Midgeholme, tucking Ursula under her arm. "Unless you mean to go by way of the lane?"

The lane, which served the little house rented by Miss Patterdale, at the corner, and, farther down and facing the common, Mr. Warrenby's residence, led, by way of a stile, to the footpath which flanked the Haswells' large garden, and ran on beside the Squire's eastern plantations to join the northern and secondary road to Bellingham. There was a gate at the bottom of the Haswells' garden, but although this would certainly have been Mr. Drybeck's shortest route he would have thought it very improper to have presented himself at the house by way of a private back-gate. So he politely fell into step beside Mrs. Midgeholme, and accompanied her down the road to where the main village street intersected it. Since the Pekes had to be continually admonished, conversation was of a desultory nature. Mr. Drybeck, wincing at his companion's frequent shrieks to Umbrella, Umberto, and Uppish, was forced to remind himself, not for the first time, that Flora Midgeholme was a goodnatured and a plucky woman, who bore uncomplainingly the hardships of a straitened income, eked it out by dispensing with the services of a maid and by breeding dogs, and always presented to the world the part of a woman well-satisfied with her lot. Only he did wish that she wouldn't call her dogs such absurd names.

But this was unavoidable. On his retirement from the army, Major Midgeholme had built a bungalow in Thornden, at the end of the village street, where the tarred road ended and a mere cart-track led across the fields to a small farm. Mrs. Midgeholme had conceived the pretty idea of calling the bungalow Ultima Thule; and when, in course of time, she began to breed Pekes Ultima had seemed to her the only possible patronymic to bestow upon them. Ultima Ulysses and Ultima Una, the progenitors of a long and lucrative line, received their alliterative names in a moment of impulsive inspiration. Ursula, Urban, and Urania had followed, and by that time the custom of alliteration had been established, and the supply of proper names was running out. Umberto, Uriah, and Ulrica exhausted it, and succeeding generations of puppies received their names from the pages of a dictionary. "But, after all," said Mrs. Midgeholme, looking on the bright side, "they *are* rather quaint, aren't they? And Unready won two firsts and two seconds at Cruft's."

In the intervals of summoning Umberto, Umbrella, and Uppish out of other people's gardens, Mrs. Midgeholme confided to her companion that although she had been invited to The Cedars to watch the tennis, and to take tea, she had been obliged to refuse. "For I don't mind telling you, Mr. Drybeck, that I doubt if I could trust myself."

"Dear me!" said Mr. Drybeck, startled.

"Not," said Mrs. Midgeholme, her eye kindling, "if I am expected to speak to Mr. Warrenby. And if he's there, which of course he will be, nothing would stop me giving him a piece of my mind! So I'm not going."

"I am exceedingly sorry. I was unaware that there was any—ah—estrangement getween you and Warrenby."

"No, well, it only happened yesterday. Not but what I never have liked the man, and between you and me and the gatepost his behaviour to Lion during the War, when Lion was absolutely *running* the Home Guard, *finished* him for me! But that he could be cruel to dumb animals I did *not* suspect."

"Dear, dear!" said Mr. Drybeck. "One of your dogs?"

"Ulysses!" said Mrs. Midgeholme. "*Ulysses!* I popped in to speak to that unfortunate niece of Mr. Warrenby's about the Conservative Whist Drive, and took the dear old fellow with me. That brutal man kicked him!"

"Good gracious!" said Mr. Drybeck. "You don't mean it?"

"I do mean it. He actually boasted of it! Had the effrontery to tell me, when I demanded to know why my angel had

9

yelped, and come limping into the house, that he had kicked him off one of the flower-beds. I fairly exploded!"

Mr. Drybeck could believe it. The mere recollection of the outrage caused Mrs. Midgeholme's ample bosom to swell, and her rather florid complexion to assume an alarmingly high colour. He made soothing noises.

"I should have said a great deal more than I did if I hadn't been sorry for poor little Mavis!" declared Mrs. Midgeholme. "It wasn't her fault; though, if you were to ask me, I should say that she's a perfect fool not to put her foot down! However, if she likes to make a doormat of herself it's no concern of mine. But when it comes to ill-treating one of my Peekies it's a very different matter! Not one word will I speak to him until he's apologized, and so I told him. And if I were to go to The Cedars and find him there I should tell him exactly what I think of him, which would make things uncomfortable for Mrs. Haswell. So I'm not going." She gave Ursula a hitch, tucking her more securely under her arm, and added: "What's more, it will serve him right if Mavis runs off with that Pole—not that I think she would, and I hope very much she won't do anything silly, because he hasn't got any prospects that I know of, besides being a foreigner. But there it is!"

"Pole?" repeated Mr. Drybeck blankly.

"Oh, don't you know him? He works at Bebside's, and lives in the end one of the row of cottages beyond you," said Mrs. Midgeholme. "At least, he lodges there. Old Mrs. Dockray," she added, for his further enlightenment.

"I fancy I have not met the young man," said Mr. Drybeck, in a tone that gave little indication of his wishing to do so.

"Well, I daresay you wouldn't have. He hasn't been here long, and though I believe he's quite all right—I mean, his father is supposed to have had estates in Poland, and that sort of thing—one never knows with foreigners, does one? Actually, I met him at the Lindales', but, of course, he isn't generally received. I don't know how Mavis came to know him, but I'm sure I don't grudge her a little fun, for it's not much she gets. He's very attractive. So good-looking, and such lovely manners! I'm not surprised poor Mavis is a bit smitten."

"Are you perhaps referring to a dark youth who rides a particularly noisy motor-bicycle?" enquired Mr. Drybeck, in repulsive accents.

"Yes, that's the one. Ladislas Zama-something-or-other: I never can get my tongue round it. There's Lion! Look who's coming, Peekies! Run and meet Father!"

They had by this time reached the cross-road. To the left could be seen the unimpressive figure of Major Midgeholme, trying to preserve his white flannels from the excited advances of the Ultimas, who were barking and jumping at him; to the right the village street led, past the Church and the Vicarage, to the lane winding up to the front drive of The Cedars. Beyond this lane, the street continued, serving a few small shops and picturesque cottages, and Mr. Gavin Plenmeller's Queen Anne house, which was set back from it in a walled garden. It then ran between hedges through open country until it came to an end at the imposing, though sadly worn gates of Old Place, the Squire's home.

Thornden could boast of no village green, or ancient stocks, but it contained, in addition to several houses built in more elegant ages, which any house-agent would have described as gentlemen's residences, a good many half-timbered cottages of honest antiquity, and a Perpendicular Church with a Jacobean rood screen, photographs of which had been reproduced in at least three books on Ecclesiastical Architecture. The Vicarage was of Victorian date, and had apparently been designed to accommodate a large family; but besides Old Place, which had all the charm of a house built in the sixteenth century and enlarged by succeeding generations, there was Gavin Plenmeller's rose-red gem in the High Street; Mr. Henry Haswell's solid Georgian mansion at the end of Wood Lane; the rather older but less important house inhabited by Sampson Warrenby, in Fox Lane; and Mr. Drybeck's unpretentious but seemly residence on the Trindale-Bellingham road. The village, which included Old Place, with its wide domain, lay in the broad half of the triangle of the roads connecting Bellingham with Trindale, on the south, and Hawkshead, on the north, the narrow part of the triangle being occupied by common-land, which was, in fact, intersected by the northern road. Miss Patterdale's old-world and extremely inconvenient cottage faced on to his; and also Mr. Warrenby's Fox House. It was a gravel common, with one or two pits, and a great many gorse-bushes; and it provided the youth of the village with football grounds and cricket pitches, and Miss Patterdale with grazing for her two goats.

Major Midgeholme, having repelled the Pekes, joined his helpmate and Mr. Drybeck, as they stood together at the corner of the street. He was a slight man of medium height, with grizzled hair, and a toothbrush moustache. It was tacitly assumed, since he had been retired with the rank of Major, that his military career had been undistinguished, but when the Local Defence Volunteer organisation had been formed in the second year of the War he had surprised his neighbours by disclosing unsuspected talents. As the only military man in the district who was not of fighting age it had fallen to him to raise and train the first recruits. This he had done with conspicuous success, even inducing the two most noted poachers in the neighbourhood not only to join the force, but to present

11

themselves occasionally at drill-parades. There was no doubt that he had been in his element, and had enjoyed the War very much. With the peace he had sunk back into the position of playing second fiddle to his wife, who, ironically enough, never ceased to regale her acquaintance with tales of his military efficiency, sage civil judgment, and general competence to deal brilliantly with any situation that might arise.

She greeted him now with bright affection. "Well met, Lion! Just off to The Cedars? Give my love to Mrs. Haswell. Any news?"

This question was uttered rather tensely. The Major, bestowing a nod and a small, perfunctory smile upon Mr. Drybeck, replied undramatically: "No, I don't think so."

"Thank God!" uttered Mrs. Midgeholme, supplying all that was lacking in her husband's tone. "I was of two minds about leaving the house, for I thought she seemed the wee-est bit restless." She directed a conspiratorial smile at Mr. Drybeck, and admitted him into the mystery, saying archly: "A Happy Event! My treasured Ullapool's first litter!"

Mr. Drybeck could think of nothing better to say than: "Indeed!" and the Major, whose consciousness of his wife's absurdities impelled him to do what he could to justify them, said apologetically: "Delicate little beggars, you know!"

"No, Lion! *Not* delicate!" said Mrs. Midgeholme. "But with a first litter one can't be too careful. Ullapool will be looking for Mother to come and hold her paw. I must away! Play well, both of you! Come, Peekies! Come with Mother!"

With these words, and a wave of one hand, she set off down the street, leaving the two men to proceed in the opposite direction, towards Wood Lane.

"Extraordinarily intelligent, those Pekes," said the Major, in a confidential tone. "Sporting, too. You wouldn't think it to look at them, but if you take them on the common they're down every rabbit-hole."

Mr. Drybeck, schooling his features to an expression of spurious interest, said: "Really?" and tried unavailingly to think of something to add to this unencouraging response. Fortunately, they had reached the first of the shops, which combined groceries with haberdashery and stationery, and also harboured the Post Office, and a diversion was created by the emergence from its portals of Miss Miriam Patterdale, vigorously affixing a stamp to a postcard. She accorded them a curt nod, and thrust the card into the letter-box, saying cryptically: "*That's* to the laundry! We shall see what excuse they can think up this time. I suppose you're going to the Haswells'? You'll find Abby there. I'm told she plays quite a good game."

"Very creditable indeed," agreed Mr. Drybeck. "A strong backhand, unusual in one of her sex."

12

"Nonsense!" said Miss Patterdale, disposing of this without compunction. "Time you stopped talking like an Edwardian, Thaddeus. No patience with it!"

"I fear," said Mr. Drybeck, with a thin smile, "that I am quite an old fogy."

"Nothing to be proud of in that," said Miss Patterdale, correctly divining his attitude.

Mr. Drybeck was silenced. He had known Miss Patterdale for a number of years, but she had never lost her power to intimidate him. She was a weatherbeaten spinster of angular outline and sharp features. She invariably wore suits of severe cut, cropped her gray locks extremely short, and screwed a monocle into one eye. But this was misleading: her sight really was irregular. She was the older daughter of the late Vicar of the parish, and upon his death, some ten years previously, she had removed from the Vicarage to the cottage at the corner of Fox Lane, from which humble abode she still exercised a ruthless but beneficent tyranny over the present incumbent's parishioners. Since the Reverend Anthony Cliburn's wife was a of a shy and a retiring nature, only too thankful to have her responsibilities wrested from her by a more forceful hand, not the smallest unpleasantness had every arisen between the ladies. Mrs. Cliburn was frequently heard to say that she didn't know what any of them would do without Miriam; and Miss Patterdale, responding to this tribute, asserted in a very handsome spirit, that although Edith hadn't an ounce of commonsense or moral courage she did her best, and always meant well.

"Are we to have the pleasure of seeing you at The Cedars, Miss Patterdale?" asked the Major, breaking an uncomfortable silence.

"No, my dear man, you are not. I don't play tennis—never did!—and if there's one thing I bar it's watching country-house games. Besides, someone's got to milk the goats."

"It's a curious thing," said the Major, "but try as I will I can't like goats' milk. My wife occasionally used it during the War-years, but I never acquired a liking for it."

"It would have been more curious if you had. Filthy stuff!" said Miss Patterdale candidly. "The villagers think it's good for their children: that's why I keep the brutes. Oh, well! There's a lot of nonsense talked about children nowadays: the truth is that they thrive on any muck."

Upon which trenchant remark she favoured them with another of her curt nods, screwed her monocle more securely into place, and strode off down the street.

"Remarkable woman, that," observed the Major.

"Yes, indeed," responded Mr. Drybeck unenthusiastically.

"Extraordinarily pretty girl, that niece of hers. Not a bit like her, is she?"

"Her mother—Fanny Patterdale that was—was always considered the better-looking of the sisters," said Mr. Drybeck repressively. "I fancy you were not acquainted with her."

"No, before my time," agreed the Major, realizing that he had been put in his place by the Second Oldest Inhabitant, and submitting to it. "I'm a comparative newcomer, of course."

"Hardly that, Midgeholme," said Mr. Drybeck, rewarding this humility as it deserved. "Compared to the Squire and me, and, I suppose I should add, Plenmeller, perhaps you might be considered a newcomer. But the place has seen many changes of late years."

"And not all of them for the better," said the Major. "Tempora mores, eh?"

Mr. Drybeck winced slightly, and said in a pensive voice, as though to himself: "O tempora, O mores! Perhaps one would rather say tempora mutantur."

The Major, prevented by circumstance from expressing any such preference, attempted no response. Mr. Drybeck said: "One is tempted to finish the tag, but I do not feel that I for one have changed very much with the times. It is sometimes difficult to repress a wish that our little community had not altered so sadly. I find myself remembering the days when the Brotherlees owned The Cedars—not that I have anything to say in disparagement of the Haswells, very estimable people, I am sure, but not, it must be owned, quite like the Brotherlees."

"Not at all, no," said the Major, in all sincerity. "Well, for one thing, the Brotherlees never entertained, did they? I must say, I think the Haswells are a distinct aquisition to Thornden. Nice to see that fine old house put into good order again, too. But if you're thinking of the present owner of Fox House, why, there I'm with you! A very poor exchange for the Churnsikes, I've always held—and I'm not the only one of that opinion."

Mr. Drybeck looked pleased, but only said, in a mild voice: "Rather a fish out of water, poor Warrenby."

"I can't think what induced him to move out of the town," said the Major. "I should have said he was a good deal more in his element in the Melkinton Road than he'll ever be at Fox House. Not by any means a pukka sahib, as we used to say in the good old days. Ah, well! It takes all sorts to make a world, I suppose."

Mr. Drybeck agreed to this, but as though he found it a regrettable thing; and the two gentlemen walked on in meditative silence. As they reached the corner of Wood Lane, Gavin Plenmeller came out of the gate set in the wall of Thornden House, and limped across the road towards them. He was a slight, dark young man, a little under thirty, with a quick, lively countenance, and a contraction in one leg, which had been caused by his having suffered from hip-disease in his childhood.

It had precluded him from taking any very active part in the War, and was held, by the charitable, to account for the frequent acidity of his conversation. He had inherited Thornden House, together with what remained, after excessive taxation, of a moderate fortune, from his half-brother rather more than a year previously, and was not felt to be a newcomer to the district. He had been used to living in London, supplementing a small patrimony by writing detective stories; but he had visited Thornden at frequent intervals, generally remaining under his brother's roof until the combination of his mocking tongue and Walter's nerve-racked irritability resulted in an inevitable quarrel —if a situation could be called a quarrel in which one man exploded with exasperation, and the other laughed, and shrugged his thin shoulders. Walter had taken an all-too active part in the War, and had emerged from it in a condition nearly resembling a mental and physical wreck, his temper uncertain, and his strength no more than would allow him to pursue, in a spasmodic way, his old, passionate hobbies of entomology and bird-watching. After each rift with Gavin he had sworn never to have the young waster in the house again; but when Gavin, wholly impervious to insult, once more arrived on his doorstep he invariably admitted him, and even, for several days, enjoyed his companionship. His indifferent health made him disinclined to see society, and when he died, and Gavin succeeded to his place, even persons of all-embracing charity, such as Mavis Warrenby, could scarcely regret the change. Gavin was not popular, for he took no trouble to conceal his conviction that he was cleverer than his neighbours; but he was less disliked than his brother had been.

The two elder men waited for him to come up with them. "Coming to The Cedars?" the Major asked.

"Yes, do you think it odd of me? I expect I shall play croquet. Mrs. Haswell is sure to ask me to: she has such a kind disposition!"

"A game of considerable skill," remarked Mr. Drybeck. "It has gone out of fashion of late years, but in my young days it was very popular. I remember my grandmother telling me, however, that when it first came in it was frowned on as being fast, and leading to flirtation. Amusing!"

"I can't flirt with Mrs. Haswell: she regards me with a motherly eye. Or with Mavis: her eyes glisten, and she knows I don't mean the dreadful things I say. Besides, her uncle might take it to mean encouragement of himself, and that would never do. He would force his way into my house, and I'm resolved that it shall be the one threshold he can't cross. My brother used to say that to me, but he didn't mean it. The likeness between us was only skin-deep, after all."

15

"Oh, yours won't be the only one!" said the Major, chuckling a little. "Eh, Drybeck?"

"No, you're quite mistaken, Major. Warrenby will cross Mr. Drybeck's threshold by a ruse. He will simulate a fit at his gate, or beg to be allowed to come in to recover from an attack of giddiness, and Mr. Drybeck will be too polite to refuse him. That's the worst of having been born in the last century: you're always being frustrated by your upbringing."

"I trust," said Mr. Drybeck frostily, "that I should not refuse admittance to anyone in such need of assistance as you indicate."

"You mean you trust you won't be at home when it happens, because your fear of appearing to the rest of us to be callous might prove stronger than your disinclination to render the least assistance to Warrenby."

"Really, Plenmeller, that borders on the offensive!" protested the Major, perceiving that Mr. Drybeck had taken umbrage at it.

"Not at all. It was merely the truth. You aren't suggesting, are you, that Mr. Drybeck lived for long enough in the last century to think the truth something too indecent to be acknowledged? That seems to me very offensive."

The Major was nonplussed by this, and could think of nothing to say. Mr. Drybeck gave a laugh that indicated annoyance rather than amusement, and said: "You will forgive me, Plenmeller, if I say that the truth in this instance is that Warrenby's presence in our midst does not—though I think it hardly adds to the amenities of Thornden—occupy my mind as it seems to occupy yours. I am sorry to be obliged to tamper with the dramatic picture you have painted, but honesty compels me to say that my feeling in the matter is one of indifference."

The Major turned his eyes apprehensively towards Gavin, fearing that it could scarcely have escaped his acute perception that Mr. Drybeck's loathing of his professional rival and social neighbour was fast approaching the proportions of monomania. But Gavin only said, with a flicker of his unkind smile: "Oh, I do so much admire that attitude! I should adopt it myself, if I thought I could carry it off. I couldn't, of course: you would have to be a Victorian for that."

"Now, now, that's enough about Victorians!" interposed the Major. "Next, you'll be calling *me* a Victorian!"

"No, you have never laid claim to the distinction."

"I am not ashamed of it," stated Mr. Drybeck.

"How should you be? The Squire isn't. By what means, do you suppose, did Warrenby obtain a foothold in Old Place? The Ainstables do receive him, you know. I find that so surprising: I'm sure they wouldn't receive me if I weren't a

16

Plenmeller. Do you think Sampson Warrenby employed devilish wiles to induce the Squire to include him on his visiting list, or are we all equal, seen from the Olympian heights of Old Place? What a corruscating suspicion! I can hardly bear it."

The Major could only be thankful that they had by this time reached the front gates of The Cedars.

CHAPTER TWO

MR. HENRY HASWELL, who had bought The Cedars from Sir James Brotherlee, was one of the more affluent members of the county. His grandfather had founded a small estate agent's business in Bellingham, which had succeeded well enough to enable him to send his heir to a minor public school. Not having himself enjoyed the advantages of such an education, he regarded them with a reverence soon justified by the rapid expansion of the business under the management of his son. William Haswell made the firm important, and himself a force to be reckoned with in civic affairs; penetrated into society which his father did not doubt was out of his own reach; contracted an advantageous marriage; and presently sent his own son to Winchester, and to New College. Sticklers who looked askance at William accepted Henry as a matter of course. He knew the right people, wore the right clothes, and held the right beliefs; and, since he was an unaffected person, he did not pretend to despise the prosperous business which had made it possible for him to acquire all these advantages. He threw a large part of his energy into the task of expanding it still further, but always found time to promote charitable schemes, sit on the board of the local hospital, and hunt at least once a week. He sent his only son to Winchester and Oxford, not because he hoped for his social advancement, but because it was the natural thing to do; and although he would not have opposed any desire on Charles's part to abandon estate agency for one of the more exalted professions he would have felt a good deal of secret disappointment had Charles not wished to succeed him. But Charles, born into an age of dwindling capitals and vanishing social distinctions, never expressed any such desire: he knew himself to be fortunate to have a sound business to step into, and felt a good deal of pride in its high standing. He had just been made a full partner in the firm, and his mother had begun to tell her friends, but without conviction, that it was time he was thinking of getting married.

Henry Haswell had bought The Cedars in a dilapidated condition from the last surviving member of a very old County family; and to such persons as Thaddeus Drybeck it was ironic and faintly displeasing that he should have set it in order, and done away with all the hideous anachronisms (including a conservatory built to lead out of the drawing-room, and chocolate-painted lincrusta walton lining the hall and staircase) with which the Brotherlees had disfigured it. It was now a house of quiet distinction, furnished in excellent taste, and set in a garden which had become, thanks to Mrs. Haswell's fanatical and tireless efforts, one of the loveliest in the County.

As the three men entered the gates, and walked up the drive towards the house, they saw her approaching from the direction of the tennis-courts, a single salmon-pink poppy in her hand. She at once came to meet them, saying: "How nice! Now I can arrange a second four! How do you do, Major? How are you, Gavin? I was just thinking of you, Mr. Drybeck: how right you are not to keep cats! I don't know why it is that one can train dogs to keep off the flowerbeds, but *never* cats. Just look at this! The wretched creature must have *lain* on the plant, I should think. Isn't it a shame? Do you mind coming through the house? Then I can put this poor thing in water."

Talking all the way, in her gently amiable fashion, she led them into the cool, square hall. She was a stout woman, with gray hair, and clothes of indeterminate style and colour, betraying no sign in her person of the unerring taste she showed in house-decoration, and the arrangement of herbaceous borders. Inserting the broken poppy into a bowl of flowers in a seemingly haphazard manner which yet in no way impaired the symmetry of the bowl, she passed on into a sunny drawing-room, where, cut in the side-wall, a glass-panelled door gave access to the rose-garden. "Of course, we ought to have had this door bricked up," she remarked. "Only I do rather like being able to step out of the room into the garden, and you don't see it from the front of the house. The Brotherlees used to have a conservatory beyond it, you remember."

"One of my more treasured childhood's memories," said Gavin. "It had a warm, nostalgic smell, and spiky green things. I loved it!"

"Cacti," supplied Mrs. Haswell. "Children always love the most dreadful things. I remember despairing of Elizabeth when she was three years old, and went into raptures over a bed of scarlet geraniums and blue lobelias. She outgrew it, of course. She and her husband have just moved into a house in Chelsea. I hope they won't find it damp, but she's done wonders with her window-boxes. Charles and Abigail Dearham are playing the Lindales, but the Vicar, and Mavis Warrenby have arrived, so we shall be able to get up a second set."

"Splendid!" said the Major.

Mr. Drybeck said nothing. He foresaw that it would fall to his lot to have Mavis Warrenby for his partner, since he was a better player than the Vicar or the Major, and the prospect depressed him.

"Your husband not playing, Mrs. Haswell?" asked the Major.

19

"No, so unfortunate! Henry has had to go over to Woodhall." replied Mrs. Haswell.

Mr. Drybeck's depression became tinged by a slight feeling of affront. Henry Haswell was the only tennis-player in Thornden whom he considered worthy of his steel, and he had been looking forward to a game with him.

They had by this time come within sight of the two hard-courts which Mrs. Haswell had insisted must be placed where they would not mar the beauty of her garden. They had been laid out, accordingly, at some distance from the house, and they backed on to the wall which shut the grounds of The Cedars off from the footpath running from the northern, Hawkshead, road, past the Squire's plantations, directly south to Fox Lane, separated from it by a stile. At this point, the path, skirting the spinney belonging to The Cedars, turned sharply westward until it met Wood Lane immediately south of The Cedars' front gates. A gate set in the wall close to the tennis-courts gave access to the footpath. It was through this gate that the Lindales, who lived on the Hawkshead-Bellingham road, had come to the party. Miss Warrenby and Miss Dearham had also used it, none of these persons being so punctilious in the use of front entrances as Mr. Drybeck.

When Mrs. Haswell led the three men up to the courts only one was being used. A cheerful and hard-fought set was in progress between the son of the house and Miss Patterdale's niece on the one side, and the Lindales, a young married couple, on the other; while the Vicar, a tall, bony man with a gentle countenance and grizzled hair receding from a broad brow, engaged Mavis Warrenby in desultory conversation on a garden-seat behind the court.

"Well, I don't have to introduce any of you," said Mrs. Haswell, smiling generally upon her guests. "Or ask you what sort of games you play, which is such a comfort, because no one ever answers truthfully. Mavis, I think you and Mr. Drybeck ought to take on the Vicar and Major Midgeholme."

"I'm not *nearly* good enough to play with Mr. Drybeck," protested Mavis, with what that gentleman privately considered perfect truth. "I shall be dreadfully nervous. I'm sure they'd much rather have a men's four."

"Not, I imagine, if you are suggesting I should make the fourth," interpolated Gavin, throwing her into confusion, and watching the result with the eye of a connoisseur.

"They will be able to make up a men's four later," said Mrs. Haswell, quite unperturbed. "I'm sure you'll play very nicely, my dear. It's a pity your uncle couldn't come."

"Yes, he was so very sorry," said Mavis, her face still suffused with colour. "But some papers have come in which he said he

20

simply must deal with. So he made me come alone, and make his excuses. I don't feel I ought really to be here."

"Yes, dear, you told me," said her hostess kindly. "We're all very glad you have come."

Miss Warrenby looked grateful, but said: "I don't like leaving Uncle to get his own tea. Saturday is Gladys's half-day, you know, so he's alone in the house. But he wouldn't *hear* of letting me stay at home to look after him, so I just put the tray ready, and the kettle on the stove, and ran off to enjoy myself. But I do feel a little bit guilty, because Uncle hates having to do those sort of things for himself. However, he said he didn't mind for once in a way, so here I am. It was really awfully kind of him."

Her pale gray eyes hopefully scanned the circle, but this recorded instance of Sampson Warrenby's consideration for his niece failed to elicit comment from anyone but Mrs. Haswell, who merely said: "It won't hurt your uncle to get his own tea. I shouldn't worry about him, if I were you."

She then handed Mr. Drybeck a box of tennis-balls, saw all four players pass through the wire gate on to the court, and sat down on the garden-seat, inviting Gavin to join her there. "It's a pity Mrs. Cliburn is late," she observed. "If she were here they could have a proper mixed doubles, and it would make a more even game. However, it can't be helped. I'm glad Sampson Warrenby didn't come."

"You said you were not."

"Yes, of course: one does say that sort of thing. I had to ask him, because it would have looked so pointed if I'd left him out. You can't leave people out in a small community: it makes things awkward, as I told Henry."

"Oh, is that why he went to Woodhall?" asked Gavin, interested.

"And if I left Mr. Warrenby out," pursued Mrs. Haswell, apparently deaf to this interruption, "I should be obliged to leave Mavis out too, which I should be sorry to do."

"I wish you had left him out."

"She leads a wretched enough life without being ostracized," said Mrs. Haswell, still deaf. "And you never hear her say an unkind word about him."

"I never hear her say an unkind word about anyone. There is no affinity between us."

"I wonder what is keeping the Ainstables?"

"Possibly the fear that nothing has kept Warrenby."

"I'm sure I said half-past three. I hope Rosamund hasn't had another of her bad turns. There, now! the young people have finished their set, and the others have only just begun theirs; I wanted to arrange it so that Mr. Drybeck should play with the *good* ones! . . . Well, how did it end, my dears? Who won?"

"Oh, the children!" said Kenelm Lindale, with the flash of a rueful smile. "Delia and I were run off our feet!"

"You are a liar!" remarked Abigail Dearham, propping her racquet against a chair, and picking up a scarlet cardigan. "We should be still at it, if it hadn't been for Charles's almighty fluke."

"Less of it!" recommended the son of the house, walking over to a table which bore a phalanx of tumblers, and several kinds of liquid refreshment. "A brilliantly conceived shot, executed with true delicacy of touch. What'll you have, Delia? We can offer you lemonade, orangeade, beer, ginger-beer and Mother's Ruin. You have only to give it a name."

Mrs. Lindale, having given it a name, sat down in a chair beside her hostess, her coat draped across her shoulders, and surreptitiously glanced at her wrist-watch. She was a thin young woman, with pale hair, aquiline features, and ice-blue eyes that never seemed quite to settle on any object. She gave the impression of being strung up on wires, her mind always reaching forward to some care a little beyond the present. Since her husband had abandoned a career on the Stock Exchange to attempt the precarious feat of farming, it was generally felt that she had every reason to look anxious. They had not been settled for very long at Rushyford Farm, which lay to the north of Thornden, on the Hawkshead road; and those who knew most about the hazards of farming in England wondered for how long they would remain. Both were energetic, but neither was accustomed to country life; and for Delia at least the difficulties were enhanced by the existence of a year-old infant, on whom she lavished what older and more prosaic parents felt to be an inordinate amount of care and adoration. Those who noticed her quick glance at her watch knew that she was wondering whether the woman who helped her in the house had remembered to carry out the minute instructions she had left for the care of the infant, or whether Rose-Veronica might not have been left to scream unheard in her pram. Her husband knew it too, and, catching her eye, smiled, at once comfortingly and teasingly. He was a handsome, dark man, some few years her senior. He had the ready laughter that often accompanies a quick temper, a pair of warm brown eyes, and a lower lip that supported the upper in a way that gave a good deal of resolution to his face. He and Delia were recognised as a devoted couple. His attitude towards her was protective; she, without seeming to be mentally dependent upon him, was so passionately absorbed in him that she could never give all her attention to anyone else if he were present.

Mrs. Haswell, who had seen her glance at her watch, gave

her hand a pat, and said, smiling: "Now, I'm not going to have you worrying over your baby, my dear! Mrs. Murton will look after her perfectly well."

Delia flushed, and gave an uncertain laugh. "I'm sorry! I didn't mean—I was only wondering."

Abigail Dearham, a very pretty girl, with a mop of chestnut curls, and wide-open gray eyes, looked at her with the interest she accorded to everyone who came in her way. "Have you got a baby?" she asked.

"Yes, a little girl. But I really wasn't worrying about her. That is to say——"

"Do you look after her yourself? Is it an awful sweat?"

"Oh, no! Of course, it does tie one, but I love doing it."

"You ought to get out more, dear," said Mrs. Haswell.

"I expect it's fun, having a baby," said Abby, giving the matter her serious consideration. "I shouldn't like to be tied down, though."

"Yes, you would. You don't mind being tied down by your old Inky," said Charles.

"That's different. I have set hours with him."

"Not much you don't!" said Charles rudely. "You're always being kept on after hours because he's in the middle of a chapter, or wants you to manage one of his beastly parties!"

His mother, not betraying the fact that she had received sudden enlightenment, said in an easy tone: "Abby is Geoffrey Silloth's secretary, Delia. So interesting!"

"No, by Jove, are you really?" said Kenelm. "What's he like?"

"Oh, quite a toot!" replied Abby cheerfully. "He's gone off to Antibes for a fortnight, which is why I've got a holiday."

This description of a distinguished man of letters was received with equanimity by Mrs. Haswell, accustomed to the phraseology of youth; with complete understanding by Charles, and the Lindales; and with patent nausea by Gavin Plenmeller, who asked in silken accents to have the term explained to him.

"Ah, here come Mrs. Cliburn and the Squire!" said Mrs. Haswell, rising to greet these timely arrivals. "Edith, how nice! But, Bernard, isn't Rosamund coming?"

The Squire, a squarely built man who looked older than his sixty years, shook hands, saying: "One of her heads. She told me to make her apologies, and say she'd be along to tea, if she feels up to it. I don't think there's much hope of it, but I left the car for her, just in case."

"Oh, dear, I am sorry! You know Mrs. Lindale, don't you? And her husband, of course."

"Yes, indeed. Glad to see you, Mrs. Lindale! And you, Lindale." His deep-set eyes travelled to the tennis-courts. "Warrenby not here? Good opportunity for the rest of us to talk over this business about the River Board. Where's Henry, Adelaide?"

"Well, I expect he'll be back before you leave." replied Mrs. Haswell. "Though if it's about the this tiresome River Board affair, I do wish—However, it's not my business, so you'd better talk to Henry. I must say, it does seem a lot of fuss about very little."

"One does so want to avoid *unpleasantness*," said Mrs. Cliburn. "Of course, it isn't anything to do with us either, but Tony and I can't help feeling that it would be a shame to appoint anyone but Mr. Drybeck to act for this new River Board. I mean, he always did when it was the Catchment Board, didn't he? And he'd be bound to feel very badly about it, particularly if Mr. Warrenby was appointed instead of him. But I oughtn't to give my opinion," she added hastily.

"Well, well, it isn't such a great matter, after all!" said the Squire. "We must see what Haswell thinks."

"Dad won't support Warrenby, sir," interpolated Charles. "I know that. For one thing, he's dead against hurting poor old Drybeck's feelings."

"Charles!" said his mother, with a warning glance towards the tennis-court.

"All right, Mum: they can't hear us. And, for another, he's just about had Warrenby, muscling into every damned thing here!"

"Nor is he alone in his surfeit," said Gavin. "I too shall oppose Warrenby. I feel sure Walter would have: he always opposed people."

The Squire threw him a frowning look, but said nothing. Kenelm Lindale, lighting a cigarette, and carefully pressing the spent match into the ground, said: "Well, I don't want to hurt Drybeck's feelings either, but, to tell you the truth, I don't really know much about this River Board."

"And you a riparian owner!" said Charles, shocked. "There used to be one Catchment Board for the Rushy, here, and another one for the Crail, which for your better information is——"

"All *right*!" said Kenelm, grinning at him. "I know where the Crail runs! I also know that two old Catchment Boards have become one new River Board. What I meant was, what about the Crail half of the Board? Haven't they got a candidate for the solicitor's job?"

"The man who look after their interests has retired," said the Squire shortly. "You'd better read the correspondence. I'll show it to you, if you like to—No, now I come to think of it, I sent it on to you, Gavin. I wish you'd let me have it back."

He turned away, and began to talk to his hostess. Another game was soon arranged, he and Mrs. Cliburn taking the places

24

of Charles and Abigail, who went off with Gavin and Mrs. Haswell to engage in a lighthearted game of Crazy Croquet, which Charles insisted was the only sort of croquet he understood.

Tea was served under the elm tree on the lawn to the east of the house, the tennis-players joining the party when their respective sets ended, and hailing with acclaim the discovery that Mrs. Haswell, always a perfect hostess, had provided iced coffee for their refreshment.

Mrs. Ainstable arrived at about half-past five, leaving her car in the drive, and walking through the rose-covered archway that led to the eastern lawn. Mrs. Haswell rose at once, and went to meet her; and she said, in her rather high-pitched, inconsequent voice: "I do apologize! Don't say I'm too late to be given tea: I should burst into tears. Isn't it hot? How lovely the garden's looking! We've got greenfly."

"My dear, you don't look fit to be out!" said Mrs. Haswell, taking her hand, and looking at her in a concerned way. "Are you sure you're all right?"

"Oh, yes! Just one of my wretched heads. Better now. Don't say anything about it: Bernard worries so about me!"

This was seen to be true. The Squire had come up to them, and was anxiously scanning his wife's face. "My dear, is this wise of you? I hoped you'd have a sleep."

"I did have a sleep, Bernard, and it did me so much good that I couldn't bear to stay away from Adelaide's party. Now, don't fuss, darling, please!"

He shook his head, but said no more. Mrs. Haswell could not think it wonderful that he should be worried. Rosamund Ainstable, though more than ten years his junior, was a woman who, without having any organic disease, had never enjoyed good health. Her constitution was delicate; any exertion out of the way was apt to prostrate her; and she was the victim of sick headaches whose cause had consistently baffled her many medical advisers. She had ceased to try to discover it, saying, with her rueful laugh, that having worked her way expensively up Harley Street she had neither the means nor the stamina to work her way down it. In the popular phrase, she lived on her nerves, which were ill-adapted to bear the strain. She had endured two world wars, dying a thousand vicarious deaths in the first, when she had known that every telegram delivered to her must contain the news that her husband had been killed in action; and losing her only child in the second. Her friends had prophesied that she would not recover from this blow; but she had recovered, exerting herself to support and to comfort the Squire, whose pride and hope were buried somewhere in the North African Desert. It might have been expected that he and she, with their heir dead, would have ceased to struggle to

25

maintain an estate impoverished by the financial demands of one war, and brought almost to penury by those of a second, but, as the Squire's legal adviser, Thaddeus Drybeck, loftily pointed out to his acquaintance, Blood Told, and the Squire continued to plan and contrive as though he believed he would be succeeded by the son he had adored, and not by a nephew whom he scarcely knew, and did not much like.

Mrs. Haswell, installing her friend in a comfortable chair, and supplying her with the tea for which she said she craved, was tactful not to betray her realization that this was one of poor Rosamund's bad days. There was a glitter in those restless eyes, too high a colour in those thin cheeks, an artificial gaiety in the high-pitched voice, which she could not like, and hoped the Squire would not notice. Whether he did or not it was impossible to guess: by tradition and temperament he was a man who concealed his thoughts and his feelings.

When all the strawberries had been eaten, and all the iced coffee drunk, the Vicar solved a problem which had been exercising Mrs. Haswell's mind for some time. He said that much as he would like to engage on further Homeric struggles duty called him, and he must away, to pay a parochial visit on a sick parishioner. This left only nine potential tennis-players to be accommodated on two courts, and no one could doubt, as Gavin Plenmeller informed Kenelm Lindale under his breath, that Miss Warrenby would honestly *prefer* to watch. He was quite right, but, judging by his expression, had scarcely foreseen the immediate sequel to this act of self-abnegation. When polite opposition had been overborne, Mrs. Haswell said: "You and Gavin must keep one another company, then, dear. Rosamund, I'm going to take you into the house: it's far too hot for you to be sitting outside."

"Good God!" uttered Gavin, for Kenelm's ear. "This is where I must think fast! None of you who pity me for my disability have the least conception of the horrors to which I am subjected. I will not bear that afflictive girl company. Quick, what does A. do?"

"You can't do anything," said Kenelm, rather amused.

"You betray your ignorance of my character."

Kenelm laughed, but soon found that he had underrated Mr. Plenmeller's bland ingenuity, and had certainly been ignorant of the ruthlessness which led that gentleman to implicate him in his plan of escape. He now learned that owing to his own importunity Gavin was about to return to his home to fetch, for his perusal, the River Board correspondence; and he began to perceive why it was that Gavin was not popular with his neighbours.

"Oh, I'm sure you ought not to!" exclaimed Mavis, glancing reproachfully at Kenelm.

"But I am sure I ought. You could see the Squire was displeased with me. He felt I shouldn't have forgotten to return the papers, and I have a dreadful premonition that I shall go on forgetting."

"You needn't fetch them for my sake," interrupted Kenelm maliciously.

"No, for my own!" retorted Gavin, not in the least discomfited. "Something accomplished will earn me a night's repose. I rarely accomplish anything, and never suffer from insomnia, but Miss Warrenby has often told me what an excellent maxim that is."

"Oh, yes, but all that way just for a few papers! Couldn't someone else go for you?" said Mavis. "I'm sure I'd love to, if you think I could find them."

Kenelm, who guessed that Gavin's mocking references to his lameness masked his loathing of it, was not surprised that this well-meant piece of tactlessness met with the treatment he privately thought it deserved.

"Does it seem to you a long way to my house? I thought it was only half a mile. Or are you thinking that my short leg pains me? Do let me set your mind at rest! It doesn't. You have been misled by my ungainliness."

He turned away, and went, with his uneven gait, to where his hostess was standing. Mavis said, sighing: "I often think it does hurt him, you know."

"He has told you that it doesn't," replied Kenelm, rather shortly.

She brought her eyes to bear on his face. "He's so plucky, isn't he? People don't realize what it must mean to him, or make allowances."

Kenelm felt that he was being reproved for insensibility, and obeyed, with relief, a summons from Mrs. Haswell.

CHAPTER THREE

By the time Gavin returned to The Cedars it was half past six, and the party was beginning to break up. Mrs. Ainstable was the first to leave, driving home alone in her aged Austin, and very nearly running Gavin down as she came somewhat incautiously round the bend in the drive. She pulled up, calling out: "So sorry! Did I frighten you?"

"Yes, I gave myself up for dead," he replied, leaving the grass verge beside the shrubbery on which he had taken refuge, and approaching the car. "And me a cripple! How could you?"

"It's stupid to talk like that: you're not a cripple. You deserved to be frightened, anyway, for behaving so atrociously. You didn't take anyone in, you know. It was as plain as a pikestaff you didn't want to sit out with Mavis Warrenby. She is dull, of course. I can't think why very good people so often are. Why on earth didn't you pretend you had to go home early, and just leave?"

"That would have looked as if I were not enjoying the party."

"Well, it would have been better than hatching up that quite incredible story about having to fetch a lot of unimportant papers for Bernard!" she said tartly.

"You wrong me. May I hand over to you the proofs of my integrity?" he said, drawing a long, fat envelope from the inner pocket of his coat, and giving it to her, with his impish smile. "Is the Squire still playing tennis?"

"Yes. It's no use my waiting for him. He's going home the other way, so that he can look at what's been done in the new plantation. So foolish of him! He'll only wear himself out to no purpose. How insufferably hot it is!"

"Is it? It doesn't seem so to me. Are you quite well, Mrs. Ainstable? Well enough to be driving alone?"

"Thank you, perfectly well! Is this your way of asking for a lift?"

"No, I should be afraid," he retorted.

"Oh, don't be so silly!" she said, rather roughly putting the car into gear.

He watched her sweep through the gates on to the lane, and walked on to rejoin the rest of the party.

One of the sets had come to an end, and Delia Lindale, who had been playing in it, was taking leave of her hostess. Since it was past Rose-Veronica's bedtime, Mrs. Haswell made no attempt to detain her. Her husband waved to her from the other court, and she sped away through the gate into the public footpath.

"I ought to be going too," said Abby.

"No, you oughtn't: I'm going to run you home," said Charles.

"Oh, rot! I can easily walk."

"You can do more: you can walk beautifully, but you aren't going to."

She laughed. "You are an ass! Honestly, there's no need to get your car out just to run me that little distance."

"Of course not, and I shouldn't dream of doing so. I'm doing it for Mr. Drybeck," said Charles, with aplomb.

"Really, that is very kind of you, my dear boy," said Mr. Drybeck. "I am far from despising such a welcome offer. A most enjoyable game, that last."

"Well, if you're going to motor Abby and Mr. Drybeck home, you could give the Major a lift too," suggested Mrs. Haswell. "You won't mind waiting till the other game finishes, will you? Mavis, now that I've got you both here, I want you and Mrs. Cliburn to help me over the prizes for the Whist Drive. I ought to get them on Monday, I think, but we never settled what we ought to spend on them. It won't take many minutes. Ah, I see the game has ended! Who won? You looked to be very evenly matched."

"Yes, a good ding-dong game," said the Squire, mopping his face and neck. "Midgeholme and I just managed to pull it off, but it was a near thing. I'm not as young as I was. Hallo, you back, Plenmeller? Thought you'd gone."

"But could you have doubted that I should, sir? Your words struck home: I have fetched the correspondence which has for too long languished on my desk. I have no excuse: I didn't even find it interesting."

The Squire stared at him under his bushy brows, and gave a grunt. "No need to have rushed off for it then and there. However, I'm obliged to you. Where is it?"

"Can it be that I have erred again? I gave the envelope into Mrs. Ainstable's keeping."

"Pity. Lindale could have taken it home, and run his eye over it. If you're going my way, I'll walk along with you, Lindale."

"I'm afraid I'm not, sir. We didn't come in the car. I'm going by way of the footpath."

"Yes, yes, that's all right, so am I. Going to have a look at my new plantation. My land stretches as far as the path, behind this place, you know."

"Now, nobody must go before they've had a drink," interposed Mrs. Haswell hospitably.

"Nothing more for me, thank you," Mr. Drybeck said. "I must not hurry my kind chauffeur, but I have promised my housekeeper I will not be late. She likes to go to the cinema in

Bellingham on Saturday evening, you know, and so I make it a rule to have an early supper to accommodate her."

"By Jove, yes!" said the Major, glancing at his watch. "I must be getting along too!"

"Perhaps I had better go quietly away," said Gavin, setting down his empty glass. "Something tells me I am not popular. Of course, I see now: I should have presented those papers to the Squire on bent knee, instead of handing them casually to his wife. It is all the fault of my upbringing."

"If you want a lift, it'll be a bit of a tight squeeze, but I'll see what I can do," said Charles, disregarding this speech.

"No, I shall wend my lonely way home, a solitary and pathetic figure. Goodbye, Mrs. Haswell: so very many thanks! I enjoyed myself enormously."

He followed the car-party to the drive, and saw them set off before limping in their wake.

"I say, is it all right? I mean, oughtn't you to have given him a lift?" asked Abby, who was sitting beside Charles in the front of the sports car. "Does it hurt him to walk?"

"Lord, no!" said Charles. "He can walk for miles. Just can't play games."

"It must be fairly rotten for him, I should think."

"Oh, I don't know!" said Charles, with cheerful unconcern. "He's always been like it, you see. Trades on it, if you ask me. People like my mother are sorry for him, and think they've got to make allowances for him. That's why he's so bloody rude."

"I must say, it was the outside edge to walk off like that, and leave Mavis stranded," admitted Abby.

"Yes, and absolutely typical. Does it for effect. Walter Plenmeller was a God-awful type too, though I daresay being smashed up in the War had something to do with that. I say, sir," he called over his shoulder to Mr. Dyrybeck, "were all the Plenmellers as bad as Walter and Gavin?"

"I was not acquainted with all the Plenmellers," replied Mr. Drybeck precisely. "The family has been established in the county for five centuries."

"Probably accounts for it," said Charles. "Run to seed."

"Tragic affair, Walter Plenmeller's death," remarked the Major. "Never more shocked in my life! I must say, though I don't like Gavin, I was damned sorry for him. Of course, the poor chap wasn't in his right mind, but it can't have been pleasant for Gavin."

"He committed suicide, didn't he?" said Abby. "Aunt Miriam's always a bit cagey about it. What happened?"

"Gassed himself, and left a letter to Gavin, practically accusing him of having driven him to it," said Charles briefly, swinging the car round the corner into the High Street. "It was all rot, of course: he used to have the most ghastly migraines, and I suppose they got to be a bit too much for him."

"Set me down at the cross-roads, Charles," said the Major, leaning forward to tap him on the shoulder. "No need to come any farther."

"Sure, sir?" said Charles, beginning to slow down.

"Quite sure—and many thanks for the lift!" said the Major, as the car stopped. "Goodbye, Miss Dearham: I hope we shall have the opportunity of playing again before you go back to town. Goodbye, Drybeck. Right away, Charles!"

They left the Major striding off in the direction of Ultima Thule, and turned the corner into the Trindale road. A few hundred yards along it, Charles stopped again to set down Mr. Drybeck, and then drove forward, and into Fox Lane.

"Come in and have a drink!" invited Abby. "Aunt Miriam would adore you to. She never drinks anything herself, but she's firmly convinced I can't exist without having gin laid on, practically like running hot and cold water, so she lays in quantities whenever I come to stay. She's an absolute toot, you know. Most people's aunts disapprove madly of cocktails, and say 'Surely you don't need another, dear?' but she never does. In fact, you'd think she was a confirmed soak, the way she fills up the glasses."

"Of course I'm coming in," said Charles, swinging his long legs out of the car, and slamming the door. "That's why I brought you home."

"I've a good mind not to ask you."

"Wouldn't be any use at all. I've been hopelessly in love with your Aunt Miriam for years, and I shan't wait to be asked. What's more, she's my Aunt Miriam too."

"She is not!"

"You ask her! She adopted me when I was a kid," said Charles, opening the wicket-gate into the neat little garden of Fox Cottage, and stooping to thump with hearty goodwill, apparently much appreciated, the elderly and stout black labrador, who had advanced ponderously to greet him. "You see! Even Rex knows I'm persona grata here, and you wouldn't say he was bursting with intelligence, would you? Go on, you old fool, get out of the light!"

"No, and I wouldn't say he had any discrimination either," replied Abby, with spirit. "He'd welcome any tramp to the house."

She glanced up to see how this retort was being received, and found that Charles was looking at her with a smile in his eyes, and something more than that. "Would he?" he said.

"Yes, he's—he's disastrously friendly," she said, aware of a rising blush. "Oh, there's Aunt Miriam, at the window, beckoning to us! Come on!"

Charles followed her into the cottage.

Miss Patterdale, in happy unconsciousness of having timed her interruption inopportunely, greeted them with a nod, and said, addressing herself to Abby: "Well? Had a good time?"

"Lovely!" replied Abby.

"She can't very well say anything else," Charles pointed out. "I was her host."

"I don't suppose that would stop her. Have some gin!" said Miss Patterdale, supporting the character given her by her niece. "You'd better mix it yourself: I bought the things the man said people put in gin. I hope they're all right."

Charles grinned, surveying the array of bottles set forth on the Welsh dresser. "Something for every taste. You *have* been going it, Aunt Miriam! Let's experiment!"

"What on earth is it?" asked Abby, presently receiving a glass from him, and cautiously sipping its contents.

"The discovery of the age. And a glass of nice, moderately pure orangeade for Aunt Miriam," Charles said, putting a glass into Miss Patterdale's hand, and disposing his large person on the sofa beside her.

"You haven't put anything in it, have you?" said Miss Patterdale suspiciously.

"Of course I haven't! What do you take me for?"

Miss Patterdale regarded him with grim affection. "I'm not at all sure. You were one of the naughtiest little boys I ever encountered: that I do know!"

"That was before I came under your influence. Best of my Aunts."

"Get along with you! Who was at your party? Besides Thaddeus Drybeck, and the Major! I know they were there."

"Everyone was at our party, except you and Our Flora. In fact, it was the success of the season. The Major told us that Our Flora was expecting a litter. No, I don't mean that, though she looks so like an Ultima herself that I almost might."

"Ullapool," said Miss Patterdale. "I ran into Flora on the common, and she told me."

"Ullapool!" exclaimed Charles reverently. "That's a new one on me, and it has my unqualified approval."

"It isn't as good as Ultima Uplift," objected Abby. "That's my favourite, easily!"

"What, more than Umbrella?" said Charles incredulously.

This, naturally, led to a lively discussion on the respective merits of all the more absurd names which Mrs. Midgeholme had bestowed on her Pekes. Miss Patterdale, entering into the argument, said in her incisive way: "You're both wrong. Ultima Urf was the best."

"Ultima *what*?" demanded both her hearers.

"Urf. It was the runt of the litter, you see. It died."

"Angel, I *don't* see!" complained Abby.

"It means a stunted child," explained Miss Patterdale. "Not bad, really, except that one would feel such a fool, shouting Urf, Urf, Urf, in the street. At least, I should. Not that I've any right to poke fun at Flora. Anything more unsuitable for a couple of goats than Rosalind and Celia I've yet to discover. I must have been out of my mind. Celia got loose this afternoon, and strayed. That's how I met Flora. She was giving some of her dogs a run on the common."

"Has Ullapool had her puppies? I'd love to see them," said Abby.

"You wouldn't be able to for several weeks. No, she hasn't. Flora doesn't think they'll arrive until tomorrow. It wasn't really that which kept her away from the party. She didn't want to meet Mr. Warrenby. They've had a violent quarrel. He kicked Ulysses off one of his flower-beds."

"Beast!" said Abby.

"Yes, I'm not at all in favour of that," said Charles. "I shall pay a visit of condolence. I like Ulysses. He's a dog of dignity. Ready for another Haswell Special, Abby?"

She handed him her glass. "Thanks. As a matter of fact, Mr. Warrenby wasn't there. He had to do some work, or something. Mavis was rather dim and boring about Poor Uncle having to get his own tea."

"Do him good!" said Miss Patterdale. "If Mavis had an ounce of commonsense—but she hasn't, and she never will have! The longer I live the more convinced I become that self-sacrificing people do a great deal of harm in the world."

Charles choked over the Haswell Special. Abby, regarding her aunt with indulgent fondness, said: "You're a nice one to talk!"

"If you mean by that that I'm self-sacrificing, you are mistaken."

"Aunt Miriam! You spend your entire life slaving for the indigent, and the sick, and every charity that raises it head——"

"That isn't self-sacrificing. It comes of being a parson's daughter, and acquiring the habit young. Besides, I like it. Shouldn't do it, if I didn't. When I talk of self-sacrificing people, I mean people like Mavis, making doormats of themselves, and giving up everything they like to satisfy the demands of thoroughly selfish characters like Sampson Warrenby. Making a virtue of it, too. It isn't a virtue. Take Sampson Warrenby! If he weren't allowed to ride roughshod over Mavis, he'd be very much better-behaved, and consequently much better-liked."

"He might be," said Charles dubiously. "Speaking for myself, I find him even more unlikable in his ingratiating moments than when he sees himself as Lord of all he surveys. You ought to hear Dad on the subject of his antics on the Borough Council!

He says Warrenby would like to be a sort of puppet-master, pulling strings to set the rest of 'em dancing to his tune. Peculiar ambition!"

"Power-complex," said Abby, nodding wisely. "I expect my old toot would find him an interesting study."

"I may be out of date," said Miss Patterdale, "but I do *not* think you ought to call Geoffrey Silloth a toot—whatever a toot may be!"

"But he is a toot, angel! You are too, and it's someone lamb-like, and altogether a good-thing-and-memorable!"

"I have never met Mr. Silloth, but I know what I look like, and it isn't a lamb. Not at all sure it isn't rather like a goat," said Miss Patterdale reflectively. "Not Celia, but Rosalind."

This unflattering self-portrait met with such indignant refutation that Miss Patterdale, though maintaining her customary brusqueness, turned quite pink with pleasure. Another drink was clearly called for by the time her young admirers had, as they hoped, convinced her that she bore no resemblance to a creature it would have been the height of mendacity to have called a pet animal; and Charles got up to mix it. It was as he was handing her glass to Abby that an interruption occurred. The garden-gate was heard to click, and Abby, glancing over her shoulder, saw through the open casement Mavis Warrenby, coming in a stumbling run up the flagged path, one hand pressed to her panting bosom, and her whole appearance betokening extreme agitation.

"Good lord, what's up?" exclaimed Abby. "It's Mavis!"

The front-door of Fox Cottage stood hospitably open, but it was seen that even in emergency Miss Warrenby was not one to burst in uninvited into a strange house. A trembling knock was heard, accompanied by a tearful voice uttering Miss Patterdale's name. "Miss Patterdale! Oh, Miss Patterdale!" it wailed.

Charles, who was standing by the dresser, with the gin-bottle in his hand, cast a startled and enquiring look at his hostess, and then set the bottle down, and went out into the narrow front passage. "Hallo!" he said. "Anything wrong?"

Mavis, who was leaning in a limp way against the door-post, gasped, and stammered: "Oh! I didn't—I don't know what to do! Miss Patterdale—Oh, I don't know what to do!"

"What's the matter?" asked Miss Patterdale, who had by this time joined Charles in the passage. "Come inside! Good gracious, are you ill, child?"

"No, no! Oh, it's so awful!" shuddered Mavis.

"Here, hold up!" said Charles, seeing her wilt against the wall, and putting his arm round her. "*What's* so awful?"

"Bring her into the parlour!" commanded Miss Patterdale. "Abby, run up and get the sal volatile out of my medicine-chest! Now, you sit down, and pull yourself together, Mavis! What has happened?"

"I ran all the way!" gasped Mavis. "I shall be all right. I didn't know what to do! I could only think of getting to you! I felt so sick! Oh, Miss Patterdale, I think I am going to be sick!"

"No, you aren't," said Miss Patterdale firmly. "Lay her on the sofa, Charles! Now, you keep quiet, Mavis, and don't try to tell me anything until you've got your breath! I'm not surprised you feel sick, running all the way from Fox House in this heat. That's right, Abby: put a little water in it! Here you are, child! Swallow this, and you'll feel better!"

Miss Warrenby gulped the dose down, and shuddered, and began to cry.

"Stop that at once!" said Miss Patterdale, recognizing the signs of hysteria. "No! It's no use trying to tell me what is wrong while you're sobbing in that silly way: I can't make out a word you're saying. Control yourself!"

This bracing treatment had its effect. Mavis made a great effort to obey, accepted a proffered handkerchief, and after mopping her face, and giving several gulps, sniffs, and sobs, grew more composed. "It's Uncle!" she managed to say. "I didn't know what to do: I thought I was going to faint, it's so awful! I could only think of getting to you, Miss Patterdale!"

"What's he been doing?" demanded Miss Patterdale.

"Oh, no, no! It isn't that! Oh, poor Uncle! I *knew* I oughtn't to have left him alone like that! I shall never forgive myself!"

"Look here!" said Charles, who was becoming bored with Mavis's exclamatory and obscure style of narrative. "Just what has happened to your uncle?"

She turned dilating eyes towards him. "I think—I think he's *dead!*" she said, shuddering.

"Dead?" Charles repeated incredulously. "Do you mean he's had a stroke, or something?"

She began to cry again. "No, no, no! It's much, much more dreadful. He's been shot!"

"Good God!" said Charles blankly. "But——"

"For heaven's sake, girl!" interrupted Miss Patterdale. "You say you *think* he's dead. Surely you didn't come here, leaving the unfortunate man alone, without making certain there was nothing you could do for him?"

Mavis covered her face with her hands. "I—I know he's dead. I thought he was asleep, and it seemed so unlike him, somehow. I went up to him, and then I saw!"

"You saw what?" said Miss Patterdale, as Mavis broke off. "Try to pull yourself together!"

"Yes. I'm sorry. It's been such a shock. In the side of his head—just here——" she pressed her left temple—"a—a hole!

35

Oh, don't ask me! And I heard it! I didn't think anything about it at the time. I was just getting over the stile at the top of the lane, and I heard a gun fired. It made me jump, because it sounded quite close, but of course I only thought it was somebody shooting rabbits. And then I opened the garden-gate, and saw Uncle on the seat under the oak-tree. . . ."

"Gosh!" uttered Abby, awed. "Who did it? Did you see anyone?" Mavis shook her head, wiping her eyes. "No one hiding in the garden? Round the back? If you were in the lane they couldn't have escaped that way, could they?"

Mavis looked at her in a bemused fashion. "I don't know. I was so shocked I never thought of anything but that poor Uncle was dead."

"But didn't you even *look*?" insisted Abby. "I mean, it had only just happened, and whoever did it can't possibly have managed to get away! Well, not far away, at all events!"

"No, I suppose—But I didn't think about that! I only thought of Uncle."

"Yes, well, all right!" said Charles. "I suppose that's fairly natural, but when you realized he was dead what did you do?"

She pushed her rather lank hair back from her brow. "I don't know. I think I was sort of stunned for a few minutes. It seemed so *impossible*! My legs were shaking so that I could hardly stand, and I felt so sick! I managed to get to the house, and I'm afraid I *was* sick."

"Yes, that's not what I mean," said Charles, trying not to speak impatiently. "Have you rung up the police? the doctor?"

She blinked. "No—oh, no! I *knew* it was no use sending for the doctor. I didn't think about the police. Oh, *need* we do that? It seems to make it worse, somehow. I mean, Uncle would have *hated* it! Having an inquest, and everyone talking about it!"

"Merciful heavens!" ejaculated Miss Patterdale. "Have you *no* sense, Mavis? You know very well I'm not on the telephone, and you come running here before ever you've—now, don't, for goodness' sake begin to cry again! Charles, where are you going?"

"Fox House, of course. I'll ring up the police-station from there, and stand by till they arrive."

"Yes, that's the best thing," she approved. "I'll come with you."

"Better not, Aunt Miriam."

"Nonsense! There may be something we can do for the poor man. You don't imagine I mean to be sick, do you?"

"Oh, Aunt Miriam, couldn't *I* go with Charles?" begged Abby. "I know all about First Aid, and——"

"Certainly not! You'll stay here and look after Mavis."

"I can't—I mean, you'd do it much better! Do let me be the

36

one to go with Charles!" Abby said, following them down the garden.

"Absolutely *not*!" said Charles, in a voice that admitted of no argument. "Hop in, Aunt Miriam!"

He slammed the car-door on Miss Patterdale, got into his own seat, and started the engine. As the car shot forward, he said: "Of all the damned, silly wet hens, that girl takes the biscuit! A child in arms would have had sense enough to have rung the police! Blithering idiot! I say, Aunt Miriam, what on earth do you think can have really happened?"

"I have no idea. It sounds as though somebody *was* shooting rabbits. I'm not at all surprised. I've often thought it most dangerous to allow it on the common."

The distance between Fox Cottage and Fox House was very short, and they had already reached their goal. The house was set back from the lane, from which it was separated by a low hedge. It had no carriage sweep, a separate gate and straight gravel drive having been made beside the garden to enable Mr. Warrenby to garage his car in a modern building erected a little to the rear of the house. Charles drew up outside the wicket-gate giving access to a footpath leading to the front-door, and switched off his engine. In another minute he and Miss Patterdale had entered the garden, and were bending over the lifeless form of Sampson Warrenby, slumped on a wooden seat set under an oak-tree, and at right angles to the lane.

Warrenby, a short, plump man, dressed in sponge-bag trousers, an alpaca coat, and morocco-leather slippers, was sitting with his head fallen forward, and one hand hanging limply over the arm of the seat.

Charles straightened himself after one look, and said, rather jerkily: "Who was his doctor?"

"Dr. Warcop, but it's no use, Charles."

"No, I know, but probably we ought to send for him. I'm not familiar with the correct procedure on occasions like this, but I'm pretty sure there ought to be a doctor here as soon as possible. Do you know which room the telephone's in?"

"In the study. That one, on the right of the front-door."

He strode away across the lawn to the house. It was built of mellow brick, in the form of an E, and the principal rooms faced across the garden to the lane, and the rising ground of the common beyond it. The long windows on the ground-floor stood open, and Charles stepped through one of these into Sampson Warrenby's study. The telephone stood on the knee-hole desk, which also bore a litter of papers and documents. Charles picked it up, and dialled Dr. Warcop's number.

When he rejoined Miss Patterdale, a few minutes later, that redoubtable lady was staring fixedly at a bed of snapdragons. "Well? Find Dr. Warcop in?" she said.

37

"Yes. Surgery-hour. He's coming at once. Also the police, from Bellingham."

Miss Patterdale cleared her throat, and said in a fierce voice: "Well, Charles, there's nothing you or I can do for the poor man. He's dead, and that's all there is to it."

"He's dead all right," said Charles grimly. "But if you imagine that's all there's going to be to it, Aunt Miriam, you'd better think again!"

CHAPTER FOUR

Miss Patterdale let her monocle fall, and, picking it up as it swung on the end of its thin cord, began to polish it vigorously. "You don't think it can have been an accident, Charles?"

"How could it have been?"

She glanced rather vaguely round. "Don't understand ballistics myself. People do go out with guns, though, after rabbits."

"But they don't aim at rabbits in private gardens," said Charles. "What's more, rabbits aren't usually seen in the air!"

She looked fleetingly at the still figure on the seat. "He was sitting down," she pointed out, but without conviction.

"Talk sense, Aunt Miriam!" Charles begged her. "Any fool could see he's been murdered! You don't even have to have a giant intellect to realize where the murderer must have been standing." He nodded towards the rising commonland beyond the lane, where the gorse-bushes blazed deep yellow in the late sunshine. "Bet you anything he was lying up in those bushes! The only bit of bad luck he had was Mavis being in the lane at the time—and even that wasn't really bad luck, because she was too dumb to do him any harm."

"Can't be surprised the girl was too much shocked to think of looking for him," said Miss Patterdale fairmindedly. "It isn't the sort of thing anyone would expect to happen! I suppose it wouldn't be any use going to search those bushes?"

He could not help laughing. "No, Best of my Aunts, it wouldn't! I don't know how long it took Mavis to assimilate the fact that Warrenby was dead, *and* to be sick, *and* to rush off in search of you, but it was quite long enough to give the unknown assassin ample time to make his getaway."

She went on polishing her monocle, her attention apparently rivetted to this task. Finally, screwing it into place again, she looked at Charles, and said abruptly: "I don't like it. I'm not going to say who I think *might* have done it—or, at any rate, wanted to do it!—but I shouldn't be surprised if it leads to a great deal of the sort of unpleasantness we don't want!"

"I do love you, Aunt Miriam!" said Charles, putting an arm round her, and giving her the hug of the privileged. "A turn in yourself, that's what you are! Don't you worry! Abby and I are your alibis—same like you're ours!"

"Don't be silly!" she said, pushing him away. "You know what I mean!" She cast another glance at the corpse, and said with some asperity: "I shall be glad when *someone* comes to relieve us! If there were anything one could do! But there isn't.

In fact, I imagine that the less we do the better it will be. Standing about to keep watch over a dead man! It's all very well for you to laugh, but I wasn't brought up to this sort of thing."

However, when Charles suggested that she might as well return to her home, she gave a scornful snort, and resumed her scrutiny of the flower-beds. Fortunately, they had not long to wait before relief came in the substantial form of Police-Constable Hobkirk, a stout and middle-aged man who inhabited a cottage in the High Street, and devoted as much of his time as could be spared from his not very arduous police-duties to the cultivation of tomatoes, vegetable-marrows and flowers which almost invariably won the first prizes at all the local shows.

He came up the lane on his bicycle, very hot, for he had been pedalling as vigorously as was suitable for a man of his girth, and a little out of breath. Alighting ponderously from his machine, he propped it against the hedge, and, before entering the garden, removed his cap, and mopped his face and neck with a large handkerchief.

"Good lord! I forgot all about Hobkirk!" exclaimed Charles, conscience-stricken. "I expect I ought to have notified him, not Bellingham. He looks a bit disgruntled, doesn't he? Hallo, Hobkirk! I'm glad you've turned up. Bad business, this."

" 'Evening, sir. 'Evening, miss," said Hobkirk, a note of formality in his voice. "Now, just how did this happen?"

"Good lord, I don't know!" replied Charles. "Miss Patterdale doesn't either. We weren't here. Miss Warrenby found the body, just as you see it, and came to Fox Cottage for help."

"Oh!" said Hobkirk noncommittally. He produced a small notebook from his pocket, and the stub of a pencil. "At what time would that have been?" he asked.

Charles looked at Miss Patterdale. "Do you know? I'm hanged if I do!"

"Come, come, sir!" said Hobkirk.

"It's no use saying come, come, in that reproving way. No doubt, if Miss Warrenby had rushed in to tell you her uncle had been shot, you'd have taken note of the time: you're a policeman. The trouble is I'm not, and I didn't."

"Ah!" said Hobkirk, pleased with this tribute to his superior ability. "That's where it comes in, doesn't it? It'll have to be established, you know, because it's a very important circumstance."

"Well, I daresay we can work it out," said Miss Patterdale, pulling an oldfashioned gold watch out of her waistband, and consulting it. "It's ten past eight now—and I know that's right, because I set my watch by the wireless only this morning—and I should think we must have been here at least half an hour."

"Twenty minutes at the outside," interpolated Charles.

"It seems longer, but you may be right. When did Mavis reach us?"

"I haven't the ghost of an idea," said Charles frankly. "I should make a rotten witness, shouldn't I? What a good job it is that I shan't be expected to know when the murder was committed!"

"I wouldn't say that, sir," said Hobkirk darkly. "And when you found him, the deceased was sitting like he is now?"

"Hasn't moved an inch," said Charles.

"Charles!" said Miss Patterdale. "This is not a moment for flippancy!"

"Sorry, Aunt Miriam! The worst is being roused in me."

"Then overcome it!" said Miss Patterdale severely. "Neither Mr. Haswell nor I have touched the body, Hobkirk, if that, as I suppose, is what you want to know. Miss Warrenby may have touched, though I should doubt it."

"I don't have to tell you, miss, that it is very highly improper for anyone to go touching anything on the scene of the crime." The constable's slow-moving gaze travelled to a sheaf of typewritten papers, clipped together at one corner, and lying on the grass beside the corpse's right foot. "Those papers, now: I take it they was there, laying on the ground?"

"Yes, and do you know what I think?" said Charles irrepressibly. "I believe the deceased must have been reading them—no, I mean *perusing* them, at the time he was shot."

"That's as may be, sir," replied Hobkirk, with dignity. "I don't say it wasn't so, but things aren't always what they seem, not by any means they aren't."

"No, and life is not an empty dream, either. Are you supposed to be in charge of this investigation?"

Hobkirk, in his unofficial moments, rather liked young Mr. Haswell, whom he considered a well-set-up young gentleman, with friendly manners, and one, moreover, who could be relied upon to do great execution, with his inswingers, amongst the batsmen of neighbouring villagers; but he now detected in him a certain lack of respect, combined with a deplorable levity, and he answered with quelling coldness: "I'm here, sir, to take charge of things till relieved. Properly speaking, you had ought to have notified me of this occurrence, when I should, in accordance with the regulations, have reported same to my headquarters in Bellingham."

"At the end of which exercise we should have been precisely where we are now," said Charles. "Still, I'm sorry you aren't going to remain in charge! I say, Aunt Miriam, is it really past eight? I'd better go and give my Mama a ring: we dine at eight, and she always pictures me in the local hospital, with every bone in my body fractured, if I don't show up when I said I would."

He strode off towards the house. Hobkirk watched him go, his countenance betraying some uncertainty of mind. In all the uneventful years of his service no case of murder had previously come his way, so that he had only a half-forgotten memory of text-book procedure to act upon. He felt vaguely that young Mr. Haswell should not be allowed to make use of the telephone belonging to the deceased. But as he had already made use of it, to summon the police, it was difficult to know on what grounds he could now be restrained. Constable Hobkirk held his peace therefore, and was secretly glad of the diversion afforded by the arrival at that moment of Dr. Warcop, in his aged but still reliable car.

Dr. Edmund Warcop, who resided in a comfortable Victorian house, inherited, like his practice, from his long-dead father, and situated on the outskirts of Bellingham, on the Trindale-road, was sixty years of age and as unaccustomed as Constable Hobkirk to dealing with cases of murder. His professional methods, which were oldfashioned, might be the despair of younger and more progressive colleagues, but he enjoyed a very respectable practice, his simpler patients being as conservative as he was himself, and thinking it scarcely possible that they could be born or die without a Warcop to attend them; and the more sophisticated believing that they must be safe in the hands of a man who rode so well to hounds, and who had been established in the district for as long as most of them could remember. He held himself in high esteem, rarely called in a second opinion, and had never been known to admit himself to have been at fault. No one, observing his demeanour as he walked across the lawn towards the oak-tree, would have guessed that this was the first case of its kind which he had attended. A stranger would more readily have supposed that he was a police-surgeon of extensive experience. He nodded to Hobkirk, but favoured Miss Patterdale with a civil good-evening, and a handshake, for she was one of his patients. "I'm sorry you should have been brought into this," he said. "Shocking business! I could scarcely believe it, when young Haswell told me what had happened. Almost under the eyes of Miss Warrenby, I understand."

He then bent over the corpse, while Miss Patterdale walked away to inspect yet another flower-bed, and the constable respectfully watched him. He glanced up after a brief examination, and said: "Nothing for me to do here. Instantaneous, of course. Poor fellow!"

"Yes, sir. How long would you say he's been dead?"

"Impossible to say with any certainty. More than a quarter of an hour, and not more than an hour. We must bear in mind that the body has been all the time in hot sunshine."

42

These remarks he repeated five minutes later, when a police-car set down at Fox House, Detective-Sergeant Carsethorn, accompanied by a uniformed constable, and two men in plain clothes. The Sergeant asked him whether there was anything else he could tell them about the murder, adding, but without malice, that Dr. Rotherhope, who, besides constituting Dr. Warcop's chief rival in Bellingham was also the police-surgeon, had been called out to a confinement, and was thus not immediately available.

Beyond informing the Sergeant that the bullet had entered the skull through the temporal bone, and would be found lodged in the brain, Dr. Warcop had nothing more to tell him. It was the Sergeant himself who observed that the shot had not been fired at very close quarters, no powder-burns being discernible.

By this time Charles had rejoined the group on the lawn. When he saw the Sergeant he was surprised, and said: "Hallo! You're not the chap who dealt with that pilfering we had at the office. What's become of him?"

"Detective-Inspector Thropton, sir. He's away, sick."

"He *will* be fed-up!" remarked Charles. "Mama says I'm to bring Mavis home with me, Aunt Miriam, for the night."

"I shall be requiring to ask Miss Warrenby a few questions, sir, before she leaves the house."

"She isn't here: she's at my house," said Miss Patterdale. "She came running to me for help, and I left her there, in charge of my niece. Can you interview her there?"

"Certainly, madam, that will be quite agreeable to me," said the Sergeant politely. "The young lady will prefer not to return until the body of the deceased has been removed to the mortuary. Very understandable, I'm sure. The ambulance is on its way."

He turned aside to confer with his subordinates, one of whom was preparing to photograph the corpse, issued some low-voiced directions, and then announced that he would like to see Miss Warrenby without further loss of time.

"What ought we to do about the house?" asked Miss Patterdale. "There's no one inside, and although I don't suppose anybody would burgle it, we can't leave it like this, can we? At the same time, I don't like to shut the front-door, because I don't think Miss Warrenby had her handbag with her, in which case she won't have the key."

"One of my men will be staying here to keep an eye on things, madam," replied the Sergeant. "Everything will be quite safe."

"Then, if you have no objection, I'll go with you," said Miss Patterdale. "Are you coming, Charles?"

He nodded, and accompanied her out into the lane. The Sergeant waited until he had skilfully turned his car in the narrow space afforded for this manoeuvre, and then started up the engine of the police-car. Miss Patterdale was thus able to reach Fox Cottage far enough in advance of him to give her time to prepare Mavis's mind for the coming ordeal, which, as she trenchantly observed to Charles, was an extremely desirable circumstance.

However, when they stood once more in the low-pitched parlour they found that Miss Warrenby had regained her composure, and was drinking tea, a stimulant she had preferred to gin. She received the news that she was to be questioned by the police with a wan smile, and said that she had known this must happen, and had been doing her best to collect her thoughts. When the Sergeant arrived, and offered her a formal apology for being obliged to trouble her at such a time, she said that she quite understood, and was anxious to be as helpful as possible. Since she had already discussed her part in the affair with Abby, going over her every movement and mental reaction in exhaustive detail, she was able to tell her story fluently, and even to establish the approximate time of the murder.

"You see, Mrs. Cliburn and I stayed on after the others had gone, to talk about the prizes for the village whist-drive," she explained. "And I know it was ten past seven when I left The Cedars, because I caught sight of the clock in the drawing-room, and that's what it said. I'd no idea it was as late as that. I told Mrs. Haswell I must simply fly, or Poor Uncle would be wondering what had become of me, and I ran across her garden to the gate on to the footpath, and came home that way. And it only takes about five minutes to reach the stile from there, so it must have been about a quarter past seven, or perhaps twenty past when it happened."

"Thank you, miss: that's very clear. And after you heard the shot, you didn't hear or see anything else?"

"No, only a sort of smack, and I didn't think anything of that at the time. I mean, it was so soon after the bang that it seemed part of it, in a way."

"You didn't see anyone? No one on the common, for instance?"

"No, I'm sure I didn't. Of course, I wasn't looking particularly, but I should have been bound to have noticed if there had been anyone."

"You didn't look particularly?" repeated the Sergeant. "The shot was fired from close enough to give you a fright, wasn't it, miss?"

"Yes, but, you see, I didn't know that. I'm afraid I'm silly about guns. I can't bear sudden bangs. I just thought it couldn't have been as close as it seemed."

The Sergeant made a careful note in his book, but offered no comment on this explanation. After a minute, he said: "Do you

44

know of any person, miss, who had a grudge against your uncle?"

"Oh, *no*!" she replied earnestly.

"You know of no quarrel with any person?" She shook her head. "To your knowledge, he had no enemies?"

"Oh, I'm sure he hadn't!"

There was little more to be elicited from her; and after a few further questions the Sergeant took his leave, telling her that she would be advised of the date of the inquest.

The prospect of having to give evidence at an inquest seemed to affect Miss Warrenby almost as poignantly as its cause, and it was several minutes before she could be reconciled to it. She reiterated her conviction that her uncle would have strongly disliked it, and was only partly soothed by an assurance from Miss Patterdale that neither the post-mortem examination nor the inquest would preclude her from burying her uncle with all the ceremonial she seemed to consider was his due. When Charles conveyed his mother's message to her, her eyes filled with grateful tears, and she begged him to thank Mrs. Haswell very, very much for her kindness, and to say how deeply touched she was by it. But she was quite sure Uncle Sampson would have wished her to remain at Fox House.

Nobody could imagine on what grounds she based this conviction. Abby, who was quite uninhibited, asked bluntly: "Why on earth?"

"It has been our home for such a long time," said Mavis, visibly investing it with ancestral qualities. "I *know* he would hate to think I couldn't bear to live there any more. Of course, it will be dreadfully painful just at first, but I've got to get over that, and I believe in facing up boldly to unpleasant things."

The slight discomfort which was too often provoked by Miss Warrenby's nobler utterances descended upon the company. After an embarrassed silence, Charles said, in a practical spirit: "Have you got to get used to living there alone? I suppose it's been left to you, but will you be able to keep it up?"

She looked startled, and a little shocked. "Oh, I haven't thought of such things! How could I? *Please* don't let's talk about them! It seems so sordid, and the very last thing one wants to think about at such a time. I just feel it's my duty to stay at home. Besides, I have to remember poor Gladys. She'll be coming out on the last 'bus, and I couldn't bear her to find the house all locked up and deserted. Whatever would she think?"

"Well, she couldn't think of much worse than the truth," said Miss Patterdale. "However, that certainly is a point: you don't want to lose a good maid on top of everything else. I was thinking you'd be alone in the house: I'd forgotten about your Gladys. If you'd really prefer to go back, you'd better stay here until later, and then I'll take you home, and stay with you till Gladys

45

arrives. Good gracious, look at the time! You must all be famished! Charles, you'd better stay to supper: luckily it's cold, except for the potatoes, and they're all ready to put in the deep-fryingpan. Abby, lay the table, there's a good child!"

"I don't think I could eat anything," said Mavis, rather faintly. "I wonder if I might go upstairs and lie down quietly by myself, Miss Patterdale? Somehow, one feels one would like to be alone at a moment like this."

To the imperfectly disguised relief of Charles and Abby Miss Patterdale raised no objection to this, but took her young friend up to her own bedroom, drew the curtains across the windows, gave her an aspirin, and recommended her to have a nice nap.

"Not but what I've no patience with these airs and graces," she said severely, when she came downstairs again. "Anyone would think Sampson Warrenby had been kind to the girl, which we all know he wasn't. If he's left his money to her, which I should think he must have done, because I never heard that he had any nearer relations, she's got a good deal to be thankful for. I can't stand hypocrisy!"

"Yes, but I don't think it is, quite," said Abby, wrinkling her brow. "I mean, she's so frightfully pi that she thinks you jolly well ought to be sorry if your uncle dies, and so she actually *is*!"

"That's worse! Don't forget the spoon and fork for the salad!" said Miss Patterdale, disappearing in the direction of the kitchen.

The murder of Sampson Warrenby naturally formed the sole topic for conversation over the supper-table, Miss Patterdale making no attempt to restrain the enthusiasm of her niece and (adopted) nephew, but maintaining her own belief that it would lead to unpleasantness. Charles was able to perceive, academically speaking, that there might be a great deal of truth in this; but Abby said simply that she had never hoped to realize an ambition to be, as she phrased it, mixed up in a murder-case. Miss Patterdale, regarding her with a fondly indulgent eye, very handsomely said that she was glad it had happened while she was there to enjoy it.

The subject was still under discussion when, having washed up all the plates and cutlery, the party sat down to drink coffee in the parlour. Miss Patterdale had just ascertained that Mavis, under the influence of aspirin, had sunk into a deep sleep, when a knock on the door heralded the arrival of Gavin Plenmeller, who had come, as he unashamedly confessed, to Talk About the Murder.

"Good heavens, is it all over the village already?" exclaimed Miss Patterdale, ushering him into the parlour.

"But could you doubt that it would be? We had the news in the Red Lion within ten minutes of Hobkirk's setting out for the scene of the crime. Mrs. Hobkirk brought it to us, and very grateful we were. News has been coming in for the past hour and more: I was quite unable to drag myself away, though there was a duck and green peas waiting for me at home. Instead, I ate a singularly nauseating meal at the Red Lion. I can't think how we ever came to be famed for our hostelries. Thank you, I should love some coffee! Where is the heroine of this affair?"

"Lying down upstairs," answered Abby. "How did you know she was here?"

"It is easy to see that you are a town-dweller," said Gavin, dropping a lump of sugar into his cup. "I used to be one myself, and I'm so glad Walter made it possible for me to return to Thornden. Life is very dull in London. You are dependent on the Radio and the Press for all the news. Of course I know that Mavis Warrenby is here! I'm delighted to learn, however, that she's lying down upstairs: I didn't know that, though I suppose I might have guessed it. Now we can talk it all over without feeling the smallest *gêne*."

"How much is known in the village?" asked Charles.

"Oh, much more than the truth! That's why I came. I want to know what really happened. Now, don't tell me it was an accident! That was the first rumour that reached the Red Lion, but nothing would induce me to lend it ear. Of course Sampson Warrenby was murdered! He is recognizable as a character created only to be murdered."

"You mean if he'd been a character in one of your books," said Abby.

"Well, he may yet be that."

"Charles thinks he must have been shot from the bushes opposite the house, on the common," said Miss Patterdale.

Gavin turned his eyes enquiringly to Charles, who briefly explained his reasons for holding this opinion. "He was sitting in the garden with his profile turned to the lane, presumably reading some papers he's taken out with him. It wouldn't have been a very difficult shot."

"But where was Mavis while all this markmanship was going on? Report places her actually on the scene of the crime."

"No, she wasn't quite that, though darned nearly. According to her story, she was getting over the stile at the top of the lane when she heard the shot. That's where the murderer was in luck: a second or two later and she *would* have been on the spot —might even have stopped the bullet."

"No, she mightn't," contradicted Abby. "That's fatuous! The man wouldn't have fired if she'd been in the way!"

"Who knows?" murmured Gavin. "I shall go and view the terrain tomorrow morning. Can't you see the stile from the common? I rather thought you could."

"Yes, I thought of that too," agreed Charles. "Several

explanations possible. The murderer may have been too intent on taking aim to look that way. He may have been lying with the gorse bushes shutting off the stile from his sight."

"I find both those theories depressing. They make it seem as if the murderer is a careless, slapdash person, and that I refuse to believe."

"But that's what they usually are, aren't they?" asked Abby. "Real murderers, I mean, not the ones in books. I know I've read somewhere that they nearly always give themselves away by doing something silly."

"True enough," said Charles. "It 'ud be nice if ours turned out to be a master of crime, but I'm bound to say I haven't much hope of it."

"If you have cast your mind round the district one can only be surprised that you have any," remarked Gavin. "Which brings us to the really burning question exercising all our minds: *who did it?*"

"I know," said Abby sympathetically. "I've been thinking of that, and I haven't the ghost of a notion. Because it isn't enough to dislike a person, is it? I mean, there's got to be a bigger motive than that."

"Besides," said Charles caustically, "we have it on Mavis's authority that her uncle had no ememies."

"Did she say that?" asked Gavin, awed.

"Yes, she did," nodded Miss Patterdale. "When the detective questioned her. I must say, I thought that was going too far. Silly, too. The police are bound to find out that no one could bear the man."

"But did you all stand by and allow this flight of fancy to go unchallenged?"

"Yes," said Abby, "though I should think the detective must have known it was a whopper, if he happened to be looking at Charles when he said it. His jaw dropped a mile. The thing is you can't very well chip in and say the man was utterly barred, when his niece thinks he wasn't!"

"Well, I very nearly did," confessed Miss Patterdale. "Because it's nonsense to say that Mavis thought he was liked in the neighbourhood. She knew very well he wasn't. It's all on a par with pretending to be heartbroken that he's dead. I don't say she isn't *shocked*—I am, myself—but she can't be *sorry*! I'll do her the justice to admit that she has always put a good face on things, and not broadcast the way he treated her, but I know from what she's told me, when he's been worse than usual, that she had a thoroughly miserable time with him."

Gavin, who had been listening to this speech with a rapt look on his face, said: "Oh, I am glad I came to call on you! Of course she did it! It's almost too obvious!"

Abby gave an involuntary giggle, but Miss Patterdale said sharply: "Don't be silly!"

"All the same, it's a pretty fragrant thought," said Charles, grinning.

"It's nothing of the sort! Now, I won't have you making that kind of joke, any of you! It's in very bad taste. Mavis says those things because she thinks one ought not to speak ill of the dead, that's all."

"In what terms does she speak of the Emperor Domitian, and the late Adolf Hitler?" enquired Gavin, interested.

"That," said Miss Patterdale severely, "is different!"

"Well," said Gavin, setting down his empty cup, and dragging himself out of his chair, "if I am not to be allowed to suspect Mavis, I must fall back upon my first choice."

"Who's that?" demanded Abby.

"Mrs. Midgeholme—to avenge the blood of Ulysses. I won't deny that I infinitely prefer her as a suspect to Mavis, but there's always the fear that she'll turn out to have an unbreakable alibi. Mavis, we all know, has none at all. That, by the way, will be our next excitement: who had an alibi, and who had none. You three appear to have them, which, if you will permit me to say so, is very dull and unenterprising of you."

"Have you got one?" Abby asked forthrightly.

"No, no! At least, I hope I haven't: if that wretched landlord says I was sitting in the Red Lion at the time I shall deny it hotly. *Surely* the police cannot overlook my claims to the post of chief suspect? I write detective novels, I have a lame leg, and I drove my half-brother to suicide. What more do the police want?"

"You know," said Charles, who had not been attending very closely to this, "I've been thinking, and I shouldn't be at all surprised, taking into account the time when it happened, if quite a few people haven't got alibis. Everyone was on the way home from our party—the Squire, Lindale, the Major, old Drybeck!"

"Don't forget me, and the Vicar's wife!" interrupted Gavin.

"I don't mind adding you to the list, but I won't have the Vicar's wife. She *can't* have had anything to do with it, and only confuses the issue."

"What about the Vicar himself?" asked Abby, her chin propped on her clasped hands. "Where was he?"

"Went off to visit the sick, didn't he? Anyway, he's out of the running too."

"So are Major Midgeholme, and Mr. Drybeck," Abby pointed out. "We ran them home."

"On the contrary! I set the Major down at the cross-road, because he told me to. I don't know what he did when I drove on. Not that I think he's a likely candidate for the list, but we

49

must stick to the facts. I then set old Drybeck down outside his house. We left him waving goodbye to us: we didn't actually see him enter his house, and for anything we know, he didn't."

"No, that's true," agreed Abby, her eyes widening. "And he really is a likely candidate! Gosh!"

"Now, that's quite enough!" Miss Patterdale interposed. "Talk like that can lead to trouble."

"That's all right, Aunt Miriam," said Charles. "I bet he isn't the only one who *might* have done it."

"Well, just you remember that!" she admonished him. "It's all very well to talk like that about people like poor old Thaddeus Drybeck, but you wouldn't think it nearly so amusing if someone were to do the same about your father, for instance."

Charles stared at her. "Dad? But he wasn't there!"

"Of course he wasn't. But what would you feel like if we started to make up stories of where he *might* have been? You shouldn't let your tongue run away with you."

She appealed to deaf ears. Young Mr. Haswell, betraying an unfilial delight in this novel aspect of his parent, gave a shout of laughter, and gasped: "Dad! Oh, what a rich thought! I *must* ask him if he can account for his movements!"

CHAPTER FIVE

By noon on the following day, the Chief Constable was listening to a report from Detective-Sergeant Carsethorn, who had spent a busy but unpromising morning; half an hour later he expressed a desire to be allowed to think the thing over; and within ten minutes he had reached a not unexpected but not very welcome decision. "And I don't mind telling you, Carsethorn," he said, as he sat waiting to be connected with a certain London telephone number, "that I should do exactly the same if Inspector Thropton hadn't chosen this moment to go down with German measles!"

"Yes, sir," said the Sergeant, torn between a natural desire to achieve promotion through his brilliant handling of a difficult case, and an uneasy suspicion that the problem was rather too complicated for him to tackle.

It was therefore with mixed feelings that, shortly before four o'clock, he made the acquaintance of a bright-eyed and cheerful individual, who was ushered into the Chief Constable's room at the police-station, a tall and rather severe man at his heels.

"Chief Inspector Hemingway?" said Colonel Scales, rising behind his desk, and holding out his hand across it. "Glad to meet you! Heard of you, of course. I warned Headquarters this would need a good man, and I see they've sent me one."

"Thank you, sir!" said the Chief Inspector, without a blush. He shook the Colonel's hand, and indicated his companion. "Inspector Harbottle, sir."

"'Afternoon, Inspector. This is Detective Sergeant Carsethorn, who has been in charge of the case."

"Very happy to work with you," said the Chief Inspector, briskly shaking the Sergeant's hand. "Of course, I don't know much about it yet, but I'm bound to say it sounds like a nice case, on the face of it."

"Eh?" ejaculated the Colonel, startled by this view of a case which he (like Miss Patterdale) feared would lead to much unpleasantness. "Did you say *nice*?"

"I did, sir. What I meant was that it's out of the ordinary."

"In a way I suppose it is. The murder itself does not present us, I think you will agree, with any unusual features, however."

"Plain case of shooting, isn't it, sir? No locked rooms, or mysterious weapons, or any other trimmings?"

"The man was shot in his own garden," said the Colonel, looking at him rather uncertainly. It appeared to him that

51

Chief Inspector Hemingway approached his task in a disquiet-ingly lighthearted spirit. He recalled that he had been warned by an old friend at Scotland Yard that he would find the Chief Inspector a little unorthodox.

"Ah!" said Hemingway. "What you might call a nice, wide field."

"No, a garden," said the Colonel.

"Just so, sir,"

"I'd better tell you exactly what has happened to date. Sit down, all of you! I'm going to light a pipe myself. You can do the same. Or there are cigarettes in that box."

He sat down, and began to fill his pipe from an old-fashioned rubber pouch. The Chief Inspector took a cigarette, and lit it; and his subordinate, offered the box by Sergeant Carsethorn, said in a deep voice that he never smoked.

Having, by the expenditure of several matches, got his pipe going, it did not take the Colonel long to lay the bare facts of the case before Hemingway. It took rather longer to enumerate and to describe the various persons who made up the society of Thornden; and here it was seen that the Colonel was picking his words carefully. Inspector Harbottle, who had been sitting with his eyes fixed on the opposite wall with an immobility strongly suggestive of catalepsy, suddenly bent a gloomy gaze upon him; but his superior maintained his air of bird-like, uncritical interest.

"Dr. Rotherhope performed the autopsy this morning," concluded the Colonel. "Perhaps you'd like to read the report. Nothing much to it, of course: the cause of death was never in doubt."

Hemingway took the report, and ran through it. "No," he agreed. "The only information it gives us which we didn't know before is that the bullet was probably fired from a .22 rifle, and that's a bit of news I could have done without. Not but what I daresay I should have guessed it. Oh, well! I don't suppose there are more than forty or fifty .22 rifles knocking around the neigh-bourhood. It'll make a nice job for my chaps, rounding them up. Cartridge-case been found, by any chance?"

"Yes, sir," said Carsethorn, not without pride. "It's here. Took a lot of time to find it. It was in the gorse-bushes you see on the plan."

"Nice work!" approved Hemingway, putting a tiny magni-fying glass to one eye, and closely scrutinizing the cartridge case through it. "Got some clear markings on it, too, which all goes to show you should never make up your mind in advance. I thought it wouldn't show anything much: nine times out of ten a .22 rifle is so worn it doesn't give you any help at all. We ought to be able to identify the gun this little fellow was fired from. Supposing we were to find it, which I daresay we shan't. If I didn't know that the easier a case looks at the start the worse it turns out to be in the middle, I should say this one's a piece of cake."

"I hope you may find it so," said the Colonel heavily.

"Yes, sir, but it's standing out a mile I shan't. From what you've told me I can see we've got a very classy décor, and, in my experience, that always makes things difficult."

"Does it?" said the Colonel, staring.

"Stands to reason, sir," said Hemingway, flicking over a page of the police-surgeon's report. "For one thing, these people you've been telling me about—Squire, Vicar, family solicitor, retired Major—will all stand by one another. I'm sure I don't blame them," he added cheerfully, oblivious of a slight stiffening on the Colonel's part. "They don't want to have a lot of nosy policemen prying into their affairs. They weren't brought up to it, like the more usual kind of criminal. And, for another, they're apt to have a lot more sense than the criminal classes. In fact, it's a good thing they don't take to crime more often. Yes, I can see this isn't going to be all beer and skittles, not by a long chalk it isn't!" He laid the report down. "Bit coy about the time of death, your Dr. Rotherhope, sir. Any doubt about that?"

"Dr. Rotherhope was unfortunately prevented from seeing the corpse until some hours had elapsed. Dr. Warcop—the deceased's medical adviser—was called in by young Haswell. It is true that he did not commit himself to any very precise time, but he is a man of strict integrity, and the time was, in any event, fixed by Miss Warrenby's evidence."

"Any reason, barring a bit of professional jealousy, sir, why Dr. Rotherhope doesn't what-you-might-call confirm that?"

A laugh was surprised out of the Chief Constable. "You're very acute! None at all! Dr. Warcop has been for long established in Bellingham, and is perhaps thought by his colleagues to be a trifle—er—out of date! But a perfectly sound man!"

"I see, sir. Is it known yet who stands to benefit by this death?"

"Barring a few very minor legacies, his niece. His Will was in the safe at his office. If you want to go into his business affairs, you'll find his head clerk very helpful. Coupland's his name: decent little chap, lived in Bellingham pretty well all his life."

"On good terms with him, sir?"

"Oh, I think so! Speaks very nicely about him. He comes in for a small legacy—a couple of hundred pounds, I think: nothing much! A good deal shocked by the murder, wasn't he, Sergeant?"

"Yes, sir, he was. Well, he's a very respectable man, Mr. Coupland is, so it's natural he would be shocked. Setting aside that it's a pretty serious thing for him. Head clerkships don't grow on every tree, as you might say, and I'm sure I don't know where he's to find another. Not in Bellingham, he won't, for even if Throckington & Flimby wanted a new head clerk it isn't quite the kind of business he'd fancy, and Mr. Drybeck's had his head clerk with him for thirty years."

"Drybeck," repeated Hemingway. "That's the gentleman you told me was given a lift to his home after this tennis-party. Where does he live?"

The Sergeant placed a spatulate finger on the plan. "Here sir, nearly opposite the opening into Fox Lane. As far as we can make out, he must have been set down there at about seven o'clock, or just after. He sat down to his supper at half past seven. That's corroborated by his housekeeper. What he was doing before that she doesn't know, not having seen him."

"What does he say he was doing?"

The Sergeant consulted his notes. "He states that he let himself into the house, and went straight upstairs, and had a shower. Which he might have done, because he's got one of those oldfashioned baths with a shower fixed up at one end of it. After that, he went out into the garden to water his flowers. According to his story, that was what he was doing when the housekeeper sounded the gong for his supper. She states that she had to sound it twice, him not hearing it the first time."

"Where was the housekeeper all this time?"

"Between the kitchen and the dining-room, getting supper ready, and laying the table. The dining-room's at the front of the house, and the kitchen's behind it, at the back. There's a pantry between the two, with communicating doors. She states that she always goes from one room to the other through the pantry, which would account for her not having seen Mr. Drybeck. What I mean is, she never went into the hall during that half-hour, so there was no reason why she should have seen him."

"If the kitchen's at the back doesn't it overlook the garden?"

"No, sir, not properly speaking. There's just a bit of ground outside the kitchen-window, like a gravel-yard, and then there's a laurel-hedge, shutting off the kitchen from the garden."

"Nice, cheerful look-out," commented Hemingway, his eyes on the plan. "So what it boils down to is that from about seven o'clock to seven-thirty this Mr. Drybeck might have been anywhere. If this plan of yours is accurate, I make it under half a mile from his place to Fox House."

"Yes, sir. He'd have had to pass Miss Patterdale's cottage, of course."

"Any reason why he shouldn't have walked across this common?"

"He could have done that," admitted the Sergeant.

"Well, that isn't to say he did," said Hemingway, in consoling

54

accents. "I can see he isn't a popular candidate for the chief rôle in this highly interesting drama. What terms was he on with Sampson Warrenby?"

The Sergeant hesitated, casting a glance at Colonel Scales. But the Colonel did not raise his eyes from his pipe, which had gone out, and needed attention. The Sergeant said, a little awkwardly: "Well, sir, I wouldn't say they was on good terms. I don't want to put it too high, but it's a fact that Mr. Warrenby has done Mr. Drybeck a good deal of harm, professionally speaking—him being what you might call very go-ahead, and Mr. Drybeck more oldfashioned, like. Very successful, Mr. Warrenby has been."

"All right," said Hemingway, apparently dismissing Mr. Drybeck. "Tell me a bit about the rest of the dramatis personae! You can skip this Miss Patterdale of yours, and young Mr. Haswell, and the niece—I've forgotten her name, but as she's got an alibi, same like the other two, I daresay it doesn't matter."

The Colonel looked up. "You have a good memory, Chief Inspector!"

Inspector Harbottle, casting upon his superior a look of vicarious and slightly melancholy pride, made his voice heard. "He has that, sir."

"That'll be all from you, Horace!" said the Chief Inspector conclusively. "Let's take this Pole of yours first, Sergeant! If I'd been told there was a Pole mixed up in this case I'd have reported sick. What's his unnatural name?"

The Sergeant once more consulted his notes. "Zamagoryski," he enunciated painstakingly. "Though they mostly seem to call him Mr. Ladislas, that being his Christian name."

"Well, we'll call him that too, though a more unchristian name I never heard!" said Hemingway. "The sooner we can be rid of him the better. I've had one case with a Georgian mixed up in it, and two more with Poles, and they pretty nearly gave me a nervous breakdown. This Ladislas, now, who was seen riding his motor-bike up Fox Lane shortly after five-thirty, how does he come into the picture?"

"Well, sir, they do say, in the village, that he's running after Miss Warrenby, and that her uncle wouldn't have him, not at any price. He's some sort of an engineer by profession, and he's got a job at Bebside's. He lodges with Mrs. Dockray, in one of the cottages beyond Mr. Drybeck's house. *That* one," the Sergeant added, indicating it on the plan. "Nice-looking young fellow, in his way, but a bit excitable. By what he told me, though I'm bound to say I wasn't attending very closely, it not being any of my business, he used to be very well-off before the War. Estates, and such, in Poland. He was so keen on telling me I thought it best to let him get it off his chest. One or two of the gentry have taken him up, but most of them don't know

55

him. He got to know Miss Warrenby, through meeting her at the Vicarage, and it seems she took a fancy to him. She's a very kindhearted young lady. She told me she was sorry for him in the first place, and got to like him enough to be very friendly. Quite frank she was about it. Said it was true her uncle had forbid her to have anything to do with him, but that she hadn't held with that kind of snobbishness. Seems they used to go for walks together, and to the pictures once or twice, when Mr. Warrenby was away. Well, it was like I told you, sir. He was seen turning into Fox Lane on his motor-bike, round about five-thirty, by Miss Kingston. She keeps the sweet-shop in the village, and she'd gone out for a bit of an airing on the common, after she closed the shop. Quite definite it was him. Well, you wouldn't mistake him: he's a very dark, handsome sort of chap, and foreign-looking."

"Didn't see him come out of the lane again?"

"No, sir. She wouldn't have, though, being on her way back to the village."

"What's his story?"

"First he swore he hadn't been near Fox Lane, but I don't set much store by that, because by the time I saw him it was all over the village Mr. Warrenby had been shot, and I don't doubt he had the wind up. After we got through with that, and with him working himself into a state because of him being foreign and everyone against him, he admitted he had gone to Fox House, to try if he could see Miss Warrenby. He didn't know she'd gone to a tennis-party. On account of its being Saturday, and Mr. Warrenby likely to be at home, he says he left his bike a little way away from the house, and went in the side-gate that leads to the kitchen, meaning to ask the maid if he could have a word with Miss Warrenby. Only, Saturday's her half-day, so she wasn't in. He says he knocked on the kitchen-door, and when he got no answer he went away again. Swears he was back at Mrs. Dockray's before six, and never stirred out again. But as she'd gone off to the pictures, here in Bellingham, leaving him a bit of cold supper, she can't corroborate that."

"Does he own a rifle?"

"He says not, sir. So far, I haven't been able to discover that he does. Mrs. Dockray said she'd seen him with one once, but that turned out to have been a couple of weeks ago, and was Mr. Lindale's .22, which he lent him, and which was subsequently returned to him. Corroborated by Mr. Lindale. He's the gentleman who owns Rushyford Farm—this place, on the Hawkshead-road."

"Well, let's take him next," said Hemingway. "I see his farm is very conveniently placed for this footpath which leads to the stile at the top of Fox Lane. Any reason why he should want to murder Sampson Warrenby?"

The Colonel answered this. "None at all, on the face of it. He's a newcomer to the district. Bought Rushyford Farm a matter of two years ago. Used to be a stockbroker. Got a very pretty wife, and one child. I fancy they're fairly newly-wed: the child's only an infant."

"That's right, sir," corroborated the Sergeant. "There doesn't seem to be any reason to think he could have had anything to do with the murder, barring the fact that he didn't like the deceased, which he makes no bones about, and having been pestered by him a bit to try to get him appointed as solicitor to the new River Board. Mr. Warrenby seems to have been set on that, but by what I can make out they none of them wanted him."

"Who are 'they'?" demanded Hemingway. "Shouldn't have thought it was much of a job to be after, but I don't know a lot about River Boards."

"Oh, no, it isn't!" said the Colonel. "That is to say, there's not a great deal to be got out of it, but it would make quite a pleasant addition to his business. My own view of the matter is that he wanted it for social reasons. It would bring him into contact with the sort of people he was ambitious to know. Give him more of a finger in county affairs, too. Pushful sort of man, you understand. The appointment is pretty well in the hands of just those people: the Squire, Gavin Plenmeller, Henry Haswell, and Lindale. They're all riparian owners, and they represent the interests of the Fishery rights. The Rushy runs through the Squire's and Lindale's lands; and Haswell and Plenmeller both own property on it. I can't see what bearing a thing like that has on murder. If Lindale hadn't been at that party, he wouldn't, in my opinion, have come into the case at all."

"Well, sir, seeing as his movements, between the time he left The Cedars, at 6.50, as near as I can get at it, till close on 7.30, aren't corroborated by any witness——"

"Oh, yes, yes, Carsethorn, you were quite right to interrogate him!" the Colonel said impatiently.

"What does he say his movements were?" asked Hemingway.

"At or around 6.50," said the Sergeant, his eyes on his book, "he left The Cedars, in company with Mr. Ainstable, by way of the gate on to the footpath. Mrs. Lindale had gone off home by the same route about a quarter of an hour earlier. The woman who works for her daily isn't prepared to swear to the time when she got back to the farm, but she says she'd been in a considerable time by seven o'clock, which is when the woman leaves. Of course, she could have gone out again later, but it don't seem likely, not with the baby. She's not one to leave her

57

baby. Mr. Lindale accompanied Mr. Ainstable a little way up the path. Then the Squire turned off to look at his new plantation, and Mr. Lindale walked on to Rushyford Farm. He says he didn't go into the house immediately, but went off to see whether his chaps had finished a job they had to do, repairing some fencing in one of his water-meadows. That's some little distance from the house. The men had gone off by that time, of course, and he didn't meet anyone. He says he went home by way of his wheat-field, and was in by 7.30. Which Mrs. Lindale corroborates."

"Well, that's all right, as far as it goes," said Hemingway. "What about this Squire you talk of?"

"Mr. Ainstable. It's like I told you, sir. He went off to look at the plantation, and didn't get home till about a quarter to eight. Mrs. Ainstable, I should mention, had left the party early, by car, at 6.30. That's corroborated by Mr. Plenmeller. He met her in the drive—he'd been back to his house to fetch some papers the Squire wanted—and she stopped to have a word with him. Seems she wasn't very well: he says she looked bad, and was very nervy. She's a bit of an invalid. Another person who went away early was Mr. Cliburn, the Vicar. He went directly after tea, to visit a sick parishioner. I should say that's all right, sir. I haven't yet checked up on him, but——"

"Well, don't, unless you're hard up for a job," Hemingway advised him. "Of course, we may have to fall back on him, but if we do, all I can say is I shall be surprised, and it takes a lot to surprise me. I might be able to swallow the Vicar's wife, at a pinch, but even that'll take a bit of doing."

"Mrs. Cliburn and Miss Warrenby were the last to leave, sir," said the Sergeant, uncertain how to take the Chief Inspector. "They both left at ten past seven, Miss Warrenby going by way of the garden-gate, and Mrs. Cliburn down the drive to Wood Lane. I've checked up on that. There's an old chap who lives in one of the cottages in the High Street, facing Wood Lane. He was sitting on his doorstep, and he saw Mrs. Cliburn come down the lane. He couldn't say what time that was, because he wasn't noticing particularly, but it seems Mrs. Cliburn stopped to pass the time of day with him, and then went straight into the Vicarage. He says he saw Mr. Plenmeller too, and that he didn't go to Thornden House but along the street to the Red Lion. And he didn't have a rifle, because that's something old Rugby would have been bound to have noticed."

"Well, we can rule out Mrs. Cliburn, too," said Hemingway. "Which brings us to this chap with the queer name. I've heard it before, but I don't seem able to put a face to it."

"I suppose you might have heard it," said the Colonel grudgingly. "He writes detective stories. Don't read 'em myself, but I'm told they're very ingenious."

58

"Yes, I thought this case sounded a bit too good to be true," said Hemingway. "So I'm stuck with one of these amateur crime-specialists, am I, sir? Has he got an alibi?"

"There seems to be some doubt about that," replied the Colonel, on a dry note. "You'd better tell him what Plenmeller said to you, Sergeant. He may as well know what he's up against."

"Well, sir, it's a fact I don't know what to make of him," confessed the Sergeant. "Anyone would think there was nothing he liked better than to be mixed up in a case of murder! I ran him to earth at the Red Lion this morning, drinking a pint with Major Midgeholme, just after twelve. Quite the life and soul of the bar, he was, holding forth about the murder, and saying how he was sure the Major's wife had done it, because of Mr. Warrenby having been brutal to one of her little dogs. All by way of a joke, of course, but you could see the Major didn't like it. So then Mr. Plenmeller started in to prove how he might have done it himself. Very humorous he was, I'm sure, but not having the whole day to waste I stepped up to the bar, and told him who I was, and said I'd like a word with him. And if you was to ask me, sir, that was all he needed to make him quite happy. Anyone would have thought the whole thing was a play, and we was having drinks between the acts, and talking it over. Indecent, I call it, not to say coldblooded! Naturally I'd no thought of asking him questions in a public bar: my idea was we'd step up to his house, but that wouldn't do for him. 'Oh', he says, 'you want to know where I was at the time the crime was committed, and I'm sure I haven't got an alibi!' The Major took him up pretty sharp on that, and said as how he knew very well he was on his way home when the rest of them—him, and Mr. Drybeck, and Miss Dearham—set off in young Mr. Haswell's car. 'Ah!' says Mr. Plenmeller, 'but how do you know I did go home? I might have been anywhere,' he says, 'and Crailing—that's the landlord of the pub—will swear I didn't come in here till close on eight last night!' Which, however, Crailing didn't do, not by a long chalk! He said he was positive Mr. Plenmeller came in long before that, though he couldn't be sure what the exact time was. Then I'm blessed if Mr. Plenmeller didn't tell him not to go saddling him with an alibi he didn't want. Before I could say anything, the Major spoke to him, very military. Told him not to make a fool of himself, and to stop trying to turn the whole thing into a farce. So then he laughed, and said it was all such good copy he wasn't going to be pushed out of it, and it was going to be very valuable to him to know how it felt to be what he called a hot suspect. However, he got a bit more serious after that, and he said that actually he had gone home before stepping down the street to the Red Lion, though he didn't think he could prove it, because

59

so far as he knew Mrs. Blindburn—that's his housekeeper—couldn't have seen him, being in the kitchen, and certainly wouldn't have heard him, because she's as deaf as a post. Which is true enough: she is."

"I see," said Hemingway, somewhat grimly. "I've met his sort before! Oh, well, with any luck we may be able to pin the murder on him!"

The Colonel smiled, but Sergeant Carsethorn looked a little shocked. "Well, I daresay he *could* have done it," he said dubiously, "but I can't say I know why he should want to."

"The Chief Inspector wasn't speaking seriously, Sergeant."

"No, sir. That's about the lot, then, as far as we've had time to discover."

"What about young Mr. Haswell's father?" enquired Hemingway. "Or is he out of the running?"

"He wasn't there, sir. He went off to Woodhall that afternoon, and didn't get home till half past eight. Woodhall's a good fifteen miles from Thornden: it's a big estate which he looks after for the owner. He's an estate agent, and he does a good bit of that sort of work."

"Was he on good terms with Mr. Warrenby?"

The Sergeant hesitated. "I wouldn't say that exactly, but on the other hand I wouldn't say that there was anything definite, if you take my meaning. They were both on the Council, and I believe they had a few differences of opinion."

"Tell me something else!" invited Hemingway. "Do you know of anyone who *was* on good terms with this character?"

The Sergeant grinned. Colonel Scales said: "Yes, you've hit the mark, Chief Inspector. He was a nasty piece of work, and no one could stand him! I don't mind telling you that I couldn't myself. He was one of those men who not only want to have a finger in every pie, but who are never content until they're top-dog. Sort of pocket-Hitler! A bumptious little upstart who wanted to be the kingpin in the district, and would go to any lengths to muscle in on things that were no concern of his, and which you wouldn't have thought he'd want to be bothered with! He even got himself on to the committee for the charity-ball Lady Binchester organized, a year ago. I don't know how he managed that, but I've no doubt he thought it would give him a foothold in that set. More fool he!"

"It sounds to me, sir, as though this place where he lived can't have been the only place where he made enemies. We've gone into all the Thornden people. What about the people he must have rubbed up against here, where he had his business?"

"We've thought of that, naturally, but setting aside the fact that Carsethorn hasn't heard of any Bellingham-man being seen in Thornden at the time—of course, it's possible to get to Fox House across the common, I know—I don't know that he had any serious quarrel with anyone. There was a good deal of jealousy, a lot of people disliked him, we should most of us have been glad to have seen him leave Bellingham. He was the best-hated man in the district, but you don't murder a man you just don't like: there has to be some motive! And that, Chief Inspector, is why I thought it wisest to call in Scotland Yard at once: no one has anything that *begins* to look like a sufficient motive!"

"There's the Pole that seems to have been making passes at the niece, isn't there?" suggested Hemingway mildly. "What's more, there's the young lady herself. If she inherits his money, I should call that a pretty good motive."

"You'd better go and make Miss Warrenby's acquaintance!" recommended the Colonel, with a bark of laughter.

"I will, sir," said the Chief Inspector.

CHAPTER SIX

"THE trouble with you, Horace, is that there's no pleasing you," said the Chief Inspector, some little time later. "I bring you down, in the middle of the summer, to as nice a part of the country as you could wish for, set you up in a pub which, as far as I can see, never got around to reading the Rationing Orders, and all you do is to sit there looking as though you'd been dragged to one of the Distressed Areas. I'll trouble you for the butter, my lad!"

The Inspector handed him a green dish fashioned into the semblance of a lettuce-leaf. "It *is* butter, to," he said severely. "About a week's ration."

Hemingway helped himself generously. Both men were sitting down, in the otherwise deserted coffee-room, to a high tea reminiscent of an almost forgotten age of plenty. The Sun, though perhaps its oldest, was by no means Bellingham's most fashionable hostelry. It was situated in a back street, and catered for Commercials; the rigours of its beds were alleviated by feather-mattresses; it had one bathroom, containing an antiquated painted bath, with an oldfashioned plug, and a wooden surround; and several of its tiny lattice windows could, by the exercise of careful force, be induced to open. Since its clients were not persons of leisure, only one sitting-room had been provided for them, and that the coffee-room, which contained, besides one long table, a number of horsehair chairs; a massive and very yellow mahogany sideboard, supporting an aspidistra, a biscuit-tin commemorating the coronation of Edward VII, and an array of sauce-bottles and pickle-jars; several steel-engravings in maplewood frames; and a tall vase full of pampas-grass. Meals were not served with elegance, or dignified by menu-cards, but the food itself was excellent, and prepared by a large-minded person. An order for tea was understood by this person to include a plate piled with bacon, eggs, sausages, tomatoes, and chips, three or four kinds of jam, scones, a heavy fruit cake, a loaf of bread, a dish of stewed fruit, and one of radishes. Sergeant Carsethorn had recommended the Sun to Hemingway, a circumstance which was causing that cheerful officer to take what his assistant considered a roseate view of his ability.

"And I'd like to know how they come by all that bacon," added Harbottle, in a sinister voice.

The Chief Inspector poured himself out another cup of tea, and lavishly sugared it. "Why you ever went in for homicide beats me," he remarked. "What you ought to have done was to have got yourself a job as snooper for the Ministry of Food. What's it matter to you where they come by their bacon? I didn't hear you making any bones about eating it. Have another cup of tea!"

Harbottle accepted his offer, and sat for some minutes stirring the brew meditatively. "It's all very well being sent into the country," he said suddenly, "but I don't like this case, Chief!"

"That's because you've got an inferiority-complex," responded Hemingway, unperturbed. "I thought there'd be trouble when they started talking about the Squire. It set you off remembering the days when you were one of the village lads, carting dung, and touching your forelock to the Squire."

"I did no such thing!" said his indignant subordinate. "What's more I never carted dung in my life, or touched my forelock! I hadn't got one, and I wouldn't have touched it if I had had!"

"One of the Reds, were you? Well, it's no use brooding over the equality of man here, because that won't get us anywhere." He observed that the Inspector was breathing heavily, and added soothingly: "All right, Job! you cool off, or you'll very likely burst a blood-vessel."

"Why Job?" demanded the Inspector suspiciously.

"If you read your Bible you'd know that the poor chap suffered from a horrible disease. Amongst other things, which I've forgotten for the moment."

"Now, look here!" exploded Harbottle. "What am I supposed to be suffering from, I'd like to know?"

"Me, mostly," replied Hemingway serenely.

A reluctant grin greeted this sally. "Well, you're the boss, so it won't do for me to contradict you, sir. But what you see in this case to be pleased about I can't make out! Seems to me it's either going to be easy that this local Sergeant you think so well of might just as well have solved it for himself; or it's going to be such a snorter that we shall never get to the bottom of it."

"It's got class," said Hemingway, selecting a radish from the dish. "It's got a good décor, too, and, barring the Pole, I like the sound of the dramatis personae. It isn't every day you get a murder amongst a lot of nice, respectable people living in a country village. Of course, I daresay Snettisham will dig up some character with a record as long as your arm, here in Bellingham, who'll turn out to be the guilty party, but so far it looks a lot more promising than that. It's got what you might call possibilities."

The Inspector frowned over these. "The Pole—which you wouldn't like!—and the niece, which the Chief Constable laughed at. I didn't reckon much to any of the others. Except that I'd like to know why the Chief Constable shut up so tight when Carsethorn started on the solicitor—Drybeck!"

"Because Drybeck's his own solicitor, and he plays golf with him every weekend," replied Hemingway promptly.

"Did Carsethorn tell you that, sir?"

"No, he didn't have to. It's standing out a mile the Chief Constable's on friendly terms with most of the people mixed up in the case. That's why he was so prompt in calling us in, and I'm sure I don't blame him."

Harbottle shook his head over this evidence of the frailty of human nature, but he appeared to accept it, and relapsed once more into meditative silence. The frown deepened between his brows; he presently said abruptly: "There's one thing that strikes me about this case, Chief!"

"What's that?" asked Hemingway, not looking up from his study of the plan of Thornden.

"Well, it seems to be fairly well established that the shot was fired from close to that clump of gorse. How did the murderer know that the deceased was going to be so obliging as to sit down on that seat in his garden at just that time of day?"

"He didn't," replied Hemingway. "He probably didn't even know he was going to have the luck to find Warrenby in the garden at all. You think it over, Horace! If the murder was committed by one of the people at that tennis-party, he knew Miss Warrenby wasn't in the house, and it's a safe bet he also knew it was the maid's day out. He may have thought Warrenby was likely to be in the garden on a hot June evening, but it wouldn't have mattered if he hadn't been. You've seen the house: it came out good and clear in one of the photographs. It's got long french windows, which would be bound to be standing open on a day like that. As for the time, that didn't matter either. If the Pole did it, obviously he couldn't have, because he must have had to lie up, waiting for Warrenby to show himself, for nearly a couple of hours. Which is one reason why I don't, so far, much fancy young Ladislas."

"The more I think of it, the more I can't help feeling it must have been someone who wasn't at that party at all," said Harbottle. "If it was one of them, where was the rifle? If it had been a cricket-match, we could assume it had been all the time in the murderer's cricket-bag; but what would anyone take to a tennis-party which could possibly hold a rifle?"

"Nothing, of course. That's quite a good point, Horace, but there's an easy answer to it. If the murderer was at that party, he knew the locality well, and somewhere between the Haswells' place and Warrenby's he had that rifle cached where he could pick it up easily at the right moment. You're a country-man! You ought to know it isn't very difficult, where you've got woods, and hedges, and ditches. I'd choose a ditch, myself, at

64

this time of the year, when the grass is long, and everything a regular tangle of dog-roses, and meadowsweet, and the rest of it."

"Yes," admitted Harbottle. "If it turns out to be like you describe."

"Well, we shall soon see," said Hemingway. "Carsethorn's coming round here before six to pick us up, and take us out to Thornden. They've had a chap keeping an eye on Fox House ever since yesterday, and Miss Warrenby wants him to be removed as soon as convenient, on account of the maid, who says she can't stay there with a policeman on the premises. Nice reputation the police have got in these parts!"

"People don't like having police in the house," said the Inspector seriously. "It isn't respectable."

"Well, once I've had a look at the scene, and gone through any private papers there may be in the desk, he can be taken off. I don't want to lose that girl a maid, even if she did murder her uncle, which we don't know, after all. Warrenby had a London solicitor, but beyond having drawn up his Will he doesn't seem to have done much for him. He's fishing in Scotland at the moment, anyway: the Chief Constable had a word with his clerk, and then with Miss Warrenby, who said she was sure her uncle wouldn't have minded us doing whatever it was our duty to do. So we don't have to lug this bird back from Scotland before we can get on with the job."

"What about the Will?" objected Harbottle.

"That was in Warrenby's safe at his office. This London lawyer is one of the executors, according to what his clerk told the Colonel, and Miss Warrenby's the other. Which made it all plain sailing. It was opened in her presence, and I can go through any papers there may be, in her presence, too. And when we get through at Fox House, we'll call on Mr. Drybeck. We don't want to start a scandal in his office, by going to interview him there tomorrow."

This programme was carried out. At the appointed hour Sergeant Carsethorn arrived with a police-car, and twenty minutes later the Chief Inspector was enjoying his first view of the village of Thornden. A game of cricket was being played on the common, where a level piece of the ground beside the Trindale-road had been turned into a playing-field; but the village itself was wrapped in a Sunday stillness. The Sergeant drove up to the cross-road, to enable Hemingway to see where Wood Lane turned out of the High Street, and then turned, and drove back to Fox Lane.

Before entering the garden of Fox House, the three men, leaving the car, climbed the rising ground of the common to where the flaming gorse bushes stood. From this point of vantage quite an extensive view could be obtained over the common, which stretched away eastward in the general direction of Bellingham. It was dotted over with similar clumps of gorse, and a great many blackberry bushes, with here and there one or two trees, mostly silver birches. Away to the north, close to the Hawkshead-road, some fencing railed off a gravel-pit which, the Sergeant told Hemingway, had recently been opened up by the Squire. He explained that the common was not Crown land, but manorial waste. "All the land here used to belong to the Ainstables, except what the Plenmellers had, west of the village, but you know how things have been for people like them, ever since the First War. They say young Plenmeller doesn't care, and from what I've seen of him I shouldn't think he cares about anything much; but the Squire's a very different sort of man. Quite one of the old school, as you may say. He'll carry on while he lives, but it's likely to be a bad look-out when he dies, because it's not to be expected that the next man will work like he does to keep things going. Lost his son in the last war, you know. I'm told the place'll go to a nephew or a cousin, or something, who never comes near it. Well, he couldn't, really: he lives in Johannesburg. Not at all the sort of Squire Thornden's accustomed to. I reckon you've got to hand it to Mr. Ainstable. It fairly knocked him out, the young chap's being killed, but he's carried on, stiff-backed as you please, doing everything he can, like starting up that gravel-pit, to keep up the estate. Over there's his new plantations: he's had to sell a lot of timber."

Hemingway nodded. "Not many left now like him," he remarked, turning to survey the garden of Fox House. "Well, it would have been an easy shot," he said, his eyes on the seat under the tree. They travelled on, up the lane, to the stile at the top of it.

"You see, if you was to crouch down you couldn't be seen from the stile," the Sergeant pointed out.

"No. Seems to be woodland beyond it."

"That's right: Mr. Haswell's spinney. The footpath skirts it. It used to be all woodland from the common up to the Vicarage meadow—you can't see that from here, but it's behind the grounds of Fox House. Of course, that's a long time ago now, but they say those fine old trees you can see were once part of it. Makes you think, doesn't it?"

The Chief Inspector was certainly thinking, but if the subject of his thought was an ancient forest he did not say so. After looking about him in silence for a few moments, he said briskly: "Well, let's get on!" and led the way down into the lane again.

The arched and massively built front-door of Fox House stood open, in the country-way, allowing a view of the hall, and of the carved staircase at the end of it. The floor was of black oak, and had two Persian rugs thrown down on it. An old chest stood under the window opposite the front-door; there was a warped gateleg-table in the centre, and several highbacked Jacobean chairs were ranged against the walls. One or two sporting prints completed an interior that seemed in some indefinable way to represent a period piece rather than the owner's individuality.

"Mr. Warrenby furnished the place regardless, when he bought it," confided the Sergeant. "He had a man down from London to advise him, even."

There was an iron bell hanging beside the front-door, and this the Sergeant tugged. The effect was instant and unexpected. Furious yapping arose, and through the half-open doorway on the left of the hall skidded two tawny and determined defenders. One of these made threatening darts at the intruders; the other, a more elderly gentleman, contented himself with standing squarely before them, and uttering slightly wheezy barks.

"Now, now, Peekaboos!" called a fondly chiding voice. "Naughty! Come back to Mother at once!"

"Mrs. Midgeholme!" whispered the Sergeant.

The look he cast at Hemingway was pregnant with meaning, but he had no time to explain the reason for his patent horror: Mrs. Midgeholme, overpowering in lilac foulard, came out of the drawing-room, and explained: "Oh! It's the police! Well, *really*! On a Sunday!"

"Good afternoon, madam. This is Chief Inspector Hemingway, from Scotland Yard. And Inspector Harbottle. They wish to see Miss Warrenby, if convenient, please."

"Scotland Yard!" ejaculated Mrs. Midgeholme, apparently regarding this institution in the light of a Gestapo headquarters. "That poor child!"

"That's all right, madam," said Hemingway soothingly. "Properly speaking, I only want to have a look through her uncle's papers. There *are* one or two questions I'd like to ask her, but don't you worry! I shan't go upsetting her."

"Well," said Mrs. Midgeholme, with an air of noble resolution, "if you *must* see her, I shall insist on being present! She is alone in the world, and she has had a terrible shock. I refuse to abandon her!"

"And I'm sure it does you credit," said Hemingway affably. "I've got no objection." He bent to stroke the elderly Peke, who was sniffing his shoe. "Well, you're a very handsome fellow, aren't you?"

The Peke, his eyes starting angrily, growled at him. However, Hemingway was scratching the exact spot on his back which afforded him the most gratification, so he stopped growling, and faintly waved his plumed tail. This circumstance struck Mrs. Midgeholme forcibly. She exclaimed: "He's taken a fancy to you! Ulysses! He hardly ever allows strangers to touch him!

67

Do you like that kind of policeman, then, my precious? Oh, *Untidy*! You mustn't let her bother you!"

By this time, the younger Peke, encouraged by the example set her by her grandfather, was effusively making the Chief Inspector welcome. Sergeant Carsethorn heaved an exasperated sigh, but no one could have supposed from Hemingway's demeanour that he had come to Thornden with any other purpose in mind than to admire Mrs. Midgeholme's Pekes. Within a few minutes he and Mrs. Midgeholme were fast friends; and he could have answered an examination-paper on Ulysses's superlatively good points, the number of prizes he had won, and the number of prize-winners he had sired. It was on a wave of good-will that he was finally ushered into the drawing-room. Here, seated in a wing-chair, with her hands folded in her lap, was Mavis Warrenby. Not being one of those who considered no wardrobe complete that did not contain at least one Good Black Frock, she had been unable to array herself in mourning, but had compromised by putting on a very unbecoming dress of slate grey. She got up, as the party entered, and said, casting a somewhat spaniel-like glance at Mrs. Midgeholme: "Oh, what——?"

"Now, there's nothing to be nervous about, my dear!" said that lady bracingly. "These are two detectives from Scotland Yard, but you've no need to be alarmed! They're very nice, and I shall remain with you all the time!"

"Oh, thank you! I'm sorry to be so silly," Mavis said, with a fleeting look at Hemingway. "I think it must all have been a little too much for me. Of course, I know I must be prepared to answer questions, and I shall do my best to help you in any way I can. I know it's my duty to, however painful it may be."

She then proceeded, with very little encouragement, to relate the whole story of her activities on the previous afternoon, not omitting a description of her qualms at leaving the late Mr. Warrenby alone in the house, and what she had said to Mrs. Haswell on perceiving how late it was. Not unnaturally, since she had by now told her story a good many times, it had grown a little in its details, and she had talked herself into almost believing that she had had a premonition of evil when she had left the house. But in two essentials the tale was identical with the version Sergeant Carsethorn had already heard: she knew of no one who could have had any reason to kill her uncle; and she had seen no one at the time when she had been startled by the shot.

"Do you know," she said simply, "I can't help feeling glad I didn't see anyone? It would be such a terrible thing to *know*! I mean, it can't bring Uncle back, and I'd much, much rather not know!"

"We know just how you feel, dear," Mrs. Midgeholme

assured her. "But you wouldn't want your uncle's murderer to go unpunished! Besides, we can't have a killer allowed to wander about our dear little village. We should none of us be able to sleep in our beds. I don't believe in trying to conceal things. I was just talking it over with Miss Warrenby when you arrived, Inspector, trying to think who *might* have done it."

"I don't think one ought to," said Mavis, in a troubled tone.

"Well, if you'll pardon me," said Hemingway, "that's where you're wrong! If you do know of anyone who might have done it, it's your plain duty to talk about it to me!"

"Oh, but I don't! I can't *imagine!*"

"Really, Mavis, that's going too far!" protested Mrs. Midgeholme. "It's all very well to be loyal to your uncle's memory—not that you've any reason to be!—but when you tell the Inspector that your uncle had no enemies—well, it just isn't true, dear, because you know very well that he had! I don't say it was his fault—though of course it was—but facts are facts! Heaven knows I'm not one to gossip about my neighbours, but I should very much like to know what Kenelm Lindale was doing after he left that party. I've always said there was something fishy about the Lindales. The way they live, never going anywhere, or taking a real part in Thornden society. It's all very well for Mrs. Lindale to say she can't leave the baby, but I think she's just stand-offish. Why, when they first came to Rushyford Farm I went to call *immediately,* and did my best to be a friend to her, but she was quite unresponsive: in fact, she made it very clear that she'd rather I *didn't* drop in at the Farm without being invited."

"I'm sure she's always been very nice to *me*," said Mavis repressively.

"Oh, I'm not saying she isn't perfectly polite, but do you *get* anywhere with her?" demanded Mrs. Midgeholme. "When I asked her about her people, and where she came from, and how long she'd been married, she was evasive. There's no other word for it: *evasive!* I wondered at the time if she had anything to hide. Well, it isn't natural for a girl—for that's what she is to me!—not to talk about her people! And I'll tell you another thing," she added, rounding on Hemingway, "they never have anybody to stay! You'd think her mother and father would visit her, or *his* mother and father, or a sister, or something, wouldn't you? Well, they don't! Not once!"

"Perhaps they're dead," suggested Hemingway.

"They couldn't *all* be dead!" said Mrs. Midgeholme. "Everybody has *some* relations!"

"Oh, Mrs. Midgeholme, please don't talk like that!" begged Mavis. "Now Poor Uncle has passed over I haven't any relations either. Not ones I *know!*"

"But you're not married, dear," said Mrs. Midgeholme,

somewhat obscurely, but with an air of one who had clinched the matter.

At this point, the Chief Inspector intervened, He said that he would like to go through the late Mr. Warrenby's papers, and in Miss Warrenby's presence.

"*Must* I?" Mavis asked, shrinking from the prospect. "I'm sure Uncle wouldn't have liked me to pry into his desk!"

"Well, it's not to be supposed he'd have liked any of us to do so," said Hemingway practically. "However, that can't be helped, and as I understand you're an executor to his Will, I think you'd better come and keep an eye on me."

A biddable girl, she rose to her feet, saying as she did so: "I couldn't believe it, when Colonel Scales told me that! I never had the least idea Uncle meant to appoint *me*. I'm afraid I don't know what executors do, but I'm so touched it makes me want to cry!"

She then led the way across the hall to the large, sunny room on the other side of it, which Mr. Warrenby had appropriated as his study. She paused on the threshold, and smiled wanly upon Hemingway. "I expect you'll think me very foolish, but I hate going into this room! Of course, I know he wasn't—I know it didn't happen there, but still—I can't help looking for him when I go in. And I want to get rid of that seat in the garden at once. That is, if the police don't mind? I know nothing must be touched until you say so."

"No, I don't mind: very natural you should want to get rid of it," said Hemingway, stepping into the study, and looking round.

"Every time I see it it reminds me!" said Mavis, shuddering. "My uncle very rarely sat out of doors. It was really *my* favourite seat, which seems to make it worse somehow. Doesn't it seem dreadful to think that if it hadn't been so terribly hot I don't suppose he ever would have taken his work out into the garden, and then none of this would have happened?"

The Chief Inspector, who was growing tired of these gentle inanities, agreed to this, and nodded to the constable who had been sitting in the room, reading a newspaper.

"I thought it best to leave a man on duty till you came, sir," explained Sergeant Carsethorn. "We couldn't very well seal the room, on account of the telephone. It's the only one in the house."

A slight twinkle was in the Chief Inspector's eye as his gaze alighted on the instrument, which stood on Sampson Warrenby's desk. It appeared to him that Miss Warrenby must have been obliged to enter the study a good many times since the murder of her uncle. As though she read his thought, Mavis said: "I've come to dread the sound of the telephone-bell."

The room, which had obviously been swept and dusted, was

very neat, the papers on the top of the desk, on which Sampson Warrenby had been working, having been collected into one pile, and tied up with red tape, and all the drawers in the desk sealed. The Sergeant explained that the papers had been scattered over the top of the desk, the fountain-pen, now lying tidily amongst several pencils in a little lacquer tray, uncovered beside them.

Hemingway nodded, and sat down in the chair behind the desk, an action from which Mavis averted her eyes. "Well, now, Miss Warrenby, I take it I have your permission to see if there's anything here that might have a bearing on the case?" he said, cutting the tape round the papers.

"Oh, yes! Though I'm sure there can't be anything. I should so like to feel that the whole thing was an accident, and the more I think about it the more I believe it was. People are always shooting rabbits here—in fact, I know my uncle several times complained to Mr. Ainstable about it, and said he oughtn't to allow it on the common. Poachers, too. Don't *you* think it might have been an accident?"

Hemingway, disinclined to enter into argument, said that it was too early for him to give an opinion. He ran quickly through the sheaf of documents, which concerned the efforts of a landlord to dislodge a tenant, and stretched over several months. Hemingway recalled that the letters which had been found, clipped together, at Sampson Warrenby's feet, had been written by this tenant, presumably before Sampson Warrenby had been called into the dispute, since the papers attached to them were copies of the landlord's own, acidly worded replies. It was the old story of a tenant protected by the Rent Restriction Acts, and the correspondence was increasingly acrimonious. But since Sampson Warrenby had merely acted in it in the rôle of legal representative to the landlord it was difficult to perceive what bearing it could have upon his murder. Hemingway laid the papers aside, and began to go through the contents of the drawers in the desk. One of these contained only such oddments as paper-clips, sealing-wax, spare nibs, and pencils, two others held virgin stationery; and another a collection of different sized envelopes. Two other drawers were devoted to bills and receipts; below these, a third held nothing but account-books and used cheques; and the fourth, on that side, contained bank-sheets. Such private correspondence as Sampson Warrenby had preserved was found thrust into the long central drawer at the top of the desk. Unlike the other drawers, it was in considerable disorder. Before touching its contents Hemingway considered it with a look of bird-like interest. "Would you say your uncle was a tidy man, Miss Warrenby?"

"Oh, yes! Uncle *hated* things to be left about."

"Is this how you'd expect to find a drawer in his desk?"

She blinked at it. "I don't know. I mean, I never went to his desk. I shouldn't have dreamed of opening any of his drawers."

"I see. Well, if you've no objection, I'll pack this lot up, and go through it at my leisure. Then you won't have to have the house cluttered up with policemen any longer. Everything will be returned to you in due course." He got up. "See to it, will you, Harbottle? Now, Miss Warrenby, are there any other papers? No safe in the house?"

"Oh, no! Uncle kept all his important papers at the office, I think."

"Then I won't be taking up any more of your time," he said.

She escorted him into the hall, where they were immediately joined by Mrs. Midgeholme and the Ultimas. Delicacy had prevented Mrs. Midgeholme from accompanying them to the study, but she was plainly agog with curiosity, and would have done her best to ferret out of the Chief Inspector the discovery of a possible clue had not Miss Patterdale at that moment walked in at the open front-door. As she was accompanied by her lumbering canine friend, a scene of great confusion followed her entrance, Mrs. Midgeholme uttering dismayed cries, and both the Ultimas bouncing at the labrador, Ulysses in a very disagreeable way, and Untidy in a spirit of shameless coquetry. Rex, though goodnatured, took very little interest in the Ultimas, but Mrs. Midgeholme was obsessed by the fear that he would one day lose patience with their importunities and maul them hideously. By the time she had succeeded in catching her pets, and scooping them up into her arms, assuring them, quite unnecessarily, that there was nothing for them to be afraid of, Mavis had explained to Miss Patterdale that the stranger was a detective from Scotland Yard; and Miss Patterdale, screwing her glass still more firmly into her eye, had looked him over and said that she was sorry to hear it.

"I knew that this was going to lead to a lot of unpleasantness," she said. "Well, it has nothing to do with me, but I do trust you won't wantonly stir up any scandal in Thornden!"

"Oh, Miss Patterdale, I'm sure there isn't anything like that to stir up!" said Mavis.

"Nonsense! Everyone has something in his life he'd rather wasn't made public. Isn't that so—What's your name?"

"I'm Chief Inspector Hemingway, madam. And I'm bound to say there's a great deal in what you say. However, we do try to be discreet."

"For my part," said Mrs. Midgeholme, "I often say my life is an open book!" She added, with a jolly laugh: "Which anyone may read, even the police!"

"I don't suppose the police have the slightest wish to do so," replied Miss Patterdale, correctly assessing the Chief Inspector's feelings. "I looked in to see how you're getting on, Mavis, and

72

to ask you if you'd like to come down to the cottage to share my supper. Abby's gone to the Haswells."

"My own errand!" exclaimed Mrs. Midgeholme, struck by the coincidence. "And Lion would be only too pleased to escort her back later, but will she be sensible, and come? No!"

"It's very, very kind of you both," said Mavis earnestly, "but somehow I'd rather stay at home today, by myself."

"Well, I shall leave Miss Patterdale to deal with you, my dear!" said Mrs. Midgeholme, perceiving that Hemingway was about to leave the house, and determined to accompany him.

The Ultimas still tucked under her arms, she sailed down the garden path beside him, saying mysteriously that there was something important she felt she ought to tell him. "I couldn't say anything in front of Miss Warrenby, so I just bided my time till I could get you alone," she said confidentially.

The Sergeant could have told Hemingway that Mrs. Midge-holme was unlikely to have anything of the smallest interest to impart. He grimaced expressively at Harbottle, but that saturnine gentleman merely smiled grimly, and shook his head.

Encouraged by an enquiring look from Hemingway, Mrs. Midgeholme said: "To my mind, there isn't a shadow of doubt who shot Mr. Warrenby. It's one of two people—for although I always think Delia Lindale is a *hard* young woman, I don't think she would actually shoot anyone. No, I never quite like people with those pale blue eyes, but I beg you won't run away with the idea that I have the least suspicion about her! It's her husband. What's more, if he did it, it's my belief she knows it. I popped in to see her this morning, just to talk things over, and the instant I opened my mouth she tried to turn the subject. She gave me the impression of being in a very nervy state—not to say scared! She didn't talk in what I call a natural way, and she didn't seem able to keep still for as much as five minutes. Either she thought she heard the child crying, or she had to go out to speak to Mrs. Murton, her daily woman. Something fishy here, I thought to myself." She nodded, but added surprisingly: "But that's not what I wanted to say to you. It *may* have been Kenelm Lindale, but only if it wasn't someone else. Ladislas Zama-something-or-other!"

"Yes, I wondered when we were coming to him," said Hemingway, with deceptive affability.

"Now, I couldn't say a word about him in front of Miss Warrenby, because the poor girl, I'm afraid, is very fond of him. I always did think it would be a most unsuitable match, and, of course, if he killed Mr. Warrenby, it really wouldn't do at all."

"Well, if he did that, madam, he won't be in a position to

73

marry Miss Warrenby, or anyone else," Hemingway pointed out. "But what makes you think he did?"

"If you knew the way he's been running after the girl, you wouldn't ask me that!" said Mrs. Midgeholme darkly.

"I daresay I wouldn't, but then, you see, I'm new to these parts."

"Yes, that's exactly why I'm being perfectly frank with you. My husband says the least said the soonest mended, but there I disagree with him! It's one's duty to tell the police what one knows, and I know that *never* would Sampson Warrenby have consented to such a marriage. He forbade his niece to have anything to do with Mr. Ladislas, and if he'd so much as guessed she was still seeing him behind his back—well, there would soon have been an end to that young man!"

"You think he'd have done the shooting instead?"

"No, I don't go as far as that, for though I've no doubt he'd have been capable of it, he was far too sly and clever to do anything like that. Mr. Ladislas would have found himself out of a job, and been obliged to leave the district. Don't ask me how Warrenby would have managed that! I only know he would. He was that kind of a man. And of course Mr. Ladislas must have guessed he'd leave his money to his niece, even if he didn't know it for a fact, which he may have done. And he was actually seen turning into this lane that afternoon! If he didn't know Miss Warrenby was at the Haswells', all I can say is that I'm surprised. I won't put it any more strongly than that: just *surprised*! So there we have him, *on* the spot, *with* a motive, and, I ask you, what more do you want?"

"Well, just a few things!" said Hemingway apologetically. "Not but what I'm much obliged to you, and I'll bear all you've said in mind. Now, I wonder what Ultima Untidy has found to roll in?"

This ruse was successful. Mrs. Midgeholme, who, once clear of the garden, had set the Ultimas down, turned, and hurried with admonishing cries towards Untidy. The Chief Inspector swiftly joined his subordinates in the car, and said: "Step on it!"

CHAPTER SEVEN

THE Sergeant, concerned, said: "I'm sorry we walked into Mrs. Midgeholme, sir, wasting your time like that! If I'd known, I'd have warned you about her."

"You'd have been wasting *your* time to have done so," said Harbottle, from the seat beside the police-driver. "The Chief likes talkers."

He spoke in the resigned voice of one forced to tolerate a weakness of which he disapproved, but Hemingway said cheerfully: "That's right, I do. You never know what they'll let fall. I picked up quite a lot from Mrs. Midgeholme."

"You did, sir?" said the Sergeant, faintly incredulous.

"Certainly I did. Why, I didn't know one end of a Peke from another when I came to Thornden, and I could set up as a judge of them now, which will probably come in useful when I'm retired."

The Sergeant chuckled. "She wins a lot of prizes with those dogs of hers," he remarked. "That I will say."

"Well, you have said it, so I can't stop you, but you don't need to say any more. I've got a very good memory, which means I don't have to be told things more than once in one afternoon," said Hemingway unkindly. "Strictly speaking, it wasn't the Pekes I meant, either. Or that unnatural Pole. It was what she had to say about the Lindales that interested me."

"Well, sir, but—just a bit of spite, wasn't it?"

"She doesn't like them, if that's what you mean, but I wouldn't call her spiteful. And I don't think she said anything about them that wasn't true. Or at anyrate what she believes to be true. Of course, you can say that it's quite enough to make anyone nervy to have her bursting in on them, and I'm bound to agree that I should think up a lot of jobs to do myself if it happened to me. On the other hand, it isn't in human nature not to want to have a good gossip about a thing like this. Provided you know you're in the clear, that is. Anything known about these Lindales?"

"Why, no sir! I mean, there isn't any reason why we should know anything about them, barring what everyone knows. Seem to be quiet, respectable people, generally well-liked in the neighbourhood. They don't get about much, but I don't know that it's to be expected they would. Not with him having his hands full with the farm, and her with a baby, and only one daily woman to help her."

"Fair enough," agreed Hemingway. "And what do you make of them never having anyone to stay?"

"I don't know," said the Sergeant slowly. "What do you make of it, sir?"

"I don't know either," said Hemingway. "But I think it'll bear looking into. You can attend to that, Horace. If Lindale was a member of the Stock Exchange it won't be difficult to get his dossier."

"You mean," said the Sergeant, his brow furrowed, "that Warrenby might have known something to Mr. Lindale's discredit, and was blackmailing him?"

"Well, from all I've been able to gather about this bird that sounds like just the sort of parlour-trick he would get up to."

"Yes, but whatever for?" objected the Sergeant.

"That's another of the things I don't know. Might not have been blackmailing him at all. If he happened to let on to Lindale that he knew something really damaging about him, Lindale might have shot him to make sure he didn't pass his information on. Depends on what it was, and what sort of chap Lindale is."

"I wouldn't have said he was that sort at all," said the Sergeant.

"You may be right," said Hemingway, as the car pulled up outside Mr. Drybeck's house. "But I once arrested one of the nicest, kindest, most fatherly old codgers you ever saw. You'd have said he couldn't have hurt a fly. Well, I don't know what he was like with flies: it wasn't the right time of the year. I arrested him for sticking a dagger into his brother's back."

With this encouraging reminiscence, he got out of the car, and trod up the path to Mr. Drybeck's front-door.

It was by this time past seven o'clock, and Mr. Drybeck, whose housekeeper did not allow him to dine at a late hour, was just sitting down to an extremely depressing Sunday supper of cold ham, salad, and a pallid shape accompanied by a dish of custard. No one could be surprised that he showed no reluctance to leave this meal. Upon being informed that two gentlemen from Scotland Yard wished to see him, he threw down his napkin, and went at once into the hall, and primly made these visitors welcome.

"I was not unexpectant of a visit from the C.I.D.," he said. "A very shocking affair, Chief Inspector. I am able to state with certainty that such a thing has never before sullied the annals of our parish. I shall be happy to render you whatever assistance may be within my power. You will first, of course, wish me to account for my own movements at the time of this outrage. That is perfectly proper. Fortunately my memory is a good one, and, I trust, exact. The result of legal training."

He then, in the most precise terms, repeated the story he had told Sergeant Carsethorn already. At only one point did

76

Hemingway intervene. He said: "You didn't hear the gong when it was sounded the first time, sir?"

"No, Chief Inspector, I did not, but that is not quite such a wonderful matter as it may appear. With your permission, we will put it to the test. There is the gong in question. If Sergeant Carsethorn will remain here, and in a few minutes' time sound it, moderately—for that, she tells me, is how Emma sounded it on that first occasion, believing me to be within the house—we three will repair to the part of the garden which I was watering at the time, and the Chief Inspector may judge for himself whether or not it can be heard."

"I don't think that'll be necessary, sir," said Hemingway.

Mr. Drybeck raised his hand. "Pardon me, I should prefer you to put my word to the proof!" he said sternly.

He then led the two Inspectors out into the back garden, through a small garden-hall. "My domain is not extensive," he said, "but you will observe that it is intersected by several hedges. That one for instance, shuts off the vegetable garden, and this one, which we are approaching, encloses my little rose-garden. Here, gentlemen, I was engaged in watering when I was summoned to supper. Let us enter it!"

He stood back, and waved to them to precede him through an arch in the tall yew hedge into a pretty, square plot, laid out in rose-beds, with narrow grass walks between, and a tiny artificial pond in the centre. Once inside, he surveyed the garden with simple pride, and said: "You may be said to be seeing it at its best. A wonderful year for roses! You are looking at those red ones, Chief Inspector. Gloire de Hollande: quite one of my favourites."

"And I'm sure I'm not surprised, sir," said Hemingway. "You've certainly got a rare show here. And there's the gong, by the way."

"I heard nothing!" declared Mr. Drybeck suspiciously.

"I didn't either," confessed Harbottle. "Not to be sure."

"You must have imagined it!" said Mr. Drybeck, inclined to be affronted. "I do not consider myself hard of hearing, not at all!"

"Well, I've got very quick ears, sir, What's more, I was listening for it. I'm quite prepared to believe that if you were busy with your roses here you mightn't have heard it. In fact, I always was, but I'm glad you made me come: it's been worth it." He strolled forward to inspect a bed planted with Betty Uprichard. "I noticed some nice roses at Fox House, but nothing to compare with yours."

"That I can well believe!" said Mr. Drybeck. "I fancy my friend Warrenby cared very little for such things.

"Did you know him well, sir?"

"Dear me, no! I can lay claim to nothing but the barest
77

acquaintance with him. To be frank with you, I did not find him congenial, and considered him quite out of place in our little coterie here."

"Seems to have been unpopular all round," commented Hemingway.

"That is true. I should be surprised if I heard of his having been liked by anyone in Thornden. But pray do not misunderstand me, Chief Inspector! I flatter myself I know Thornden as well as any man, and I know of no one in my own circle who had the smallest cause to commit the terrible crime of murdering him. I am very glad you have come to see me, very glad indeed! There is a great deal of talk going on in the village, and I have been much shocked by some of the wild rumours I have heard. Rumours, I may say, that are set about by irresponsible persons, and have not the least foundation in fact. Imagination has run rife. But to the trained mind I venture to say that this case presents no very difficult problem, and is not susceptible to any fantastic solution."

"Well, I'm glad of that," said Hemingway. "Perhaps I'll be able to solve it."

"I fear you will find t all too easy to do so. I have myself given the matter a good deal of thought, regarding it, if you understand me, in the light of a chess-problem. I am forced to the conclusion—the very reluctant conclusion!—that all the evidence points one way, and one way only. *One* person had the opportunity and the motive, and that person is the dead man's niece!"

Inspector Harbottle's jaw dropped. Recovering his countenance, he said in accents of strong disapprobation: "Setting aside the fact that it is rarely that a woman will use a gun——"

"That," interrupted Mr. Drybeck smartly, "is what is said every time a woman does use a gun!"

"Setting that aside, sir," said Harbottle obstinately, "I never saw a young lady less like a murderess!"

"Pray, is it your experience, Inspector, that murderesses—or, for that matter, murderers—look the part? It is my belief that Miss Warrenby is a very clever young woman."

"Well, now, that's highly interesting," said Hemingway. "Because I'm bound to say she doesn't give that impression."

Mr. Drybeck uttered a shrill little laugh. "I've no doubt she impressed you as a woman overcome by the death of a dear relation. Bunkum, Chief Inspector! Bosh and bunkum! She talks as if Warrenby rescued her from destitution when she was a child. You may as well know that she has only lived with him for rather less than three years. He offered her a home when her mother died, and she accepted it, although I happen to know that she has a small income of her own, and was certainly of an age to earn her own living. No doubt she had her reasons

78

for preferring to take up the position of an unpaid housekeeper and hostess in her uncle's house. Indeed, one is tempted to say that one now sees she had! If rumour does not lie, she has lately become attracted by a young Pole, who rides about the country on a noisy motor-cycle. I need scarcely say that the popular theory in the village is that this man is the guilty party. My own belief is that such a theory will not hold water. If it is true that the young man went to Fox House at the hour stated, I find it impossible to believe that he can have waited until twenty minutes past seven before shooting Warrenby. Consider! The house contained none but Warrenby himself; not only the front-door, but the windows on the ground floor also, stood open. Why, then, did this man wait until Warrenby stepped into the garden?"

"Why indeed?" said Hemingway.

"The trained mind, therefore rejects the theory," said Mr. Drybeck, rejecting it. "Consider again! Let us follow Miss Warrenby's own story step by step!"

"Well, if it's all the same to you, sir, I've done that twice already today and though I'm sure it's highly instructive——"

"She leaves The Cedars alone, and by the garden-gate," pursued Mr. Drybeck, disregarding the interruption, and stabbing an accusing finger at Hemingway. "In spite of the fact that during the course of the afternoon she repeatedly told us of her qualms at leaving her uncle alone, she remained on at The Cedars after all the other guests, with the single exception of Mrs. Cliburn, had left. She thus makes sure that she will not meet any of the party on her way home. She states that she climbed the stile into the lane, and entered Fox House through the front gate. It may have been so, but I incline, myself, to the belief that she approached the house from the rear. A hedge separates its grounds from the footpath that runs between them and the spinney attached to The Cedars: not, you will agree, an insuperable obstacle! In this way she is able to abstract her uncle's rifle from the house without his knowing that she had in fact returned from the tennis-party. No doubt she regained the footpath by the same route, having ascertained that her uncle was conveniently seated in the garden. Then, and then only does she cross the stile."

"Always supposing her uncle happened to have a rifle," interpolated Hemingway. "Of course, if he didn't, it upsets your theory a bit. Did he?"

"I am not in a position to say whether he had a rifle or not," said Mr. Drybeck testily. "A .22 rifle is a very ordinary weapon to find in a country house!"

Inspector Harbottle looked rather grimly at him, his eyes narrowed; but Hemingway said blandly: "Just so. Mind you, it hasn't come to light, but, there! it's early days yet."

"Ah!" said **Mr. Drybeck** triumphantly. "You are forgetting one significant circumstance, Chief Inspector! If we are to believe that Warrenby was shot at twenty past seven—and I see no reason for disbelieving this—what was Miss Warrenby doing between that time and the time when she reached Miss Patterdale's house?"

"When was that?" asked Hemingway.

"Unfortunately," said Mr. Drybeck, "it seems to be impossible to discover exactly when that was, but my enquiries lead me to say that it cannot have been less than a quarter of an hour later. I am much inclined to think that Miss Warrenby made a fatal slip when she correctly stated the time when she—as she puts it—'heard the shot'. Before she went to Miss Patterdale, the rifle had to be disposed of."

"The young lady came over faint, and small wonder!" interjected Harbottle.

"Nonsense, Horace! she was burying the rifle in the asparagus-bed! Well, sir, I'm sure I'm much obliged to you. Wonderful, the way you've worked it all out! I shall know where to come if I should find myself at a loss. But I won't keep you from your dinner any longer now."

He then swept the fulminating Harbottle out of the rose-garden, bade Mr. Drybeck a kind but firm farewell, and joined Sergeant Carsethorn in the waiting car.

"Where to now, sir?" asked the Sergeant.

"What's the beer like at the local?" demanded Hemingway.

The Sergeant grinned. "Good. It's a free house."

"Then that's where we'll go. The Inspector's a bit upset, and needs something to pull him round."

"Well you know that I never drink alcohol!" said Harbottle, under his breath, as he got into the car beside him.

"Who said anything about alcohol? A nice glass of orangeade is what you'll have, my lad, and like it!"

"Give over, sir, do!" Harbottle besought him.

The Sergeant spoke over his shoulder. "Did you get anything more than I did out of Mr. Drybeck, sir?"

"Yes, I got the whole story of the crime," said Hemingway cheerfully. "What you boys wanted me and Harbottle for when you had Mr. Drybeck beats me! He's got a trained mind, and he's bringing it to bear on this crime."

"A trained mind!" snorted the incensed Inspector. "You haven't that, of course, Chief!"

"You're dead right I haven't!"

"He fairly turned my gorge!" said the Inspector, ignoring this piece of facetiousness. "Him and his trained mind! A real, wicked mind, that's what he has! Trying to cast suspicion on a nice young lady!"

"Taken your fancy, has she?" said Hemingway. "I'm bound to say she didn't take mine."

"You aren't going to tell me that you think a gentle little thing like that could have anything to do with this?" said the Inspector, shocked.

"No, I'm not. I've got what wouldn't hurt you: an open mind! There's a great deal in what Drybeck says, and the fact that he said it because he's in the devil of a funk is neither here nor there."

"He was that all right."

"Of course he was. So would you be in his shoes. He's worked it all out, and whether he shot Warrenby or not I don't know, because I haven't got second sight, but what I do know is that he's proved to himself that he *could* have done it, in the time. Which saves me having to prove it for myself."

"He made one slip," said the Inspector, with satisfaction. "How did he know Warrenby was shot with a .22 rifle?"

"Yes, I can see you think he knew that because it was him did the shooting. You may be right, but it wouldn't surprise me if the whole village knows it."

"If they do, it's Dr. Warcop who's told them!" said the Sergeant, who had been listening intently. "Him or that fool, Hobkirk! The pair of them are so pleased with themselves for having been in on this that I wouldn't be surprised if they started giving talks about it on the air! A fat chance we shall have of rounding up all the .22's now that everyone's been tipped off! I ought to have done it the instant we got that bullet."

"Well, don't take on about it!" recommended Hemingway. "Unless this bird we're after has broken loose from Broadmoor, you never had a chance of rounding up anything but a lot of innocent rifles. The best you could ever hope for was to find someone who did have a .22, and has unaccountably mislaid it. What are we sitting here for?"

"Red Lion, sir," ventured the driver.

"You should have said so before. Come on, Horace! We'll see what the lads of the village have got to say about this horrible crime. Properly speaking, we ought to leave you outside, Carsethorn, because you'll very likely cramp my style. However, I daresay they've all had a good look at the car by now, so you may as well go in with us."

"Well, there's one person as has seen us, sir," said the Sergeant, after a glance at the Red Lion. "That's Mr. Plenmeller, sitting in the window. I don't know but what I wouldn't as soon wait in the car."

"What you want to do is to get the better of these prejudices of yours," said Hemingway severely. "What with you having it in for this author, and the Inspector getting a down on poor old Mr. Drybeck—as helpful a gentleman as I ever met—

you'll very likely infect me, between the pair of you. You come and introduce me to the local crime-expert!"

This, in the event, proved to be unnecessary. No sooner had the three officials entered the bar-parlour than Gavin Pienmeller, who was standing drinks to Miss Dearham, Major Midgeholme, and young Mr. Haswell, hailed them with every evidence of delight."If it isn't my friend, Sergeant Carsethorn, with—unless my instinct betrays me, which it rarely does—dignitaries from Scotland Yard! Come over here, Sergeant! You'll never guess what we've been talking about! George, serve these gentlemen, and chalk it up to my account! That," he added, addressing himself to Hemingway, after one piercing scrutiny of his face, "is to put you under a sense of obligation, in case you decide to arrest me. You're Chief Inspector Hemingway: you had charge of the Guisborough case. At some future date, I shall do my best to get you into a malleable condition: I would give much to know the details of the evidence which was suppressed. I was in court every day. Let me make you known, by the way, to Miss Dearham! She, like Mr. Haswell here, doesn't come into this case, much to her regret, and quite unlike Major Midgholme, whose motive for shooting Sampson Warrenby, though obscure, you will no doubt discover."

"Really, Plenmeller, your tongue runs away with you!" said the Major stiffly. "Good-evening, Chief Inspector. Sad business, this."

"What a mendacious thing to say!" remarked Gavin. "When we are all perfectly delighted! Or did you mean sad for Warrenby?"

"Yes, I rather got the impression that Mr. Warrenby wasn't what you might call popular," said Hemingway. "Good-evening, Major: I've had the pleasure of meeting Mrs. Midgeholme already."

The Major looked startled. "You've been to see *my wife*?"

"Not properly speaking, sir: no. I met her up at Fox House. With Ulysses and Untidy," he added calmly. "Very handsome little dogs. Prizewinners, I understand."

"The way the police ferret out information!" murmured Gavin, causing the Major to flush slightly. "But I don't think Mrs. Midgeholme ought to have forced Ulysses to visit the scene of his humiliation. Rather sadistic, don't you agree?"

"No, I do not!" snapped the Major.

Abby turned her candid gaze upon Gavin, and spoke with paralysing frankness. "Definitely unfunny," she said. "Why don't you try to find out who really did it, instead of making up fantastic stories about people who couldn't possibly have done it? You ought to be able to: you write awfully clever thrillers. I haven't read any of them myself, actually, but that's what everyone says."

82

"Attagirl!" said Charles admiringly.

"What a low, nasty backhander!" remarked Gavin. "I shall ignore it. When I write my clever thrillers, ducky, I have the advantage of knowing from the start who did the murder. In fact, I know who is going to do it. It makes quite a difference, and serves to show how depressingly unlike life is fiction. My suspects all have lovely motives, too. You never met such a set of crooks as I can (and do) assemble in one restricted scene. Why, I once wrote a good stabbing-mystery set in a village just like this, and even the verger turned out to have the murkiest kind of past! The people of Thornden are too respectable for me. I won't say dull, leaving that to be inferred."

"Would you describe yourself as dull, sir?" enquired Hemingway. "It isn't the word I'd have chosen."

"No, or respectable either, but when I tried to cast myself for the rôle of chief suspect I met with nothing but discouragement. The Sergeant even snubbed me. I wonder that beer isn't choking you, Sergeant."

"What you did, sir, if you'll pardon me saying so, was to try to pull my leg," retorted the Sergeant.

"Not at all. As an amateur of crime, I felt I ought to be the culprit. Now, don't, anybody, talk to me of that Pole, said to be walking out with Mother's-good-girl! Any student of crime knows that the guilty man is never the mysterious foreigner. Besides, he's so obvious! If I can't have myself or Mrs. Midgeholme, I'll have the Squire, I think."

"Here, I say! Draw it mild!" protested Charles.

"It's silly," said Abby flatly. "He's just about the most unlikely person you could possibly think of."

"He is *quite* the most unlikely person I can think of," Gavin corrected her. "Therein lies his charm. I am not interested in the obvious. Have another pint, Chief Inspector!"

"No, I won't do that, thank you, sir. But I find all you're saying very interesting—speaking as a professional. Speaking as an amateur, why do you feel you ought to be the culprit?"

Gavin regarded him with approval. "You're restoring my shaken faith in the police-force, Chief Inspector. Or are you merely humouring me?"

"Oh, no, sir! It isn't every day I meet one of you gentlemen who write about crime, and I'd like to know how a real crime strikes you."

"Disappointingly. There is nothing to solve except the comparatively uninteresting matter of the identity of the murderer. No hermetically sealed room, no unusual weapon, too few seemingly unshakeable alibis."

"Well, I think the identity of the murderer is far more interesting than those other things," objected Abby. "*Fascinating*, when one actually knows all the people!" she added naïvely.

83

"Ah, yes, but you, my sweet, are a female! Persons are more interesting to you than problems. Will you mind very much if the guilty man proves to be some quite low, insignificant creature you've never even heard of?"

"No, of course I shan't. I should be glad, but I've got a feeling that won't happen."

"I have the greatest respect for womanly intuition; I have a great deal of it myself. But doesn't yours inform you that I am a person easily capable of performing a murder?"

"No, of course not!" Abby said, flushing.

"Then it is underdeveloped. I assure you that I am."

"Yes, probably," Charles intervened. "But not this murder! You'd go in for something a bit more subtle."

"Why, Charles, I did not look for this tribute from you!" Gavin said mockingly.

"You can take it that way if you like. I'd be willing enough to consider you for the star part in this drama if I could think of any conceivable reason why you should want to murder Sampson Warrenby. As I can't, you'll have to go on being a super, as far as I'm concerned."

"But doesn't your dislike of me make it possible for you to picture me in the star rôle?" Gavin asked softly.

"No."

"Oh, you are a very poor hater, Charles! Or are you maliciously attempting to make the Chief Inspector lose interest in me? I believe you are. I shall have to tell him that I have already committed one murder, and I meant to let him find that out for himself."

"On paper. That's different."

"Many, on paper. Only one in actual fact."

"Look here, don't you think this has gone far enough?" said the Major uncomfortably. "It isn't quite a fit matter for joking, you know!"

"But I wasn't joking. It is well known that I murdered my half-brother."

The Major was stricken to silence; Charles said, under his breath: "*Must* you always dramatize yourself?" and Hemingway, with an air of cosy interest, said conversationally: "Did you, though, sir? And how did you manage that, or is it a secret?"

"It's a lot of nonsense!" muttered Sergeant Carsethorn, glowering at Gavin.

"I induced him to kill himself, Chief Inspector, thus succeeding to his property. I won't say to his debts, for they were really almost negligible—unlike the liabilities which attach to any estate in these delightful times. Of course, had I known that Walter's money was almost wholly tied up in land—did I say that reverently enough, Charles? I've been practising ever since I succeeded Walter, but I fear I still haven't got it right—well,

84

had I known this, I'm not at all sure that I should have driven him to suicide."

"If you don't like living at Thornden House, why don't you clear out?" demanded Charles.

"Find me a buyer!"

The Major rose to his feet. "I must be getting along," he said. "If I may say so, Plenmeller, you're talking plain balderdash!"

"What a lovely word! May I use it, or is it copyright?"

The Major ignored him, saying to Hemingway: "The late Mr. Plenmeller, as I have no doubt the Sergeant will tell you, was a bit of a war-casualty, and took his own life while temporarily of unsound mind."

"Leaving a letter accusing me of having driven him to it. Don't forget that!"

"It's a pity you can't," said the Major, with unaccustomed sternness. "Mistake to keep on brooding over things. Good-night, Abby!" He nodded to the rest of the company, said: "'Night!" in a general way, and departed.

"Ought we to be going too, Charles? Your mother invited me for eight, and I don't want to keep her waiting," said Abby, who, like most of her generation, had very good manners.

He glanced at his watch, and rose, "Yes, it's about time we pushed off," he agreed. "I say, Chief Inspector, is it true that Warrenby was shot with a .22 rifle? Or oughtn't I to ask?"

"Oh, I don't mind your asking, sir! But you want to go and ask Sergeant Knarsdale, not me: he's the expert on ballistics."

Charles laughed. "All right! But, if it's true, you've got the hell of a job on your hands, haven't you? Crowds of people have them here. I've got one myself. First gun my father ever gave me. I used to pot rabbits with it."

"Do you still use it, sir?"

"No, I haven't lately: too short in the stock for me now. My father had it altered for me when I was a kid, but it's knocking around somewhere."

"Do you mean you don't know where it is?" demanded Abby.

He looked smilingly down at her. "Don't sound so accusing! It's either amongst my junk, or in the gunroom. If Mother didn't shove it up in the attics, with my old trainlines."

"But don't you see?" exclaimed Abby, her eyes brightening. "Someone could have pinched it!"

"Don't be a goop!" he besought her. "They'd have to have a nerve, snooping round the house looking for a stray rifle! Come on, we must push off!"

"But I like that theory," said Gavin. "It brings Mavis Warrenby back into the picture, and she was one of my first fancies. Try as I will—not that I would have you think I've tried very hard—I can't believe in so much saintliness. You ought to have seen her after church this morning! Such a brave little woman, nobly doing her best to bear up under heavy sorrow! A schoolboy's gun would have been just the thing for her. Oh, I must go home, and work on this new theory!"

"I would," said Hemingway cordially. "You might tell me before you go whether you've got a .22 as well as Mr. Haswell?"

"I haven't the least idea, but I should think very probably. I don't shoot myself, but my half-brother had several sporting guns. Would you like to come and see for yourself?"

"Thank you, I would, sir," said Hemingway, getting up. "No harm in making sure, and no time like the present. You two can wait here for me," he added, to his subordinates. "I shan't be long. I understand you live quite close, don't you, sir?"

"A hundred yards up the street," Gavin answered, pulling himself out of his chair with one of his awkward movements, and limping across the floor.

Outside the inn, having parted from Charles and Abby, the Chief Inspector set a moderate pace, and was rewarded for his consideration with a snap. "Let me assure you that ungainly though my gait may be it does not necessitate my walking at a snail's pace!" said Gavin, an edge to his voice.

"That's good, sir," said Hemingway. "A war-injury?"

"I took no part in the War. I was born with a short leg."

"Very hard luck, sir."

"Not in the least. I'm sure I should have disliked soldiering heartily. It does not discommode me in the saddle, and since hunting is the only sport I have the least desire to engage in, any sympathy you may be silently bestowing on me is entirely wasted."

"Do you get much hunting, sir?"

"No, I cannot afford it. It doesn't run to more than one decent hunter. Not a bad-looking horse, and not a bad performer on his going-days. Other times, it's hit 'em and leave 'em, but he hasn't gone back on me yet."

"Your brother didn't hunt?"

"No, he was such a dreary type, always either treacling trees, or observing the habits of some birds, and shooting others."

"What made him commit suicide—if I may ask?"

"I've told you: I did. With his dying breath he told me so, and you have to believe dying words, don't you?"

"Well, I wouldn't so to say bank on them—not under those circumstances. In my experience, the sort of messages suicides leave behind them would be better put straight on the fire, because they only bring a lot of misery on people that in nine cases out of ten don't deserve it."

"Oh, would you put it as strongly as that? I thought it was so annoying of him: like uttering a dirty crack, and then walking

86

out of the room before it can be answered. We have now reached my ancestral home: go in!"

The Chief Inspector stepped through the gate in the wall, and paused for a moment, looking at the gracious house before him.

"Like it?" Gavin asked.

"Yes, sir. Don't you?"

"Aesthetically, very much; sentimentally, a little; practically, not at all. The plumbing is archaic; the repairs—if I could undertake them—would be ruinous; and to run it properly a staff of at least three indoor servants is necessary. I have one crone, and a gardener-groom, who also does odd jobs." He led the way up the flagged path to the front-door, and opened it. "The room my brother used, amongst other things, as his gun-room, is at the back," he said, limping past the elegant staircase to a swing-door covered in moth-eaten brown baize. "Kitchen premises," he said over his shoulder. "Here we are!" He opened a door, and signed to the Chief Inspector to enter. "A disgusting room!" he remarked. "It reeks of dogs, and always will. My brother's spaniels used to sleep in it. A revolting pair, gushingly affectionate, and wholly lacking in tact or discrimination! Guns over here." He went to a glass-fronted case, and opened it. "Quite an armoury, as you perceive. Including a couple of hammer-guns, which must have belonged to my father. Yes, I thought Walter would probably have a .22. Take it, and do what you will with it!" He lifted it out of the case as he spoke, but paused before handing it to Hemingway, and said, with a twisted smile: "Oh, that was unworthy of the veriest tyro, wasn't it? Now I've left my finger-prints on it. That might be quite clever of me, mightn't it?"

"Not so very clever," said Hemingway. "Something tells me that the gun I'm after won't have any prints on it at all. Mind if I borrow this, sir?"

"No, and much good would it do me if I did mind! Would you like to fire it into my marrow-bed? I expect we can find some ammunition for it."

"Not my department, sir," Hemingway said, tucking the rifle under his arm. "I'm much obliged to you, though."

He took his leave of Gavin on the doorstep, and found, when he stepped through the gate again, that the police-car was drawn up outside. He got into the back, beside Inspector Harbottle, and propped the rifle up between them. "Well, I'll say this for you, you're a zealous lot of chaps," he remarked. "Or did they throw you out of the pub for getting noisy?"

"Where do wish to go now, sir?" asked Harbottle severely.

"Back to Bellingham. We've done about enough for today, and given ourselves plenty to think about. Also I've picked up the first of the rifles we aren't looking for."

"You don't think it could be that one, sir?" asked the Sergeant. "I mean, you've got some reason?"

"No, I haven't got any reason, but if I've hit the right one, first crack out of the bag, it'll be a miracle, and I don't believe in them. Step on it a bit, son: no one will have you up!"

"You have now seen a few of the people you have to deal with," said Harbottle, with gloomy satisfaction. "Are you still liking the case, Chief?"

"Of course I am! Why shouldn't I, when I've got half a dozen people doing my job for me?"

This drew a smile from Harbottle, but slightly puzzled the Sergeant, who did not recall having seen quite so many persons in the Chief Inspector's train. "Half a dozen, sir?" he repeated.

"Well, that's what's called a conservative estimate," said Hemingway. "From what I've seen, I shouldn't think there's a house or a cottage in Thornden where they aren't chewing over the crime at this very moment. If your Mr. Drybeck hasn't solved the whole mystery by tomorrow, very likely that nice young couple will have done it, and then we can go back to London, and take all the credit."

CHAPTER EIGHT

WHATEVER may have been the topics under discussion in other houses, nothing but the murder of Sampson Warrenby was considered worthy to be talked about at The Cedars, where the son of the house and Miss Dearham were regaling Mrs. Haswell, over cocktails, with a description of the encounter at the Red Lion. Mrs. Haswell, beyond entertaining a vague hope that no one she knew would prove to be the guilty person, took really very little interest in the affair. She inclined to the belief that the murder had probably been committed by a Bellingham man, and was a good deal more exercised in her mind over the disquieting symptoms suddenly evinced by one of her rarer plants. However, she and Miss Patterdale were agreed that although it was disagreeable to persons of their generation to have a murder committed in their midst, it was very nice for the children to have something to occupy them, Thornden being such a quiet place, with really nothing to do in it at this season except to play tennis. Miss Patterdale went so far as to say that if it had had to happen she was glad it had happened during Abby's visit, because she was always so afraid Abby would grow bored when she stayed with her. Mrs. Haswell said, Yes, she felt the same about Charles; but privately she thought a murder had not been necessary to keep either Charles or Abby from a state of boredom.

"I rather liked the Chief Inspector, didn't you?" Abby said. "The other one had a quelling sort of face, though. Much more like what one imagines. I do wonder what they're doing!"

"I thought the Chief was leading us all on to talk. I was afraid you were going to come out with your theory."

"Like Gavin. You are a beast, Charles! As though I would! All the same, I bet I'm right."

"Abby thinks old Drybeck did it, Mum."

"Oh, no, dear, I shouldn't think so!" said Mrs. Haswell, quite unperturbed. "He's lived here for *years*!"

Charles, accustomed to the workings of his mother's mind, grinned appreciatively, but said: "The end of it will be, of course, that he'll have her up for slander."

Again Mrs. Haswell demurred, this time on the ground that Mr. Drybeck was Miss Patterdale's solicitor.

"Yes, and if I'm right he won't be able to have me up for anything," Abby pointed out. "He's the one person who fits in."

"No, he isn't," Charles contradicted. "He doesn't fit in half as well as Mavis."

"Oh, do shut up about Mavis!" begged Abby. "She couldn't possibly have done it! She's far too dim!"

"If you ask me, she's a dark horse. It's a pity you shirked coming to church this morning. I don't like Gavin, but he was dead right about her! Talk of overacting! She was doing the heartbroken heroine all over the shop, accepting condolences, and drivelling about her dear uncle's kindness, and being alone in the world, until even Mummy felt sick!"

"Well, no, darling, not sick exactly," said Mrs. Haswell. "It was all a little insincere, but I expect she feels that's the way she ought to behave. There's something about death that turns people into the most dreadful hypocrites. I can't think why. I was just as bad when your grandfather died, until your father pointed out how disagreeable and exacting he'd been for years, wearing poor Granny out, and never being in the least pleased to see any of us."

"You weren't the same as Mavis at all!" said Charles. "*You* didn't pretend he'd been a saint, and tell everyone you wished he hadn't left his money to you!"

"No, darling, but I always knew he must have done that, and in any case it didn't come to me till Granny died. Not that I should have said anything so silly."

"Yes, but that's just the kind of thing one would expect Mavis to say!" Abby pointed out. "There was a girl at school awfully like her, always saying 'Oh, I don't think we ought to!' and being kind and forgiving to everyone, and saying improving things. She was the most ghastly type! And the worst thing about people like that is that they actually believe in their own acts. I wouldn't mind half as much if they were doing it deliberately, and stayed honest inside, but they don't. Geoffrey Silloth says hypocrisy is a deadly drug which finally permeates the whole system. And, in any case," she added, struck by a powerful thought, "*can* you see Mavis firing a gun?"

"I *didn't* see it," said Charles, with emphasis. "All I know about her is that she chose to come down here and act as a sort of unpaid drudge for an out-and-out swine, who wasn't even decently polite to her, rather than get a job and be able to call her soul her own. And I never knew why till yesterday!"

"Well, dear, until yesterday you never really thought about it at all, did you?" interpolated his mother mildly.

"She said she felt it was her duty to look after Dear Uncle," said Abby.

"Boloney!" said Charles scornfully. "I may not have thought much about it, but I do recall that in one of her expansive moments she disclosed that it was *such* a surprise to her when Dear Uncle wrote to offer her a home, because she had never even met him. So if you're nourishing a vision of Warrenby being the prop of his sister-in-law's declining years, can it! He

90

offered Mavis a home because, for one thing he needed a hostess in his big social climb, and, for another, he thought it would be grand to have a housekeeper and general dog's body he wouldn't have to pay, and could bully!"

"Yes, that's perfectly true," conceded Abby. "But I still say she didn't do it. Do you know what I did when you were all at Church this morning? I walked down to Mr. Drybeck's house, and then cut back to Fox House, across the common, timing myself, and I found he could have done it *easily*! It took me exactly six minutes to reach the gorse bushes. What's more, there's plenty of cover, because there are lots of bushes and things on that part of the common."

"I don't say Drybeck couldn't have done it in the time, but I don't suppose he'd walk as fast as you did. He's too old."

"What rot!" said Abby scornfully. "He's as thin as a herring, and look at him on the tennis-court!"

At this moment, Mr. Haswell walked into the room, saying, as he shut the door, that if Charles must borrow his clothes he did wish he would sometimes put them back where they belonged, instead of leaving them all over the house. He said this without ill-will, and certainly without any hope that his words would bear fruit; and his son replied, as he invariably did: "Sorry, Dad!" and then dismissed the matter from his mind.

Mr. Haswell, having by this time observed that a guest was present, shook hands with Abby, favouring her with an appraising look, which rather surprised her, since she was well-acquainted with him and quite unaccustomed to exciting more interest in him than he felt for any of his son's young friends, all of whom he received in an uncritical and incurious spirit. Fortunately for her self-possession she did not know that this keen scrutiny was due to certain mysterious words uttered by Mrs. Haswell into his private ear on the previous evening. He was a well-built man, with a square, rather impassive countenance, and a taciturn disposition; and although he was a pleasant host, and accepted with perfect equanimity all the young people who invaded his house, and danced to the radio, or argued loudly and interminably on such subjects as Surrealist art, Anglo-Soviet Relations, and The Ballet, most of Charles's friends stood in considerable awe of him. Appealed to now by Charles to state whether he thought old Drybeck had murdered Sampson Warrenby, he replied calmly: "Certainly not," and poured himself out a glass of sherry.

"Well, that's Abby's theory. I think it's possible, but my own bet is that it was Mavis. What's your view, Dad?"

"That you'd both of you do better to leave it to the police, and not talk quite so much about it," replied his father.

Abby, who had been very well brought-up, would have

abandoned the entrancing topic at once, but Charles, though extremely fond of his parents, naturally held them in no exaggerated respect. He said: "You know perfectly well we're bound to talk about it. It's quite the most interesting thing that's ever befallen Thornden."

"Oh, Mr. Haswell!" said Abby, feeling that Charles had broken the ice, "there's a Chief Inspector from Scotland Yard, and we actually talked to him, at the Red Lion!"

"Did you indeed?" he said, smiling faintly. "That must have been a thrill for you! I hope you didn't tell him what your theories are?"

"No, we were madly discreet," she assured him.

"I didn't have to tell him my theory," said Charles. "Gavin did that for me. Oh, I say, Mummy, do you know what became of my old .22, by any chance? The one Daddy got for me when I was at school?"

"Do you mean the one you used to shoot rabbits with, darling? Yes, I lent it to old Newbiggin's grandson: the one with the extraordinary ears, who was so helpful that time Woodhorn was ill, and I couldn't get the car to start."

"Good lord! Did he bring it back?"

"Oh, yes, I'm sure he must have!" said Mrs. Haswell, folding up her tapestry-work, and removing the thimble from her finger. "Why? You don't want it, do you, Charles?"

"No, but it looks as if the Chief Inspector will. Gavin had the bright idea that it would have been just the rifle for Mavis to handle, and I should think they're bound to follow that up. And if it's sculling about the village——"

"No, it isn't. I remember now!" said Mrs. Haswell. "Jim Newbiggin returned it one day when I was in London, and Molly put it in the cloakroom. I meant to put it with the rest of your stuff, in the attic, and then I forgot, and I don't know what became of it."

"Lord-love-a-duck!" said Charles inelegantly, and immediately left the room.

He returned in a very few minutes, carrying in one gloved hand a light rifle. "Shoved at the back of the coat-cupboard," he said briefly. "Now, where would be a safe place to put it? I haven't touched it, and no one must, because of finger-prints. Look, Mummy, I'll put it on the top of the cabinet for the time being."

"*Must* you use my gloves?" asked his father.

"Sorry, Dad! There weren't any others, and it isn't greasy."

He then deposited the rifle well out of any housemaid's reach, stripped off the glove, and dropped it on a chair. Mr. Haswell observed this with disfavour, but as the gong sounded at that moment he said nothing, merely picking his glove up on his way out of the room, and restoring it to the cloakroom himself.

Since only one of her three servants was on duty on Sunday evenings, supper at The Cedars was cold, and no one waited at table. There was thus no other bar to exhaustive discussion of the murder than Mr. Haswell's silent disapproval. And as it was Mrs. Haswell who set the ball rolling again, by saying that she really didn't think Mavis was the kind of girl to borrow things without asking if she might, Abby felt herself at liberty to pursue her own theory. Exhaustively searching the inside of a large lobster-claw with a silver pick, she said: "Of course she wouldn't! Gavin only said it to be clever. Like saying that if he couldn't have Mavis, or himself, for the murder he'd have Mr. Ainstable."

"What?" said Mr. Haswell, looking up.

"Yes, because he was the most unlikely person he could think of."

"Do you mean to say that Plenmeller said that in front of this Chief Inspector you say you met?"

"Oh, lord, yes!" replied Charles, turning the contents of the salad-bowl over in chase of an elusive olive. "I thought it was a bit thick myself, but I don't suppose it really mattered much. Too fatuous!"

"Besides, he didn't mind Mr. Warrenby nearly as much as most people did," Abby remarked. "I mean, he and Mrs. Ainstable have him to parties, don't they? *Had* him, I mean."

"Yes—and, come to think of it, *why?*" said Charles slowly. "He was about the last man on earth you'd expect the Ainstables to have had any time for at all, and it wasn't even as though he was their solicitor. Why did they take him up, Dad?"

"I have no idea, nor should I have said that they did more than show him a little ordinary civility."

Charles was frowning. "Well, I think they did. The Squire quite definitely introduced him to you, didn't he, Mummy? And he'd never have wormed his way into the Club if the Squire hadn't sponsored him."

"I expect the Ainstables felt it was their duty to be neighbourly," said Mrs. Haswell placidly.

"Well, they didn't feel it was their duty to be neighbourly to those ghastly people who evacuated themselves here from London during the blitz, and took Thornden House for the duration!" said Charles. "They never had anything to do with them at all!"

"No, but that was different," replied his mother. "They weren't permanent residents, and they got things on the Black Market, and said that if you knew your way about you could always get extra petrol. You couldn't expect the Ainstables to have anything to do with them!"

"No, but that's just the type of man Warrenby was too," Charles said.

"We don't *know* he was, dear: he wasn't here during the War."

"At all events, he wasn't the kind of man the Squire usually encourages."

"Oh, no, not in the least! I must say," remarked Mrs. Haswell reflectively, "I have sometimes wondered why he bothered to be nice to him, particularly when poor Mr. Drybeck disliked him so much."

"He *did* dislike him, didn't he?" said Abby eagerly.

"Well, dear, I'm afraid we all did."

"But Mr. Drybeck much more than most people. Charles, I can't think how you can be so dim about this! Going on and on about Mavis, when all the evidence points to Mr. Drybeck!"

"It doesn't. Besides,——"

"Yes, it does," Abby insisted. "He had a motive, for one thing. Not just hating Warrenby, but being done down by him, which I know from things Aunt Miriam's told me. Losing clients to him, and Warrenby pulling fast ones on him."

"Abby, me sweet, be your age!" Charles besought her. "*Look* at poor old Thaddeus! The most respectable body!"

"Like Armstrong!" she flashed. "That's what's been in my mind all day! He's a solicitor, too, and it's almost the same motive. Armstrong was a respectable little man no one ever dreamed would murder anyone, but he did, so it's no use saying the motive isn't strong enough!"

"I agree with all that, but you're forgetting that it was Armstrong's *second* murder—at least, he did'i't pull it off, did he? I remember he was tried for having poisoned his wife, and he had a much stronger motive for that. I don't suppose he'd have tried to do in his rival if he hadn't got away with the first murder. Probably made him think he was so damned clever he could get away with any number of murders. Like the Brides in the Bath man. Isn't it true, Dad, that if a murderer gets away with it he very often commits another murder? Sort of blood to the head?"

"So I believe," replied his father. "But if you are suggesting that Drybeck has already murdered someone it's high time you curbed your imagination."

"I'm not. I'm merely pointing out to Abby where Drybeck's resemblance to Armstrong ceases."

"Well, whatever you're doing, I think we've had about enough of the subject," said Mr. Haswell. "Did you get any tennis this afternoon?"

This question, impartially addressed to both the young people, put an effectual end to the discussion. It was not re-opened, the rest of the evening being spent in playing Bridge. Only when Charles motored her back to Fox Cottage did Abby say: "Was your father annoyed with us for talking about the murder?"

"Oh, no!" said Charles. "I think he's afraid we shall be indiscreet in the wrong company, that's all. Like Gavin."

She wrinkled her brow. "He isn't indiscreet. He's waspish."

"Baiting the Major? I don't think he's doing anyone any harm, you know. Merely being witty, and showing-off."

"He was definitely waspish about Mavis," she insisted.

"And who shall blame him? So am I."

"Yes, but you wouldn't set the police on to her," she said seriously.

"Under certain circumstances I might."

"What circumstances? I don't believe you would!"

"Like a shot I would! If I thought the police were after me, or my people." He paused, rounding the corner into Fox Lane. "Or you," he added.

"Thanks awfully! Big of you!"

"I'm like that," he said unctuously, pulling up outside Fox Cottage. "Nothing I won't do for the people I love!"

"Go to the stake for them, I wouldn't wonder!" she returned, with an uncertain little laugh.

"With enthusiasm—for you!"

"D-don't be so silly! Oh, look! here comes Aunt Miriam!"

"Blast Aunt Miriam!" said Charles savagely.

"Hallo, Charles!" said Miss Patterdale, opening the gate, and coming up to the car with a large cardboard dress-box under her arm. "I thought you'd bring Abby back, so I packed up the things for your mother's Sale of Work. Will you give them to her, please?"

He took the box from her, and threw it somewhat unceremoniously on to the back-seat. "All right, Aunt Miriam. Is that ghastly Sale upon us again already? Hell! What about running down to the sea tomorrow, after tea, Abby? I'll look in in the morning on my way to the office, and see how you feel about it. 'Night, Aunt Miriam!"

"Nice boy, Charles," remarked Miss Patterdale, accompanying her niece up the path to the front-door. "Did you solve the mystery between you?"

"No. Actually, Mr. Haswell rather squashed us. I say, Aunt Miriam, you know Charles and I looked in at the Red Lion for a short one before we went on to The Cedars? Well, we were having drinks with Gavin and Major Midgeholme when that detective who interviewed Mavis walked in, and whoever do you think he brought with him?"

"Two detectives from Scotland Yard," said Miss Patterdale promptly. "I met them up at Fox House."

"Oh, no, did you really? What did you think of the little one—the Chief Inspector? I rather fell for him. He's got a sense of humour, and he handled Gavin a fair treat!"

"I should say," responded Miss Patterdale grimly, "that he

95

is adept in handling people a fair treat, as you put it. You should have heard him with Flora Midgeholme! I *knew* this would lead to trouble!"

"No, why should it? Only for the murderer, and you don't mind that, do you?"

"Certainly not, but it won't be only for the murderer if I know anything about it. There won't be a skeleton in Thornden that isn't dug up. Don't tell *me*! Your Chief Inspector said that they always tried to be discreet. I don't know whether he thought I believed him. I suppose you know he called on Thaddeus Drybeck?"

"No! What happened? Tell me!"

"I don't know, except that he's made Thaddeus behave like a cat on hot bricks. He came up here after supper with one of the feeblest excuses I've ever heard, and tried to make me remember what time it was when Mavis came to tell me her uncle had been killed. I'm not surprised he's losing ground in his practice: make him grasp that I wasn't likely to remember something I'd never known I could not! I couldn't think what he was after. You'd never guess what it turned out to be! He's trying to prove that Mavis killed her uncle! Silly old fool! The fact of the matter is he's lived the whole of his life wrapped up in cottonwool, and this affair has frightened him out of his wits."

Abby, who was trying to pour out a glass of lemonade without allowing the scraps of peel to slide out of the jug, suspended her operations to stare at her aunt. "Is he really scared?" she asked. "Then it all goes to *show*! Why should he be scared if he had nothing to do with it? Trying to divert suspicion on to someone else, too!"

Miss Patterdale was rather amused by this. "Well, you all of you seem to suspect someone, so why shouldn't he?"

"No, only Charles and me, really, because Gavin isn't serious. The Haswells don't suspect anyone, and the Major doesn't either."

"Flora does," said Miss Patterdale, with a short bark of laughter. "Lord, what a fool that woman can be! She can't make up her mind whether that Pole did it, or the Lindales—either one of them or both."

"The Lindales," repeated Abby, considering this suggestion dispassionately. "I don't know them well enough to say. Why does Mrs. Midgeholme think they might have?"

"No reason at all. Mrs. Lindale has been a little stand-offish to her. Don't blame her!"

"What do the Lindales themselves say about it?"

"My dear girl, you don't suppose I've been up to Rushyford, do you? I've no idea."

"Oh, no, I just thought you might have seen them after church!"

"They aren't churchgoers. At least, he isn't. I don't know what she may do: I believe she's an R.C."

"Oh! Aunt Miriam, why did the Ainstables take Warrenby up?"

"It's news to me that they did," said Miss Patterdale curtly.

"*Aunt Miriam!* I distinctly remember you saying once that you couldn't imagine why the Squire tolerated him!"

"Tolerating people isn't the same as taking them up. Who's been putting this idea into your head?"

"Gavin more or less started it——"

"He would!" interrupted Miss Patterdale, her eyes snapping.

"Oh, he didn't say anything about that! He was only talking rot about the Squire having done the murder because he was the least likely person," said Abby, not very lucidly. "And that made Charles ask his father exactly what I've asked you."

"It did, did it? And what did Mr. Haswell say?"

Abby laughed, and gave her a hug. "He was rather snubbing. Like you, angel!"

"So I should hope! Now, Abby, I've nothing to say against your playing at detection, but you stick to Thaddeus! Do him good to be harried a little, old stick-in-the-mud! Leave the Ainstables alone! They've had enough trouble, poor things, without being worried by policemen. I should be seriously annoyed if I found you'd said anything to that Scotland Yard man which put a lot of false ideas into his head. If the Ainstables were kinder than most of us to that odious man, it was because they always feel they have a duty towards everyone in the district."

"It's all right: I'm not going to do anything snakeish," Abby assured her. "All the same, you *do* think it was funny of the Ainstables, don't you? Funny-peculiar, I mean."

"Whatever I may have thought on that subject, I most certainly don't think it had anything to do with Warrenby's murder. Come along, it's time we went to bed!"

CHAPTER NINE

BEFORE he went to bed that night, Inspector Harbottle, who had spent some part of the evening at the police-station, studying the Firearms Register, was able to inform his chief, with a certain gloomy satisfaction, that thirty-seven persons, living within reasonable distance of Thornden, possessed .22 rifles. "And that, mind you, is only within a twenty mile radius," he added, unfolding a piece of paper.

Hemingway, who had himself been engaged with the papers he had taken from Sampson Warrenby's desk, perceived that he was about to read his list aloud, and instantly discouraged him. "I don't want to hear you reciting the names of a lot of people I've never heard of, Horace! Checking up on the rifles is a nice job for the locals, and one that'll just about suit them. You tell me who owns a .22 in Thornden! That'll be enough to be going on with."

"It wouldn't surprise me if we had to throw the net much wider," said Harbottle. "You're very optimistic, Chief, but——"

"Get on!" commanded Hemingway.

The Inspector cast such a glance upon him as Calvin might have bestowed on a backslider, but replied with careful correctitude: "Very good, sir. According to the Register, there are eleven .22 rifles in Thornden. That includes three belonging to farmers, living just outside the village, which I daresay you aren't interested in."

"You're right. And if I have any cheek from you, Horace, I'll give you the job of checking up on the whole thirty-seven!"

Cheered by this threat, the Inspector permitted himself to smile faintly. "Well, the Squire has one," he offered. "Likewise a chap called Eckford, his agent; and a John Henshaw, game-keeper. Setting aside the possibility that someone might have got hold of their rifles unbeknownst, there doesn't seem to be any reason, from what Carsethorn tells me, to think they could have had anything to do with the case. Next, there's Kenelm Lindale: he has one."

"Which he lent to Ladislas the Pole not so long ago. I re-member that one," interpolated Hemingway.

"I thought you would," said Harbottle, eyeing him with melancholy pride. "Then there's young Mr. Haswell's, which he spoke about; and Mr. Plenmeller's, which you picked up. Josiah Crailing has one—he's the landlord of the Red Lion; and the last belongs to Mr. Cliburn, the Vicar. Mr. Drybeck's got a shot-gun only; and Major Midgeholme's hanging on to his Service revolver, and six cartridges, which there's a fight about every time his Firearms Licence is due for renewal. So far he's managed to keep them." He folded his list, and put it back in his pocket. "That's the lot, Chief—so far as the Register goes. Do you want Carsethorn to pull them all in?"

"What, the whole thirty-seven?"

"Eleven," Harbottle corrected him.

"Call it eight, Horace! If all else fails, maybe I'll start to take an interest in these three farmers of yours, but so far I've got enough on my hands without annoying people that very likely wouldn't have recognized Warrenby if they'd met him in the street. Tell Carsethorn to make the usual enquiries, and not to go cluttering poor old Knarsdale up with a lot of rifles which their owners can account for." He paused, and considered for a moment. "No sense in us treading on one another's heels—nor in getting ourselves disliked more than we probably are already. I'm going to Thornden myself tomorrow, and I shall be paying a call on the Vicar. Tell Carsethorn I'll bring in that rifle if I see fit. He'd better pull in the Squire's, Lindale's, and young Haswell's first thing. He seems a fairly sensible chap, but you'd better warn him to do the thing tactfully—particularly when he gets to the Squire. The usual stuff about persons unauthorized perhaps having got hold of it."

The Inspector nodded, but said: "You're going to see the Vicar?"

"Yes, and his rifle gives me a nice excuse."

"Carsethorn did check up on his alibi. It seems all right, Chief."

"That's why I need an excuse. By what the Colonel tells me this Reverend Anthony Cliburn is just the man I want to give me the low-down on this high-class set-up. So far, I've had to listen to Mrs. Midgeholme, who thinks Lindale murdered Warrenby, because Mrs. Lindale gave her a raspberry; and to Drybeck, who's in a blue funk; and to Plenmeller, who wants to be funny; and I'm getting muddled. When you want to know the ins and outs of village-life, Horace, go and talk to the Vicar! Not that it's any use telling you that, because you haven't got the art of making people talk, which is what becomes of drinking sarsaparilla instead of an honest glass of beer."

"Anything in Warrenby's papers, sir?" said the Inspector coldly.

"Nothing that looks like doing us any good. We may find something at his office tomorrow, but I shall be surprised if we do."

The Inspector grunted, and sat down. He watched Hemingway collect the papers into a pile, and then said: "There is something that strikes me, Chief."

"Second time today. You're coming on," said Hemingway encouragingly. "Go on! Don't keep me on tenterhooks!"

"From the moment I was told the shot was probably fired from a .22 rifle," said the Inspector, "I've been turning it over in my mind, wondering what was done with that rifle. Because it seems to me it would be taking a big risk to walk away with it over your shoulder, or under your arm. Who's to say you'd meet no one? But I watched you go off up the street with Plenmeller, Chief, and it came to me then that if anyone could walk about with a rifle concealed he could push it down his left trouser-leg, and, with that queer limp of his, no one would notice a thing."

"Not bad at all, Horace!" approved Hemingway. "Now tell me why he takes it home, and puts it back in the gun-cabinet, instead of dropping it in the river, or somebody's backyard—which is just the sort of little joke that would appeal to him, I should think. He inherited his guns from that brother of his; he doesn't shoot himself—which I believe, because, for one thing, he's not the kind of fool who'd tell lies to the police which they could easily disprove, and, for another, I noticed that the guns in that cabinet were showing signs of rust—and if he'd chosen to say that he didn't know where the rifle was, and hadn't even known it wasn't in the cabinet, it would have been a difficult job to prove it hadn't been pinched. Because it could have been, easy! His door's kept on the latch, and he's got a deaf housekeeper." He got up, glancing at the marble clock over the fireplace. "I'm going to turn in, and you'd better do the same, or you'll start brooding, or get struck by another idea, which would be bad for my heart."

The Inspector rose, and after eyeing his chief for a pregnant moment, addressed himself to the vase of pampas-grass in a musing tone. "If I had to explain why I like my present job, I'm blessed if I could do it!"

"If you're thinking the B.B.C. is going to ask you to take part in a programme, you needn't worry!" retorted Hemingway. "They won't!"

"How Sandy Grant put up with it as long as he did I *don't* know!" said Harbottle.

"That's all right, Horace: he knew if he stuck to me he'd precious soon get promoted."

"It's a fact your assistants do," admitted Harbottle grudgingly.

"Of course they do! Recommending them for promotion is the only way I can get rid of them. Come on up to bed!"

On the following morning, Inspector Harbottle betook himself to Sampson Warrenby's office, and Hemingway went round to the police-station, where, after putting through a call to Head-quarters, he had an interview with the Chief Constable, and received a brief report from Sergeant Knarsdale.

The Sergeant had already despatched the bullet, with its cartridge-case, which he had fired from Gavin Plenmeller's rifle, to London, but said frankly that he was not hopeful. "I wouldn't like to say, not for sure, without seeing them under the comparison-microscope," he told Hemingway, "but I think they'll find there's some marks on this cartridge-case I couldn't spot on the other. Got any more for me, sir?"

"Sergeant Carsethorn will be bringing in three more this morning, unless they've got unaccountably mislaid."

Knarsdale grinned. "Regular arsenal we'll have here!"

"You don't know the half of it! The Inspector's got thirty-seven on his list."

"Ah, well! we'll be able to get up a competition," said the Sergeant, who knew his Chief Inspector.

"That's right: I'm just off to Woolworth's to buy some nice prizes for you!" said Hemingway, and left him chuckling gently.

Ten minutes' walk brought the Chief Inspector to Sampson Warrenby's office. A guide was offered, but as he was informed that he had only to cross the market-place to South Street, which was the main shopping-street in Bellingham, and to walk down it until he reached East Street, which intersected it, he declined the offer, and set off alone. A large number of country omnibuses were ranked in the market-place, and South Street was already congested with all those who had come into the town to do the week's shopping. Hemingway caught a glimpse of Miss Patterdale, stalking into a grocer's, with a large basket on her arm; and a minute later he met Gavin Plenmeller, emerging from the portals of a bank.

"Good heavens! Scotland Yard in person!" exclaimed Gavin, causing everyone within earshot to turn and stare avidly at Hemingway. "But what are you doing, frittering away your time in idle sight-seeing, Chief Inspector?"

"Yes, it's easy to see why you aren't, so to say, popular with Sergeant Carsethorn, sir," said Hemingway, eyeing him grimly. "Pity you forgot your megaphone!"

Gavin laughed. "I *am* so sorry!" he mocked, and passed on up the street.

Hemingway proceeded on his way, and soon arrived at Sampson Warrenby's office in East Street. Here he was received by a junior clerk, and afforded two stenographers and the office boy their second thrill of the day. All three contrived to catch a glimpse of him, as he was led to Sampson Warrenby's room, and although the glimpse was a brief one it was sufficient to enable the elder of the two damsels to state that he had eyes that looked right through you, and to convince the younger that if she were summoned before him to answer any questions she wouldn't be able to speak a word, on account of her being very

101

high-strung, as anyone who knew her could testify. The office-boy said in a very boastful way that it would take more than a C.I.D. man to scare him, after which he went off to the Post Office with two unimportant letters, his mind being troubled with a horrid fear that from so high-ranking an official not one of his youthful peccadilloes could remain hidden.

Meanwhile, the Chief Inspector had joined his subordinate in Sampson Warrenby's room, and had made the acquaintance of Mr. Coupland, the head clerk.

Mr. Coupland was a thin little man, with sparse, grizzled hair, and anxious face. He greeted the Chief Inspector nervously, and said: "This is a shocking business! I can't get over it. As I've been saying to the Inspector, I don't know what's going to happen, I'm sure, Mr. Warrenby not having a partner. It's very worrying, very! I really don't know what I ought to do. Not when we've cleared up what we have on hand."

"Well, I'm afraid I can't help you there," said Hemingway. "Busy practice, this?"

"Oh, very! Very busy indeed!" Mr. Coupland said earnestly. "The biggest practice in Bellingham, and growing so—well, Mr. Warrenby was talking of having to take a partner. And now this! Well, I don't seem able to believe it's happened, and that's a fact!"

"Came as a surprise to you, did it?"

The clerk blinked at him. "Oh, yes, it did indeed! More like a shock, really. Well, as I say, I can't realize it. I keep thinking Mr. Warrenby will come walking in any moment, wanting to know if the Widdringham lease has been posted, and—But, of course, he won't."

He glanced up, with an uncertain smile, and was disconcerted to find himself the object of a bright, piercing scrutiny. He did his best to meet it, the smile fading from his face.

"Been his head clerk for long?"

"Ever since he started practice in Bellingham," said Mr. Coupland, with a touch of pride.

"And you didn't know that he had any enemies?"

"No—no, indeed I didn't! Mr. Warrenby wasn't one to take people into his confidence. Even in practice, there were always some things he preferred to deal with himself. He was a—a very energetic, forceful man, Chief Inspector."

"By what I've heard he was a man who made a lot of enemies."

"Yes, I believe—that is, as to his private affairs I couldn't say, but professionally, of course, he wasn't well-liked. He was very successful, you see, and that made for a good deal of jealousy. On the Council too, and all the committees he sat on—well, in everything, really, he would have his own way, and—perhaps I shouldn't say this, but—but I fear he wasn't always very scrupulous in his methods. He once said to me that there were few things he enjoyed more than making people dance when he pulled their strings, and, of course, that sort of thing doesn't make a man popular. He always treated me very well, and all the staff, but I couldn't but wonder sometimes at the trouble he'd go to to discover everything about the people he came into contact with. I ventured to ask him once, but he only said you could never know when it might be useful."

"Blackmail?" asked Hemingway bluntly.

"Oh! Oh, no, I wouldn't say that! I never saw anything to make me suspect—it always seemed more to me as though it amused him to make people he didn't like uncomfortable by letting them see he knew something about them they wouldn't wish to be known. Oh, quite trivial things—I don't mean to suggest—I daresay you know the sort of thing I mean, Chief Inspector. There aren't many of us who haven't ever done anything we wouldn't be a bit ashamed to have known. If you understand me!"

"I understand you all right. And you were surprised when you heard someone had shot this pocket-Hitler of yours?"

Mr. Coupland looked startled. "Yes, indeed, I was! Oh, dear, I hope I haven't given you a wrong impression! I didn't mean to say that Mr. Warrenby did anything to make anyone want to *murder* him! Often he would say things more by way of a joke than anything: twitting one about some little misfortune, or mistake. Well, he's done that to me, and I won't deny it *did* make one angry, but—but there was nothing in it really!"

"I see," said Hemingway. "Well, Mr. Coupland, I don't have to tell you that it's your duty to give me any assistance or information you can, so I'll put it straight to you: have you any reason to suspect that he may have been blackmailing—or whatever you like to call it!—anyone, at the time of his death?"

"No, Chief Inspector! No, no, none at all—I assure you! Well, I couldn't have! I never knew him *privately*, and in his practice—oh, *no!*" said Mr. Coupland, looking frightened and unhappy.

Hemingway, who had been watching him with his head a little on one side and an expression in his eyes which reminded Harbottle irresistibly of a robin on the watch for a tit-bit, nodded, and said briefly: "All right!"

At this point, the junior clerk slid into the room through as narrow an opening of the door as was possible, and stood hesitating on the threshold. Mr. Coupland glanced at the Chief Inspector for guidance, but as Hemingway did not seem to think that the intrusion in any way concerned him, he cleared his throat, and said, in rather a strained voice: "Yes, what is it?"

The youth trod delicately up to him, and murmured something to him, of which the only words which Hemingway heard were "Sir John Eaglesfield." They appeared to exercise a powerful influence on Mr. Coupland, for, after exclaiming in a dismayed and startled way, he said: "I wonder if you would excuse me for a few minutes, Chief Inspector? One of Mr. Warrenby's most valued clients——!"

"That's all right," said Hemingway. "You go and deal with him!"

Not unthankfully, Mr. Coupland removed himself. When the door had closed behind him and his junior, Harbottle, who had remained seated at Warrenby's desk throughout his chief's interview with the head-clerk, silent and observant, said: "What do you make of him, sir?"

"Oh, perfectly honest!" Hemingway replied, going to the desk, and looking at the mass of papers on it. "How are you doing, Horace? You seem to have got enough to keep you occupied!"

"I have," said Harbottle, on a mordant note. "That chap was just explaining to me, when you came in, that things aren't as straight as he'd wish, owing to the office being so cramped. Which it certainly is. He was telling me that Warrenby was determined to get an office next to the Town Hall, which he says is the best pitch in the whole of Bellingham, and wouldn't be content with anything else."

"And I don't doubt he would have got it," remarked Hemingway.

"Nor I. I wish he had, for I should have found my job easier," said Harbottle, casting a glance round the room, which was indeed crammed with cupboards, shelves with labelled deed boxes piled on them, a safe, standing open, two filing-cabinets, and a large bookcase. "If there's any scheme in this town he hadn't got a finger in, I can't think what it could be. That cupboard over there is full of the stuff, and I take it I'd better go through it. He seems to have kept all his private business-letters and such here. Mostly in the safe, but this lot comes from the cupboard under the books. That's what you want me to work on, isn't it?"

Hemingway nodded. "Yes, don't try to meddle with the deed-boxes belonging to his clients: you'll be getting into hot water if you do, and wasting your time as well. Well, I've seen some solicitors' offices which I thought were so cluttered up no one could ever find a thing in them, but this fairly takes the cake! Poor old Horace!"

"Oh, it isn't in a muddle!" Harbottle said. "Everything's docketed, and bundled up. The trouble is there's so much of it, and what he's written on his bundles doesn't always convey as much to me as it no doubt did to him."

"Coupland no use to you?"

"Not on all these side-lines. He only knows about the real business of the office. I've got hold of one bit of information I

104

think'll interest you, Chief. Did you know Warrenby was the Clerk of the Peace?"

"No, but I'd have betted any money on it."

"He was appointed last year," said Harbottle. "I got it out of Coupland. Old Drybeck was laid up when the appointment fell vacant. Used to be held by some old solicitor, who died just before Quarter Sessions. Warrenby slid into the job when Drybeck was convalescing in Torquay."

"Probably murdered the old Clerk to get the job," commented Hemingway, who had picked up a sheaf of letters, and was running a rapid and practised eye over them.

"I could tell from the way Coupland spoke Drybeck thought he ought to have been appointed."

"Well, I don't know that I blame them for choosing Warrenby. I should think he was an efficient bloke, which is more than I'd be prepared to say of Drybeck—on the evidence I've got so far. Yes, yes, Horace, I know what you're after! It gives Drybeck a bit more motive. You may be right, but I should think he must have got used to seeing Warrenby grabbing every job in sight. Don't tell me he didn't get himself appointed Town Clerk, Coroner, Sexton, Welfare Officer, and Town Crier as well, because I wouldn't believe it!"

"He was the Coroner, but as for the rest of them, he was not, and couldn't have been," said the Inspector austerely.

"You don't know what the poor fellow would have managed to be if he hadn't been cut off in his prime. Have you come upon anything that might be of use to us?"

"Not unless you're interested in a letter about Mr. Ainstable's gravel-pit, or the negotiations for the purchase of Fox House. You might like to see that: it gives you a fair idea of what the deceased was like. The way he beat the owner down! But it's old stuff."

"What was he writing about the Squire's gravel-pit? Trying to buy that too, at cost-price?"

"No, it's only a letter from some firm of London solicitors, which is an answer to one from him on behalf of a client. There ought to be a copy of that, but I haven't found it yet. Must have slipped out of the clip."

"You don't seem able to find the answer either," remarked Hemingway, watching him scuffle through the heaps of papers on the desk. "What was it about?"

"Seems Warrenby had a client who was interested in gravel, and he was making enquiries on his behalf."

"The hobbies people go in for!"

"For goodness sake!" snapped the Inspector, exasperated by his own failure to lay his hand on the letter he wanted. "I put it aside to show you, but there's no room to turn round in here! His client wanted a licence, of course!"

"Temper!" said Hemingway reprovingly. "What had these London solicitors got to do with it? I thought Drybeck was the Squire's solicitor. In fact, the Chief Constable told me he was."

"I don't know anything about that, sir, but these people seem to be the solicitors for the estate, or some such thing. Ah!"

"Found it?"

"No, but this must be the copy of Warrenby's letter. Got into the wrong lot. Here you are, sir!"

Hemingway took the copy, and read it, while the Inspector continued his search. "Two years old, I see. You were quite right, Horace: he *had* a client who was interested in the Squire's gravel-pit! He was informed they were the proper people to apply to, and would be glad, etc., etc. Next instalment in tomorrow's issue—with luck! Go on, Horace! I can hardly wait!"

The Inspector cast him a fulminating look, and said coldly: "I have it here. You put those letters you were reading down on top of it."

"That's right: you can't learn too early how to pass the buck, if you want to get on in life," said Hemingway encouragingly. He read the letter, a crease between his brows. "Well, they seemed quite willing to do business, but I don't get the hang of this tenant-for-life business. The licence would have to be by arrangement with the tenant-for-life—oh, I see, it's the Squire! some sort of an entail, I expect. And all moneys would have to be paid to these people for apportionment as between the tenant-for-life and the Trust funds. Well, I daresay it's all very interesting. Any more of it?"

"I've found nothing more so far."

"No letters from the unnamed client?"

"No. Which is why I thought it worth while to show you those two. Looks as if nothing came of the proposal. I wondered if perhaps the Squire refused to do business, and whether there might have been bad blood between him and Warrenby over it," said Harbottle slowly, frowning over it.

"And then Warrenby started pinching the gravel for his client when no one was looking, and so the Squire up and shot him. Really, Horace, I'm surprised at you!"

"If I'd meant anything of the kind, you might well be! Unless you think such folly is catching!" retorted Harbottle.

Hemingway laughed. "Not bad!" he said. "But I've got something better to do than to stay here listening to you being insubordinate. Keep at it! you may find something, though I doubt it. I'll send young Morebattle in to give you a hand."

"You're not taking him to Thornden, sir?"

"No, I don't need him. He's all yours, Horace."

"I shall be glad of him," admitted the Inspector, casting a jaundiced eye over the work awaiting him.

Hemingway left him, and walked back to the police-station. Sergeant Carsethorn had not yet returned from Thornden, but the Station-Sergeant had news for the Chief Inspector. He said, with a twinkle in his eye: "Got a message for you, sir."

Hemingway regarded him shrewdly. "You have, have you? Now, come on! Out with it, and don't stand there grinning!"

"Sorry, sir! It's from Mr. Drybeck," said the Sergeant solemnly.

"Oh, well, that's different! What's he want?"

"Told me to give you this, sir—and to be careful how I handled it, because he found it close to the scene of the crime. In some long grass by the gorse-clump. He was quite put out not to find you here. Said at first that he'd look in later, but I told him we wasn't expecting you in, not till this evening."

"You're wasted down here, my lad," said Hemingway approvingly. "What's he found? A hairpin, which he thinks must have belonged to Miss Warrenby?"

The Sergeant, who had produced from the drawer of the high desk some small object wrapped in a linen handkerchief, looked up quickly. "If I may say so, sir, you're on to things pretty sharp!"

"I've no objection, but you're not going to tell me that *is* what he found, are you?"

"No, sir," said the Sergeant, unfolding the handkerchief. "But when he decided to leave it in my charge he told me to draw your attention to the initial."

"You'd have to, wouldn't you?" said Hemingway, surveying with an expression of revulsion a powder-compact made of pink plastic with the letter H superimposed in imitation rubies.

"He said," continued the Sergeant carefully, "that it was not for him to draw conclusions, and he would leave the matter in your hands."

"Well, that's handsome of him, at all events. I'd give something to see Sergeant Carsethorn's face when he hears he missed this in his search for that cartridge-case. You'd better put a notice outside the station saying a valuable compact has been found. I daresay some girl's boy-friend gave it to her, and she'd like it back."

"Do you mean that, sir?"

"Of course I mean it! You don't think I want it, do you?"

"I must say it didn't seem likely to me it was the sort of compact Miss Warrenby would have," admitted the Sergeant.

"It isn't the sort any young lady in her walk of life would have. I never saw such a nasty, cheap job!"

"No. Of course, there *is* the initial. But you know best, sir!" he added hastily.

"You may take it from me that I do! How many girls in Bellingham have got names beginning with M, do you suppose?

That compact wasn't by those gorse-bushes when Carsethorn and his chaps searched the ground, and it wasn't there when I went out to Fox House. But I'll tell you what was there then, or very shortly afterwards, and that was sightseers, very likely come out from this place to look at the scene of the crime. There was a couple hovering back-stage while I was there: I saw them. By Sunday evening it was probably all over the town there'd been a murder, and a lot of us had come down from Headquarters to take over. Miss Warrenby's probably had them picnicking on the front lawn, poor girl. What's more, she doesn't use powder: I've seen her! And finally, if she did, where do girls keep their compacts? In their handbags! All I can say is, if you think she powdered her nose before shooting her uncle you ought to go and get yourself certified!"

"Yes, sir," said the Sergeant, grinning broadly.

"And if that's Mr. Drybeck's handkerchief, give it back to him! Hallo, here's Carsethorn. Well?"

"I've brought in the three you wanted, sir."

"Good man! Any difficulty?"

"Not with Mr. Ainstable, sir, nor yet at The Cedars. Mr. Ainstable quite saw why we wanted his rifle, and made no objection at all. It was in his estate room. That's not part of Old Place: just a small kind of summerhouse, which was converted, so as Mr. Eckford, the Squire's agent, wouldn't have to go through the house every time he went there. I had a look at it, the Squire taking me to it, and I wouldn't like to say the rifle couldn't have been lifted, and put back later, because I think—if you knew when the estate room was likely to be empty—it might have been. Young Mr. Haswell left his rifle wrapped up in a bit of sacking, and told Mrs. Haswell to give it to us if we called asking for it. Now, that rifle was found by him in the cupboard in the cloakroom, sir, and could easily have been taken by anyone at that tennis-party—if they could have hidden it, which I *don't* think."

"What about Lindale's?"

"Yes, sir, I have that too. He wasn't best pleased: said no one could possibly have borrowed it without his knowing. But it wasn't him that made the real trouble over it. That was Mrs. Lindale. He wasn't in when I called, and had to be fetched off the farm. She sent the daily woman to find him, thought I told her I only wanted to test the rifle, as a matter of routine. Very hostile she was. Scared, I thought. Started tearing me off the strip, the way women do when they've got the wind up. Only then her husband came in, and she quietened down as soon as he spoke to her. Very gone on one another they are, I'd say. He said if it was really necessary for me to take the rifle I could do so, but he'd be obliged to us if we wouldn't come bothering his

108

good lady, because she's very nervous, and things like this murder upset her."

"In that case," said Hemingway, "I'm going to be unpopular, because I'm going to go out there to bother her this afternoon."

CHAPTER TEN

THE Chief Inspector was taken to Thornden by the young constable who had driven him there on the previous day; but since Rushyford Farm was his first objective Constable Melkinthorpe took the right fork out of Bellingham, which led to Hawkshead. This road, after a few miles, intersected the common, north of the Trindale-road, and, about a quarter of a mile before it reached Rushyford, passed the Squire's gravel-pit. Men were working there; Hemingway asked whose men they were, and Melkinthorpe replied with the name of a local firm, adding that they did say that Mr. Ainstable made quite a good thing out of it. Constable Melkinthorpe, who was enjoying his present assignment more than any that had previously fallen to him, and dreamed of vague heroic deeds, turned circumspectly into the rather narrow entrance to Rushyford Farm, and asked hopefully if the Chief Inspector wanted him to go with him into the house.

"Not unless you hear me scream," said Hemingway, getting out of the car. "Then, of course, you'll come in double-quick to rescue me." He slammed the car-door, and paused for a moment, surveying the house before him, which was a rambling, picturesque building set in a small garden, and with its farm-buildings clustered to one side of it. The front-door stood open on to a flagged passage, but Hemingway very correctly knocked on it, and awaited permission to enter. He had to knock twice before he could get a response. Then Mrs. Lindale came running down the uncarpeted oaken stairway, hastily untying an apron as she descended, and casting it aside. "Sorry!" she said. "My daily has gone into Bellingham to get the rations, and I couldn't come down before. Do you want Mr. Lindale?"

"Well, I should like a word with him, madam," said Hemingway. "My name's Hemingway—Chief Inspector, C.I.D. Perhaps you'd like to have my card."

She made no attempt to take it, but stood in the doorway as though she would have denied him ingress. "We've already had one detective here today! What on earth can you want? Why do you come badgering us? My husband was barely acquainted with Mr. Warrenby! I think it's the limit!"

"I'm bound to say it must be a nuisance for you," admitted Hemingway. "But if we weren't allowed to make enquiries we wouldn't get much farther, would we?"

"Neither my husband nor I can possibly be of any use to you!" she said impatiently. "What is it you want to know?"

"Oh, I just want to ask you both a few questions!" he replied. "May I come in?"

She seemed to hesitate, and then, reluctantly, stood aside for him to pass, saying ungraciously, as she pushed open a door on the right of the passage. "Oh, all right! Go in there, will you? I'll send to fetch my husband."

She then walked away down the passage, and could be heard a minute later shouting to one Walter to tell the master he was wanted up at the house. When she came back to the sitting-room, she still wore a defensive look, but said, with a perfunctory smile: "Sorry if I bit your head off! But, really, it's a bit much! We've already told the police all we know about what happened on Saturday, and the answer is nothing. I left The Cedars just after half-past six, and came straight back here to put my baby to bed. I can't tell you the exact moment when my husband left: he was still playing tennis when I went away: but I happen to know he wasn't anywhere near Fox Lane when Mr. Warrenby was shot!"

Hemingway, who rarely found it necessary to consult his notes, said affably: "Ah, that's a bit of evidence the local police must have forgotten to give me! It's a good job I came. How do you happen to know it, madam?"

"Because he was down by the water-meadows," she replied, boldly meeting his eyes. "I saw him there!"

"You did?" said Hemingway, all polite interest.

"I'll take you up and show you the window, if you like. You can see the water-meadows from one of the attics. I happened to run up to get something—we keep a lot of junk stored in the attics—and I distinctly saw my husband!" She paused, and added: "I'm sure I told the other detective, when he first came to see us! I'd be ready to swear I did!"

"I don't doubt that for a moment," said Hemingway. "Or you might have had your reasons for not telling Sergeant Carsethorn at the time."

"What possible reason could I have had?"

"Well, I don't know, but perhaps you hadn't realized, when the Sergeant first called on you, that you *could* see the water-meadows from that attic window," suggested Hemingway.

Her colour rose, flaming into her naturally pale face. "Of course I knew it! If I didn't tell the Sergeant—but I'm nearly sure I did!—it must have been because I was so shocked and startled by the news that Mr. Warrenby had been shot that it momentarily slipped my mind!"

"What brought it back to your mind—if I may ask?" said Hemingway.

"When I had time to think—going back over what I did after I got home on Saturday——" She broke off, her knuckles whitening as she gripped her thin hands together.

111

Hemingway shook his head. "You shouldn't have kept it from the Sergeant when he came to pick up your husband's rifle this morning," he said, more in sorrow than in anger.

"If you like to come upstairs you can see for yourself!"

"I don't disbelieve you," said Hemingway, adding apologetically: "That you can see the water-meadow from the attic, I mean."

There was a moment's silence. "Look here!" said Delia Lindale fiercely. "I can tell you now that you're wasting your time! We hardly knew Mr. Warrenby, and we can't tell you anything! Why don't you ask Mr. Ainstable what he did after he parted from my husband on Saturday? Why didn't he go home in the car, with his wife? Why did he suddenly decide to visit his plantation? I suppose, just because the Ainstables have lived here for centuries, they're above suspicion! Like Gavin Plenmeller! You might find out what *he* was up to, instead of coming here to badger me! Why shouldn't it have been he? He *loathed* Mr. Warrenby! Ask Miss Patterdale if it isn't true that he said steps would have to be taken to get rid of him! I was standing beside her when he said it, at a cocktail-party the Ainstables gave last month, and so was Mr. Cliburn! The Warrenbys were both at the party, and I can tell you this!—everyone was saying how extraordinary it was of the Squire to have invited them! Particularly when he knew that Mr. Warrenby was pretty well barred in the neighbourhood!"

"Why was that?" enquired Hemingway.

"Because he was a bounder, I suppose. The sort of person the Ainstables look down their noses at. They don't welcome Tom, Dick, and Harry to Old Place, I assure you! In fact, I'm dead sure Mrs. Ainstable wouldn't have called on me if it hadn't been for Miss Patterdale's asking her to! She as good as said so! I—I don't want to try to cast suspicion on anyone, but I do wonder whether Mr. Warrenby had some sort of a hold over the Squire. Since this happened, I've naturally thought about it a good deal, trying to think who might have had a reason for shooting Mr. Warrenby, and remembering all sorts of little incidents, which, at the time, I didn't attach any importance to——"

"Such as?" interpolated Hemingway.

"Oh——! Mr. Ainstable trying to get my husband to back Warrenby for the River Board lawyer, for instance! I can't see what it matters, *who* gets the job, but no one but the Squire wanted it to be Warrenby. And now, when I think it over, I wonder why the Squire wanted him instead of Mr. Drybeck? Mr. Drybeck is his own solicitor, and an old friend, and he wants the appointment, too."

The sound of a firm step on the flagged passage made her break off, and turn her head towards the door. Kenelm Lindale came into the room, a slight frown between his eyes. He was dressed in ancient grey slacks, and a coloured shirt, open at the throat, and he looked to be both hot and annoyed. "Police?" he said shortly.

"It's a Chief Inspector from Scotland Yard," his wife warned him. "I've told him we can't help him!"

He dug a handkerchief out of his trouser-pocket, and wiped his face, and the back of his neck. "All right," he said, looking at Hemingway. "What is it you want to know? We've started to cut the hay, so I shall be glad if you can make it snappy."

"I just want to check up on your evidence, sir," said Hemingway mendaciously. "We do have to be so careful, in the Department. Now, I think you said you left that tennis-party at about ten-to seven, didn't you?"

"As near as I can make it: I don't know exactly, but I think it was about then. Mr. Ainstable and I left together, by the garden-gate. He may know when it was. I haven't asked him."

"When did you part from Mr. Ainstable, sir?"

"Couple of minutes later, I suppose. He turned off into his new plantation, which runs behind The Cedars. I went on. You'll see that one of my farm-gates opens on to the road opposite the footpath leading to the village. It's about a hundred yards up the road from here. I came in by that gate, and went to see how my chaps had got on with a job I set them to do in one of my water-meadows. I was in the house by half-past seven: that I do know, because I happened to look at the clock in the passage."

"Oh, darling, were you going by the grandfather?" said Mrs. Lindale quickly. "I thought you were relying on your watch! That clock was ten minutes fast: I put it right when I wound it up yesterday. I'm sorry: I ought to have told you, but I didn't know you were going by it."

Her husband looked at her, and after a tiny pause said lamely: "Oh!" He went to the fireplace, and selected a pipe from a collection on the mantleshelf, and took the lid off an old fashioned tobacco-jar. As he began to fill the pipe, his eyes on his task, the frown deepened on his brow. He said deliberately: "I don't think it can have been as fast as all that, Delia. I could hardly have been down to the water-meadows and got back here by twenty-past seven."

She swallowed. "No. Of course not. Which is why I should think you really left The Cedars earlier than ten-to seven. Time's so deceptive, and when you've got no particular reason for looking at your watch. . . ." Her voice tailed off uncertainly and she did not finish the sentence.

"And did you happen to notice what the time was when you saw Mr. Lindale down in the water-meadow, madam?"

113

asked Hemingway, his eyes not on her face, but on her husband's.

Lindale looked up quickly. "What's this?"

"Kenelm, you know I told you I'd caught sight of you from the attic-window!"

If Lindale felt exasperation, no hint of it appeared in his face. He put an arm round Delia's shoulders, and hugged her slightly. "You silly kid!" he said. "You mustn't try to mislead the police, you know: you'll get had up for being an accessory after the fact, won't she, Chief Inspector?"

"Weil, I might charge her with trying to obstruct me in the execution of my duties," agreed Hemingway.

Lindale laughed. "Hear that? Now, you go and attend to Rose-Veronica before you get yourself into trouble! She was making a spirited attempt to tip the pram up when I came in."

"But, Kenelm——"

"You don't want my wife, do you, Chief Inspector?" Lindale interrupted.

"No, sir, not at the moment."

"Then you trot off, darling, and leave me to have a talk with the Chief Inspector," Lindale said, propelling her gently but firmly to the door.

She looked up at him, a little flushed, her mouth unsteady. Then she jerked out: "All right!" and left the room.

Lindale shut the door behind her, and turned to look at Hemingway. "Sorry about that!" he said. "My wife is not only extremely highly-strung, but she's also firmly convinced that anyone not provided with a cast-iron alibi must instantly become a red-hot suspect, in the eyes of the police. Queer things, women!"

"I could see Mrs. Lindale was very nervous, of course," said Hemingway noncommittally.

"As a matter of fact, she's very shy," explained Lindale. "And she didn't like Warrenby. I can't make her believe that that doesn't constitute a reason for suspecting either of us of having shot him."

"Do I take it that you didn't like him either, sir?"

"No, I didn't like him. No one did here. Bit of an outsider, you know. Not that we ever had much to do with him. We don't go out much: no time for it."

"I understand you haven't lived here long?"

"No, we're newcomers. I bought this place a couple of years ago only."

"It must be a change from stockbroking," remarked Hemingway.

"After the War, I couldn't settle down to the Stock Exchange again. I did have a shot at it, but what with one thing and another I was thankful to get out. Things aren't what they were."

He struck a match, and began to light his pipe. "That chap—don't remember what his name is—who came to pick up my .22 this morning! I take it you want to test it, and I've no objection to that, but I think it's only fair to say that I don't see how anyone could have taken it without my knowing. I keep it in the room I use as my office, and there's a Yale lock on the door. I don't run to a safe yet, you see, and I often have quite a bit of cash in the house. Wages, and that sort of thing, which I have to put in my desk."

"Yes, sir, Sergeant Carsethorn did tell me that you said no one could have got hold of your rifle."

"Well, he asked me several questions about it which led me to think he had young Ladislas in mind. I expect you know about him: one of these unfortunate expatriates. It's quite true that I lent the rifle to him a little while ago—which I know is a technical misdemeanour—and that I also gave him some cartridges. I should like to make it quite plain that he returned the rifle to me the same evening, and gave me back all the unused cartridges."

"Been up here worrying you about it, has he?" said Hemingway sympathetically. "Very excitable, these foreigners. That's all right, sir: I shan't arrest him because he borrowed your rifle a few weeks ago."

"I can't be surprised that he's got the wind up. It seems that that Sergeant put him through it pretty strictly, and there's no doubt there's a lot of prejudice against the Poles."

"Well, I shan't arrest him for that reason either," said Hemingway.

"There's apparently a lot of talk going on in Thornden about his having run after Mavis Warrenby," said Lindale. "That's what's upset him. Says he meant nothing, and I believe him! Nice enough girl—kindhearted and all that sort of thing—but she's no oil-painting. It's not my affair, but if I were you I wouldn't waste my time on Ladislas." He bit on his pipe-stem for a moment, and then removed the pipe from his mouth, saying bluntly: "Look here! I don't want to meddle in what's no concern of mine, but I've got a certain amount of fellow-feeling with young Ladislas! I've had some! It's come to my ears that because my wife and I are a damned sight too busy to buzz around doing the social the village gossips are spreading it about that there's something queer about us! Mystery-couple! Mystery my foot! The fact that you've turned up today shows me clearly enough that you've heard this tripe. Well, I've just about had it! I was barely acquainted with Warrenby; it doesn't matter two hoots to me whether he's alive or dead. If you're looking for a likely suspect, you find out what Plenmeller was up to at twenty-past seven on Saturday!"

"Thank you, sir, I hope to. Can you help me?"

"No, I can't. I was on my own land at that time. I'm not even sure when he left The Cedars, though I have an idea we most of us left in a bunch—the Squire and I by the gate on to the footpath, the others by the front drive. I only know that he's apparently been occupying himself ever since the murder with casting suspicion on most of his neighbours—which may be his idea of humour, or not!"

"On you, sir?"

"God knows! I shouldn't be surprised. He wouldn't dare do so to my face, of course."

"Well, you may be right," said Hemingway, "but I'm bound to say that when I met Mr. Plenmeller he was sitting with Major Midgeholme, and he didn't make any bones about telling me I should soon discover what the Major's motive was for having shot Mr. Warrenby."

Lindale stared at him. "Poisonous fellow! He knows better than to try that sort of thing on with me."

"Do you know of any reason why he should have wanted Mr. Warrenby out of the way, sir?"

"No. Nor am I saying that I think he's your man. But I fail to see why he should have the sole right to fling mud about! What's he doing it for? I call it damned malicious—particularly if it's true that he's made that unfortunate girl, Mavis Warrenby, one of his targets. I shouldn't have said anything if it hadn't been for his behaviour, but if that's his line, all right, then, I'd like to know first why he had it in for Warrenby more than anyone else, and then why he made an excuse to leave that party on Saturday after tea!"

"Did he, sir?" said Hemingway. "I thought he left when you and Mr. Ainstable did, not to mention Miss Dearham and Mr. Drybeck?"

"Finally, yes. Before that, he made a futile excuse to go home and fetch something the Squire wanted."

"What would that have been, sir?"

"Some correspondence to do with the appointment of a new solicitor to the River Board. The Squire wanted me to take a look at, but any time would have done!"

"This River Board does keep cropping up," remarked Hemingway. "Were you one of the Riparian Owners that were anxious to keep Warrenby out of the job!"

"I can't say I cared much either way," said Lindale, shrugging. "I expect I should have allowed myself to be guided by the Squire: he knows more about it than I do, and he seemed inclined to think Warrenby would be a suitable man to appoint."

"I see, sir. And when did Mr. Plenmeller leave The Cedars to go and fetch this correspondence—which I take it was in his possession!"

"When the sets were being arranged after we'd all finished tea. I should say it was at about six. As far as I remember he was gone about half an hour. He got back before my wife left: that I do know, because she told me so."

"His house being half a mile from The Cedars, if I remember rightly," said Hemingway.

"Oh, don't run away with the idea that I'm suggesting he didn't go to his house! I think he did. It could take him half an hour, and he could have done it in less time if he'd been put to it. That short leg of his doesn't incapacitate him as much as you might think."

"No, he told me it didn't," said Hemingway mildly. "So what is it you *are* suggesting, sir?"

Lindale did not answer for a minute, but stood frowning at his pipe, which had gone out. He looked up at last, and said: "Not suggesting anything except a possibility. Which is that he might have gone home to pick up his rifle—if he had one, but that I don't know: I've never seen him with a gun. And to cache it somewhere along the footpath, near The Cedars' front-gate."

Hemingway eyed him speculatively. "Found he'd come out without it, so to speak?"

"No. Not having known, until he got to The Cedars, that he would have the opportunity to use it!" said Lindale. "Warrenby had also been invited to that party, and he cried off at the last moment. Which meant that he was certain to be at home, and alone. Now do you get it? Plenmeller left when young Haswell motored Abby Dearham and old Drybeck, and the Major home. Who's to say that he didn't nip into the footpath once the car was out of sight? What was he doing between the time he left The Cedars, at the end of the party, and the time—whenever that was—he turned up at the Red Lion?"

Hemingway shook his head. "I'm no good at riddles: you tell me!"

"I can't tell you, because I'm no good at riddles either, but it seems to me it's something the police might look into instead of nosing round my place, and scaring my wife!" said Lindale, his eyes smouldering. "I don't know whether Plenmeller did it, or even if he had any reason to do it—not that I think that 'ud worry him! I've often wondered whether these fellows who are so damned clever at murdering people on paper ever put their methods into practice—but I can see how he could have concealed a light rifle without exciting any suspicion, supposing he'd walked into someone. Ever thought that that limp of his might be turned to good account!"

"Well, it's the sort of thing that's bound to strike one sooner or later, isn't it?" said Hemingway, picking up his hat.

Lindale escorted him out to the waiting car. "No doubt you

think I shouldn't have said any of this. I daresay I shouldn't have, if I didn't know that Plenmeller himself had no such scruples! You can tell him, if you like: I've no objection."

"Well, from what I've seen of him," said Hemingway, "I don't suppose he'd have any objection either. I hope we shall be able to let you have your rifle back in a day or two. Good-day to you, sir!"

Constable Melkinthorpe, sedately driving towards the gate, hoped that his unconventional passenger might tell him what had been the outcome of his interview, but all Hemingway said was: "Can we get to the Ainstables' house from where we are?"

"Old Place, sir? Yes, sir: there's an entrance on to this road. Matter of a mile farther on. Shall I drive there now?"

Hemingway nodded. "Yes, but you can pull up first by this footpath I've heard so much about."

Melkinthorpe obeyed. turning to the right as he emerged from the farm, and stopping a hundred yards up the road. Hemingway alighted, and slammed the door. "Right! You wait here!" he said, and walked off down the footpath.

On his left lay the common; on his right, for about a hundred yards, a ditch surmounted by a post-and-wire fence separated the path from a plantation of young fir-trees. A lichened stone wall marked its southern boundary, and this wall then flanked the path for perhaps fifty yards. Hemingway knew that behind it lay part of the garden of The Cedars, and took note of the position of the gate, set in it at its southern end. Just beyond the gate, the wall turned at right-angles again, completely shutting the gardens from view. The path then continued for another fifty yards between the common and a small spinney, before curving sharply westward to join Wood Lane at a point immediately south of The Cedars' front-gate. Where it turned to the west, a stile had been set, giving access to it from Fox Lane.

Hemingway paused there for a few minutes, thoughtfully considering the lie of the land. He glanced along the path, but a bend in it hid Wood Lane from his sight. Over the stile Fox House could be seen, through the trees in its garden, and so too could the gorse clump on the rising common, gleaming gold behind the bole of an elm-tree growing beside the lane. Uncultured voices, and the flutter of a summer-frock, informed the Chief Inspector that in one of his surmises at least he had been right: Fox Lane had suddenly become attractive to sightseers. He pursed up his mouth, shook his head slightly, and walked back to the main road, disappointing his chauffeur by saying nothing more, as he got into the car, than: "Go ahead!"

The Hawkshead-road entrance to Old Place consisted merely of a white farm-gate, opening on to a narrow, unmade road, with grass growing between the wheel-ruts. Melkinthorpe explained that it was only a secondary way to the house, the real entrance, which he described as proper big gates, with a lodge and all, lying at the end of Thornden High Street.

"Nice place," commented Hemingway, as they drove along the track. "Mixture of park and woodland. Does it end at the road, or was that the Squire's land beyond the road, where they've been felling all those trees?"

"I believe his land stretches as far as the river, sir. He owns a lot of the houses around here, too."

"That's no catch, these days," said Hemingway.

He said no more, but when the car presently drew up before the house his quick eye had absorbed more than the indestructible beauty of the park. The road had led them past a small home-farm (with two more gates to be opened and shut), and what had once been an extensive vegetable-garden, with an orchard beyond it; and had reached the front-drive by way of the stable-yard, where weeds sprouted between the cobblestones, and rows of doors, which should have stood with their upper halves open, were shut, the paint on them blistered and cracked. Where half a dozen men had once found congenial employment one middle-aged groom was all that was to be seen. "Progress," said Chief Inspector Hemingway. But he said it to himself, well-knowing that his companion, inevitably reared in the hazy and impracticable beliefs of democracy-run-riot, would derive a deep, if uninformed, gratification from the reflection that yet another landowner had been obliged, through excessive taxation, to throw out of work the greater part of his staff.

As though to lend colour to these sadly retrogressive thoughts, Constable Melkinthorpe said, as he drew up before the house: "They say the Squire used to have half a dozen gardeners, and I don't know how many grooms and gamekeepers and such. Of course, things are different now."

"They are," said the Chief Inspector, getting out of the car. "And the people as notice it most are those gardeners and grooms and gamekeepers. So you put that into your pipe, my lad, and smoke it!"

With which damping words he left Constable Melkinthorpe gaping at him, and walked up to the door of Old Place.

A tug at the iron bell-pull presently brought to the door a grizzled servitor, who, upon learning his name and calling, bowed in a manner that contrived to convey to the Chief Inspector his respect for the Law, and his contempt for its minions. Combining courtesy with disdain, he consigned the Chief Inspector to a chair in the hall, and went away to discover what his employers' pleasure might be.

When he returned he was accompanied by Mrs. Ainstable, two Sealyham terriers, and a young Irish setter, who effusively made the Chief Inspector welcome.

"Down!" commanded Mrs. Ainstable. "I'm so sorry! *Down,* you idiot!"

Hemingway, having wrestled successfully with the setter's advances, and brushed the hairs from his coat, said: "Yes, you're a beauty, aren't you? Now, that'll do! Down!"

"How nice of you not to mind him!" said Mrs. Ainstable. "He isn't properly trained yet." Her tired, strained eyes ran over the Chief Inspector. "You want to see my husband, I expect. He went down to the estate room a little while ago, so I'll take you there, shall I? It'll save time, and since that's where he kept his rifle I'm sure you'd like to see the place."

"Thank you, madam."

Her light laugh sounded. "I don't think we've ever had so much excitement in Thornden before!"

"I should think you must hope you never will have again," said Hemingway, following her down a passage to a door opening on to a rather overgrown shrubbery.

"I must admit that I wish it had never happened," she replied. "So horrid to have a murder in one's midst! It worries my husband, too. He can't get over his belief that he's responsible for Thornden. Have you any idea who did it? Oh, I mustn't ask you that, must I? Particularly when my husband is one of the possibles. I wish I'd waited for him, and made him drive home with me."

"You left the tennis-party early, didn't you, madam?"

"Yes, I only looked in for tea. I'm rather a crock, and don't play tennis. And it was so insufferably hot, that day!"

"Do you know what time it was when you left, madam?"

"No, I don't think I do. Does it matter? Sometime after six, I should say. Ask Mr. Plenmeller! I met him just as I was starting. He might know when that was."

"That would have been when he was returning with some papers for your husband?"

Again she laughed. "Yes, were you told about that?"

"I was told he made an excuse to leave the party after tea, and came back half an hour later. I didn't know he had met you, madam."

She paused, turning her head quickly to look at him. "That sounds as if someone were trying to make mischief! Well, it serves him right! Hoist with his own petard. Were you told why he made an excuse to go away?"

"No, I can't say I was, madam. Do you know why?"

"Yes, of course: everyone knew! It was quite atrocious and entirely typical. When they made up two sets after tea, Miss Warrenby was one over, and she elected to sit out. Which meant she would talk to Gavin Plenmeller. So he said he must go home to fetch some papers for my husband. You can't be surprised that he makes enemies."

120

"No," agreed Hemingway. "And you think everyone knew why he went away?"

"Oh, well, everyone who heard him! Mrs. Haswell said that he and Miss Warrenby must keep one another company, upon which he told Mr. Lindale, in what he may have meant to be an undertone but which was all too audible, that this was where he must think fast. Whether Miss Warrenby heard it, I don't know: I did! Here we are: this is the estate room. Bernard, àre you very busy? I have brought Chief Inspector Hemingway to see you."

Two steps led up to the open door of the room, which was a large, square apartment, severely furnished with a roll-top desk, a stout table, some filing cabinets, and several leather-seated chairs. A map of the estate hung on one wall, and a door at one side of the room gave access to another and smaller office. The Squire was seated at the table, official forms spread before him. He looked up under his brows, and favoured Hemingway with a hard stare before rising to his feet. "Scotland Yard?" he said brusquely. "You ought to be resting, Rosamund."

"Nonsense, dear!" said Mrs. Ainstable, sitting down, and taking a cigarette from the box on the table. "Resting, when we actually have the C.I.D. on the premises? It's far too interesting! Like living in one of Gavin's books."

He looked at her, but said nothing. Glancing up, as she lit her cigarette, she smiled at him, reassuringly, Hemingway thought.

The Squire transferred his attention to Hemingway. "Sit down, won't you? What can I do for you?"

The tone was more that of a commanding officer than a man undergoing interrogation. Hemingway recognized it, appreciated it, and realized that the Squire was not going to be an easy man to question. But those responsible for putting him in charge of this case had not chosen him at random. "Old County families mixed up in this business. Likely to be sticky," had said the Assistant Commissioner, to Hemingway's immediate superior and lifelong friend, Superintendent Hinckley. "I think we'll send Hemingway down. I don't pretend to know how he does it—and probably it's just as well that I don't, for I've no doubt he behaves in a thoroughly unorthodox fashion—but he does seem to be able to handle that kind of difficult witness." To which Superintendent Hinckley had replied, with a grin: "He *can* be exasperating, can't he, sir? Still, there it is! Myself, I've got a notion it's those unconventional ways of his that kind of take people off their guard. And it's a fact, as you said yourself, that he does bring home the bacon. He's got what he calls——" But at this point the Assistant Commissioner had interrupted him, uttering savagely: "Flair! You needn't tell me! And it's perfectly true, blast him!"

The Chief Inspector would have had no hesitation in ascribing the first question he put to the Squire to his mysterious flair. Taking a chair on the opposite side of the table, he said, at his most affable: "Thank you, sir. Well, I thought I'd best come up to have a chat with you, because I understand you were by way of being a friend of Mr. Warrenby's."

This unexpected gambit had the effect of producing a silence which lasted just long enough to satisfy the Chief Inspector. No one, watching him, would have supposed that he was paying any particular attention to either of his auditors, but although he choose that moment to pat one of the Sealyhams, who was sniffing his trouser-leg, he missed neither the Squire's stare, nor the slight rigidity which held his rather restless wife suddenly still, her gaze lowered to an unblinking scrutiny of her burning cigarette.

The Squire broke the silence. "Don't know that I should put it as high as that," he said. "I got on perfectly well with him. No sense in living at loggerheads with one's neighbours."

"No," agreed Hemingway. "Though, by all accounts, he wasn't an easy man to get on with. Which is why I thought I might find it helpful to have a talk with someone who wasn't what you might call prejudiced against him. Or for him, if it comes to that. What with Miss Warrenby on the one side, and pretty well everyone else on the other, the thing I want is an unbiased view. How did he come to get himself so much disliked, sir?"

The Squire took a moment of two to answer this, covering his hesitation by pushing the cigarette-box towards Hemingway, and saying: "Don't know if you smoke?"

"Thank you, sir," said Hemingway, taking a cigarette.

"Difficult question to answer," said the Squire. "I never came up against Warrenby myself: always very civil to me! but the fact of the matter was that he was a bit of an outsider. Pushing, and that sort of thing. No idea how to conduct himself in a place like this. Got people's backs up. Before the War, of course,—but it's no use thinking backwards. Got to move with the times. No use ostracizing fellows like Warrenby, either. Got to accept them, and do what one can to teach them the way to behave."

Yes, thought the Chief Inspector, you're a hard nut to crack, Squire! Aloud, he said: "Would you have put it beyond him to have gone in for a bit of polite blackmail to get his own way, sir?"

The ash from Mrs. Ainstable's cigarette dropped on to her skirt. She brushed it off, exclaiming: "What a lurid thought! Who on earth did he find to blackmail in these respectable parts?"

"Well, you never know, do you?" said Hemingway thoughtfully. "I've been having a talk with his head clerk, and it set me wondering, madam."

"No use asking me!" said the Squire harshly. "If I'd had any reason to suspect such a thing, shouldn't have had anything to do with the fellow."

"You're trying to make out why we did have anything to do with him, aren't you?" said Mrs. Ainstable, her eyes challenging the Chief Inspector. "It was my fault. I couldn't help feeling sorry for his unfortunate niece! That's why I called on them. It's all very silly, and feudal, but if we receive other people follow our lead. But do tell us more about this blackmailing idea of yours! If you knew Thornden as I do, you'd realize what an entrancingly improbable thought that is! It's all getting more and more like Gavin Plenmeller's books."

Out of the tail of his eye Hemingway could see that the Squire's gaze was fixed on his wife's face. He said: "I can see I shall have to read Mr. Plenmeller's books. Which puts me in mind of something I had to ask you, sir. Did you ask Mr. Plenmeller to fetch some papers from his house, during the tennis-party on Saturday?"

"No, certainly not!" said the Squire curtly. "I asked him to let me have them back, but there was no immediate hurry about it. He chose to go for them at once for reasons of his own. Damned rude reasons, too, but that's his own affair! Don't know what you're getting at, but it's only fair to say that he was back at The Cedars before I left the party. Met my wife on the drive, and gave the papers to her. Might have given them to Lindale, and saved me the trouble, but that's not his way!"

"Something to do with this River Board I hear so much about, weren't they, sir? I understand a solicitor's wanted, and Mr. Warrenby was after the post?"

The Squire stirred impatiently in his chair. "Yes, that's so. Don't know why he was so keen on being appointed: there's nothing much to it. However, he had a fancy for it, and as far as I was concerned he could have had it. Not worth worrying about."

"Well, that's what it looks like to me," confessed Hemingway. "Not that I know much about such matters. Mr. Drybeck wanted it too, I understand."

"Oh, that's nonsense!" said the Squire irritably. "Drybeck's well-enough established here without wanting jobs like that to give him a standing! As I told him! However, I daresay he'd have got it in the end! There was a lot of opposition to Warrenby's candidature."

"Well," said Hemingway, stroking his chin, "I suppose he *has* got it, hasn't he, sir?—the way things have turned out."

"What the devil do you mean by that?" demanded the Squire. "If you're suggesting that Thaddeus Drybeck—a man

123

I've known all my life!—would murder Warrenby, or anyone else, just to get himself appointed to a job on a River Board——"

"Oh, no sir! I wasn't suggesting that!" said Hemingway. "Highly unlikely, I should think. I was just wondering what made you back Mr. Warrenby, if Mr. Drybeck wanted the post."

"Quite improper for me to foist my own solicitor on to the Board!" barked the Squire. "What's more——Well, never mind!"

"But, Bernard, of course he minds!" interrupted his wife. "Mr. Drybeck is the family solicitor, Chief Inspector, but—well, he isn't quite as young as he was, and, alas, not nearly as competent as Mr. Warrenby was! Yes, Bernard, I know it's hideously disloyal of me to say so, but what *is* the use of making a mystery out of it!"

"No use talking about it at all," said the Squire. "Got no possible bearing on the case." He looked at Hemingway. "I take it you want to know where I went and what I did when I left The Cedars on Saturday?"

"Thank you, sir, I don't think I'll trouble you to go over that again," replied Hemingway, causing both husband and wife to look at him in mingled surprise and doubt. "The evidence you gave to Sergeant Carsethorn seems quite clear. You went to cast an eye over that new plantation of yours. I was looking at it myself a little while back. Don't know much about forestry, but I see you've been doing a lot of felling."

"I have, yes," said the Squire, his brows lifting a little, in a way that clearly conveyed to the Chief Inspector that he failed to understand what concern this was of his.

"You'll pardon my asking," said Hemingway, "but are you selling your timber to a client of Mr. Warrenby's?"

"To a client of Warrenby's?" repeated the Squire, a hint of astonishment in his level voice. "No, I am not!"

"Ah, that's where I've got a bit confused!" said Hemingway. "It was the gravel-pit he was interested in, wasn't it? There's some correspondence in his office, dealing with that. I don't know that it's important, but I'd better get it straight."

"I have had no dealings whatsoever with Warrenby, in his professional capacity," said the Squire.

"He wasn't by any chance acting for this firm that's working your pit, sir?"

"Certainly not. I happen to know that Throckington & Flimby act for them. In point of fact, no solicitors were employed either by me or by them."

"You didn't get your own solicitors to draw up the contract, sir?"

"Quite unnecessary! Sheer waste of money! Very respectable firm. They wouldn't cheat me, or I them."

"Then, I daresay that would account for your solicitors not

seeming to know you'd already disposed of the rights in the pit," said Hemingway.

"If you mean Drybeck, he was perfectly well-aware that I had done so," said the Squire, his eyes never shifting from the Chief Inspector's face.

"No, not him, sir. Some London firm. Belsay, Cockfield & Belsay I think their names are."

A draught from the open door stirred the papers on the table. The Squire methodically tidied them, and set a weight on top of the pile. "Belsay, Cockfield & Belsay are the solicitors to the Trustees of the Settlement of the state," he said. "The details of any transactions of mine would naturally be unknown to them. Do I understand you to say that Warrenby had been in communication with them?"

"That's right, sir. And seeing that it seems to have been pretty inconclusive I thought I'd ask you for the rights of it."

"May I know the gist of this correspondence?"

"Well, it seems Mr. Warrenby had a client who was interested in gravel, sir. He wrote to these solicitors, making enquiries about terms, having been informed—so he wrote—that they were the proper people to approach in the matter. Which they replied that they were, in a manner of speaking, but that any arrangements would have to be with you. And, as far as the documents go, there it seem to have petered out. For I gather he didn't approach you, did he, sir?"

It was not the Squire but Mrs. Ainstable who answered, exclaiming: "No, he approached me instead! *Really*, what an impossible person he was! It's no use frowning at me, Bernard: he may be dead, but that doesn't alter facts! So typical of him to find out from me that you'd already leased the gravel-pit, instead of asking you! I can't bear people who go about things in a tortuous way for no conceivable reason! So dreadfully underbred!"

"He asked you, did he, madam?"

"Oh, not in so many words! He led the conversation round to it."

"When was that?" asked Hemingway.

"Heavens, I don't know! I'd forgotten all about it until you told us all this. He was the most inquisitive man—and quite unsnubable!" She laughed, and stubbed out her cigarette. "I wonder who his client was? It sounds rather as if it must have been some shady firm he knew my husband wouldn't have had anything to do with. What fun!"

"No doubt that would have been it," agreed the Chief Inspector, rising to his feet.

CHAPTER ELEVEN

It was five o'clock when Hemingway reached the Vicarage, and he found the Vicar in conference with one of the Church-wardens, Mr. Henry Haswell. An awed and inexperienced maidservant ushered him straightway into the Vicar's study, saying with a gasp: "Please, sir, it's a gentleman from Scotland Yard!"

"Good gracious me!" ejaculated the Vicar, startled. "Well, you'd better show him in, Mary—oh, you *are* in! All right, Mary: that'll do! Good-afternoon—I don't know your name?"

Hemingway gave him his card, which he put on his spectacles to read. "Chief Inspector Hemingway: dear me, yes! You must tell me what I can do for you. Oh, this is one of our Church-wardens—Mr. Haswell!"

"Perhaps you'd like me to clear out?" said Haswell, nodding briefly to the Chief Inspector.

"Not on my account, sir," said Hemingway. "Very sorry to come interrupting you, Vicar. It's quite a small matter, really. I see by the Firearms Register that you own a .22 rifle. Could I have a look at it?"

"Rifle?" said the Vicar blankly. "Oh, yes, so I do! But it is really my son's. That is to say, I got it for him originally, though of course he has no use for it now he lives in London. Still, one never knows when he might like to have it, beside getting a little sport when he comes to visit us. I don't shoot myself."

"No, sir. Might I see it?"

"Now let me think!" said the Vicar, looking harassed. "Dear me, this is very awkward! I wonder——? Excuse me, I'll go and look! Do take a chair!"

Hemingway watched him leave the room, and said, with a resigned sigh: "Yes, I can see this is another rifle which has been allowed to go astray. I think you were responsible for the first, sir."

"Not unless you consider me responsible for my wife's—misdemeanours, Chief Inspector," replied Haswell calmly. "Nor can I agree that the rifle in question has gone astray. It is true that it was lent—improperly, of course—to the local plumber, who once got my wife's car to start for her; but it is equally true that he returned it some days ago, since when it has not, to my knowledge, been out of the house."

"Yes, that's all very well, sir," retorted Hemingway, "but my information is that it was left hanging about in a cupboard in your cloakroom, so that as far as I can make out anybody could have borrowed it without you being the wiser!"

"Quite so, but may I point out that it was found in that cupboard no later than yesterday evening? While I can—with some difficulty—visualize the possibility of its having been abstracted by one of the people who came to my wife's tennis-party, I am quite unable to arrive at any satisfactory explanation of how anyone knew that there was a rifle at the back of a coat-cupboard, or how he or she could have restored it without having been seen by any member of my household. Have you collected the rifle? My son left it ready for you."

"No, I didn't, sir, but Sergeant Carsethorn did, which is how I come to know what happened to it."

Haswell smiled faintly. "You must admit we've kept nothing from you, Chief Inspector!"

"Very open and above board, sir. Is there a door into your cloakroom from the garden?"

"No. The only entrance is through the hall, and the ventilation is by ventilator, above a fixed, frosted-glass window. In fact—taking into consideration my son's alibi—there seems really to be only one person who might, without much difficulty, have both removed the rifle from the cupboard, and restored it. Myself, Chief Inspector—as I feel sure you've realized." He paused, and his smile grew, a tinge of mockery in it. "But I don't think I should have put it back," he added. "Cliburn, have your sins found you out?"

"They have, they have!" said the Vicar, who had come back into the room, an expression of guilt in his face. "I am exceedingly sorry, Inspector, but I fear I cannot immediately lay my hand upon the weapon. If one could but see the pitfalls set for one's feet! Not but what I am aware that I have erred, well-aware of it!"

"All right, sir! You've gone and lent it to someone," said Hemingway. "Which, of course, you've got no business to do."

"I cannot deny it," said the Vicar mournfully. "But when one possesses a sporting gun—selfishly, I feel for I have no use for it—it seems churlish to refuse to lend it to lads less fortunate, particularly when the example is set me by our good Squire, who allows shooting on his waste-land, and is always the first to encourage the village-lads to spend their leisure hours in sport rather than the pursuits which, alas, are by far too common in these times! Splendid fellows, too, most of them! I've watched many of them grow up from the cradle, and I can assure you, Inspector, though I have undoubtedly broken the law in lending a rifle to any unauthorized person, I should not dream of putting it into the hands of anyone I could not vouch for."

"Well, sir, whose hands *did* you put it into?" asked Hemingway patiently.

"I *think*," said the Vicar, "and such, also, is my wife's recollection, that I lent it last to young Ditchling. One of my choir-boys, till his voice broke, and a sterling lad! The eldest of a large family, and his mother, poor soul, a widow. He has just received his call-up papers, and I fear that in the excitement of the moment he must have forgotten to return the rifle to me, which was remiss of him, and still more so of me, for not having reminded him. For young people, you know, Inspector, are inclined to forget things."

"They are, aren't they, sir?" agreed Hemingway, with commendable restraint. "Did you say he was the eldest of a large family? With a whole lot of young brothers, I daresay, who have been having a high old time with a gun that doesn't belong to them, and have very likely lost it by this time!"

The Vicar, much dismayed, said: "Indeed, I trust not!"

"Yes, so do I," said Hemingway grimly. "Where does this large family live?"

"At No. 2 Rose Cottages," replied the Vicar, regarding him with an unhappy look in his eye. "That is the row of cottages facing the common, on the Trindale-road."

"It is, is it?" said Hemingway, his excellent memory at work.

"I know what you are thinking," said the Vicar, sitting down heavily in the chair behind his desk. "I can never sufficiently blame myself for having been the cause—unwitting, but equally unpardonable!—of bringing suspicion to bear upon a member of a gallant and a persecuted nation, and one, moreover, of whom I know no ill!"

"Well, I won't deny, sir, that it did come into my mind that this Pole with the unnatural name whom you all call Ladislas lodges in one of those cottages," admitted Hemingway. "But if you know what I'm thinking it's more than I do myself, because I've always found it a great waste of time to think about things until I've got a bit more data than I have yet. However, I'm glad you've mentioned him, because what any gentleman in your position has to say about one of his parishioners seems to me well worth listening to."

"I cannot, I fear, describe Ladislas as my parishioner," said the Vicar deprecatingly. "He is not, you know, of my communion. One is apt, of course, to look upon every soul living in one's parish as a member of one's flock, and particularly in such a case as this, when the young man is so tragically bereft of family, home, even country, one feels impelled to do what one can to bring a little friendliness into a lonely life."

"And I'm sure it does you credit, sir," said Hemingway cordially.

"I am afraid it rather does Ladislas credit," said the Vicar, with a sudden smile. "We had Poles stationed in the vicinity during the War, and the impression they made upon us was not entirely happy. One makes allowances, of course, but still —— No, *not* entirely happy! Indeed, to my shame I must confess that I was far from being pleased when I heard that one had come to live permanently amongst us. However, I thought it my duty to visit the young man, and I was agreeably surprised by him. A very decent fellow, determined to make his way in his job, and combating, I grieve to say, a good deal of insular prejudice. I had no hesitation in introducing him to one or two people whom I thought he might find congenial, and I have had no reason to regret having done so. I should add, perhaps, that his landlady, our good Mrs. Dockray—a most respectable woman!—is quite devoted to him, and that is a more valuable testimony than mine, Inspector!"

"I wouldn't say that, sir, but at least it means he hasn't been spending his spare time getting all the village girls into trouble—not to mention the wives whose husbands are doing their military service," said Hemingway.

Haswell, who had retired to the window-seat, laughed suddenly; but the Vicar, though he smiled, shook his head, and said that when he thought of the infants, of what he must call mixed parentage, whom he had been obliged to baptize, he felt more like weeping. From this reflection he was easily led to talk about the humbler members of his flock, the Chief Inspector listening to his very discursive descriptions with great patience, mentally sifting possible grains of wheat from obvious chaff, and guiding him adroitly, by way of Mrs. Murton, who obliged for Mrs. Lindale, into the higher ranks of Thornden society. But the Vicar could not tell him very much about the Lindales. Like Ladislas, Mrs. Lindale was not of his communion, and her husband, although brought up in the Anglican faith and a very good fellow, was not, alas, a churchgoer. It was a pity, the Vicar thought, that such pleasant young people should live such retired lives. It was rarely that one had the pleasure of meeting them at any of the little entertainments in the neighbourhood. Mrs. Lindale was thought to be stand-offish; he himself believed her, rather, to be shy. Miss Patterdale—whom he always called the good angel of the parish—had been most neighbourly, and spoke well of Mrs. Lindale. Indeed, she had persuaded Mrs. Ainstable to call, but nothing had come of it, Mrs. Lindale excusing herself from accepting invitations on the score of being unable to leave her little girl. A pity, he could not but think, for although the Ainstables were not of the Lindales' generation, and did not, nowadays, entertain a great deal, they must be considered, in every sense of the word, valuable connaissances.

"Yes, I've just been having a chat with them," said Hemingway. "A gentleman of the old school, Mr. Ainstable.

The Chief Constable was telling me that he lost his only son in the war, which must be just about as bad a thing for Thornden as it was for him, I should think."

"Indeed, indeed you are right, Inspector!" said the Vicar earnestly. "One of the finest young men I have ever known, and one, moreover, who would have upheld traditions which are so fast vanishing. The flowers of the forest . . . ! A bitter blow for the Squire! One must hope that the present heir will prove a worthy successor, but I fear there will be a sad change in the relationship between the Squire and the village. Thornden does not readily accept strangers."

"Nor any other place I ever heard of," said Hemingway. "Still, we'll hope it won't happen for a good many years to come. The Squire looks pretty hale and hearty—more so than Mrs. Ainstable, I thought."

The Vicar sighed. "'For thou knowest not what a day may bring forth,'" he said, as though he spoke to himself.

"Well, no, sir," said Hemingway, startled but respectful. "That's true enough, but——"

"The Squire has angina pectoris," said the Vicar simply.

"You don't say so!" exclaimed Hemingway, shocked.

"There is no reason to suppose that the Squire won't live for a great many years yet," said Haswell.

"Indeed, we must all pray that he will, my dear Haswell!"

"Yes, but I see what the Vicar means," said Hemingway. "With that disease—well, you *don't* know what a day may bring forth, do you? I'm not surprised Mrs. Ainstable looks so anxious. And he's not the sort to spare himself, by what I can see."

"He is not an invalid," said Haswell shortly. "He has been an energetic man all his life, and it would be extremely bad for him not to take the sort of exercise he's accustomed to."

"True, very true!" the Vicar said. "One wishes, though that he had fewer cares to weigh upon him. I am almost tempted to say, that he were less conscientious, but one should not, and indeed one does not, wish that."

"Struggling to keep up an estate which some kind of a cousin or nephew who lives in South Africa will inherit," said Hemingway slowly. "And I should say it is a struggle." He glanced at Haswell. "I saw he'd been cutting down a lot of timber."

"Also planting new trees, however."

"Yes, I saw that too."

"The Squire is a remarkable man," said the Vicar warmly. "Indeed, I tell him sometimes that he has all the enterprise of a man half his age! I remember when he first made up his mind to turn the common to account—I should explain, Inspector, that the common——"

"Talking about the common," interrupted Haswell, "can anything be done, Chief Inspector, to dissuade people from trailing across it, dropping litter all over it, and staring over the hedge at Fox House? It's extremely unpleasant for Miss Warrenby, to say the least of it."

"Poor girl, poor girl!" exclaimed the Vicar. "This is most disgraceful! One wonders what the world is coming to! This unmannerly craving for sensationalism! Gavin Plenmeller said something to me about it this morning, but I paid little heed, since the way in which he phrased it led me to believe that he was merely indulging in one of those jokes which I, frankly, neither like nor find in any way amusing. Inspector, something must be done!"

"I'm afraid there's nothing the police can do about it, sir— not as long as people stick to the common and the public road, and don't go creating obstructions, which they really can't be said to do, right up the end of a blind road," replied Hemingway.

An anxious look came into the Vicar's face. "I wonder, if I were to go up, and address a few words to them, pointing out to them how very——"

"Some of them would giggle, and others would be extremely rude to you," interposed Haswell. "You'd do better to persuade Plenmeller to take on that job he'd enjoy it, and might even succeed in dispersing the mob. Unless they lynched him."

"Haswell, Haswell, my dear friend!" the Vicar reproved him.

Haswell laughed. "Don't worry! Can you imagine him lifting a finger on behalf of Warrenby's niece?"

The Vicar shook his head, and said that their poor friend had a very unkind tongue, but one must strive to make allowances, and the heart knew its own bitterness.

"Well, I daresay it would sour one a bit, to be as lame as he is," said Hemingway. "It's certainly an education to hear him talk, and the things he can find to say about pretty well everyone he lays his tongue to fairly made me sit up. However, I don't know that I set much store by it. It wouldn't surprise me if he was living up to a reputation for coming out with something shocking every time he opens his mouth."

The Vicar bent an approving look upon him, and said, in his gentle way that he was a wise man. "I have been much distressed at the attitude he has seen fit to assume over this shocking affair," he said. "Upon the lack of Christian charity, I will not enlarge, but from the worldly point of view I have ventured to warn him that the unbridled exercise of his wit is open to misconstruction. In the event," he added, inclining his head in the suggestion of a bow, "I perceive that my fears were groundless."

"Thank you very much, sir," said Hemingway cheerfully. "Come to think of it, I might feel a lot more suspicious if Mr.

Plenmeller had seen fit to change his tone, because from what I'm told he's been saying for months that Mr. Warrenby would have to be got rid of. What I haven't yet been able to make out is why he had it in for Mr. Warrenby more than anyone else—which is saying something, according to what I'm told." He paused, but the Vicar merely sighed, and Haswell gave a laugh and a shrug. "Or even," he continued thoughtfully, "if the only difference between him and the rest of the good people here who couldn't stand Mr. Warrenby was that he said just what he thought, and they didn't."

"I fear so, I fear so!" said the Vicar mournfully.

There was a decided twinkle in the Chief Inspector's eye. "You too, sir?"

"I cannot deny it," replied the Vicar, sinking deeper into dejection. "One has tried not to entertain uncharitable thoughts, but the flesh is weak—terribly weak!"

"You will soon find yourself regarding with suspicion anyone who did not dislike Warrenby, Chief Inspector," said Haswell. "Let me hasten to assure you that I found him quite as objectionable as the Vicar did!"

Hemingway laughed, and got up. "He does seem to have made himself unpopular," he agreed. "I won't take up any more of your time now, sir."

"Not at all," said the Vicar courteously. "My time is at the disposal of those who may need it."

He then escorted Hemingway to the front-door, shook hands with him, and said that he could have wished to have met him on a happier occasion.

Constable Melkinthorpe then drove away, asking the Chief Inspector, as he halted the car in the Vicarage gateway, which way he was to go. He was told to drive to Rose Cottages, and, after allowing a boy on a bicycle to pass down the High Street, he swung his wheel over to the left, and was just changing gear when the Chief Inspector told him to stop. He obediently pulled in to the side of the street, and saw Major Midgeholme crossing the road towards the car.

"Good-evening, sir!" said Hemingway. "Want me?"

"Yes," said the Major, with an air of resolution. "I have been turning it over in my mind, and I think it's my duty to put you in possession of a piece of information. Mind you, it may be nothing! I don't say I attach much importance to it, but one never knows, and in such cases as this I consider it to be every man's duty to tell the police whatever he may know."

"Quite right, sir," said Hemingway, and waited.

But the Major seemed still to be a little undecided. "Can't say I like talking about my neighbours!" he said. "But when it comes to murder, things are different. My feeling is that if what I have to say is irrelevant, there's no harm done; and if it isn't—

well! There's no denying that this business has made us all sit up—do a bit of thinking! I'm not going to pretend I know who did it, because I don't. Between you and me and the gate-post, there's a bit too much amateur detection going on in Thornden! Shouldn't like you to think I was trying to do your job for you, but of course I've thought about it a good deal, and talked it over with one or two people. As a matter of fact, I was discussing it with my wife last night—she's got her own theories, but I shan't go into that, for I don't agree with her. Point is, it's been in my mind all along that the two people who disliked Warrenby the most were Drybeck and Plenmeller. Now, when Drybeck and I were on our way to The Cedars on Saturday, Plenmeller joined us, and one of the things he said was that his was the only threshold in Thornden which Warrenby couldn't cross." The Major paused impressively. "Well, I happened to mention that to my wife, and she told me that she had seen Warrenby go into Thornden House on Saturday morning! Of course, she doesn't know what he went for, or for how long he was with Plenmeller, for she was shopping, and she thought no more about it. I didn't set much store by it myself when she first told me, but I've been turning it over in my mind, and I've come to the conclusion you ought to know about it. As I say, there may be nothing in it. On the other hand, queer thing to do—boast that Warrenby had never crossed his threshold when he'd done so that very morning! Almost as if he wanted to make sure no one should think he'd had any dealings with the fellow."

Constable Melkinthorpe, glancing at the Chief Inspector to see what effect this disclosure had upon him, was not surprised to perceive that his calm was quite unruffled.

"I see," said Hemingway gravely. "He'd have to be a bit of an optimist, wolldn't he, sir, to think no one would notice Mr. Warrenby going to call on him, on a Saturday morning, right on the village street?"

"Well," said the Major, shrugging, "I've told you for what it's worth, that's all!" He looked up, and stiffened a little. Gavin Plenmeller, coming from the direction of his house, was crossing the road diagonally towards them.

"Undergoing interrogation, laying information, or just passing the time of day, Major?" enquired Gavin. "I'm glad to see you here, Chief Inspector, and I'm sure the whole village shares my feeling. We confidently expected to see you in our midst at crack of dawn, but it was not to be. I may add that a certain amount of dissatisfaction has been felt. Action is what we want, and we did think that a real detective from London would provide us with plenty to talk about."

"Well, I must be getting along," said the Major, not quite comfortably.

Gavin looked at him, a glint in his eyes. "Now, why are you

suddenly in a hurry to go away?" he wondered. "Can it be—can it possibly be—that you were telling the Chief Inspector something damaging about me?" He watched a dull red creep into the Major's cheeks, and laughed. "Splendid! What was it? Or would you prefer not to tell me?"

It was patent that the Major would very much have preferred not to tell him, but he was an officer and a gentleman, and he was not going to turn and run in the face of fire. He said boldly: "Seems to me that you've done so much talking yourself about people that you can't very well object if the tables are turned."

"Of course I don't object!" said Gavin cordially. "I merely hope that you've dug up something good about me."

"I haven't dug up anything. Not my business to pry into your affairs! And if you want to know what's been sticking in my mind, it's this!—Why did you tell me that Warrenby had never crossed your threshold?"

"Did I?" said Gavin, faintly surprised.

"You know damned well you did!"

"I don't. It's quite possible, of course, and I shouldn't dream of denying it, but when did I make this momentous statement?"

"You said it to Drybeck and to me when we were walking up Wood Lane on Saturday. You said that yours was the only threshold he couldn't cross."

"I spoke no less than the truth, then. Yes, I remember: our Thaddeus wasn't a bit pleased, was he? But what is this leading up to?"

"That won't wash, Plenmeller!" said the Major, gaining assurance with indignation. "Warrenby had crossed your threshold that very morning!"

"Take note, Chief Inspector," said Gavin quite unmoved, "that I instantly and categorically deny this infamous accusation!"

"It may interest you to know, however, that my wife saw him go into your house!"

"She lies in her throat," said Gavin amiably. "She may have seen him enter my garden. In fact, if she was in the High Street at the time, I should think she could hardly have escaped seeing that. She may even have noticed his very vulgar car parked at my gate. Now tell me how she saw through a brick wall and I shall be all interest!"

The Major looked a good deal taken aback, and a little sceptical. "Are you telling me he didn't enter your house?"

"You oughn't to need telling," Gavin reporoved him. "He found me in the garden, and in the garden we remained. I don't say he didn't make a spirited attempt to cross my threshold, for he did. He had the impertinence to suggest that we should go into the house, which forced me to disclose to him that to admit him would be to break a solemn vow."

The Major gasped. "You can't have said such a thing!"

"Nonsense, you know very well that I find not the smallest difficulty in saying to people's faces precisely what I say behind their backs!"

The Chief Inspector intervened at this point. "Why did he want to cross your threshold, sir?"

"Vaulting ambition, perhaps. It may be said to have o'er-leapt itself. Or do you want to know why he wanted to see me?"

"That's it," said Hemingway.

"Ah! Well, he came to remonstrate with me. At least, that was how he phrased it. He seemed to think I had been inserting a spoke into his wheel on various occasions, and it had come to his ears—one wonders how!—that I had spoken of him in opprobrious terms. So I told him that these allegations were true, and he then asserted that he would know how to put a stop to my activities. How he proposed to do any such thing I am unable to tell you, and, of course, we shall now never know what Napoleonic scheme he may have had in mind. I can only say that he failed to convince me that he had evolved any form of counterattack whatsoever. The remonstrance somewhat rapidly deteriorated into sound and fury. He favoured me with a catalogue of the services he had rendered to the county, adding, a trifle infelicitously, I felt, a list of the distinguished persons whom he had—as he regrettably put it—forced to play ball with him. After that he became incoherent, and I showed him off the premises."

"Well, by Jove!" exclaimed the Major, bristling with suspicion. "Seems a queer thing you didn't tell Drybeck and me that you'd had this quarrel with Warrenby!"

"My very dear Major," said Gavin sweetly, "in the first place, there was no quarrel: I never gratify my enemies by allowing them to lure me into losing my temper. In the second place, I have not so far been conscious of the smallest impulse to confide my minor triumphs to a Drybeck or a Midgeholme. And, in the third, I have long realized that in my not wholly unsuccessful attempts to depress Warrenby's pretensions I have been playing a lone hand."

"You're the most offensive fellow I have met in all my life!" said the Major, his face by this time richly suffused with colour. "I'll be damned if I'll stand here bandying words with you!"

"No, I didn't think you would," said Gavin. He watched the Major stride off down the street, and said pensively: "It's a mystery to me that so many persons find it impossible to shake off crashing bores. Did you ever see a fish take the fly more readily?"

Hemingway said, ignoring this question: "What made you dislike Mr. Warrenby so particularly, sir?"

"Sheer antipathy, Chief Inspector. Mixed with a certain

135

amount of atavism. The blood of the Plenmellers arose in me when I saw that repulsive upstart storming every citadel, including the Ainstables'. When he lived, I rarely managed to earn my brother's approval, but now that he is dead I feel sure I'm behaving just as he would have wished. Which is what people so often do, isn't it? There's a moral to be drawn from that, but I beg you won't! Do you want to know any more about Warrenby's ill-advised visit to me, or have you had enough of it?"

"I'd like to know how he thought he could make you stop running him down," said Hemingway, fixing Gavin with a bright, enquiring gaze.

"So would I, but it was never disclosed. I discount his veiled threat to take me into court on a charge of uttering slander. My imagination boggles at the thought of such a man as Warrenby complaining publicly of the things I've said about him. Not quite the kind of notoriety he craved for, you know!"

"Oh, he did threaten to take you into court, sir?"

"He did, and I promised him that I should do my best to ensure his winning his case. He was not in the least grateful. In his blundering way he was not devoid of intelligence. Tell, me, Chief Inspector!—have you in your diligent research come upon the name of Nenthall?"

"Why do you ask me that, sir?" countered Hemingway.

There was a derisive gleam in Gavin's eyes. "I'm not at all sure, but I see that you haven't. Well, when you have finished following up the theories put forward by the village half-wits, you might find it profitable to discover what was the significance of that name. I can't help you: I never heard it until it was tossed, with apparent carelessness, into the conversation at the Red Lion, one evening about a month ago."

"Who by?" asked Hemingway.

"By Warrenby, upon receiving a well-merited snub from Lindale. He asked Lindale if the name conveyed anything to him. Lindale replied that it did not, but it was all too apparent that it conveyed a great deal to him."

"Oh! And what happened then?"

"Nothing happened. Our curiosity remained unsatisfied. Warrenby said that he had just wondered, and the incident terminated. It appeared to me, however, that the question had had a profound effect upon Lindale—and I just wonder, too."

"When you talk of a profound effect, sir, what exactly do you mean?"

"Well," said Gavin thoughtfully, "it did occur to me for one moment that I might be going to witness a murder. But you have to bear in mind, of course, that I am by profession a novelist. Perhaps I allowed my imagination to get the better of me. But I still wonder, Chief Inspector!"

He removed his hand from the door of the car, favoured Hemingway with one of his sardonic smiles, and limped away.

Constable Melkinthorpe's feelings got the better of him. He drew an audible breath. "*Well!*" he uttered. "He's a one, and no mistake! Blessed if I know what to make of him!"

"As no one wants you to make anything of him, that needn't keep you awake! Get on with it!" said Hemingway tartly.

CHAPTER TWELVE

A FEW minutes later, the police-car was standing outside Rose Cottages, and the Chief Inspector was making the acquaintance of Mrs. Ditchling and five of her seven children, who ranged in age from Gert, who was twenty, to Jackerleen, who was six. He would willingly have dispensed with the introductions which were forced upon him, but while Mrs. Ditchling was cast into housewifely distraction by his visit, because she was afraid he would find the place a bit untidy—which was her way of describing a scene of such chaos as might be expected to exist in a very small cottage inhabited by seven persons, most of whom were of tender years—it was obviously considered by the rest of the family to constitute a red-letter day in their lives, Alfie, a young gentleman in velveteen knickers and Fair Isle jersey, going so far as to dash out into the garden at the back of the cottage yelling to his brother Claud to come quick, or else he wouldn't see the detective.

In describing the scene later, to Inspector Harbottle, Hemingway admitted that he lost his grip at the outset. The Ditchlings were not only friendly: they were garrulous and inquisitive, and they all talked at once. The Chief Inspector, stunned by his reception, found himself weakly admiring a hideous toy rabbit made of pink plush, shown him by Jackerleen—or, as she was mercifully called, Jackie; answering questions fired at him with the remorselessness of machine-guns by Alfie, and his brother Claud; and endorsing Mrs. Ditchling's opinion that for Edie to leave her nice, steady job at Woolworth's to become a film-star would be an act of unparalleled folly. He was also put in possession of much information, such as the entire history of the late Mr. Ditchling's untimely demise; of the rapid rise, in Millinery, of Gert; of the medals Claud had won as a Boy Scout; of the trouble his mother had had over Alfie's adenoids; of the letter Ted had written from his training-camp; and of the high opinion his employer held of Reg, who, unfortunately, was going to the pictures that evening, and so had not come home after work. "He *will* be upset!" said Mrs. Ditchling.

Everyone seemed to feel that the absent Reg was missing a rare treat, Gert saying that it *was* a shame, Claud asserting that he would be as sick as muck, and Jackerleen asking her mother several times, with increasing tearfulness, if Reg wouldn't come home to see the pleeceman.

When the Chief Inspector at last managed to make known the reason for his visit, the confusion grew worse, for Mrs.

Ditchling, shocked to learn that his rifle had not yet been returned to the Vicar, related in detail the circumstances of Ted's call-up, Gert asserted several times that Ted had told Reg particular not to forget to take the rifle back for him, Edie said that that was Reg all over, Claud and Alfie argued shrilly with one another on the certain whereabouts of the weapon, and Jackerleen reiterated her demand to know if Reg was not coming home to see the pleeceman.

"Well, I hope to God he's not!" said Hemingway, plucking the two boys apart, and giving each a shake. "Stop it, the pair of you! You shut up, Alfie! Now then, Claud! If you're a Wolf Cub, you just tell me where your brother put the Vicar's rifle—and if I see you try to kick Alfie again, I'll tell the Scoutmaster about you, so now!"

Thus admonished, Claud disclosed that Ted put the gun in his workshop, to be safe; and the whole party at once trooped out into the narrow strip of garden at the rear of the cottage. At the end of this was a wooden shed, which, Mrs. Ditchling proudly informed Hemingway, Ted had erected with his own hands. But as the door into it was locked, and the key—if not mislaid, or taken away in a moment of aberration by Ted—was in the absent Reg's possession, Claud's statement could not be verified. A suggestion put forward by Alfie, who wanted action, that the lock should be forced, was vetoed by the Chief Inspector. He issued instructions that Reg was to bring the Vicar's rifle to the police-station in Bellingham on his way to work on the following morning, refused the offer of a cup of tea, and left the premises. He was accompanied to the door by the entire family, who saw him off in the friendliest way, the two boys begging him to come to see them again, and Jackerleen not only saying goodbye to him on her own behalf, but adding by proxy, and in a squeaky voice, the plush rabbit's farewell.

This scene so much astonished Constable Melkinthorpe that instead of showing his efficiency by starting his engine, and opening the door for Hemingway to get into the car, he sat staring with his mouth open.

"Yes, you didn't know I was their long-lost uncle, did you?" said Hemingway. "For the lord's sake, start her up, and look as if you were going to drive me to Bellingham, or we shall have Claud and Alfie trying to storm the car!"

"Where *am* I to drive you, sir?" asked Melkinthorpe.

"To the end of the row. I'm going to call on Ladislas, but I don't want that gang flattening their noses against the window."

Fortunately the ruse succeeded, and by the time the car had reached the end of the row the Ditchlings had retired again indoors. Hemingway got out of the car, and walked back to Mrs. Dockray's cottage.

It was by this time nearly six o'clock, and Ladislas had

returned from work. Ushered into the front sitting-room, by Mrs. Dockray, who eyed him with considerable hostility, the Chief Inspector found that Ladislas was entertaining two unexpected visitors. Mavis Warrenby, attired from head to foot in funeral black, and Abby Dearham, had called to see him, on their way back, by country omnibus, from Bellingham. It did not seem to Hemingway that their visit was affording Ladislas any pleasure. He was a handsome young man, with dark and romantically waving locks, and brown eyes, as shy as a fawn's. He was plainly frightened of the Chief Inspector, and lost no time in telling him, in very good English, that the ladies had just looked in on their way home. Miss Warrenby enlarged on this, saying in her earnest way: "Mr. Zamagoryski is a great friend of mine, and I felt I must show him that I *utterly* believe in him, and *know* he had nothing to do with my poor uncle's death."

Looking anything but grateful for this testimony, Ladislas said: "It is so kind!"

Bestowing a smile of quiet understanding on him, Miss Warrenby took his hand, and pressed it in a speaking way. "You must have faith, Laddy," she said gently. "And shut your ears to gossip, as I do. I often think how much better the world would be if people would only remember the monkeys."

"But what good shall it do to remember monkeys?" cried Ladislas, recovering possession of his hand. "Pardon! This is not sensible, to talk of monkeys!"

"You don't understand. Three little monkeys, illustrating what I always feel is a maxim we ough to try to——"

"*I* get it!" interrupted Abby triumphantly. "See no evil, Hear no evil, Speak no evil! It's all right, Ladislas: it's only a saying, or something. Come on, Mavis! If the Chief Inspector wants to talk to Ladislas, we'd better clear out!"

Ladislas looked uncertainly from Hemingway to the ladies. Mavis said that perhaps he would prefer her to remain, her voice conveying so strong a suggestion that there existed between them a beautiful understanding that he looked more frightened than ever, and made haste to disclaim any desire for her support. So Mavis began reluctantly to collect her numerous parcels, and the Chief Inspector, retrieving from under the table a paper-carrier, handed it to her, saying that she seemed to have been doing a lot of shopping.

"Only mourning," Mavis replied reverently, and with a slightly reproachful inflection. "I know it's out of date to go into mourning, but I think myself it is a mark of respect. So I asked Miss Dearham if she would go into Bellingham with me, because I didn't quite feel I could go alone—though I know I must get used to being alone now."

As she spoke, she turned her eyes towards Ladislas, who

avoided her gaze, looking instead, and with considerable trepidation, at Hemingway.

"Quite so," said Hemingway. "Did you respect your uncle, miss?"

This direct question made her blink at him. "What an *extraordinary* thing to ask me!" she said. "Of course I did!"

"Do you mean really, or because he's dead?" asked Abby, unable to suppress her curiosity.

"Abby, I know you don't mean it, but I do so hate that *cynical* sort of talk! I was very, very fond of Uncle Sampson, and naturally I respected him."

"Well, that interests me very much," said Hemingway. "Because, if you don't mind my saying so, miss, you seem to be about the only person I've met who did respect him."

"Perhaps," she suggested, "I knew him better than anyone else did."

"Just what I was thinking," agreed Hemingway. "So perhaps you can tell me why he managed to get himself disliked. Now, don't say he wasn't disliked, because I know he was and you must have known it too!"

If he had hoped to startle her out of her self-possession by these bludgeon-like tactics, he was destined to be disappointed. She only looked at him in a soulful way, and said: "I always think it's such a pity to judge by exteriors, don't you? My dear uncle had lots of little foibles, but under them he had a heart of *gold*. People just didn't *know* him. Of course, he wasn't perfect—everyone has *some* faults, haven't they? But it's like that beautiful little verse I learned when I was at school, and made up my mind I'd try to live up to." She sighed, smiled and, to the acute discomfort of Miss Abigail Dearham, recited in a rapt tone: " 'There is so much good in the *worst* of us, And so much bad in the *best* of us, That it hardly becomes *any* of us To talk about the *rest* of us.' "

"Gosh!" uttered Abby, revolted. "Did they really make you learn rancid things like that at your school? Mine was much better! We used to learn really good things, like 'Fair stood the wind for France', and 'Edward, Edward', and 'Lord Randal, my son'. There was some sense in that! Come on, we must go!"

The Chief Inspector raising no objection, she then hustled Mavis out of the room, and was heard adjuring her, in the passage, not to talk such ghastly tripe, because it made everyone want to be sick.

The Chief Inspector was left confronting Ladislas, who appeared to believe that he had fallen into the hands of the Gestapo. "I can tell you nothing!" he declared, standing with his back to the wall. "It does not matter what you do to me, I can tell you nothing, for I know nothing!"

"Well, if that's so it wouldn't be any use doing anything to

141

you," remarked Hemingway. "Not that I was going to. I don't know what antics they get up to in Poland, but in England you don't have to be afraid of the police. Are you and Miss Warrenby going to get married, may I ask?"

"No! A thousand times no!"

"All right, all right, there's no need to get excited about it! Just a friend of yours?"

"She is most kind," said Ladislas, more quietly, but watching him suspiciously. "I do not have many friends here. When I am presented to her, I am pleased, for she is sympathetic, she asks me about my own country, and she herself is not happy, for that one, her uncle, is a tyrant, and, like me, she does not have friends. I do not think of marriage. I swear it!"

"Her uncle was unkind to Miss Warrenby, was he?"

"But yes! She does not say so—she is very good, she makes no complaint—but I have eyes, I am not a fool! She does even the work of a servant, for it is a large house, that, and there is only one servant who is in it, living in it! Miss Warrenby has told me that when the other became married to the gardener Mr. Warrenby would not have another to replace her, for he was not generous, and he said Miss Warrenby had nothing to do, so she could do work in the house. And always she must be obedient, and she must be at home to wait on this uncle, and to be polite to his friends, but her own friends she must not have, no!"

"Didn't like her making a friend of you, in fact?" Hemingway paused, but Ladislas only glared at him. "How was that?"

"I am Polish!" Ladislas uttered bitterly.

"He didn't, by any chance, get it into his head that you wanted to marry Miss Warrenby?"

"It is untrue!"

"All right, don't get excited! Did you see Mr. Warrenby when you went to the house on Saturday?"

"No!"

"Yes, you did. What was he doing?'

Ladislas broke into impassioned speech, the gist of the torrent of words which burst from him being that if he were not a foreigner the Chief Inspector would not dare to question him, or to doubt his word.

"In my job, we get into the way of doubting people's words," said Hemingway equably. "Besides, you've got a trick of telling first one story and then another, which confuses me. You told Sergeant Carsethorn you didn't go to Fox House, and when he didn't believe that, you said you did. You told him you went to the back-door. Which leads me to think that you knew Mr. Warrenby was in the house, because you'd seen him. I daresay you reconnoitred a bit, and I'm sure I don't blame you, for he seems to have been the sort of man no one would have wanted

142

to meet if they could have avoided it. So now you tell me just what *did* happen!"

This matter-of-fact speech appeared to damp Ladislas's passion. After staring at Hemingway for a moment, he said in a flattened voice: "When I say I did not see him, I mean— I mean——"

"You mean you did," supplied Hemingway. "Comes of being foreign, and not being able to speak English right, I daresay."

Ladislas gulped. "He was in his study. He was reading some papers."

Hemingway nodded. "At his desk? You could see him from the road, easy, if that was where he was. So then, according to what you told Carsethorn, you slipped up to the back-door, which, I must say, seems to me a silly thing to have done, because, for one thing, I've seen the path which the tradesmen use, and it runs up that side of the house, so that I should have thought you'd have caught Mr. Warrenby's eye; and, for another, unless he was uncommonly deaf, I should have expected him to have heard you knocking on the back-door. However, if that's your story, I don't mind: it doesn't seem to me to matter much."

"Now I shall tell you the truth!" said Ladislas impulsively. "I did not go to the door! I went away, because I do not wish to make trouble for Miss Warrenby, and if her uncle is at home it is plain to me that she cannot go with me anywhere. It makes nothing!"

"Only a bit of extra work for the police, and that's fair enough, isn't it?" said Hemingway.

He left Ladislas hovering between doubt and relief, and went out to find that Constable Melkinthorpe was no longer alone. He had left the car, and was standing beside it, grinning down at an aged and disreputable individual in a much-patched suit of clothes and a greasy cap, which he wore at a raffish angle wholly inappropriate to his advanced years. Beside him stood a buxom lady, who appeared to be torn between anxiety and annoyance; and, eyeing them both in a boding fashion, was a stout and middle-aged constable. As the Chief Inspector paused for a moment, surveying the group, the buxom lady tried to take the old gentleman's arm, and besought him urgently to give over, and come off home to his tea.

"You lemme go, or I'll fetch you a clip!" said the Oldest Inhabitant, in shrill but slightly indistinct tones, and brandishing a serviceable ash-plant. "Wimmen! I 'ates the sight of them! I'm a-going to 'ave a few words with the Lunnon 'tec, and it 'ud take more than a nasty, meddling female to stop me! Ah! *And* more than a muttonheaded flat-foot wot never got no promotion, and never would, not if he lived to be as old as wot I

143

am, which 'e won't, becos 'e eats too much—unless it ain't fat, but dropsy 'e's got."

"*Father!*" expostulated his daughter, giving his arm a shake. "You've got no call to be rude to Mr. Hobkirk! If you don't stop it——"

"You give me any more of your imperence, Biggleswade, and you'll wish you'd kept a civil tongue in your head!" interrupted Constable Hobkirk, swelling with wrath.

"*Mr.* Biggleswade to you, Mr. Hobkirk!" instantly responded the lady, with a sudden veering of sympathy. "Ninety years old he is, and I'll thank you to remember it! Now, come along with you, Father, do!"

"What's all this about?" demanded Hemingway, stepping up to the group.

Constable Melkinthorpe so far forgot himself as to wink at his superior, but Hobkirk replied in official accents: "Police Constable Hobkirk, sir, reporting——"

"You shut your gob, young feller!" commanded Mr. Biggleswade. "You ain't got nothing to report. It's me as'll do the reporting. I'm going to 'ave me pitcher in the papers, and a bit wrote about me underneath it."

"All right, grandfather!" said Hemingway goodnaturedly. "But give the constable a chance! What's the matter, Hobkirk?"

"If there was anything the matter, which there ain't," said the obstreperous Mr. Biddleswade, "it wouldn't do you no good to go asking 'im, because 'e ain't seen beyond that great stomach of 'is for years—not but wot that's far enough. Nor I won't 'ave me words took out of me mouth by 'im, nor by you neither, becos the police never 'ad nothing on me, and I ain't afraid of any of you!"

"You're a wicked old man, that's what you are!" exploded the sorely-tried Hobkirk. "Before you got so as you couldn't do more than hobble about with a stick, you was the worst poacher in the county, and well I know it!"

Mr. Biggleswade's villainous countenance creased into a myriad wrinkles, and he gave vent to a senile chuckle. "That's more than you could prove, my lad," he said. "I don't say I weren't, nor yet I don't say I were, but wot I do say is that I were a sight too smart for all them gurt fools to catch."

"Don't pay any heed to him, sir!" begged his horrified daughter. "He's getting to be a bit childish! I'm sure I ask your pardon for him coming worriting you like this, but he's that obstinate! And coming up here to talk to you without his teeth!"

A vicious dig from her sire's elbow put her temporarily out of action. "My darter," explained Mr. Biggleswade. "Lawful," he added. "Which is wot makes 'er so blooming upperty! I got others. Ah, *and* sons! First and last——"

"Listen, grandfather!" interposed Hemingway. "There's

nothing I'd like better. than to hear your life-story, but the trouble is I've got work to do. So you just tell me what you want to see me about, will you?"

"That's right, my lad, you listen to me, and you'll get made a Sergeant!" said Mr. Biggleswade approvingly. "Cos I know who done this 'ere murder!"

"You do?" said Hemingway.

"He don't know anything of the sort, sir!" expostulated Hobkirk. "He's in his dotage! *Sergeant!* Why, you silly old fool——"

"You leave him alone!" said Hemingway briefly. "Come on, grandfather! Who did do it?"

An expression of intense cunning came into the wizened countenance of Mr. Biggleswade. "Mind, I'll 'ave me pitcher in the papers!" he warned the Chief Inspector. "And if there's a reward I'll 'ave that too! Else I won't tell you nothing!"

"That's all right," said Hemingway encouragingly. "If you can tell me the name of the man I'm after, I'll take a photo of you myself!"

Much gratified, Mr. Biggleswade said: "You're a smart lad, that's wot you are! Well, if you want to know 'oo done it I'll tell you! It were young Reg Ditchling!"

"*Father!*" said his daughter imploringly. "It isn't *right* to go taking that poor boy's character away from him! I keep *telling* you you've got it all wrong!"

"Reg Ditchling," repeated Mr. Biggleswade, nodding his hoary head mysteriously. "And don't you let no one tell you different! I was up on that there common—ah, and not so far from Fox Lane neither!—and I 'eared a shot. Plain as I 'ear you yammering now I 'eard it, and don't none of you start talking to me about no backfires, 'cos there ain't any man living knows more about gunshots than wot I do—I didn't pay no 'eed, 'cos it weren't none of my business, but 'oo do you think I seen not ten minutes later, 'iding be'ind a blackberry bush?"

"Reg Ditchling," replied Hemingway promptly.

"You leave me tell it you meself!" said Mr. Biggleswade, affronted. "Reg Ditchling it was! 'And wot might you be up to?' I says to 'im. 'Nuthin',' 'e says, scared-like. 'Oh, nuthin' is it?' I says to 'im. 'And 'oo give you that rifle, my lad?' I says. Then 'e 'ands me a lot of sauce, and makes off, and I went up to the Red Lion to 'ave a pint afore me tea."

"Yes!" interjected his daughter. "And when I went up to fetch you home it was all of seven o'clock, and Mr. Crailing told me you'd been there half an hour!"

Hobkirk, who had edged himself up to the Chief Inspector, said for his private ear: "That's right, what she says, sir, but make the silly old fool listen to a word of sense I can't! I'll have a few words to say to Reg Ditchling when I get hold of him,

145

borrowing guns he's got no right to have, but *if* he did any shooting on the common that day it was a good hour before Mr. Warrenby was killed. And I wouldn't believe that old rascal, not if he was to swear to it on his Bible-oath! It's all on account of old Mr. Horley being interviewed for the local paper the day *he* was ninety! Nothing'll do for Biggleswade but to get into the papers as well, *with* his picture!"

"Well, I hope he manages to pull it off," said Hemingway, watching appreciatively the spirited way in which Mr. Biggleswade was resisting his daughter's attempts to drag him homewards. "A very lively old gentleman, I call him. He deserves to get his picture in the papers."

Hobkirk eyed him doubtfully. "If you had to see as much of him as I do, sir—"

"Lord bless you, he wouldn't worry me! Have you had many of the villagers trying to do a bit of detection?"

"Sir," said Hobkirk earnestly. "you wouldn't believe it! Something chronic, it is! I've had to choke off more silly fat-heads who saw people they don't like not more than half a mile from Fox House nowhere near the time Mr. Warrenby was shot—well, as I say, you wouldn't hardly credit!"

"That's where you're wrong, because I would," said Hemingway. "Now then, grandfather! You go off home and have your tea, and don't you worry any more about it! I won't forget what you've told me! Come on, Melkingthorpe! Bellingham!"

At the police-station, he found the Chief Constable awaiting him, and chafing a little. He said cheerfully: "Sorry sir! Did you want to speak to me? I've been a bit held up by the local talent." He saw that he had puzzled the Colonel, and added: "Amateur detectives, sir: the place is swarming with them."

"Oh!" said the Colonel rather blankly. "Damned annoying! Got anything to tell me?"

"No, sir, I can't say I have. The soup's thickening nicely, which is as far as I'm prepared to go at the moment."

"You seemed pleased!" said the Colonel.

"I am," admitted Hemingway. "In my experience, sir, the thicker it gets the quicker you'll solve it. Can you tell me anything about the way Mr. Ainstable's estate is settled?"

"No," replied the Colonel, looking at him narrowly. "I can't. Except that the heir is Ainstable's nephew. Do you mean it's entailed?"

"Not exactly, no. At some date a settlement was made, but what the terms of it were I don't know. The Squire doesn't own the estate, that's all I know."

"Good God! I had no idea—are you sure of your facts, Hemingway?"

"I'm sure he's only the tenant-for-life, sir, and I know the

146

name of the firm of solicitors who act for the trustees of the settlement. But that's just about all I do know. How old was Mr. Ainstable's son when he was killed?"

The Colonel reflected. "He and my boy were at school together, so he must have been nineteen and—no, he was a few months older than Michael. About twenty."

"Not of age. Then the estate must have been settled by his grandfather, or resettled by him. It can't have been resettled by this man while his son was still a minor. I'm not very well up in these things, but I did once have a case which hinged on the settlement of a big estate."

"How did you find all this out?" demanded the Colonel. "I should doubt whether anyone except, I suppose, Drybeck, knows anything about Ainstable's affairs. And, good God, he wouldn't talk about a client's private business!"

"Properly speaking," replied Hemingway, "it was Harbottle who discovered it. And Mr. Drybeck wasn't the only person who knew there'd been a settlement. Sampson Warrenby knew it. And unless I'm much mistaken, Mr. Haswell knows it too—or at any rate suspects it."

"I should have said that Warrenby was the last man in the world Ainstable would have confided in! But go on!"

"I'm dead sure he didn't confide to him, sir. Warrenby found it out. There's a copy of a letter he wrote to the solicitors of the trustees, saying that he had a client that was interested in Mr. Ainstable's gravel-pit, and that he was informed they were the proper people for him to apply to. And there's an answer from this firm, all very plain, stating that although any money would have to be paid to them, acting for the trustees, to be apportioned as between the tenant-for-life and the trust funds, all such contracts were a matter for Mr. Ainstable only. Now, on the face of it, it looks as if Warrenby must have approached Mr. Drybeck, knowing him to be Mr. Ainstable's solicitor, and been passed on by him to this London firm."

"I suppose so," said the Colonel, staring at him.

"Yes, sir, only I've met a lot of false faces in my time, and it's my belief this is one of them. I don't doubt Warrenby got the information he wanted out of Mr. Drybeck, but I should say he didn't appear in the matter himself. In fact, I don't know how he managed it, which is probably just as well, because I've got a strong notion that if ever I got to the bottom of the methods the late lamented employed to find out things about his neighbours I'd very likely get up a subscription for the man who did him in, instead of arresting him."

"I don't follow you," the Colonel said. "Why should Warrenby not appear in the matter? It seems to me that if he had a client——"

147

"Yes, sir, but another strong notion I have is that he hadn't got any such thing. Seems highly unnatural to me that Mr. Drybeck should never have mentioned the matter to the Squire, and that he didn't I'm quite satisfied. It came as news to Mr. Ainstable—and not such very pleasant news either."

The Colonel stirred restlessly. "What makes you think there was no client?"

"The fact that we don't hear anything more about him, sir. Having gone to the trouble of finding out who was the right person to apply to, Warrenby didn't apply to him."

"He might, surely, have discovered that the lease of the pit had already been granted," objected the Colonel.

"I'll go further than that, sir. He might have known it all along. In fact, he must have known it. Everyone in Thornden couldn't help but know it. I think something made him suspect the Squire's estate had been settled, and he wanted to know just how the land lay. He hadn't a hope of getting Mr. Drybeck to tell him anything, so he went about the job in a different way."

"I should like you to tell me exactly what's in your mind, Hemingway," said the Colonel, in a level voice.

"Well, sir, taking one thing with another, it wouldn't surprise me to learn that the Squire's committing waste—and has been doing so ever since his boy was killed. Now, as I say, I'm not an expert, but I do know that if you've got a settled estate, and you go selling its capital, in a maner of speaking—timber, mineral rights, and such-like—about two-thirds of what you make out of it has to be put into the estate funds." He paused, but the Colonel said nothing. "And if you put the whole sum into your own pocket—or perhaps invest it so that your wife will be left comfortably off when you're dead—well, that's committing waste."

The Colonel raised his eyes from their frowning contemplation of the blotter on his desk. "That's a pretty serious charge, Chief Inspector."

"It is, sir. Only, of course, I'm not concerned with what Mr. Ainstable may be doing with his estate, except in so far as it might have a bearing on this case. It isn't a criminal offence."

"What do you mean to do?"

"Get the Department to make a few discreet enquiries for me. There won't be any noise made over it, but it's got to be done."

"Of course," said the Colonel, a little stiffly. "If you think you have enough evidence to justify an enquiry."

"Well, I do think so, sir. To start with, I've got reason to suspect that Warrenby had some sort of a hold over the Squire. To go on with, I've had a look at that estate, and I can see there's precious little money being spent on it, and a tidy sum being taken out of it. Then I find that it's going to a nephew

148

who, by all accounts, is next door to being a stranger to the Squire. And I don't mind saying that I've got a lot of sympathy for the Squire, because he's been hamstrung by a settlement that was meant to make everything safe and snug. If the boy had lived to be twenty-one, I don't doubt the estate would have been resettled, and provision made for Mrs. Ainstable. But he didn't, and it looks to me very much as if the Squire knows that nephew of his wouldn't look at it the same way his son would have. Well, when I saw Mr. and Mrs. Ainstable, I thought she looked a lot more likely to die than he did. But when I left Old Place, I went and paid a call on the Vicar, and that's where I learned that the Squire has a bad heart."

"Angina," said the Colonel shortly. "But, as far as I know, he's only had two not very severe attacks."

"Yes, Mr. Haswell, who happened to be with the Vicar when I called, said there was no reason why Mr. Ainstable shouldn't live for a good many years yet. On the other hand, you don't have to be a doctor to know that he might go very suddenly. That adds quite a bit of colour to what I'd already noticed. Which was that when I mentioned those two letters Harbottle found in Warrenby's office I knew I'd given the Squire and Mrs. Ainstable a nasty jolt. I got the impression that the last thing either of them wanted me to do was to start nosing round that gravel-pit, or all the timber he's been felling. And on top of that, when the Vicar started to say something about the gravel-pit, Mr. Haswell nipped in as neat as you please, and flicked his mind off on to something quite different. Which leads me to think that he's got pretty much the same idea as I have about what the Squire's up to."

There was a short silence. The Colonel broke it. "This is a damned, nasty affair, Hemingway! Well—it's up to you, thank God! If you're right—if Warrenby was blackmailing the Squire, not for money, but merely to force him to sponsor him socially—does that, in your view, constitute a sufficient motive for murder?"

Hemingway rose to his feet. "I don't remember, offhand, how many cases I've had, sir," he said dryly. "A good few. But I couldn't tell you what constitutes a motive for murder, not yet what doesn't. Some of the worst I've handled were committed for reasons you wouldn't even consider to be possible— if homicide didn't happen to be your job. You don't need me to tell you that, sir."

"No," said the Colonel. "But it depends on the type of man involved."

"That's right, sir: it does."

The Colonel glanced up. "Blackmail," he said heavily. "Yes, that's a motive, Chief Inspector—a strong motive."

"Yes, and it gives us a nice wide field," agreed Hemingway.

"Because, unless I miss my bet, I don't think the Squire was the only person Warrenby was putting the black on." He glanced at his watch. "If you'll excuse me, sir, I'll be leaving you. I told my chief I'd be giving him a ring about now." He walked over to the door, and looked back, as he opened it, a twinkle in his eye. "I've got upwards of half a dozen people who could have committed this murder, as far as their alibis go, which is nowhere," he remarked. "At least four of them have got what'll pass for motives, and the end of it will very likely be that it'll turn out to be someone I haven't begun to consider yet."

"I hope to God you may be right!" said the Colonel.

CHAPTER THIRTEEN

THERE was no one in the small office temporarily allotted to the Chief Inspector, but he saw that Harbottle had been there before him, for a pile of papers had been laid on the desk. He sat down, pushed the papers to one side, and drew the telephone towards him.

He was speedily connected with his immediate superior, Superintendent Hinckley, and was greeted by him with asperity, and a total lack of formality, the Superintendent saying, with awful sarcasm, that it was nice to hear his voice, and adding that there was nothing he liked better than to be kept hanging about at Headquarters, particularly when he happened to have a date. To which the Chief Inspector replied suitably, not omitting to animadvert upon persons who sat all day with their feet on their desks. After which interchange of civilities, the Superintendent laughed, and said: "Well, how's it going, Stanley?"

"I've seen worse. What have you got for me?"

"Nothing that's likely to interest you, I'm afraid. Seems quite straightforward. Born in 1914, in Nottinghamshire. Only son of the Reverend James Arthur Lindale. Father still living, mother died in 1933; two sisters, one married, the other single. Educated at Stillingborough College. Joined his uncle's firm of Lindale & Crewe, stockbrokers, in 1933. Became a member of the Stock Exchange, 1935. Called up in 1939, and served with the R.A. until 1946, when he was demobilized—do you want his military record? He served all over the place, and picked up a D.S.O. Ended up as a Major, with the Army of Occupation, in Germany."

"No, I don't think that's likely to be of much use. What's he been doing since he was demobilized?"

"He went back to the Stock Exchange for nearly five years. Lived in bachelor chambers, in Jermyn Street. There's nothing known about him, barring the bare facts I've given you. Hasn't even had his driving licence endorsed. He left the Stock Exchange at the end of 1950. That's all I've got for you."

"I'm bound to say it isn't promising," said Hemingway. "What about his wife?"

"He hasn't got one."

"Yes, he has!" Hemingway said impatiently. "*And* a baby! I told you so, and what's more I asked you to look into her record too!"

"I know you did, but I haven't got anything here about her."

151

"Who handled this?" demanded Hemingway suspiciously.

"Jimmy Wroxham."

"Oh!" said Hemingway. "Well, it's not like him to miss anything that's wanted. You did tell him to look into the wife, Bob?"

"Yes, I did, and if I ever see half a chance of getting you dismissed from the service with ignominy——"

"You won't," interrupted Hemingway. "No, look here, Bob, Jimmy must have slipped up! I've seen the set-up: husband and wife, and one baby, a year old. By what Lindale told me, I should say he was married about two years ago."

"No record," replied the Superintendent. "Jimmy had a talk with one of the partners of the firm he used to be with, and he didn't seem to know where he was now, or what he was doing. Said he left the Stock Exchange because he was unsettled by the War."

"That's pretty much what Lindale told me. But, by what you've just read out to me, it looks as though it took him five years to decide he couldn't stick city life any longer. Did you say he had a couple of sisters living?"

"Yes. The elder one lives with the father—he's got a parish somewhere in the Midlands—and the younger one's married to a shipowner. Lives up near Birkenhead."

"Birkenhead. . . . Well, that's some way off. Might account for her never having been seen in these parts. I should have thought the other one would have visited him, though. Oh, well! Perhaps she can't leave the old man. Did Jimmy see the uncle?"

"No, he died in the last year of the War. No Lindales at all in the firm since your man pulled out."

"Pity. He might have been able to wise us up. Something odd about this."

"I don't see anything odd about it. The woman you've seen must be his mistress. It does happen, you know!"

Hemingway was frowning, and ignored this frivolity. "It hasn't got that appearance," he said. "She isn't that type at all. It isn't that kind of household, either. Well, never mind! I've got another job I want done. Now, listen, Bob!"

He was still talking to Hinckley when Inspector Harbottle came into the office. The Inspector wore his usual air of inpenetrable gloom, a circumstance which prompted his superior to tell the Superintendent that he must now ring off. "Because Dismal Desmond's just come in, and I can see he's suffered a bereavement. So-long, Bob!"

"If that was the Superintendent," said Harbottle, eyeing him severely, "has he had the report on any of the bullets yet, sir?"

"Only the first. Nothing like the one we're after. We shall be getting the rest tomorrow."

"It was not fired from Plenmeller's rifle?" said Harbottle, a strong inflexion of disappointment in his voice. "Well, I'm surprised!"

"I'm not," replied Hemingway. "I fancy I see that bird leaving the rifle in the case for me to pick up, if he'd shot Warrenby with it!"

"Well," said Harbottle, dissatisfied, "of all the people I've seen down here, I'd say he was the likeliest. I don't mind telling you, Chief, I took a dislike to him the instant I laid eyes on him."

"I know you did, and I'll do my best to bring it home to him," said Hemingway, who was jotting down various items in this notebook.

"It's no laughing matter," said the Inspector austerely. "A wicked tongue shows a wicked nature! When he told you he had murdered his brother, I was never more shocked in my life. Even you, sir, would not talk about a thing like that as if it was a good joke!"

"Now, look here!" exclaimed Hemingway wrathfully.

"And, what is more," continued the Inspector, paying no heed to him, "whatever I may have believed at the time, I believe him now!"

"You can believe what you like, but I'm not here to investigate the other Plenmeller's death. Carsethorn tells me there was no doubt he committed suicide, anyway."

"Oh, he did that all right!" said Harbottle. "But, if you were to ask me, I should say this man was morally his murderer."

"Well, he said he drove him to it, didn't he? What have you found to put you into this taking?"

"It hasn't, strictly speaking, anything to do with this case," said Harbottle, "but I brought it along with those papers you see there, thinking you might like to read it. You'll recall that I told you Warrenby was the Coroner: well, I came upon the letter that unfortunate man wrote when he killed himself. Here it is! Now, you listen to this, sir! It's dated May 25th of the last year—that was the night he locked himself into his bedroom and gassed himself. '*Dear Gavin, This is the last letter you'll receive from me, and I don't propose ever to set eyes on you again. You only want to come here for what you can get out of me, and to goad me into losing my temper with your damned tongue, and to be maddened by you on top of all I have to suffer is too much. I've reached the end of my tether. The place will be yours sooner than you think, and when you step into my shoes you can congratulate yourself on having done your bit towards finishing me off. You will, if I know you. Yours, Walter.*'" Harbottle laid the sheet of paper down. "And he was right, poor gentleman! He does congratulate himself!"

Hemingway picked up the letter, and glanced at it. "Yes, well, I don't like Plenmeller any more than you do, but I call

153

it a damned mean thing to do, gas yourself and leave a letter like this behind you! Nice for his brother to have to listen to it being read out in court!"

"You'd have thought he'd have left the district," said Harbottle.

"I wouldn't, because, for one thing, he'd find it hard to get a price for his property here; and for another, although he may be a coldblooded devil, he's got plenty of nerve."

"Nerve enough to have shot Warrenby is what *I* think!"

"Lord, yes!" agreed Hemingway. "Nerve enough to shoot half the village, if it suited his book to do it! But if you're trying to make me believe he shot Warrenby just because he didn't happen to like him, you're wasting your time, Horace! I've been telling the Chief Constable that I don't know what constitutes a motive for murder, or what doesn't, but that was putting it a bit too high. I *do* know that no one, barring a lunatic, kills a chap because he thinks he's a pushing bounder! I daresay that's what his highness would like me to think, so as he can sit back and watch me making a fool of myself; but if he wants me to treat him as a hot suspect he'll have to give me a sniff of a real motive—*and* stop being the life and soul of the party! Did you find anything else at Warrenby's office?"

Harbottle glanced disparagingly at the papers on the desk. "I brought that lot along for you to look at, but I wouldn't say they were likely to lead you anywhere. There's some correspondence with one of the Town Councillors, which looks as if they'd had a row; and there's a whole lot of stuff about a trust for sale, which I can't say I quite get the hang of them. Seems Mr. Drybeck was the principal trustee, and had the handling of it. Warrenby was acting for someone he calls by a fancy name I never heard before." Harbottle picked up one of the clips of documents, and searched through them. "Here you are, sir! A Cestui que trust," he said, laying the letter before his chief, and pointing to the words.

"Lawyers!" ejaculated Hemingway disgustedly. "Go and see if there's a dictionary on the premises, for the lord's sake!"

The Inspector went away, returning a few minutes later with a well-thumbed volume in his hand. "It's a person entitled to the benefit of a trust," he announced.

"Good!" said Hemingway, who was running through the letters. "That's about what it looks like, from all this. This client wants his share of the trust: that's clear enough; and apparently it's all in order to sell the thing, only, for some reason or other Drybeck's being coy about doing it."

"Yes, but only because it's a bad time to sell," Harbottle pointed out. "He says so in one of the letters, and it sounds reasonable enough. You'll see that Warrenby doesn't quarrel with that at all. Writes perfectly civilly, and says he appreciates

154

the situation, but his client is anxious to receive his share of the sale without loss of time. I don't see what bearing any of it could have upon the murder, sir. In fact, I was in two minds about bringing it to you. The thing that made me wonder was that Mr. Drybeck came into the office this afternoon—nosing round, *I* thought, but he said he'd come to find out if there was anything he could do to help Coupland. He tried to get me to tell him if I'd discovered anything—at least, that's the way I read his chat, but I wouldn't be prepared to swear it wasn't just inquisitiveness. I got rid of him, of course, and it did enter my mind that perhaps he was worried about this correspondence with Warrenby. I found nothing else that was any concern of his."

"Well, that's interesting," said Hemingway. "There's no doubt that this client of Warrenby's was determined to have his share of the trust, and there's no doubt that Drybeck's stalling. Of course, it may be that he's just trying to do his best for the beneficiaries—pity we don't know what the others felt about an immediate sale!—and on the other hand it may be that he's got reasons of his own for not wanting to sell the trust."

"Good gracious, Chief, do you mean you think he's been embezzling the funds?" exclaimed Harbottle.

"No, not embezzling them, but it wouldn't surprise me if he's made a muck of the thing through being fatheaded, or half asleep. And if that's so, then I'd bet my last farthing Warrenby had got wind of it. It'll bear looking into, anyway. Is there anything in this?" He picked up an address book as he spoke, and opened it at random.

"I haven't studied it, sir. I thought I'd better do so, though."

Hemingway nodded, turning over the thin leaves in a cursory survey. "Yes, quite right. You never know what——" He broke off suddenly. "Well, I'm damned!"

"What have you found, sir?" demanded the Inspector, bending over him to see what was written on the page.

"Something I wasn't expecting, and didn't more than half believe in. Horace, let it be a lesson to you! Always pay attention to what people say to you, no matter how silly you may think it sounds!"

"You do," said Harbottle.

"I didn't this time. I had a suspicion that your friend Plenmeller was trying to see whether he could get me to follow a red herring. He told me to look for someone called Nenthall—and here he is, my lad! Francis Aloysius Nenthall, Red Lodge, Braidhurst, Surrey. Damn! I wish I'd looked at this book before I rang the Superintendent up! I'll have to get on to him again first thing tomorrow."

"What did Plenmeller say about this man?"

"He said that Warrenby once asked Lindale if the name

155

conveyed anything to him, and that it obviously conveyed a lot more than he liked—though he denied it. Which may, or may not be true. What I'm sure of is that Ultima Unlikely was right when she said there was something fishy about the Lindale set-up. There is. *She's* scared white, and *he's* playing every ball sent down to him with a dead bat. They've got something they're desperately anxious I shan't find out. So has the Squire —but I think I know what that is. This is a nice case, Horace."

"I don't see it, sir."

"No, and you never will, because you're not interested in psychology."

The Inspector, knowing his chief's foibles, looked at him with deep foreboding, but Hemingway did not pursue his favourite study. He said thoughtfully: "I don't know when I've had so many possibles to choose from. It's to be hoped I don't lose my bearings amongst them. There are three with motives that stand out a mile: the dead man's niece, who inherits his money; her glamour-boy, who says he never thought of marrying her, which I take to be a highly mendacious statement; and old Drybeck, who's been losing ground to Warrenby for years, and may—if my guess is correct—have been standing in danger of being discovered by him to have made a mess of some trust. Those are what you might call the hot suspects. After them I've got the questionables, headed by the Squire. I think he was being blackmailed by Warrenby."

"The Squire?" said Harbottle sceptically. "Blackmailed for what?"

"Committing waste. No, I know you don't know what that is, but it doesn't matter: it's a civil offence, and though it could easily land him in a packet of trouble it isn't a thing that concerns the police. I'll explain it to you presently, but don't keep on interrupting me! As I say, there's him, which makes four—and we shall have to include his wife, though I can't say I fancy her much, so that's five. Next, we've got the Lindales. Either *could* have done it; he's the type who *would*, given a sufficient motive. That tots up to four in the Questionable class. Seven altogether."

"Are you leaving out Plenmeller?" demanded Harbottle.

"Certainly not: I'm putting him at the head of the third class—those that might have done it, but who don't seem to have had any reason to have done it. Three of them. Plenmeller, easily capable of murder; Haswell, a dark horse——"

"He had an alibi, sir!"

"Not the young man: his father. I met him today, with the Vicar, and he's one of these cool, levelheaded customers who say just about as little as they need. Carsethorn verified that he did go to some place or other fifteen miles from Thornden on

156

Saturday afternoon, but we've only got his word for it that he didn't get home till eight because he stopped at his office in Bellingham on his way, to polish off some job he had on hand. They close at midday on Saturdays, so there was no one there to corroborate his story."

"What about the Vicar?" asked Harbottle. "He could have reached Fox House by way of his own meadow."

"If the Vicar did it, I'm not fit to direct traffic, let alone conduct an investigation into a case of murder! The only other possible—unless you have a fancy for Mrs. Midgeholme, because Warrenby kicked one of her dogs—is Reg."

"Who is he?"

"I haven't met him yet, but I've got reason to think he may have been cavorting about the common with the Vicar's gun on Saturday. He's a very unlikely suspect, but I'm including him because he's got that rifle hidden away somewhere. I've left orders he's to bring it in to us tomorrow on his way to work. From what I've seen of his family, I should say he would. If he doesn't, you can go and pull him in. All told, that makes nine people—but I admit I don't fancy some of them."

"You've forgotten the Major," said Harbottle drily.

"I'm keeping him up my sleeve, in case all else fails," retorted Hemingway, gathering the papers on the desk into a pile, and tying them up. "Come on! We've done enough for today."

"Are you asking for an adjournment tomorrow, sir? Who is going to preside over the inquest?"

"Fellow from Hawkshead. The Chief Constable tells me he's all right, but one of these chatty old boys that like to go into all the irrelevant details, so I daresay we shall waste the better part of the morning on the job. However, there's not much I can do till I hear from Hinckley again. Come on!"

On the following morning, Hemingway was greeted by the news, when he walked into the police station, that young Ditchling had arrived there ten minutes earlier, and was awaiting his pleasure.

"Did he bring in that rifle?" asked Hemingway.

"Yes, sir. Sergeant Knarsdale has it."

"All right. Know anything about this lad?"

"No, sir—nothing against him, that is. It's a very respectable family. All in steady jobs, and none of them been in any kind of trouble. This kid's just over sixteen. Works at Ockley's Stores, and is well spoken of by the boss. But I'd say he's pretty scared."

"Fancy that!" marvelled Hemingway. "Send him in to me!"

The youth who was presently ushered into the small office was a shockheaded boy with a slightly pimpled countenance, and the rather clumsy limbs of the rapidly growing adolescent. He entered the room with every evidence of reluctance, and

157

remained just inside it, staring at the Chief Inspector out of a pair of round, serious eyes, and tightly gripping a trilby hat before him.

Hemingway looked him over. "So you're Reg Ditchling, are you?" he said.

"Yessir," acknowledged Reg, with a gulp.

"All right. Come and it down in that chair, and tell me what you mean by not giving his gun back to Mr. Cliburn!"

This command was uttered in quite a friendly tone, but it was apparent that Reg saw the prison gates yawning wide before him. He shrinkingly approached the chair in front of the desk, and sat down on the extreme edge of it, but the power of speech seemed to have deserted him.

"Come on!" said Hemingway kindly. "I'm not going to eat you. Where was the rifle? Did you have it in that shed I saw?"

"Ted put it there, 'cos of Alfie, sir."

"Well, that was a sensible thing to do, at all events. Was the shed locked every day?"

"Yessir."

"Where do you keep the key?"

"Ted and me had a place for it the others don't know about, sir, so as Claud and Alfie couldn't get in and monkey with the tools when we wasn't there."

"Well, where was this place?"

Reg twisted his hat round and round between his hands. "Ted and me put tarred felt over the roof, to keep the rain out, sir. There's a place where you can slip the key underneath it."

Hemingway's brows snapped together. "Is that where you always put the key?"

"Yessir," said Reg nervously. "Nobody knows about it, 'cept Ted and me—honest, sir!"

Hemingway said nothing for a moment, vizualizing the row of cottages, from the upper back-windows of which, he judged, a sufficiently good view could be obtained of the line of narrow gardens. Reg swallowed convulsively, and went on twisting his hat.

"Now, look here, my lad!" said Hemingway. "I'm not going to ask you why you didn't do what your brother told you, and take that rifle back to Mr. Cliburn, because I know why you didn't. Nor am I going to tell you that you've been breaking the law by having in your possession a gun without a Firearms licence, because I've no doubt Constable Hobkirk's already torn you off the strip."

"Yessir," acknowledged the culprit, with a sickly smile. "I'm very sorry, sir."

"Well, see you don't do it again! You answer what I *am* going to ask you truthfully, and very likely you'll hear no more

158

about it. Did you have that rifle out on the common on Saturday?"

"Yessir, but *honest* I never shot the gentleman!" said Reg, sweating a little.

"What *did* you shoot?"

"Nothing, sir! It was only target-practice, like Ted told me I ought to do. It was Ted learnt me to shoot, and I only went out with him the three times. And then he got his call-up papers, and he said to take the rifle back to the Reverend, and, honest, I meant to! Only there was some cartridges left, and I thought if I was to use them for practice the Reverend wouldn't mind, and I could take the rifle back on the Sunday."

"Well, why didn't you?"

"It—it was all over the village Mr. Warrenby had been shot."

"Had the wind up, eh?"

"Well, I— Well, sir——"

"Because," pursued Hemingway relentlessly, "this target-practice of yours was quite close to Fox House, wasn't it?"

"*No*, sir!" asserted Reg, the colour rising to his face. "That's what old Mr. Biggleswade told you, but it isn't true! I went to Squire's gravel-pit, 'cos there's no one there of a Saturday afternoon, and it's a safe place. And I brought my cards, sir, just to *show* you it's true, what I'm telling you!"

With these words, he produced from his pocket several small cardboard targets, and laid them on the desk before the Chief Inspector. If they were valueless as proof that Reg had not fired the Vicar's rifle in the vicinity of Fox House, they did at least convince Hemingway that only by accident could he have shot a man through the head at a range of nearly a hundred yards. There was a decided twinkle in his eye as he looked at the targets. He said: "What was your range?"

"Twenty-five yards, sir—about," replied Reg.

"You got quite a lot of shots on the targets, didn't you?" said Hemingway gravely.

"Yessir!" said Reg, with simple pride. "I was trying to get a good group, like Ted does. If I could practise regular, I soon would."

"Well, what you want to do is to join a Rifle Club, my lad, and not go practising with other people's rifles in public places," said Hemingway, handing him back his targets. "What time was it when you were in the gravel-pit?"

"It would have been a bit after five when I got there, sir, and I wasn't there more 'n an hour, that I'll swear to, and I should *say* it was less, because I was back home by half past six. And please, sir, Mum, and Edie, and Claud will tell you the same, because——"

"Yes, well, if I want to check up on your story I'll ask them!" said the Chief Inspector hastily, mentally registering a resolve to depute this task to Harbottle. "What I want to know at the moment is what you did with the rifle when you got home?"

"I cleaned it, sir, like Ted showed me."

"Yes, and then?"

"I didn't do anything with it, sir, beyond wrap it up in a bit of sacking. Ted said——"

"Never mind what Ted said! Did you lock it up in the shed?"

"Well—well, no, sir—not at once I didn't. I mean—I *had* it in the shed, but it wasn't locked, of course, 'cos I had to do a job for Mum," said Reg apologetically. "Two, really, because Claud and Alfie went and broke one of the chairs, scrapping, you know, so I mended that, and then I got on with the plate-rack Ted and me was making for her."

"You mean you were in the shed yourself?"

"That's right, sir. I locked it up when Mum called me in to supper, which we had a bit late, on account of Claud not getting in till near a quarter to eight, because of the Outing the Wolf Cubs had."

"So that you're quite sure no one could have got hold of the rifle?"

"Well, they *couldn't*, sir not possibly! And what's more, sir, I don't see how Mr. Biggleswade could have heard me shooting, not from where he was sitting! Because when he came in to tell Mum how he'd been talking to you, which he did, right away, he told her where he'd been sitting when he heard the shot, and Mum says his own daughter told him not to talk so silly, because he couldn't have heard it, not all that way off. And it stands to reason he didn't, sir, because if he heard one shot, why didn't he hear all the others?"

Hemingway pulled open a drawer in the desk, and took from it the sketch-plan of Thornden. "Where was he sitting?" he asked. "Come and show me!"

Reg obediently got up, and stared at the plan over the Chief Inspector's shoulder. It took him a minute or two to grasp it. Then he said: "Well, sir, it's a bit difficult, because this doesn't show the trees, and the paths, and that, on the common. Only the gorse bushes beside Fox Lane. There's some trees just beyond them, about here." He laid a finger on the plan, a little to the north-east of the gorse-clump.

"Between the bushes and the gravel-pit. Yes, I saw them. And beyond them the ground falls away, doesn't it?"

"That's right, sir. You get a view over the common from there, and there's a seat, and a path leading to it. Mr. Biggleswade said he was sitting there, and I daresay he was, because it's the walk he always takes. And you can see for yourself it's a long way off the gravel-pit." He paused, a frown of deep concentration on his brow. "What's more, if he had heard me shooting, he must have known which side of him I was, and he's gone and

160

said I was firing in the very opposite direction to what I was! He must be getting barmy! But what I think, sir, is that he never heard anything, and he only said he did because of seeing me with the rifle, and wanting to get into the papers."

"Where did he see you?"

"Well, it was along the path I told you about, sir. It sort of runs into Fox Lane nearly opposite Miss Patterdale's house."

"And what made you go all that way round to get home, when you could have done it in half the time, walking straight across the common from the pit?" asked Hemingway.

Reg blushed, and replied guiltily: "Well, sir—being as it was the Reverend's gun—Well, what I mean is, it's all open in that part of the common, besides the cricket-ground—and a Saturday afternoon, too, with people about—so I thought better to go round where I wouldn't be likely to meet anyone."

"Only you met Biggleswade. And when he asked you what you were up to with a rifle, you cheeked him, and ran off. Now, it didn't seem to me that he's one who sets much store by the law, so what made you so scared of him?"

"I wasn't—not exactly, sir! Well, I wouldn't have been if it wasn't for Alfie. Alfie went and played a trick on Mr. Biggleswade the other day, and he was fair hopping, and he's such a spiteful old devil I thought he might easily go and make trouble with the Reverend, or even Mr. Hobkirk, just to get back on us!" said Reg, in a burst of candour.

"I see. That's about all I want from you at the moment, then. You'd better get off to your work—and see you don't go breaking the law again, my lad!"

"No, sir! *Thank* you, sir!" said Reg, on a gasp of relief.

He made for the door, nearly colliding with Inspector Harbottle, who came into the office at that moment. The sight of the Inspector's stern countenance quite unnerved him; he stammered something unintelligible, and fairly fled from so quelling a presence.

The Inspector shut the door. "Is that young Ditchling? You seem to have shaken him up good and proper, sir!"

"Not me! He took one look at you, and thought you were the public hangman, and I'm sure I'm not surprised. Is that the report I'm waiting for?"

"Just come in," said Harbottle, handing him a sealed envelope.

Hemingway tore it open, and drew out the single sheet it contained, and spread it open. "Not a sausage!" he said, assimilating its message.

"You mean to tell me, sir, that not one of the rifles we've tested is the one we're after?"

"Not one!" said Hemingway cheerfully. "What's more, I don't need a comparing microscope to convince me the Vicar's rifle isn't the right one either. It'll have to be tested, of course, but you can put it out of your head, Horace! If every witness was as honest as that kid you saw, you'd be a Chief Inspector, instead of stooging round with me, and thinking how much better you could do the job yourself!"

"I don't," said Harbottle, his rare smile flickering across his face. "But if the fatal shot wasn't fired from any of the rifles we've pulled in, nor yet from the one you have now, then it seems to me that we shall have to pull in some of the others which you wouldn't even let me tell you about!"

"We may," agreed Hemingway. "On the other hand, we may not. I'm beginning to get some funny ideas about this case, Horace. However, there'll be time enough to tell you what they are when we've attended the inquest." He glanced at his watch. "Which we'd better be thinking about," he added. "What will you bet me the Deputy Coroner will be playing to capacity?"

"If he is, people will be disappointed," said Harbottle. "I suppose you'll ask for an adjournment pretty quick on the doctor's evidence?"

"I probably will," said Hemingway. "It all depends."

CHAPTER FOURTEEN

THE Chief Inspector was right. As he and Harbottle elbowed their way through the throng of persons seeking admission to the court-room, he said, over his shoulder: "What did I tell you? Turning them away at the doors!"

Inside, the Chief Constable said: "It was bound to be a *cause célèbre*, of course. Half Bellingham's here. Silly fools! What do they think they're going to hear?"

Hemingway, scanning the audience, made no reply. Half Bellingham might be present, but Thornden was scantily represented. Neither the Ainstables nor the Lindales had apparently thought it worth while to attend the inquest; and of Gavin Plenmeller there was no sign. Major and Mrs. Midgeholme were seated beside Mr. Drybeck; and Mr. Haswell had found a place not far from them. Possibly he had come to hear his son give evidence.

Charles, who was suffering from a strong sense of ill-usage, had brought Mavis, Abby, and Miss Patterdale from Thornden, in his dashing sports car. So incensed was he with Abby for electing to accompany Mavis on her shopping expedition on the previous afternoon, rather than to have run down to the coast with him, as had been (he insisted) arranged, that he had invited Miss Patterdale to occupy the front seat in his car, and had even gone so far as to say that he didn't know why Abby wanted to attend the inquest at all. But Mavis, who (he savagely whispered to Miss Patterdale) had got herself up to look like a French widow, said gently that she had asked Abby to go with her, so there was nothing more to be said about that. Abby had then made a very rude grimace at him, an unendearing gesture which had had the extraordinary effect upon him of confirming him in his resolve to marry her, even if he had to drag her to the altar to do it.

When he shepherded his party into the court-room, those who had come into Bellingham on the omnibus were already ensconced in front-row seats. Besides Mr. Drybeck and the Midgeholmes, these included Mr. Biggleswade, and the late Mr. Warrenby's cook-general, a sharp-eyed damsel with tow-coloured hair cut in the style adopted by her favourite film-star. Gladys, a good cook and a hard worker, was known to be a Treasure, but she was also one of those who believed in sticking up for her rights. Not even her late employer had ever been permitted to encroach on these; and since he was well aware of the difficulty of getting servants to live in quiet villages, and set

163

a high value on Gladys's culinary skill, he had been content, after one attempt to subjugate her, to rate Mavis for being unable to manage the household better. Gladys considered it to be her unquestionable right to attend the inquest; and when Mavis had shown reluctance to grant her leave off in the middle of the morning, she had spoken so ominously about the Unsettled state of her feelings ever since Mr. Warrenby's death, that Mavis had hastily retracted her first refusal. An attempt on her part to convince Gladys that nice girls did not wish to attend sensational inquests failed entirely.

"Well, it's only natural, isn't it?" had said Gladys.

"I don't think it is, Gladys. I'd give *anything* not to have to go."

"You'll enjoy it all right once you get there, miss," had replied Gladys, briskly stacking the breakfast-china in a cupboard. "'Tisn't as though Mr. Warrenby was any loss."

"He is a great loss to *me*," had said Mavis, in a repressive tone.

"Well, it's quite proper you should say that, miss," had been the paralysing response. "It wouldn't hardly be decent not to, being as he's left you all his money. But I know what I know, and many's the time I've wondered why ever you put up with him and his nasty, bullying ways."

It was hardly surprising, after this, that Mavis had retreated from the kitchen, leaving her henchwoman mistress of the field.

The Deputy Coroner was a chubby little man with white hair, pink cheeks, and a general air of cosiness. It was plain to Inspector Harbottle, resigning himself, that he would conduct the inquest at unnecessary length, and entirely to his own satisfaction.

From the point of view of the audience, as Hemingway said in his assistant's ear, Mavis Warrenby was the biggest draw. Whether she was conscious of the stir her appearance created it was impossible to guess, for she conducted herself just as a heroine should, bravely, modestly, and with enough sensibility to win not only the sympathy of the mob, but also that of the Coroner, who handled her with the greatest tenderness, assuring her several times that he appreciated how painful it must be for her to be obliged to give her evidence.

She was followed by young Mr. Haswell, who had been so much revolted by a performance which he freely described, in a whisper, to Abby, as ham, that when the Coroner, by way of putting things on the friendly footing he apparently desired, repeated his remark about the painful aspect of having to describe what he had seen in the garden of Fox House, he replied with the utmost cordiality: "Oh, no, not a bit, sir! *I* don't mind!"

He then told the court, with admirable brevity, just how he had found the dead man, and what his own actions had been.

Chief Inspector Hemingway provided everyone with a mild thrill by rising to his feet and putting a question to him.

"When you went into the study, to use the telephone, did you touch anything on the desk?"

"No, only the telephone," Charles replied. "I took care not to. There was a mess of papers and things all over it."

"Did you see anything to make you think someone might have looked for anything on, or in, the desk?"

"No," Charles said unhesitatingly. "When I said, a mess, I meant only the sort of muddle of papers you'd expect, if a man had been working there. It looked to me, from the way the chair had been pushed back, and the fountain-pen left lying on the blotter, as though Mr. Warrenby had left the room rather suddenly, and meant to return."

"Now, what do you mean by that?" asked the Coroner chattily.

Charles glanced at him. "Well—just that, sir. It was a blazing hot day, and that room had had the sun on it for hours. It was pretty hot still when I was in it. I thought, from what I've told you, and from the fact that Mr. Warrenby was wearing morocco slippers, and had a clip of papers at his feet, that he'd strolled out for a breath of air. That's all."

The Chief Inspector sat down, and the Coroner told Charles that he might leave the box. Dr. Warcop was summoned to take his place. The Chief Inspector leaned across his assistant to speak to Sergeant Carsethorn. "Who's the blonde sitting three from the end of the row behind us, next to a fat girl in blue?"

The Sergeant turned his head, and was able to identify the blonde as Gladys Mitcham, cook-general at Fox House. Hemingway nodded, and sat back. Inspector Harbottle asked softly: "What is it, Chief?"

"Something young Haswell said made her sit up. Looked as though, for two pins, she'd have chipped in," replied Hemingway briefly.

"Are you going to ask for an adjournment?"

"Soon as the doctors have had their innings. The police surgeon won't keep us long: he's all right. This old dodderer will hold the stage for as long as he's allowed to, from the looks of him."

This prophecy was soon found to have been correct. Dr. Warcop proved to be the worst kind of medical witness, and he seemed to be labouring under the delusion that he was addressing a class of students. Since he had been prevented by an emergency call from one of his more valued patients from assisting at the autopsy, even the Coroner, himself a talkative man, felt that his evidence might have been compressed into a very few sentences. He was extremely pompous, and when

165

asked by the Chief Inspector if he could state the approximate time of the murdered man's death, he explained at great length, and with many scientific terms, why it was impossible for him—or, he dared to add, for anyone—to pronounce with certainty on this point. He then perceived that his colleague, Dr. Rotherhope, was gazing abstractedly at the ceiling, a smile of dreamy pleasure on his face, and he said with meaning emphasis that he had had many years of experience, and had learnt the danger of asserting as incontrovertible facts statements which, in his humble opinion, were open to doubt. He was prepared to enlarge on this theme, but was balked by the Chief Inspector, who cut in neatly when he paused to draw breath, said: "Thank you, doctor," and sat down.

"Er—yes, thank you very much, doctor!" said the Coroner, as Dr. Warcop turned towards him, with the evident intention of continuing his lecture. "That's quite clear: more than a quarter of an hour, but less than an hour, you think. If the Chief Inspector has no further question he wishes to put to you, we need not keep you any longer."

Dr. Rotherhope rose briskly to his feet as his name was called.

His evidence was brief, technical, and, to the general public, very uninteresting. The Chief Inspector asked him no questions, but the Coroner was inspired to ask if he was able to give an opinion on the probable time of Warrenby's death.

Dr. Rotherhope was swift to seize opportunity. "No, sir," he replied. "A considerable time had—unfortunately—elapsed before I saw the body."

He then stood down, bearing the appearance of a man who considered the morning not wholly wasted; and the Chief Inspector rose to ask for an adjournment.

Colonel Scales, seeking him a few minutes later, found only Inspector Harbottle, who said, in answer to his enquiry: "I don't know where he is, sir. He slid out of the court as soon as he'd asked for an adjournment, and he didn't tell me where he was going. Though I fancy I know what he was after. Did you want to see him for anything special, sir?"

"No—only to ask whether he's had the report on those bullets."

"Yes, sir, it came through this morning. None of the markings correspond at all."

"Oh! That's disappointing. What does he mean to do now?"

"I can't tell you that, sir. He didn't say, but I don't think he's disappointed."

"Well, I daresay I shall be seeing him later," said the Colonel, passing on.

Sergeant Carsethorn said: "What *did* he slip off so quickly for?"

"From what I know of him, he went to intercept that fair girl—Warrenby's cook. He's probably standing her fruit sundaes in some tea-shop by this time," replied the Inspector caustically.

"Whatever for?" demanded Carsethorn, staring.

"To get her to talk. She looked like the sort that shuts up like a clam the instant you start to ask a few straight questions, and this I will say for the Chief: to hear him getting people to tell him every last thing he wants to know, and a lot more besides, is a downright education!"

"I can see he's got a way with him," agreed the Sergeant. "Sickening, none of those bullets matched! Seems to me we're back where we started."

To this Harbottle vouchsafed no more than a grunt, and as as he saw Mrs. Midgeholme bearing down upon them, the Sergeant effaced himself.

Mrs. Midgeholme, like Colonel Scales, wanted the Chief Inspector. Unlike the Colonel, she expressed her dissatisfaction at not finding him. She said that she particularly wished to drop a word in his ear.

"Well, madam, if you care to step across the road to the police-station, you can tell me whatever it is you wish the Chief Inspector to know, and I'll see he does know it," offered Harbottle.

Mrs. Midgeholme betrayed an unflattering reluctance to accept him as a substitute. "I'd *rather* speak to the Chief Inspector," she said.

"Just as you wish, madam," said Harbottle, unmoved.

"When do you expect him back?" she asked.

"I couldn't say at all, madam."

"Oh, dear, that's *most* awkward!"

Major Midgeholme, who was looking harassed, said: "We ought to be getting along, Flora, or we shall miss the 'bus. Really, you know, I don't think it's necessary for you to meddle in what isn't our business!"

This intervention was, in the Inspector's opinion, unfortunate, for it had the effect of strengthening Mrs. Midgeholme in her resolve. "No, Lion!" she said firmly. "It is every citizen's duty to help the police as much as they can. Besides, I think it only right that he should be put on his guard. If you're quite sure there's no chance of my being able to see the Chief Inspector himself, I suppose I'd better give you a message for him," she added, to Harbottle. "Don't wait for me, Lion! I shall come out on the later 'bus."

She then accompanied the Inspector to the police-station, informing him on the way that only her sense of duty had brought her to Bellingham, one of her more valuable bitches having

167

produced her first litter during the night. Without receiving the smallest encouragement, she then described in enthusiastic detail the puppies, adding some useful tips on the correct feeding and care of brood bitches. To all of which the Inspector said, as he ushered her into Heminway's temporary office: "Yes, madam?" He then put forward a chair for her, and himself sat down behind the desk, drawing a sheet of official paper towards him, and unscrewing the cap from his fountain-pen.

"Of course, I'm not making a *statement*, exactly," said Mrs. Midgeholme, impressed by these preparations. "Not that I mind having what I say taken down."

But in the event the Inspector found it unnecessary to take any notes at all.

"As soon as I found out what was going on," said Mrs. Midgeholme, plunging into the middle of her disclosures, "I made up my mind that the Chief Inspector ought to know about it. Apart from anything else, I feel *responsible* for that poor girl. I might be her mother!"

"Are you speaking of Miss Warrenby?" asked Harbottle.

"Good gracious, whom else should I be speaking about? There she is, alone in the world, and I call it absolutely *wicked*! Mind you, I've never liked Thaddeus Drybeck, but that he would go about casting suspicion on an innocent girl I did *not* think! Believe it or not, that's what he's doing! He's been prying round Thornden, asking all sorts of questions, and trying to make out a case against the child! He even asked *me* things, because, of course, I do know Miss Warrenby better than anyone else does, and I won't deny I could tell you a lot of things about that household, and the disgraceful way Sampson Warrenby treated his niece. If she weren't a saint she'd never have put up with it! But you know what it is, with people like that!—they never have any *sense*! Which is another thing I want to speak to the Chief Inspector about, because anyone could impose on Miss Warrenby—anyone! But as for Thaddeus Drybeck, words fail me!"

The Inspector, placing no dependence on this statement, waited for her to continue.

"When I found out what he was up to—collecting information about all the times Warrenby was absolutely brutal to her, and trying to prove by time, and measurements, and I don't know what beside, that she could have shot her uncle—well, I didn't hesitate to tell him what I thought of him! You ought to be ashamed of yourself, I said to him, and I should have said a good deal more if I'd known then what I know now! Would you believe it?—he actually had the impertinence to pump Gladys! She's Miss Warrenby's cook, and I know this for a *fact*, because she was on the same 'bus this morning, and she told me with her own lips! I don't know when I've been so

168

shocked! *Well!* I said, and I decided then and there that it was my bounden duty to put the Chief Inspector on his guard. For it's nothing but spite! Thaddeus Drybeck is one of those old bachelors who never have a good word to say for the modern generation. You must warn the Chief Inspector not to believe a word he says!"

"Very well, madam," said Harbottle. "But it isn't at all necessary. If I may say so, you've no need to worry."

"It's all very well for you to say that," argued Mrs. Midgeholme, "but he *is* a lawyer, and if you can't believe what a lawyer tells you, I ask you, who *are* you going to believe?" She paused in a challenging way, but the Inspector proffered no suggestion. "It stands to reason!" she said. "Now, *I* say it's just spite, because, to my mind, he's too much of an old woman to have shot Warrenby himself, though I've no doubt he'd have liked to. Abby Dearham—she's Miss Patterdale's niece—believes he did it, and is trying to divert suspicion from himself, but although I must say she's worked it all out really very cleverly, somehow I can't credit it. No. The longer I live the more certain I am that my own theory is the right one. It was Ladislas. It's no use talking to me about the time being wrong: I don't know anything about that, but what I *do* know is that he's double-faced. There's no other word for it."

"I daresay," replied the Inspector. "In my experience, a lot more people are than you'd think. In any case,——"

"Wait!" commanded Mrs. Midgeholme. "Before any of this happened, it was common talk that he was running after Miss Warrenby. He's a handsome young man, if you admire that foreign type, and, of course, there's no denying that the poor girl took a fancy to him. Well, it's not to be wondered at, because she isn't attractive to men usually, and I daresay she was flattered. *I* think he's an adventurer. He must have guessed, if he didn't know it for a fact, that she would come into money when her uncle died. So if that isn't a motive for murdering him, I don't know what is! And no sooner is Warrenby dead than what do you think Ladislas does? Pretends he was never interested in Miss Warrenby! He was at the Red Lion yesterday, —a thing he hardly ever does, I may tell you!—trying to make everyone believe that nonsense! My husband said it was really quite ridiculous, and merely made people think he was badly frightened. Well, I might not have made anything much of that, if it hadn't been for what I discovered after dinner."

"What was that?" enquired the Inspector mechanically.

"I happened to ring Miss Warrenby up, and that maid of hers answered the call. And what do you think she said?"

"I don't know."

"She said she thought Miss Warrenby was sitting in the summer-house—you wouldn't know it: it's at the bottom of

169

the garden, at the back of the house—*talking to Mr. Ladislas!* You could have knocked me down with a feather! After all that fine talk of his, sneaking off when he knew no one would be about, to visit Miss Warrenby! I just told Gladys not to bother, and rang off, and made up my mind that the thing to do was to report it to the Chief Inspector."

"I'll tell him, madam," said Harbottle, bent on getting rid of her. "As soon as he comes in, and I'm sure he'll be very grateful to you."

"I only hope he *does* something!" said Mrs. Midgeholme, beginning, to his relief, to collect her gloves and handbag.

Ten minutes after her departure, Hemingway walked in.

"You've missed Mrs. Midgeholme," Harbottle told him.

"I told you I'd got flair. What did she want?"

"To help you do your job. I was very near to telling her you'd gone off with a blonde."

"It's a good think you didn't. She's a blonde herself, and if she once got the idea I go for blondes I'd never be able to shake her off. I was right about Gladys: young Haswell did make her sit up."

"Did you get anything important out of her?" Harbottle asked curiously.

"That I can't say. But she's got her head screwed on the right way, has Gladys. She says that if the late Warrenby was sitting in the garden with his slippers on it must have been something highly unexpected which took him out of the house."

"Why?" demanded Harbottle.

"Seems it was one of his idiosyncrasies. Another was never going out without a hat. Gladys, not having been on the scene of the crime, and not having seen the photographs either, doesn't know that he had no hat on when he was shot, which is where I have the advantage of her."

"I believe the bit about the hat," said the Inspector reflectively. "There's a lot of men never stir a step out of doors without they must put a hat on. My old father's one of them. I don't see why he shouldn't have gone out in his slippers, unless the ground was wet, which we know it can't have been."

"You don't see it, because very likely you never caught cold through getting your feet chilled. Still, you ought to know that once a man gets it into his head that something is a fatal thing to do, it gets to be an obsession with him. Gladys tells me that he's even ticked her off for popping down in her slippers to get a bit of mint, or something, out of the kitchen-garden."

"You seem to set a lot of store by what this Gladys of yours says," remarked the Inspector. "Has she got any ideas about what took him out of doors without his hat or his snowboots?"

"She has, of course, which is where she and I part company, as you might say—though I wouldn't dare to tell her so. She

170

says the late Warrenby was lured out by a trick. It's no use asking me what the trick was, or who played it, because it wasn't a notion I took any kind of fancy to, and I headed Gladys off it. And I'll thank you to stop calling her my Gladys, Horace! She's been walking out steady with a very respectable chap in the building-trade for the last two years, and you'll be getting me into trouble."

The Inspector gave a dry chuckle. "If that's so, I'll bet you know a whole lot about the building-trade you didn't know before, sir! But what do you make of this stuff she's given you?"

"I'm not at all sure," replied Hemingway frankly. "I've had a feeling ever since yesterday that I've had the wrong end of the stick pushed into my hand; and I've now got a feeling that for all I've got nine suspects there's something highly significant which is being hidden from me. What's more, while Gladys was telling me all about the late Warrenby's habits, I got another feeling, which was that if only I'd the sense to see it, she was giving me a red-hot clue."

"That *is* flair!" said the Inspector.

Hemingway eyed him suspiciously, but it was plain that he had spoken in all seriousness. "Well," Hemingway said, after a slight pause, "you're coming on, Horace! When you were first wished on to me——"

"You asked for me," interpolated the Inspector.

"If I did, it was because I've always been susceptible to suggestion. Anyway, when you first came to me, you used to think I was heading for the nearest looney-bin every time I got a hunch."

"I didn't, because Sandy Grant warned me not to be misled," retorted the Inspector. "He told me——"

"I don't want to know what he told you, for I'll be bound it was something insubordinate, not to say libellous, besides having a lot of that unnatural Gaelic of his mixed up with it. What did Mrs. Midgeholme come to tell me? Don't say Ultima Ullapool has whelped, and she wants me to be god-father to one of the pups!"

"One of her bitches has, but I don't know if it was Ullapool. I wasn't attending all that closely. She says old Drybeck's going round trying to prove Miss Warrenby murdered her uncle, and you're not to believe a word he says. And also that that Pole of yours has told everyone he's got no intentions towards Miss Warrenby, but went up to Fox House after dinner last night, and sat with her in the summer-house. I don't know whether there might be something in that."

"I've already had that from Gladys. Taking everything into account, I should say young Ladislas went up to beg Jessica's First Prayer to lay off till all this commotion has blown over. He's got intentions all right, and he's scared white I should think so. Jessica's gone up to London, by the way. I saw young Haswell driving her to the station, so it looks as if she was catching the 12.15. She may be escaping from justice; on the other hand, she may have gone up to see her uncle's solicitors, to find out how she stands, and what she's to use for money till probate's been granted. In fact, that's why she has gone, according to what Gladys tells me, which is why I didn't arrest her. Let's hope that's the Superintendent!"

The telephone-bell was emitting a discreet buzzing noise. Harbottle picked up the receiver, listened for a moment, and said: "Yes, switch it through: he's here." He handed the receiver to Hemingway. "It is the Superintendent," he said.

CHAPTER FIFTEEN

IN the early part of the afternoon the police-car was once more proceeding along the Hawkshead-road. As Constable Melkinthorpe slowed to take the turn into Rushyford Farm, Hemingway said: "No, drive on slowly! If he's haymaking, I'll find him in one of his fields."

He was right. Melkinthorpe coasted gently along, and the sound of a hay-cutter soon came to their ears. The hay was being cut in one of the fields abutting on to the road, and Kenelm Lindale could be seen, standing talking to one of his farmhands.

Hemingway got out of the car. "You stay here, Horace," he said.

The Inspector, who had been expecting this, nodded. Almost bursting with curiosity, Constable Melkinthorpe slewed himself round in the driver's seat, and opened his mouth to speak. Then he shut it again. Something told him that an indiscreet question addressed to Inspector Harbottle would earn the enquirer nothing but a blistering snub. "Hot, 'sn't it, sir?" he said weakly.

The Inspector opened the newspaper he had brought with him, and began to read it. "It often is at this time of year," he replied.

Constable Melkinthorpe, lacking the courage to venture on any further remark, had to content himself with watching the Chief Inspector walk across the field towards Kenelm Lindale.

Lindale had seen him, but he did not go to meet him. After one glance, he resumed his conversation with the farmhand. As Hemingway came within earshot, he said: "Well, get on with that job first: I'll be along presently, and we'll take another look at it. Good afternoon, Chief Inspector! What can I do for you this time?"

"Good afternoon, sir. Sorry to come interrupting you, but I'd like a word with you, please."

"All right. I suppose you'd better come up to the house."

"Provided we can get out of range of the din this machine of yours makes, I'd just as soon talk to you here."

"Infernal things, aren't they?" Lindale said, walking beside him towards the blackthorn hedge which separated the field from the one beyond it. "Give me the old-fashioned methods! But it's no use, these days. Now, what is it you want?"

"I'm going to be quite frank with you, sir, and, if you're wise, you'll be frank with me. Because what I have to ask you

173

I can quite as easily ask Mrs. Lindale, which, I take it, you'd a lot rather I didn't do."

"Go on!" said Lindale evenly.

"Is Mrs. Lindale, properly speaking, the wife of a Francis Aloysius Nenthall, living at Braidhurst?"

There was a short silence. Lindale gave no sign that the question had startled him, but walked on beside the Chief Inspector, his face a little grim, his eyes fixed on the ground before him.

"Her maiden name," continued Hemingway, "having been Soulby, and the date of her marriage the 17th October, 1942."

Lindale looked up, a smouldering spark of anger in his eyes. "You could prove it so easily if I denied it, couldn't you?" he said bitterly. "Damn you! In the eyes of the law she is, but if Nenthall weren't a Catholic, and a coldblooded bigot on top of that, she'd be mine!"

"I don't doubt you, sir."

"How did you find this out?" demanded Lindale.

"We needn't go into that," replied Hemingway. "What I want to know——"

"Yes, we dam' well need!" interrupted Lindale. "I've got a right to know who told you! Unless someone tipped you off, you can't have had the slightest reason for suspecting it, and I want to know who it was who went ferreting out my private affairs!"

"Well, you do know, don't you, sir?" said Hemingway.

"Warrenby?" Lindale said, staring at him with knitted brows. "I've reason to think he knew—God knows how!—but he can't have told you! Unless—Have you come upon some blasted enquiry agent's report amongst his papers?"

"Is that what you expected?" Hemingway said swiftly.

"Good lord, no! What on earth should he do such a thing *for*? He once said something which showed me that he knew about Nenthall, but how much he knew, or how he knew it, I couldn't tell. I got under his skin one evening at the Red Lion —I couldn't stand the fellow, you know!—and he asked me if the name, Nenthall, conveyed anything to me. I said it didn't, and there the matter dropped. He never mentioned it again, and, so far as I know, he didn't spread any kind of scandal about us, which was what I was afraid he'd do. I didn't think anyone but he knew anything about us—though I do know that that Midgeholme woman has done her best to discover all the details of our lives!"

"I don't mind telling you, sir, that I've no reason to suppose that anyone does know it, at any rate down here, except me and my Inspector. And I should think I don't have to tell you that I shouldn't, unless I had to, make it public."

"No, I believe you wouldn't, but I can see how you might

174

very well have to make it public. I've been hoping to God you'd get on to the track of the man who did do Warrenby in before you started making enquiries into my past!"

"You say Warrenby never mentioned the matter to you but the once, sir. Quite sure of that?"

"Of course I'm sure of it! Are you thinking he was blackmailing me? He wasn't. I haven't anything he wants—money or influence. What is more, had he tried that on I shouldn't have hesitated to put the matter into the hands of the police. It isn't a crime to live with another man's wife: I'd nothing to fear from the police. I can only suppose that he found it out by some accident, and let me know he'd done so to pay me out for choking him off."

"Am I to take it, then, that the only use he made of his knowledge was to get off a bit of spite?"

Lindale was frowning. "It does sound improbable, put like that," he admitted. "It's the only use he did make of it. He may have had other ideas in mind, but what they were I can't for the life of me imagine. The impression I had was that he said it partly out of spite, and partly as a sort of threat—Accept-me-socially-or-I'll-make-trouble kind of thing."

"Which he could have done."

Lindale stopped, and said: "Look here, Chief Inspector, I'd better be quite open with you! As far as I'm concerned, Warrenby was welcome to tell the whole world all he knew. Neither my—neither Mrs. Nenthall nor I have done anything to be ashamed of. There was never any furtive intrigue. We—well, we cared for one another for years, and Nenthall knew it. She married him during the War, when she was only a kid, and—well, it just didn't work out! I'm not going to say anything about Nenthall, except that if I murdered anyone it would be him! There was a child, a little boy, which made it all impossible. My wife is a woman of very strong principles. Then the kid died—meningitis, and—I shan't take you into all that. She was ill for months, and then—well, we had it out, the three of us, and the end of it was that she came to me. There couldn't be a divorce, so nothing ever got into the papers. My own view is that it's a mistake to make any secret of the situation. People aren't anything like as hidebound as they used to be. Her family, of course, have cut her out: they're Catholics, and pretty strict; and my father disapproves. But I think that most people, knowing the facts, wouldn't ostracize us—none that we've the least desire to be on friendly terms with. That's my point of view, but I said I'd be open with you, and so I'll tell you that my wife doesn't share it. She believes that she's living in sin, poor girl. We're very happy—but there's always that behind. Which is why I'd do a lot to keep the whole thing secret. A lot, but not commit murder—though I don't expect you to believe

175

that. But whatever you believe, I'm dead sure you haven't enough evidence against me to justify an arrest! The bullet wasn't fired from my rifle, and I infer that you already know that, or you wouldn't be asking me questions: you'd be clapping handcuffs on me! Well, I quite see that you'll have to try to find out more, and I've no objection to that. All I do ask is that you'll refrain from worrying my wife. I won't have her driven into another nervous breakdown: she's been through enough!"

"Well, sir, I can't promise you anything," Hemingway replied, "but I don't mind saying that I shan't worry her, unless I must. I won't keep you any longer now: you'll be wanting to get back to your hay-cutting."

"Thanks!" Lindale said, turning, and walking with him towards the gate. "I shan't run away."

They parted at the gate. Constable Melkinthorpe, straining his ears, mananged to hear a snatch of dialogue, and found it disappointing.

"Well, you've got wonderful weather," Hemingway remarked.

"Couldn't be better. Touch wood!" said Lindale, shutting the gate behind him.

Hemingway crossed the road to the car. "Take a walk with me, Horace," he said. "You can drive the car round to the end of Fox Lane, Melkinthorpe, and wait for us there."

He led Harbottle to the entrance to the footpath, and turned into it.

"Well?" said Harbottle.

"He's no fool. In fact, he's very plausible."

"Too plausible?"

"No, I wouldn't say that. He didn't overplay his part at all. What he told me tallied with what the Superintendent gave me. He also said that as far as he was concerned the whole world could know the truth about him, and I'm inclined to believe him. The trouble is—and he told me this too, which may have been honesty, or may have been because he knew I was wise to it— Mrs. Lindale doesn't look at it like that."

"I'm not surprised," said Harbottle austerely.

"Now, don't let's have any psalm-singing!" said Hemingway, with a touch of irritability. "I've got a lot of sympathy for that chap. I should say life isn't all beer and skittles for him, with a wife—or whatever you like to call her, which I can guess, knowing you!—who can't get over thinking she's a black sinner. What's more, I don't suppose it ever will be—not unless Nenthall is obliging enough to pop off. And don't give me any stuff about the wages of sin!"

"I won't. But it's true, for all that," said the Inspector. "Is this the footpath he and the Squire came along together? I've never seen this end of it till today."

"It is, and it was about here that the Squire turned off into the plantation. I should say he did, too—either when he said he did, or a bit later. Perhaps both."

"Both?"

"Well, if he's the man I'm after, he had to park the rifle somewhere, hadn't he? Seems to me his own plantation would have been as good a place as any. Easy to have picked it up, and to have nipped back to Fox Lane when Lindale was out of sight."

"But the shot wasn't fired from his rifle," objected Harbottle.

"I know it wasn't. It may be that we shall have to pull in his agent's rifle, and his gamekeeper's as well."

Harbottle frowned over this. "I don't think the Squire's the man to commit a murder with another man's gun—and that man one of his own people," he said.

"Very likely you don't. You didn't think he was the kind of man to cheat his heir either."

"You don't yet know that he is doing that, sir. And I don't mind telling you *I* wouldn't want the job of accusing him of such a thing!"

"Well, you haven't got the job. Now, this is Mr. Haswell's spinney—separated from his garden by a wall, as you see. Any amount of cover to be had. We won't follow the path to his gates, but you can see where it runs and you can see that it would have been possible for Miss Warrenby to have got home by pushing through that very straggly hedge into her uncle's grounds."

The Inspector smiled wryly. "You're forgetting, sir, that you're not to believe a word Mr. Drybeck says."

"Well, I don't believe many of them," said Hemingway, climbing over the stile. "Come on! I've got a fancy to take another look at the scene of the crime."

Together they walked down the lane for some twenty yards, and then climbed the slope on to the common. Fox House had ceased to attract sightseers, and there seemed to be no one about. Hemingway paused by the gorse-clump, and stood looking thoughtfully at the gardens of Fox House. The seat had been removed, but a bare patch in the lawn showed where it had stood.

"I seem to remember that someone told me once you were by way of being a good shot, Horace," said Hemingway. "How does a man's head, at this range, strike you, as a target?"

The Inspector, whose modest home was made magnificent by the trophies which adorned it, appreciated this, and at once retorted: "It's wonderful, how you discover things no one else has ever heard of, sir! I *have* done a bit of shooting in my time, and I should consider it a certain target."

"All right, you win!" said Hemingway, grinning. "Would you call it a certain target for the average shot?"

"I think a man would need to be a good shot, but not necessarily a crack shot. I thought so when I first saw this place, and it's one reason why I've never seriously considered Miss Warrenby. I don't say women aren't good shots: I've known some who were first-class, but they're few and far between, and we've no reason to think Miss Warrenby has ever had a gun in her hand."

"It seems to rule Reg out too," said Hemingway. "Pity you didn't see his targets! I'm always trying to find something that'll give you a laugh."

"Are you ruling out the possibility of an accident as well?"

"For the lord's sake, Horace——! If a chap was standing here, do you see him firing into a man's garden, with the owner in full view?"

"No," admitted the Inspector. "It does seem unlikely." He glanced curiously at his chief. "What's in your mind, sir?"

"I'm wondering why the murderer fired from here, instead of trying for a closer shot. Unless he was a very good shot, I think it was chancy."

"There's the question of cover," the Inspector pointed out. "If he came from the stile, he couldn't have got a shot from the lane, without coming into Warrenby's sight. I took particular note of that. Those trees at that side of the lawn make it impossible for you to get a view of the seat until you're almost abreast of it. I should say that the murderer didn't cross the stile, but climbed up on to the common beyond it, and worked his way round under cover of the bushes."

"Why?" demanded Hemingway. "How did he know Warrenby would be sitting in the garden? On what we've heard about his habits, it wasn't likely."

The Inspector thought for a moment. "That's so. But there must be an answer, because one of the few things we know about this murder is that the shot *was* fired from where we're standing. We've got proof of that, so an answer there's got to be. I think I've got it, too. It's safe to assume that the murderer was proceeding pretty cautiously, isn't it? He didn't know where Warrenby would be, but he did know that all the sitting-room windows in the house look out this way. I don't see him walking along outside that low hedge to get to the gate, and running the risk of being seen by Warrenby. Once he saw there was no one in the lane, I should think he pretty well stalked the house, if you get my meaning. Probably kept down under cover of the hedge. He could have seen Warrenby like that, but he'd have had to stand up to get a shot at him. He'd want to take careful aim too, and it's not to be supposed Warrenby would have sat still to let him do it. My idea is that he did see him, and doubled back to the stile. In fact, the long range was forced on him just because Warrenby was in the garden."

"You may be right," Hemingway said.

"I can tell you don't think so, though."

"I don't know, Horace. It sounds reasonable enough. I've just got a feeling there was more to it than that. Come on! We'll take a look at Biggleswade's favourite seat."

They walked in a north-easterly direction, to where some silver-birch trees stood. Beyond them, the ground began to fall away more steeply, and a little way down the slope a wooden seat had been placed, commanding a good view over the common. It was not unoccupied. After one keen look, Hemingway said: "If it isn't old granddad himself! You'd better mind your p's and q's, Horace: he's inclined to be testy. Good-afternoon, Mr. Biggleswade! Taking the air?"

Mr. Biggleswade looked him over with scant favour. "And why shouldn't I be?" he demanded. "Tell me that!"

"I can't. What's eating you today, grandfather?"

"If I was your granddad you'd 'ave more sense nor wot you 'ave," said the old gentleman severely. "I'm disappointed in you, that's wot. You're gormless. If you'd paid attention to wot I says to you, you'd 've 'ad the bracelets on young Reg Ditchling last night."

"Don't you worry about him!" said Hemingway. "I've got my eye on him all right."

"A fat lot of use that is!" said Mr. Biggleswade. "You 'aving your eye on 'im don't stop 'im coming up to my place, calling me out of me name—ah, an' fetching 'is ma along of 'im, and that pair of screeching Jezebels, Gert and Edie, besides. Painted 'ussies, that's wot they are, and don't you let anyone tell you different! Oo's this you got with you?"

A rheumy gaze was bent upon Inspector Harbottle; a note of disparagement sounded in the aged voice. Hemingway said promptly: "You don't have to bother about him: he's just my assistant."

"Six foot of misery, that's wot 'e looks like to me," said Mr. Biggleswade, not mincing matters. "You don't want to let 'im get near the milk-cans. Wot's more, if you'd done wot I told you, you wouldn't need no assistant. Plain as I 'ear you now I 'eard that shot, Saturday!"

"You tell me some more about this shot," invited Hemingway, sitting down beside him. "How was it you only heard one shot?"

"Becos that's all there wos to 'ear."

"But young Reg tells me he fired a whole lot of shots."

" 'E'd tell you anything, young Reg would. Ah! and you'd swaller it!"

"Now, now! He was firing at targets, you know, in the Squire's gravel-pit."

"Oh, 'e wos, was 'e? If 'e'd told you 'e was firing at a 'erd of rhinorcerusses which 'e 'appened to find in Squire's gravel-pit, you'd swaller that too! Pleecemen! I never 'ad no opinion of 'em, and I ain't got none now, and I never will 'ave. Young Reg never fired no shot in Squire's gravel-pit. 'Cos why? 'Cos if 'e 'ad, no one wouldn't 'ear it this far off. Ah! and 'e couldn't 'ave got 'isself on to this 'ere path so soon as wot 'e did do. And I'll tell you another thing, my lad! I won't 'ave you taking my character away like you're trying to!"

"I shouldn't think you've much to take away," said Hemingway frankly. "Still, I wouldn't think of taking away what you've got left of it."

"Oh, yes, you would!" said Mr. Biggleswade fiercely. "And don't you give me no sauce! I'll 'ave you know there ain't any man in Thornden wot knows more about guns than wot I do, and I won't 'ave you spreading it about I don't know where a shot's being fired from! Over there's where Reg fired Vicar's rifle!" A trembling and gouty finger pointed in the direction of Fox Lane.

"All right," said Hemingway soothingly. "So what did you do?"

"I says to meself, Someone's larking about in Mr. 'Aswell's spinney, I says. There, or thereabouts," replied Mr. Biggleswade, nodding wisely.

"That's some way off, grandfather," Hemingway suggested.

"It 'ud 'ave 'ad to 'ave been a sight further off for me not to 'ear it," said Mr. Biggleswade, with a senile chuckle. "Very sharp ears I've got! A lot of people 'ave wished I didn't 'ear so quick when I was in me prime."

"I'll bet they did. You're a wonder, that's what you are, grandfather. It can't have made much of a noise, either, at this distance."

"No one never said it did. If you'd 'eard it, you wouldn't 'ardly 'ave noticed it, I dessay. And as for that walking tombstone o' yours, 'e'd 'ave thought it was a motor-car back-firing up on the 'Awks 'ead-road as like as not."

"Oh, no, I would not!" said Harbottle, stung into a retort.

"Shut up, Horace! Don't you pay any heed to him, grandfather! What happened after the shot? Did you see anyone besides Reg Ditchling?"

"No, I didn't. I wasn't going to go poking my nose into wot wasn't none of my business. I ain't a nasty, nosy pleeceman! I set off down this 'ere path, like I told 'Obkirk, and I 'adn't gorn so very far when I 'eard someone be'ind me, same like you'd 'ear one of them gamekeepers when 'e was trying to creep on you. And I looked round, quick-like, and I see young Reg 'iding be'ind one of the bushes."

"Down the other end of the path that was, wasn't it?"

"Right down the other end," corroborated Mr. Biggleswade.

180

"How long after you heard the shot would that have been?"

"Not more'n ten minutes or so. I don't get about so fast as wot I useter," said Mr. Biggleswade, flattered to find himself with an attentive audience at last. "And there was young Reg! If you'd 'ave paid more 'eed to wot I told you yesterday, you'd 'ave 'ad 'im safe under lock and key by this time."

"Well, I might," said Hemingway, getting up. "That is, if I knew what he was doing, hanging about the scene of the crime, instead of making his getaway."

"Ah! That's telling," said Mr. Biggleswade darkly.

"It is, isn't it? I shall have to be getting along now, grand-father. Don't you go sitting in the Red Lion till that daughter of yours has to come and drag you out! Nice goings on at your time of life!"

The ancient reprobate seemed pleased with this sally, and cackled asthmatically. Hemingway waved to him, and began to walk away. " 'Ere!" Mr. Biggleswade called after him. "Will I 'ave me pitcher in the papers?"

"That's telling too!" replied Hemingway over his shoulder.

"Rogues' gallery, I should think!" said Harbottle, falling into step beside him. "What on earth made you encourage him to hand you all that lip?"

"I don't mind his lip. I reckon he's entitled to cheek the police, when they haven't been able to catch up with him in ninety years. He's a very remarkable old boy, and a lot sharper than the silly fools who say he's getting soft in the head. I wanted to hear some more about that shot of his."

"Why?" demanded the Inspector.

"Because I think he did hear one."

"Well, what of it, sir? According to what you told me, what he heard couldn't have had any bearing on the case. It was an hour too early!"

"Horace, I told you only this morning I'd got a feeling the wrong end of the stick had been pushed into my hand, and that there's something important I haven't spotted. We're now going to have a look for it!"

CHAPTER SIXTEEN

"WHERE are we off to?" enquired the Inspector. "Fox House?"

"Out of the old gentleman's sight, for a start," Hemingway replied. "I want to think."

They reached the gorse-clump again, and Hemingway stopped. The Inspector watched him curiously, as he stood there, his quick, bright eyes once more taking in every detail of the scene before him. Presently he gave a grunt, and sat down on the slope above the lane, and pulled his pipe and his aged tobacco-pouch out of his pocket. While his accustomed fingers teased the tobacco, and packed it into the bowl of the pipe, his abstracted gaze continued to dwell first on the spot in the garden where the seat had stood, and then upon the stile, just visible round the bole of the elm-tree. The Inspector, disposing himself on the ground beside him, preserved a patient silence, and tried painstakingly to discover, by the exercise of logic, what particular problem he was attempting to solve. Hemingway lit his pipe, and sat staring fixedly at Fox House, his eyelids a little puckered. Suddenly he said: "The mistake we've been making, Horace, is to have paid a sight too much attention to what you might call the important features of this case, and not enough to the highly irrelevant trimmings. I'm not sure I've not precious near been had for a sucker."

"I've heard you say as much before, but I never heard that it turned out to be true," responded the Inspector.

"Well, it isn't going to be true this time—not if I know it! This operator is beginning to annoy me," said Hemingway briskly.

The Inspector was a little puzzled. "Myself, I hate all murderers," he said. "But I don't see why this one should annoy you more than any other—for it is not as if the case was a complicated one. It isn't easy, but that's only because we have too many possible suspects, isn't it? Taken just as a murder, I'd say it was one of the simplest I've ever handled."

"When you talk like that, Horace, I think I must be losing my flair. I ought to have spotted at the outset that it was much *too* simple."

"But you can't go against the facts, sir," argued the Inspector. "The man was shot in his own garden, by someone lying up beside these bushes, at about 7.15 or 7.20, according to Miss Warrenby's evidence. You can doubt that, but you can't doubt the evidence of the cartridge-case Carsethorn's men found under the bushes. The difficulty is that the murder happened to be committed just when half a dozen people who all of them had reasons for wanting Warrenby out of the way were scattered round the locality, in a manner of speaking, and couldn't produce alibis."

Hemingway had turned his head, and was looking at him, an alert expression on his face. "Go on!" he said, as the Inspector paused. "You're being very helpful!"

Harbottle almost blushed. "Well, I'm glad, Chief! It isn't often you think I'm right!"

"You aren't right. You're wrong all along the line, but you're clarifying my mind," said Hemingway. "As soon as you said that the murder happened to be committed while a whole lot of Warrenby's ill-wishers were sculling about at large, it came to me that there wasn't any 'happen' about it. That's the way it was planned. Go on talking! Very likely you'll put another idea into my head."

The Inspector said, with some asperity: "All right, sir, I will! I may be wrong all along the line, but it strikes me that's there's a hole to be picked in what you've just said. It can't have been planned. Not with any certainty. The murderer couldn't have known Warrenby would be in the garden at that exact time; that was just luck. He must have been prepared to go into the house, or at any rate into the garden, where he could have got a shot through the study-window, and when you consider how near he came to being seen by Miss Warrenby, as things turned out, you'll surely agree that there wasn't much planning about it. If he'd been forced to enter the garden, Miss Warrenby would have seen the whole thing. As I see it, he's got more luck than craft."

"Don't stop! It's getting clearer every minute!"

"Well, do you agree with me so far?" demanded Harbottle.

"Never mind about that! You can take it I don't, unless I hold up my hand."

"I see no sense in going on, if you don't agree with anything I say, sir."

"Well, I shouldn't see any sense in us sitting here agreeing with one another," returned Hemingway. "Where's that going to get us?"

"Look here, sir!" said Harbottle. "If we're going to assume that the murder was planned to take place when all the guests at that tennis-party were on their way home, then we've also got to assume that the murderer was banking on having all the luck he did have—which seems pretty inadequate planning to me! Why, it could have come unstuck in half a dozen places! To start with, he's got to do the job quick, because it cuts both ways, having a lot of people scattered near the scene: who's to say one of them won't come down the lane? You can say it's unlikely, but it might have happened. What was a dead certainty was that Miss Warrenby was bound to arrive on the scene at any moment. So he's got to reach the house ahead of her, shoot Warrenby, and get away without losing a second of time. What would have happened if Warrenby had gone upstairs, or into the back-garden? He must have faced that possibility! He must have thought, if he planned it, that he must allow himself quite a bit of time, in case of accidents."

"Quite true, Horace. So you think that he laid his preparations—by which I mean his rifle—on the off-chance that he'd get an opportunity to shoot Warrenby?"

There was a pause. "When you put it like that," said the Inspector slowly. "No, that won't do. But my arguments still hold!"

"They do," said Hemingway. "They're perfectly sound, and they do you credit. Our operator didn't want to be hurried over the job, and it's safe to assume he wasn't going to take any unnecessary risks."

"Then what's the answer?" said Harbottle.

"Warrenby wasn't shot at 7.15, nor anything like that time."

There was another pause, while the Inspector sat staring at his chief. He said at last: "Very well, sir. I can see several reasons for thinking you're wrong. I'd like to know what the reasons are for thinking you're right, because you haven't jumped to a conclusion like that simply because you want to make out the murder was carefully planned."

"I haven't jumped at all," replied Hemingway. "I've been adding up all those bits and pieces of information which didn't seem to lead anywhere. Taking it from the start, the doctor was what you might call vague on the time of Warrenby's death."

"Yes," conceded Harbottle. "I remember it was the first point you queried, when you were going through the case with the Chief Constable. But it didn't seem to matter much, and goodness knows Dr. Warcop isn't the only doctor we've come across who's more of a hindrance than a help to the police!"

"You're right: it didn't seem to matter. The mistake I made was in accepting as a fact that the time of the murder was fixed. To go on, the next thing was that I was given a highly significant piece of information by Miss Warrenby. She told me, the very first time I saw her, that her uncle very rarely sat out of doors. Well, I didn't pay any particular heed to that, because it didn't seem to matter any more than the doctor's evidence. There the corpse was, sitting in the garden, with a bullet through his left temple; and there the cartridge-case was, lying just were you'd expect to find it, supposing Warrenby had been shot while he was on that seat."

The Inspector sat up. "Are you going to say he wasn't shot in the garden at all?"

"I should think very likely he wasn't," replied Hemingway

coolly. "We'll hope he wasn't, because if we can prove he was actually shot somewhere else we shall have gone a long way to prove he wasn't shot at 7.15 either. He was probably shot an hour earlier. Which brings me to the third bit of seemingly irrelevant information, handed to me last night by old Father Time. Only, what with his daughter and Hobkirk telling me he was soft in his head, beside being Thornden's Public Enemy No. One, and it's standing out a mile that he had a spite against Reg Ditchling—not to mention the ambition he's got to have his picture in the papers on top of that—I'm bound to say I didn't set any store by anything he said. You know, Horace, it begins to look as though it's about time I retired. There doesn't seem to be anything I haven't missed."

"I was thinking, myself, that there doesn't seem to be anything you *have* missed," said the Inspector drily. "I remember, now that you bring it to my mind, that Miss Warrenby did say that about her uncle's habits, but I shouldn't have, if you hadn't brought it up."

"If you're going to start handing me bouquets, my lad, I shall know you've got a touch of the sun, and the next thing you'll know is that you're lying in hospital with an ice-pack on your head, or whatever it is they do to sunstroke cases," said his ungrateful superior. "Besides, you're putting me out. The last bit of information I was handed came from that blonde cook of Warrenby's—which was where I began to pull myself together, because I didn't miss that. And if Warrenby never went out in his slippers, or without his hat, it looks more than ever as though he wasn't killed out of doors."

"Yes," agreed Harbottle. "I see all that, but what I don't yet see is the point of it. It seems to me that there isn't any point at all. When you get a murder faked to look as if it was committed some time later than the actual time, it's generally done to give the murderer an alibi. I heard of a case where the shooting was done with a revolver that had a silencer fitted to it, and a few minutes later, when the murderer had established an alibi, a detonator went off, leading everyone to think that was the noise of the shot."

"I was on that case," said Hemingway.

"Were you, sir? Then you'll agree it isn't on all fours with this one. For one thing, no detonator makes a noise like a .22 rifle; for another, Miss Warrenby said she heard the sound of the bullet's impact; and for a third, the fake—if it was a fake— was fixed to take place when nobody had an alibi. Nobody, that is, except young Haswell, Miss Dearham, and Miss Patterdale. Well, neither Haswell nor the girl could have committed the murder an hour earlier, because they were both at The Cedars, playing tennis; and Miss Patterdale, I take it, we needn't consider. She's never been in the running. You can say

185

that for anything we know she shot Warrenby at 6.15, or there-abouts; but she certainly didn't fire the shot Miss Warrenby heard, and if she's found out a way of faking the sound of a rifle being fired, *and* the impact of its bullet, the whole thing timed to go off an hour after it's been set, she must be a master-criminal, instead of a respectable maiden lady without a stain on her character. Yes, and besides all that, the apparatus would have had to have been removed, and disposed of. Aside from the fact that the whole idea of such an apparatus is impossible——"

"You needn't keep on trying to convince me Miss Patterdale didn't do it," interrupted Hemingway. "And you needn't prove to me that the second shot couldn't have been fired automatically either, because I know that too. Even if such an apparatus were possible, the absence of just one crucial alibi rules it out. The second shot wasn't fired for that purpose. In fact, quite the reverse. It was fired so that you and I should have a nice lot of hot suspects to occupy our minds."

The Inspector considered, deeply frowning. "Yes," he acknowledged. "That's possible, I suppose. It certainly narrows the field, if you're right, Chief. If we're to assume that the time of the murder was between 6.0 and 6.30, we're left with Gavin Plenmeller, the Pole, Mr. Haswell, and, I suppose, the Vicar. Well, naturally, the first thing that comes to one's mind is that Plenmeller was absent from The Cedars at that time."

"Which gives him an additional reason for wanting to make it appear that the murder was committed a good deal later on," interpolated Hemingway.

"It does, of course. But there's a snag, sir. I'm willing to believe—though I can't say I like the idea—that at some time or other he parked a rifle where he could pick it up easily; I'm willing to believe he again parked it, after committing the murder. But what I can't believe is that he parked it a third time! He may be a cool customer, but it just isn't in human nature to leave the fatal weapon hidden in a ditch, or some such place—and there aren't any ponds he could have thrown it into—when you know the police are going to be on the spot, and searching thoroughly, within a matter of half an hour! Whoever did it must have got rid of the rifle where it wouldn't be found—which indeed he has done!—and Plenmeller didn't have enough time to do any such thing. If the chap who owns the Red Lion is to be believed, and I don't see any reason for disbelieving him, Plenmeller was in his bar-parlour round about 7.30 to 7.45. I grant you he could have reached the Red Lion from here in that time, but that's all he could have done. And limp or no limp, you aren't going to tell me he sat in the Red Lion with a rifle stuck down his trouser-leg! You'll remember, too, that the landlord told Carsethorn he'd stayed to dinner there. Where was the rifle all that time? And whose rifle was it? We know it wasn't his own!"

Hemingway regarded him with a half-smile. "You know, Horace, there's no pleasing you at all," he said. "First, nothing will do for you but to pin this crime on to Plenmeller, and now, when it begins to look as if we might be able to do it, you turn round and argue that he couldn't have done it!"

"Now, that's not fair, Chief!" Harbottle protested. "You know very well I don't want to pin it on to anyone but the right man! All I said was that as far as appearances go he seems to me a more likely murderer than any of the others, except, perhaps, that chap Lindale. I daresay he wouldn't stick at much, but for the purposes of this argument he's out of it. I don't see how Plenmeller could have got rid of the rifle, but I do see that it wouldn't have been difficult for any one of the other three to have done so. The Vicar—mind you, I'm not saying it was him, and I don't think it was, either—the Vicar wasn't at The Cedars after 6.0, so he might have committed the murder at 6.15; and as we don't know what he was doing after he left that sick parishioner of his he might possibly have fired your second shot. Since he could have got into the grounds of Fox House from his own meadow, there would have been very little fear of his being seen; and he had all the time in the world to dispose of the rifle."

"The only difficulty being that his rifle wasn't in his possession at the time," said Hemingway. "However, the rifle is the stumbling-block in every instance, so I won't press that point."

"I've nothing more to say about the Vicar. You've met him, and I haven't. What I do think is that we can't rule out Ladislas any longer. He told you that he didn't know anything about that tennis-party. That might be true, or it might not. My experience of a place like this is that everyone knows when someone's giving a party. Say he did know! All right! He shoots Warrenby, realizes he's bound to be suspected, and so hangs about until he hears someone coming. He may even have sneaked along the common to watch the footpath, knowing that several people were likely to leave The Cedars by the garden-gate. He's got a motor-bike; his landlady was out that evening: what was to stop him driving off anywhere he pleased—perhaps to the river—and getting rid of the rifle?"

"What rifle?" asked Hemingway, all polite interest.

"I don't know. One of those we haven't checked up on, probably."

"What made him wait for three-quarters of an hour before shooting Warrenby? We know he was seen turning into Fox Lane at 5.30; if Crailing's to be believed, Father Time turned up at the Red Lion at about 6.30, which means that he must have heard the shot he did hear at about 6.15, or a few minutes earlier. I agree that the murderer didn't want to have to do the job in a hurry, but three quarters of an hour seems to me a long time to wait."

"Well, from your description of him, he sounds a temperamental, nervy sort of a chap," offered the Inspector. "Perhaps he couldn't make up his mind to do it straight off."

"Rotten!" said Hemingway. "If that's the way it was, and he'd hung about, trying to summon up enough resolution to pull the trigger, he'd have gone off home without pulling it at all!"

"There might be some other explanation."

"There might. What happened to his motor-bike all this time? Did he leave it standing in the lane for nearly two hours, just to make sure anyone that happened to have passed that way would know he must be somewhere around?"

"Of course not. He might have hidden it amongst the bushes on the common. Taken it up the path that goes to the seat where we found Biggleswade."

"Talk sense! You try and hide a motor-bike amongst a lot of bushes! That old sinner would have spotted it like a flash!"

"By the time he reached the place Ladislas would have retrieved it, and ridden off," returned the Inspector.

"Then Father Time would have heard the engine starting up, and he hasn't said a word about hearing any such thing."

"That isn't to say he didn't hear it. He's out to make a case against Reg Ditchling, and that would spoil it."

"All right, I'll concede you that point. There's this to be said in favour of suspecting Ladislas: he had a motive we don't need a strong microscope to see. What about Haswell?"

"There isn't enough about him, and, if you'll forgive me saying so, sir, that's the trouble. We don't really know where he was, or what he was doing, up till eight o'clock, when he got home."

"What we do know, though, is that he was driving himself in his car. If I've got to choose between a car and a motor-bike, I'll try and hide the motor-bike, thank you very much!"

"There must be *some* place where either could be hid," said the Inspector obstinately. "The more I think of it, the more I'm convinced transport was needed." He paused, and said suddenly: "What about the dead man's own garage? It's a double one: I noticed that. What was to stop him, as soon as he'd shot Warrenby, from driving his car in, and leaving it there until Miss Warrenby had run off to fetch Miss Patterdale?"

"And what little bird told him that's what she would do?" enquired Hemingway. "You *have* got a touch of the sun, Horace! What anyone would expect her to do was to have rung up for the police, or the doctor, not to lose her head, and go careering off as she did!"

188

"I don't know about that," said Harbottle defensively. "Girls do lose their heads, after all!"

"They do, and not only girls either. But when that happens you can't guess *what* they'll do, far less bank on them choosing any particular one of four or five silly antics!"

"No," Harbottle admitted. "Come to think of it, sir, it's funny she did lose her head, isn't it? She seems to me one of the self-possessed kind."

"No, I don't think it is," Hemingway replied. "In fact it's what I should have expected her to do. Nasty jolt for a girl who kids herself into believing that all is love and light. She was rocked right off her balance." He knocked his pipe out lightly, and got up. "Come on, now! It's no use us arguing who might have fired that shot at 6.15 until we're sure there was a shot at that time. And if there was, then what was our operator aiming at when he fired the second shot an hour later?"

The Inspector looked gloomy. "As well look for a needle in a haystack! He probably fired it into the ground." He saw Hemingway cock a quizzical eyebrow at him, and said hastily: "No, not the ground! Not if Miss Warrenby heard the impact!"

"Just in time, Horace!" remarked Hemingway. "You and your knowledge of guns! And I don't think we need go round looking for a likely haystack. What we've got to remember is that what we've all been thinking was a narrow shave for our operator was just as carefully planned as the rest of it. He wanted Miss Warrenby on the spot as a witness; he wanted the shot to sound natural; and he didn't want the bullet to be found. Well, the only safe targets I can see are the trees. Plenty of them across the lane, in the grounds of Fox House, but they're too far off to be dead-certain targets. Putting myself in his place, I should have aimed for the elm-tree. It's the only tree on this side of the lane with a big enough trunk for the purpose. Let's go and take a look at it!"

They descended into the lane, and walked up it a few yards to where the elm-tree stood. The Inspector glanced back at the gorse-bushes, silently calculating. "You're not looking high enough, Chief," he said. "If it's there, I should expect to find it a good ten feet above the ground."

"You would?" said Hemingway, staring up the bole of the tree. "You're very good, Horace: what do you make of that graze!"

The Inspector strode quickly to his side, and gazed up at a gleam of pale colour where a small splinter had been chipped from the tree-trunk. There was a good deal of surprise in his face, not unmixed with awe. "Well, I'll be——! I do believe you're right, sir!" he exclaimed.

"Well, don't say it in that tone of voice! What we want now
189

is a ladder, or a pair of steps. Got a knife on you, Horace?"

The Inspector nodded. "Yes, I've got that, but where do we find the steps?"

"We'll borrow them from the house," said Hemingway. "That is, if Gladys is in. If she's got the afternoon off, we'll see if there's a ladder in the gardener's shed."

"It'll be locked," prophesied the Inspector. "And if you ask that girl for a ladder she'll be bound to come and watch what we do with it."

"She won't, because I shall keep her in the kitchen, asking her a whole lot of silly questions."

They walked up the straight path which led from the trades-men's gate to the back-door. The sound of loud music seemed to indicate that Gladys had not got the afternoon off, but was listening to Music While You Work, turned on at full blast. So it proved. Gladys was polishing the table-silver, and came to the door with the leather in one hand. The manner of her greeting to Hemingway led the Inspector to infer that his chief had not scrupled to charm and to flatter her at their previous encounter. He cast a sardonic glance at Hemingway, but that gentleman was already engaged in an exchange of badinage. Beyond saying: "Whatever do you want a ladder for?" Gladys raised no demur at lending her employer's property to the police. She gave Harbottle the key to the gardener's shed, warning him that if he didn't put the ladder back where he found it the gardener wouldn't half raise Cain on the morrow, and invited Hemingway to step into the kitchen, and have a cup of tea. The kettle, she said, was just on the boil. When the Inspector reappeared, some fifteen minutes later, he interrupted a promising tête-à-tête, and it did not seem to him that his superior had found it necessary to ask his hostess any questions, silly or sensible. Gladys sat on one side of the table, both her elbows planted on it, and a cup of very strong and very sweet tea held between her hands, and as the Inspector came in she was giggling, and telling Hemingway that he was a one, and no mistake. "If my Bert was to hear you, I don't know what he wouldn't do!" she said.

"Ah!" said Hemingway, briefly meeting the Inspector's eyes over her head. "If I was a marrying man, I'd cut your Bert out!"

"Sauce!" said Gladys, greatly delighted. She looked over her shoulder at Harbottle, and added, politely, but without enthusiasm, "Would your friend like a cuppa?"

"No, he never drinks it," said Hemingway, rising to his feet. "Besides, two's company, and three's none. Now, I've just got to check up on one or two points. Any objection to my going into the study?"

Gladys glanced at the clock. "Fat lot of good it would be to start objecting to you policemen!" she remarked. "I don't mind, but can't you wait a bit? It's just on the quarter, and I can't miss Mrs. Dale's Diary. Sit down, the pair of you, and listen to it! It's ever so nice."

"No, we mustn't do that, because we've got to get back to Bellingham," said Hemingway. "There's no need for you to come with us to the study, though. You stay here and listen-in! I'll see the Inspector doesn't go pinching anything."

"You haven't half got a nerve! More likely him as'll keep an eye on you, I should think! You won't go turning the room upside-down, will you?"

Hemingway assured her that he would preserve apple-pie order in the room, and as, at that moment, a voice suddenly announced: "Mrs. Dale's Diary: a recording of the daily happenings in the life of a doctor's wife," she temporarily lost interest in him, and turned the face of a confirmed addict towards the radio.

The two men quietly withdrew, and went along the passage at the back of the house to the hall.

"You found it?" Hemingway said.

The Inspector opened his hand, disclosing a small piece of lead.

"Now we *are* getting somewhere!" said Hemingway. "We'll send that off to town for comparison with the one that was dug out of Warrenby's head. Knarsdale can take it up tonight."

"I wish I thought there was a hope of finding the cartridge-case of that one," said the Inspector.

"Well, there isn't, and I should say there never was. Our operator didn't leave much to chance. We were meant to find the one under the gorse-bush. We weren't meant to find the other, and we shan't."

He led the way into the study as he spoke, leaving the door open, so that he could hear any approaching footsteps.

"Over by the desk!" he said briefly. "He was probably shot while he was sitting behind it. There wouldn't have been much blood, but there must have been some."

"There was none on the papers we found on the desk," Harbottle reminded him. "And I see no sign of any on the desk itself."

"The top of it, according to young Haswell, and to Carse-thorn, was littered over with papers. I don't doubt they got spattered, and were carefully removed. We'll get Warrenby's clerk to go through the lot I took away: he may know if anything's missing. Try the window-curtains, and the woodwork of the window! I want to have a good look at the carpet."

The carpet was a thick Turkey rug, with a groundwork of red, and a sprawling pattern of blue and green. On his hands and knees, Hemingway said: "Fresh blood falling on this wouldn't show up. He might have missed it. A couple of spots is all I ask for!"

"There's nothing on the curtains," the Inspector informed him. "However, they hang well clear of the long window, so there might not be." He too dropped on to his knees and closely studied the floor-boards. "You'd expect to see a sign on the floor, though."

"The murderer must have looked to see, and if there was blood on any of the woodwork he'd have wiped it carefully. May have tied something round Warrenby's head before he moved him. Come here, and tell me what you make of this!"

The Inspector went to him, took the magnifying-glass held out to him, and through it stared at two very small spots on the carpet which showed darker than the surrounding red. "Might be," he grunted.

"Cut 'em off!" commanded Hemingway. "It's a lucky thing it's one of these shaggy rugs. Give me that glass again."

With its aid, he presently discovered another stain, fainter and rather larger, as though it had been smeared over. "And I think that proves my theory, Horace," he said cheerfully.

"If the stains turn out to be bloodstains," amended his cautious assistant, putting the tufts he had sawn off into the match-box Hemingway was holding out to him.

"That'll be a job for Dr. Rotherhope," said Hemingway. "They look remarkably like it to me." He glanced at the desk. "And it accounts for the fountain-pen left with its cap off," he remarked. "I ought to have paid more attention to that when Carsethorn told me that's how he found it. Come on! that sounds like my blonde coming to look for me!"

CHAPTER SEVENTEEN

THE two detectives, walking down the lane towards the Trindale-road, came within sight of Fox Cottage, and saw that an animated group was gathered at its gate. For the animation, what, at first glance, appeared to be a pride of Pekes was responsible. Closer inspection revealed that only five of the Ultimas were present, four of them harnessed on couplings, and winding themselves round their owner's legs, and the fifth, in whose stately mien Hemingway recognized Ulysses, the patriarch, unrestrained by a leash. Young Mr. Haswell's car was parked in the lane, but he and Mrs. Midgeholme both stood outside the gate. On the other side of it, and leaning on its top bar, were Miss Patterdale, wearing an overall and gardening-gloves, and her niece, looking remarkably pretty in a pink linen frock and an enormous and floppy sunhat. All four were engaged in discussion, Mrs. Midgeholm's demeanour being particularly impressive; and none of them noticed the approach of the detectives until Ulysses attracted attention by stalking up the lane towards the newcomers, and uttering a threatening bark.

"Now, what's the matter with you, old High and Mighty? Nice way to greet your friends!" said Hemingway, stooping to pat Ulysses.

Ulysses's eyes started with indignation at this familiarity. He growled, but he was not a dog of hasty disposition, and before proceeding to extreme measures he sniffed the Chief Inspector's hand, and realized that here was, if not a friend, at least a bowing acquaintance. His mighty mane sank, he slightly waved his tail, and sneezed.

"Isn't he the cleverest old fellow?" exclaimed Mrs. Midgeholme. "He knows you quite well!"

Her voice was drowned by frantic pleas from the four other Ultimas to their progenitor not to be taken in by the police. Ulysses, looking scornfully at them, gave further evidence of his sagacity by placing himself in a position clearly inviting the Chief Inspector to scratch his back. Hemingway very obligingly did so, while Mrs. Midgeholme unwound the other Ultimas, and besought them to be quiet.

"I guessed I should find you here," she told Hemingway. "I saw the police-car just round the corner, waiting, and I put two and two together and deduced that you were visiting the scene of the crime. So I thought I'd just pop down on the off-chance of running into you."

"Don't be a fool, Flora!" said Miss Patterdale trenchantly.

"You don't suppose the Chief Inspector wants to listen to all these idiotic theories of yours, do you? You'd be better advised to pop home, and take a look at that new litter of yours. My father once had a field spaniel who buried her first pups alive. You can't be too careful."

"My treasured Ullapool!" said Mrs. Midgeholme indignantly. "She's the most wonderful little mother! Beautiful pups, too! Tell it not in Gath, but I have a feeling that one of the dogs is going to be as big a prize-winner as Ulysses."

"I've thought of a jolly good name for you," offered Charles. "Call him Uzziah!"

Mrs. Midgehome seemed a little doubtful. The Chief Inspector said judicially: "I don't say it's a bad name, but to my way of thinking there's a better. I lay awake for a good hour last night, trying to remember it. It came in a rattling good yarn I read when I was a boy—before your time, I expect, sir. Umslopogaas!"

"Before my time nothing!" retorted Charles. "Every right-minded person knows his Rider Haggard! Damn! Why didn't I think of that? It's terrific!"

Mrs. Midgeholme, though gratified that the Chief Inspector should have expended so much thought on the Ultimas, was plainly not enamoured of the name. She said that if she bred black Pekes she might think about it; and she was just about to explain to the company her reasons for not breeding black Pekes when Miss Patterdale put a summary end to the discussion by saying with a snort: "And then call one of the bitches Ullalume, and be done with it! I don't know whether the Chief Inspector wants to waste his time choosing absurd names for your dogs, Flora, but I'm not going to waste any more of mine. I'm going to get on with my weeding."

She then favoured Hemingway with a curt nod, and strode off to where she had left her trug and gardening-fork.

Mrs. Midgeholme looked a trifle disconcerted, but laughed, and said: "Dear old Miriam! I always say, Abby, that your aunt is *quite* a character. But, of course, it wasn't the Ultimas I wanted to see you about, Chief Inspector. I did *hope* to catch you this morning, but it was not to be. You got my message?"

This question, uttered in a somewhat suspicious tone, seemed to be addressed as much to Harbottle as to Hemingway, and it was he who answered it, at his most wooden.

"Now, I know perfectly well that you think I'm interfering," said Mrs. Midgeholme, upon receiving his assurance, "but what I feel is that anyone who *lives* in Thornden is bound to know more about all the people than a stranger. You see what I mean?"

"Yes, but you can't have it both ways," interpolated Charles, evidently continuing an interrupted argument. "Old Drybeck

194

was born and bred here, so why shouldn't the Chief Inspector listen to him as much as to you?"

"Oh, that's ridiculous!" she replied. "You can't possibly count him! And, anyway, that wasn't what I was going to say. No. The thing is, I've just been giving my angels a run on the common, Chief Inspector, and I met that dreadful old man, Biggleswade, and he told me *all* about what he thinks happened on Saturday. Well, of course, it's nonsense to suppose young Ditchling had anything to do with it, because anyone who knows the family could tell you at once that they're all above suspicion. I don't mind saying that my first thought was he was lying."

"'Lied in every word,'" corrected Charles, grinning. "'That hoary cripple, with malicious eye'—I can't remember how it goes on, but it's exactly right! There's something about way-laying the traveller with his lies, too. 'If at his counsel I should turn aside Into that—something—tract'—No, I can't remember how it went on, but it's Biggleswade all right!"

"What on earth are you drivelling about?" asked Abby.

"I'm not drivelling, I'm quoting. Browning."

"Oh! 'Just for a handful of silver he left us,'" said Abby showing her erudition.

"Absolutely!" agreed Charles, his eyes dancing.

"I don't know anything about Browning," said Mrs. Midgeholme impatiently, "but, as I say, I did think at first that Biggleswade was making the whole thing up. And then it came to me in a flash!"

She paused dramatically, and Hemingway, finding that she was looking in a challenging way at him, said, with an air of interest: "It did?"

"He was going by the Church clock!" said Mrs. Midgeholme triumphantly. "Summertime, you know! It's never changed so it's an hour wrong. So when *he* thought the time was 6.15, it was really an hour later!"

It was apparent that Abby, Charles, and Inspector Harbottle were all wrestling with an unspoken problem. It was Harbottle who first reached a conclusion. "*Earlier!*" he said.

"No, she's right," said Charles. "Later!"

"Wait a bit!" commanded Abby. "Do we put the clocks *on,* or *back*?"

"Go on, Horace!" said Hemingway encouragingly. "Which?"

"On," said Charles positively. "So if the Church clock says 6.15, it's really 7.15. By summertime, I mean. So Mrs. Midgeholme *is* right."

"Well, I'm glad we've settled that point," said Hemingway. "But I don't myself see that old boy making any mistake about opening-time. Not but what I'm very grateful to Mrs. Midgeholme for the trouble she's taken. I shall have to be getting along now, but——"

"What, don't you want to hear the rest of our theories?" said Charles, shocked. "I've worked out a very classy one; Miss Dearham has proved hers up to the hilt; Gavin Plenmeller's latest proves *he* did it, but it's too ingenious; the Squire has practically settled that the murder was committed by——"

"What, has the Squire gone in for detection too?" demanded Hemingway.

"Of course he has! Everyone in Thornden has! The Squire's idea is that the murderer was a Bellingham man, who came out by car or motor-cycle, hid same in his gravel-pit, and then lay up in the gorse-bushes until the right moment."

"And what's your own theory, sir?"

"No, no!" Charles replied, laughing. "*I'm* not going to do your job for you! *Or* get myself sued for uttering slanders!"

"Perhaps you're right," agreed Hemingway.

"I wish I could ginger Mavis up to sue Mr. Drybeck!" said Abby, with feeling.

"Good lord, you haven't told her he thinks she did it, have you?" exclaimed Charles.

"*I* didn't tell her, but someone did. She said she would rather not talk about it, and one had to make allowances, and she was sure he didn't mean to hurt her feelings."

"That girl is really a saint!" declared Mrs. Midgeholme. "She may be exasperating, but you have to admit that she's an example to us all!"

The Chief Inspector was amused to perceive, from their expressions, that the example set by Miss Warrenby was not one which either Charles or Abby meant to follow. He took his leave of the party, and went away with Harbottle to where the car awaited them.

"What do you suppose they were doing up at Fox House?" said Abby, watching the two detectives turn the corner into the main road.

"Probably having another look at the terrain," said Charles.

"I only hope they haven't been pumping Gladys," said Mrs. Midgeholme worriedly. "You know what servants are! She'd be bound to make the most of every little unpleasantness there had ever been in the house, and what with all, on top of Thaddeus Drybeck's really *wicked* attempt to throw suspicion on poor Mavis, I'm very much afraid the police may be thoroughly misled. Well! I've done *my* best, and I can't do more! Come along, Ulysses! Home to Father!"

Charles, watching with approval Ulysses's first assumption of deafness and subsequent leisurely progress in Mrs. Midgeholme's wake, said: "I like that dog. He knows what is due to his own dignity. All the same, I'm damned if I'd put up with being called his father." He turned his head, and looked down at Abby. "You stood me up yesterday: what about running down to Filey Cove now?"

"Don't you ever do any *work*?" asked Abby provocatively.

"I do a great deal of work. I've been out on an important job this very afternoon. If you need reassurance, I shan't get the sack for not returning to the office. I'm a full partner, let me tell you! No, you don't!"

Miss Dearham, about to retire strategically, found her right wrist clamped suddenly to the top of the gate, and at once protested. She said that Charles was hurting her arm, upon which he lifted her wrist and kissed it. Much shaken, she could think of nothing to say, but, blushing, adorably, peeped up at him under the huge brim of her hat. Charles, quick to seize opportunity, kissed her in good earnest.

"What on earth are you doing?" demanded Miss Patterdale, suddenly emerging from her little potting-shed, and screwing her monocle into her eye, the better to observe her young friends.

"Asking Abby to marry me," responded Charles brazenly, one arm round Abby's shoulders, his other hand still clasping her maltreated wrist.

"Nonsense! You don't ask a girl to marry you in front of her aunt!"

"I've already made several attempts to ask her to marry me *not* in front of her aunt, but you always turn up just as the words are hovering on my tongue!" Charles retorted.

Miss Patterdale looked suspiciously from one flushed face to the other. "Well, I don't know what the world's coming to, I'm sure!" she said. "Kissing and cuddling across my garden-gate! If you really *are* going to marry Abby you'd better come inside, and stop making a public exhibition of yourself! Or are you pulling my leg?"

"Certainly not!" said Charles, affronted. "You don't suppose I'd kiss Abby across your gate, or anyone else's, if I didn't hope to marry her, do you?"

"As far as I can make out," said Miss Patterdale, "you're all so promiscuous these days that it would be unwise to suppose anything! *Are* you going to marry her?"

Charles looked at Abby. "Am I, my only love?"

"Yes," said Abby. "If—if you think we could make a do of it, I'd like to—awf'ly!"

"Well, if that's a proposal I'm glad I never received one!" said Miss Patterdale. "However, it'll give you both something to think of besides meddling in a murder-enquiry, so I daresay it's a good thing. I'll go and put the kettle on for tea."

"That," said Charles, releasing his betrothed, and opening the gate, "I take to be an invitation and a general blessing.

197

That's better! Now I can kiss you properly! To hell with the murder! Who cares?"

Miss Dearham returned his embrace with fervour, but said, as soon as she was able to say anything: "As a matter of fact, I've rather lost interest in it, too. Though I *should* like to know what those detectives were doing up the lane, and what they're up to now."

They were, in fact, being driven back to Bellingham; and as neither placed any great reliance on Constable Melkinthorpe's discretion, their conversation would scarcely have interested Miss Dearham. It was not until they had been set down at the police-station, and Inspector Harbottle had given the deformed bullet he had dug out of the elm-tree into the safe-keeping of Sergeant Knarsdale, that the murder of Sampson Warrenby was even mentioned. The Sergeant said: "That looks like a .22 bullet all right. Well, if the rifle wasn't the last you brought in, sir, I'm blessed if I know what to make of it!"

"What we found out this afternoon puts an entirely different complexion on things," said Hemingway. "You get going, Knarsdale! I want the report on that little fellow as soon as I can get it! Horace, ask the chaps here for the Firearms Register, and bring it along to me!"

When the Inspector presently entered the small office, he found his superior sorting the papers that had been taken from Sampson Warrenby's desk. He said, as he put them aside: "We must have Coupland on to these. There's one letter which seems to be written in answer to something I can't yet find, but it's a job for him, not for me. Got the Register? Good!"

"I don't know if you think I may have missed a .22 rifle, sir," said Harbottle, somewhat starchily, "but I can tell you now I made a list of every one within a radius of twenty miles of Thornden."

"Thirty-seven of them, which I never had any interest in, and never shall," said Hemingway. "I wish you'd pull yourself together, Horace! Up till today we've never considered any weapon *but* a rifle, because the range seemed to make it certain it could only have been a rifle shot. Which is another of the things we were meant to think. We've now got every reason to believe Warrenby was shot at much closer range, and I want to know just what lethal weapons there are in the neighbourhood."

"Carsethorn said something about the Major's army revolver, but that won't do, because——"

"Of course it won't! It's the wrong calibre! Stop trying to annoy me!" said Hemingway, opening the register.

Silence reigned for a few minutes. Suddenly Hemingway looked up. "We're getting warmer, Horace. I find here that when his firearms permit was last renewed, a couple of years back, the late Walter Plenmeller had a .22 Colt Woodsman

Automatic Pistol in his collection. Which, let me tell you, was not in the gun-cabinet at Tornden House. Now then!"

The Inspector came quickly round the corner of the desk to stare down at the entry.

"Could you carry a gun like that without anyone's knowing it?" demanded Hemingway.

"I suppose it could be done," admitted Harbottle. "But— Good Lord, sir, *what for?*"

"Seems to me it's time we did a little research into Plenmeller's affair," said Hemingway, rather grimly.

"Yes, I see we shall have to, but what I'm thinking is that no one here knows anything against him. And I can't help feeling that if there was anything we should have been told fast enough. People don't like him, and the way they've all been searching for clues and motives you'd have expected several of them to have sicked us on to him, wouldn't you?"

"No, I wouldn't. Whatever it was that Warrenby found out—if that was the motive for his murder—you can bet your life it was something no one else knew anything about. That's obvious."

"You're thinking Warrenby may have tried to blackmail him? That wasn't what was in my head, sir. To my mind, it was more likely he did Plenmeller some sort of an injury—because Plenmeller's the type of man who might easily kill out of sheer, wicked revenge. Only I haven't discovered a trace of anything like that. What's more, I put it to you, Chief, would he have gone round telling people he must take steps to get rid of Warrenby if he'd meant to shoot him? That's the last thing a murderer does!"

"Yes, my lad," said Hemingway, in a dry voice. "And that's something he knows quite as well as you do. If he's the man I'm looking for, then I freely hand it to him! He's been remarkably clever. The killing wasn't done in some highly ingenious way that might have made us pay particular attention to a man who spends his life writing detective problems; he didn't try to fake an alibi for himself; he's told me and everyone else that he hated Warrenby's guts; and he's even told us all that he's quite capable of murdering someone—which I never doubted. He's even managed to stay as cool as a cucumber throughout, which isn't usual. That's probably because he's got a very good opinion of himself, and thinks he's far too clever for me to catch up with."

"You don't think he could have done it just because he did hate Warrenby, do you?" asked the Inspector.

"No, I don't. Hating Warrenby was a lot more likely to make him think up ways of getting under his skin. Which I've a strong notion he did do. Warrenby wouldn't like that. We know what happened when he got a snub from Lindale. I'll bet he had worse to put up with from Plenmeller!"

"Now, wait a bit, Chief!" protested the Inspector. "If Warrenby was blackmailing him, he wouldn't have dared get under his skin!"

Hemingway shook his head. "I don't think it was ordinary blackmail. He hadn't anything Warrenby could want any more than Lindale had. But we know from what his clerk told us that Warrenby liked to find things out about people. He said you never knew when it might come in handy—and in the meantime it gave him a nice feeling of power. I should say he didn't really mean to let on to Lindale he knew what his secret was: he lost his temper, and out it came. Well, now, supposing he did know something to Plenmeller's discredit? Do you imagine he'd put up with Plenmeller being rude to him, shoving spokes in his wheel, and running him down to all and sundry if he could bring him to heel just by telling him that he knew what his secret was? If you ask me, Horace, he'd have thoroughly enjoyed lowering Plenmeller's crest! Anyone would, for that matter! Only that's where he slipped up: Plenmeller isn't the type it's safe to blackmail."

"That may be," agreed Harbottle, "but I'd also say he isn't the type you could blackmail easily! I mean, from the way he talks you'd think the chances are he'd be more likely to boast of having done something wrong than to try to keep it dark! Well, I ask you, sir! Look at the brazen way he told us he'd driven his brother to his death!"

"As a matter of fact," said Hemingway slowly, "I was thinking of that. All things considered, I believe I'll take a look at that case. Did you read the whole of it?"

"The inquest on Walter Plenmeller? I haven't read any of it—barring the letter he left."

Hemingway looked at him with a gathering frown. "What, didn't you even glance over the report? What made you pick the letter out?"

The Inspector blinked. "That's all there was. I found it in one of the tin boxes. I haven't been through any of the Coroner's records."

"Do you mean to tell me," said Hemingway, "that Warrenby had taken that letter out of the proper file, and put it amongst his own papers?"

"Yes, I suppose he must have, sir. I don't really know what they do with the reports on inquests. As Warrenby *was* the Coroner, I didn't make much of it, except to wonder whether he wanted that letter to taunt Plenmeller with, perhaps."

"Next time you find a document like that where it has no business to be perhaps you'll be so good as to tell me!" said Hemingway wrathfully. "I thought you'd been running through that case!" He pulled open a drawer in the desk, and turned over the papers it contained.

A good deal chagrined, the Inspector said: "I'm sorry, sir. But there was nothing *to* the case! I had a talk with Carsethorn about it, and it was a straight case of suicide all right."

Hemingway had found the letter, and was re-reading it. "Then what made Warrenby take this letter out of the record? Don't talk nonsense to me about wanting to taunt Plenmeller with it! Much he'd have cared! It must already have been read aloud in court!"

"After what Coupland said to us, sir, I only thought it was rather typical of the man to want to get his hands on something to Plenmeller's disadvantage. Which, to my way of thinking, it is, because it shows him up to be a heartless sort of man, deliberately getting on his brother's nerves. But I'm sure I'm very sorry."

"All right. I ought to have asked you where you found it. Get me that file! If the office is shut, find out where Coupland lives, and——"

"You needn't worry, sir: I'll get it," interrupted the Inspector, his back very rigid.

"And find out if the Chief Constable's in the building! If he is, I'd like a word with him, at his convenience."

A few minutes later, he was informed by the Sergeant on duty that Colonel Scales had come in a little while earlier, to do some business with the Superintendent, and had left a message in the charge-room that he would like to see the Chief Inspector before he left the police-station. "He says, would you go right in, sir?"

Colonel Scales was just nodding dismissal to a very stout Superintendent when Hemingway went to his room, and he said: "Come in, and sit down, Hemingway! Glad to hear you want to see me: I hope it means you've got something?"

"Yes, I have, sir," responded Hemingway. "Several things. I've sent one of them round to your Dr. Rotherhope by one of my chaps, and I hope he'll be able to let me have a report on it tonight. He told me he'd got a small laboratory, so I don't think I shall have to send it all the way to Nottingham to be analysed."

"What is it?"

"I can't tell you that, sir: I only know what I hope it may be. It's quite a long story."

"Then have a cigarette, or light your pipe, and tell it to me!" invited the Colonel. "Nothing more you wanted to say to me, is there, Mitcham?"

"No, sir," replied the stout Superintendent regretfully, and withdrew.

"Now!" said the Colonel.

"Well, sir, putting it baldly, Sampson Warrenby wasn't shot at 7.15; and in all probability he wasn't shot with a rifle."

"Good God! How do you arrive at that?"

Hemingway told him. He listened in attentive silence, surprise in his face, and a good deal of respect, but when Hemingway reached the end of his story, and said, with a rueful smile: "I missed a lot of points on this case, and I don't deny it," he gave a gasp, and exclaimed: "Did you, indeed? You must set yourself a pretty high standard! But this alters the whole case! If the murder was committed between 6.0 and 6.30, you've narrowed the field considerably."

"Unless it was committed by someone we know nothing about, which I don't think, sir, it's narrowed to four people, only two of whom seem at all likely. Those unaccounted for at that time are the Vicar, Mr. Haswell, young Ladislas, and Gavin Plenmeller. If the Vicar got hold of a gun on the side, and shot Warrenby, or anyone else, with it, I'm resigning before I get kicked out. I can't form an opinion about Mr. Haswell, because he's not one who gives away much, but I don't at all fancy him, for various reasons—the principal one being that I haven't discovered even a hint of a motive for his having wanted to put Warrenby away."

"I'm pretty confident you won't," said the Colonel. "I've known him for years—in point of fact, he's a friend of mine—and although a thing like that mustn't be allowed to weigh with either of us, it does enable me to say that if he murdered Warrenby I've been deceived in his character ever since I first knew him!"

"That's all right, sir: he's not my fancy by any means. Which leaves us with Ladislas, and Plenmeller. And of those two I prefer Plenmeller."

"The Pole—Ladislas, as you call him—has a definite motive," the Colonel pointed out. "Plenmeller, I agree, is perhaps the more likely of the two to have thought out and executed such a careful murder, but he seems to have had no motive at all."

"I wouldn't be too sure of that, sir. It's what I particularly wanted to talk to you about. One thing he had which, so far as we know, no one else had, and that's an automatic pistol of the calibre we're looking for. It's listed amongst his brother's guns, and it wasn't in his gun-cabinet when I went to his house. Of course, there's no saying what kind of an armoury Ladislas may have, but I never yet heard that a .22 pistol was issued by any army, English or foreign. And if it wasn't a left-over from the War, I don't know how he could have come by it, for, unless I'm very much mistaken, he's not a member of the underworld, and he wouldn't have the ghost of a notion how to get hold of an illicit gun. So that leaves Gavin Plenmeller, and it's about him I want to consult you, sir."

"I can't tell you a thing," the Colonel said. "I don't like the fellow; I agree that he'd be capable of planning such a murder; but I know of no reason why he should have done it—unless you think the thrillers he writes have gone to his head, and he wanted to prove he could baffle the police!"

"No, I don't think that, sir—though I don't doubt he thinks he can baffle us. I've got a strong suspicion it's the old story of a man getting away with one murder, and believing that because he's fooled the police once he can do it again."

The Colonel sat up with a jerk. "What? Good God, are you suggesting——?"

"I want to know just what happened when Walter Plenmeller was supposed to have committed suicide," said Hemingway.

CHAPTER EIGHTEEN

For perhaps half a minute the Colonel sat staring at him, an expression of mingled incredulity and dismay in his face. Then he said, rather explosively: "Have you any reason for making such a suggestion?"

"Yes, sir, that!" said Hemingway, laying Walter Plenmeller's letter on the desk. "It was found amongst Warrenby's papers—and I should like to know why he took it out of the file, and kept it locked up in a tin-box."

"Took it out of the file? But that is the most irregular—— Good heavens!"

"Highly irregular," agreed Hemingway. "It's safe to assume he had a good reason for doing it. I'm bound to say I don't see what it was, but I've got a hunch that letter contains the clue I'm looking for."

The Colonel had picked the letter up, and was reading it. "I remember it well," he said. "I hold no brief for Gavin, but in my opinion this is a damnable letter to have written! I thought so at the time. In fact, I was extraordinarily sorry for Gavin."

"It seems to show that his brother hated him pretty bitterly, and I suppose he wouldn't have done that without cause."

"That's nonsense!" the Colonel said. "Walter didn't hate him at all! What you've got to understand is that Walter was always an uncertain-tempered man, and after he got shot up in the War he used to fly off the handle at the smallest provocation. How much he actually suffered I don't know, and I doubt if anyone did, but he was a real case of nerves shot to pieces. He certainly used to get appalling migraines, and he was always complaining of insomnia. The London specialist he went to prescribed tablets for that. It was established that he took one on the night of his death."

"He didn't by any chance take a lethal dose?"

"No. Apart from what the post-mortem revealed, the house-keeper—she's there still, by the way—testified that when she dusted his room the morning before, she noticed that only one tablet was left in the bottle he kept on the bedside-table. Another bottle, unopened, was found in his medicine-chest."

There was a very alert look in the Chief Inspector's face. "So that although he had the means to his hand to commit suicide in the easiest and most pleasant way possible, he chose to gas himself? That seems to me quite an interesting point, sir, if you don't mind my saying so."

"You mean it's a point we should have gone into."

"I wouldn't go so far as to say that, but it does rather strike one, doesn't it?" said Hemingway apologetically.

"It didn't. And in justice to Inspector Thropton, who was in charge of the case, I must say that there was no reason why it should have. It's quite possible that Walter didn't know what the lethal dose was, or what its immediate effect might be. I don't think it's surprising that he should have preferred to take his usual dose, to send him to sleep, and turned on the gas. Surely that was as pleasant a way of killing himself as any other?"

"I should think it would be," agreed Hemingway, "if the tablet sent him to sleep in a matter of a minute or so. But if it was like any sleeping-draught I ever heard of, and took about half an hour to act—well, then I don't think it *was* such a pleasant way of dying. And, what's more, I don't see what he took it for at all."

The Colonel laid his pipe down. "Damn you, Hemingway!" he said, with an uncertain laugh. "You're beginning to make me feel uncomfortable! I suppose we ought to have considered that—but there didn't seem to be the smallest reason to suspect that there had been foul play! It's true that Gavin was his half-brother's heir, but Plenmeller wasn't a rich man! There's the house, and what's left of the estate, but I can tell you with certainty that Plenmeller found it hard to make both ends meet. Would Gavin have murdered his brother just to possess himself of a dwindling income, and a house he can't afford to run as it should be run?"

"Well, sir, I take it that would depend on what the state of his own finances were," said Hemingway. "Judging by that letter, they weren't any too healthy. '*You only want to come here for what you can get out of me,*' seems to show that he was trying to get money out of Walter. Did anything come out about that at the inquest?"

"No. I don't think anything much was said about it. It was so obvious—it *seemed* so obvious that things had got to be too much for Walter. It wasn't as though he'd never had such an idea, you know. He'd often said that he was tempted to put an end to himself. No one thought he meant it—it sounds an unkind thing to say, but he was so wrapped up in his ailments that he was sometimes quite maudlin about himself, and damned boring, too!—but it turned out that he had meant it. Or so we believed."

"Yes, I see, sir. But you said a minute or two ago that he didn't hate his brother. This letter looks to me as though he did."

"Yes, but you didn't know him," the Colonel said. "To me, this reads like Walter in one of his rages—Dr. Warcop called 'em nerve-storms. I can't tell you the number of flaming rows he had with people. He flew out at me once, in the Club, over something quite trivial. I didn't pay any heed, and it soon blew over. He was like that with Gavin, but I'm quite sure that he was fond of him, in his way. He was a good bit older, you know, and in the days before his own health was wrecked he was always very sorry for Gavin. He was proud of him, too. Used to talk a lot about his books, and how clever he was. There was nothing he liked better than hearing Gavin scoring off people. Only, of course, sooner or later, Gavin would score off *him*, and then the fat was in the fire again. It's fair to say that no one could amuse him more or infuriate him more. I can't tell you the number of times he's sworn he'd never have Gavin in his house again, and blackguarded him to anyone he could get to listen to his grievances. But it always ended in smoke. As soon as he'd cooled off, he used to start missing him, I think. You can imagine that he hadn't many real friends. People naturally shied off, and it's my belief he was lonely. Anyway, I can assure you that this sort of wild diatribe——" he flicked the letter with one finger—"didn't make much impression on those of us who'd known for years just how much his furies were worth. Why, it can't have been more than three weeks before he died that he had some sort of a row with Gavin, and bored everyone in the smoking-room one afternoon by talking in exactly the style of this letter, and swearing that *this* time he meant what he said, and that he wasn't going to *see* Gavin again, much less allow him to come down to Thornden House. Well, I can only tell you that about three days before his death he was here in Bellingham, to meet Gavin at the station, and to take him out to Thornden in a hired car, and as pleased as possible about it!"

"That's interesting," said Hemingway. "And what did Gavin do, in three days, to drive his brother into committing suicide?"

"It does sound extraordinary, of course," the Colonel admitted. "Dr. Warcop—yes, I know what you feel about him, but, after all, he was Walter's medical attendant, and he must have known a good deal about him!—Dr. Warcop, as I say, considered that the balance of his mind was disturbed at the time. How much Gavin may have had to do with that, no one can tell. He certainly thought that Walter exaggerated his ailments, and the letter Walter wrote indicates clearly that he didn't scruple to say so. He himself said at the inquest that Walter had complained of migraine on that last day. He described him as 'more than ordinarily on edge'. I remember that he was asked if there had been any quarrel between them, and he replied quite frankly that he had become so impatient with his brother for indulging in what he called 'querulous self-pity', that he had spoken his mind on the subject. Dr. Warcop's opinion, which he expressed privately to me, was that this might well have been enough, in the mood Walter was then in, to have pushed him right over the edge. You can say, morally speaking, that Gavin was at least partly responsible for his brother's death. There's no doubt he behaved quite heartlessly to him. Whether he hoped to goad him into committing suicide is a question which, thank God, lay beyond our province! In fairness to him, I should tell you, perhaps, that his subsequent conduct was meticulously correct."

"I expect he made a good witness," said Hemingway thoughtfully.

"A very good witness, under extremely trying circumstances," said the Colonel. "One could scarcely have blamed him had he destroyed that letter, but he did no such thing. He put it immediately into Inspector Thropton's hands. Of course, it's true that it was the housekeeper who first saw the letter, and gave it to him, but she gave me the impression of being fonder of Gavin than of Walter, and it's my private opinion that she might have been coaxed or bribed to say nothing about it. It's to Gavin's credit that he made no attempt to conceal it from us."

An odd little smile flickered in Hemingway's eyes. "Very proper, sir, I'm sure."

"*Now* what's in your mind?" demanded the Colonel suspiciously.

"Well, sir, it was the letter which made you all take it for granted the unfortunate gentleman had committed suicide, wasn't it?" suggested Hemingway.

A buzzer sounded in the room; the Colonel picked up one of the two telephones on his desk, listened, and said shortly: "Send him in!" He then laid the instrument down and said: "Harbottle, wanting you."

"Good!" said Hemingway. "I sent him round to Warrenby's office to pick up the file of that inquest. He must have found Coupland still there."

"I think you'd better read the transcript of the proceedings before I say anything more," said the Colonel.

"I will, sir." Hemingway picked up Walter Plenmeller's letter, and looked meditatively at it. "When you first read this, it strikes you like any other suicide-letter, doesn't it? It's only when you come to think about it that you get the idea that there's something not quite right about it."

"In what way?"

Hemingway cocked his head a little to one side, dubiously surveying the letter. " '*This is the last letter you'll ever receive from me, and I don't propose ever to set eyes on you again,*' " he read aloud. "Well, I suppose that's one way of saying you mean to do yourself in, but it doesn't seem to me a natural way to put it. '*You only want to come here for what you can get out of me, and to goad me into losing my temper with your damned tongue, and to be maddened by you on top of all I have to suffer is too much.*' " He lowered the paper. "You know, sir, the more I think about that, the less I like it. Sounds to me more as if he was telling his brother he wouldn't have him about the place any more than that he meant to kill himself."

"What about '*I've reached the end of my tether*'?" countered the Colonel. "Then, that bit about the place being Gavin's sooner than he expected?"

" '... *and when you step into my shoes you can congratulate yourself on having done your bit towards finishing me off,*' " read Hemingway. He rubbed the tip of his nose reflectively. "Doesn't say Gavin had driven him to commit suicide, does he? More like a general strafe against him for plaguing him when his health wasn't good enough to stand any worry." He saw the scepticism in the Colonel's face, and added: "Take it this way, sir! Supposing he hadn't committed suicide, and Gavin had happened to show you that letter: would you have thought that was what he'd had in mind?"

The door opened to admit Inspector Harbottle. The Colonel grunted a greeting, and took the letter out of Hemingway's hand, and read it through once more. "No," he said, having considered it for a minute or two. "I don't know that I should. I should probably have thought it was written in one of his fits of temper. But he did commit suicide!"

Hemingway turned to Harbottle, and received from him a sheaf of papers, saying briefly: "Thanks, Horace! Mind if I go through this lot now, sir?"

"No, I should prefer you to. Sit down, Inspector!"

Harbottle pulled up a chair to his Chief's elbow, and together they read the report of the inquest, while the Colonel, after watching Hemingway's face for a few minutes, chose a fresh pipe from the rack on his desk, filled and lit it, and sat smoking, and staring out of the window. For some time nothing broke the silence but the crackle of the sheets as they were turned over, and, once, a request from Harbottle, not so swift a reader as his Chief, that a page should not be turned for a moment. A frown gathered on Hemingway's brow as he read, and several times he flicked the pages back to refer to something which had gone before. When he finally laid the sheaf down there was a very intent look in his eyes, and he did not immediately speak.

The Colonel glanced at him. "Well? Quite straightforward, isn't it?"

"Wonderfully," said Hemingway. "Just as if all the wheels had been oiled—which I don't doubt they had been."

The Colonel flushed. "You believe that we missed something?"

"Sorry, sir! I do. Mind you, I'm not surprised! You'd none of you any reason to suspect Walter's letter wasn't what it seemed to be. I daresay I wouldn't have started to smell a rat, if I hadn't come upon it amongst Warrenby's own papers, where it had no business to be. It was that which set me thinking."

"But, good heavens, Hemingway, are you suggesting that Warrenby, acting as Coroner, suspected all along that the letter was a fake?" exclaimed the Colonel, in horrified accents.

"Not all along, no," replied Hemingway. "I should say it was only when he got to thinking about it more particularly that he began to have his doubts, same like me. Probably after Gavin took up his residence in Thornden, and showed clearly what sort of a neighbour he was going to be. Silly of him to have made an enemy of Warrenby. That was his conceit, of course, thinking he could run rings round anyone he chose. Well, I've got plenty of evidence to lead me to suppose that Warrenby's reaction to the sort of contemptuous way Gavin probably treated him would have been to see if he couldn't get some kind of a hold over him. He'd be bound to think over Walter Plenmeller's death. It was easy for him to go over the inquest again, at his leisure. He may have felt as I do about the letter, or there may be something in it, which I haven't spotted, that struck him as fishy. You can take it he didn't remove it from the file because he wanted a bit of bedtime literature."

"Do you believe it to be a forgery? I don't set up to be a handwriting expert, but I'd swear to it as Walter's handwriting."

Hemingway nodded. "Oh, yes, I wasn't questioning that, sir! Do you know if the envelope was preserved?"

"I can't remember that I ever saw an envelope, but if Carsethorn's in the station, we'll soon find out. He was on that case with Thropton," replied the Colonel, picking up the house-telephone.

"He is, sir," said the Inspector. "I've just been having a word with him."

The Sergeant came quickly in answer to the summons. Upon the question being put to him, his eyes narrowed, as though he were bringing a distant view into focus. After a moment's exercise of memory, he said positively: "No, sir. We never saw the envelope. Mr. Plenmeller handed the letter to Inspector Thropton, spread open, like it is now. He said something about supposing he'd got to give it to the police, though his instinct—no, his *baser self* was what he said—made him a sight more inclined to put it on the fire."

"Sounds lifelike." commented Hemingway. "If you ask me, it was his baser self that made him hand you the letter. I wish I could see the envelope, though I don't suppose there was ever a chance that anyone would have been allowed to."

"The housekeeper saw it," said the Sergeant. "I remember she told us how she was the one who saw the letter first. On the bedside-table it was. She said it had the one word, Gavin, written on it."

"It had, had it? Well, it can't be helped: it's a safe bet the housekeeper wouldn't know whether it was Walter's writing, or only a copy of it."

"What are you getting at?" demanded the Colonel. "Why do you think the envelope may have been significant?"

"Just an idea I've got at the back of my mind, sir," replied Hemingway, stretching out his hand to pick up the letter. "A little while ago, you were telling me that only three weeks before Walter's death he was saying that he wouldn't have Gavin in the house again, or even see him."

"But he did have him in the house again. Whatever the quarrel may have been, it was made up."

"Yes, sir. But it occurs to me that that's exactly what he says in this letter." Hemingway raised his eyes from the letter, one brow lifting quizzically, but no one spoke. All three men were watching him closely, and in the Colonel's face was an expression of dawning comprehension. "Well," Hemingway continued, "I've now studied this letter till I'm sick of the sight of it, and, apart from the points I've already mentioned, there's only one thing about it which looks to me a little suspicious. Walter had a sprawling sort of writing, and a trick of joining one word to the next through not bothering to take his pen off the paper. Will you take a look at the date at the top of the page, sir, and tell me what you think?"

He laid the letter down before the Colonel, and, with one accord, Harbottle and Carsethorn moved round the table to obtain a view of it. The Colonel looked closely at it, and then across the desk at Hemingway. "The figure 2 seems rather close to the 5," he said slowly.

"Look where the light, upward stroke from the Y of May reaches it!" said Hemingway. "It joins the 2 at the bottom of the figure, not, as you'd expect, at the loop at the top. How he made a 2, starting from the bottom of the diagonal line, I can't imagine. But if you carry that faint line from the Y on, in your mind's eye, the way it's going, I think you'll find it would join the 5 exactly where it should, supposing Walter had dated his letter May 5th, and not May 25th."

The Sergeant drew in his breath with a hissing sound; Harbottle cast a glance of grim, vicarious pride at his Chief; the Colonel sat back rather limply in his chair, and said; "Good God! You think this letter may have been written at the time of the quarrel I told you about——But it's diabolical!"

"Well, it'll have to go up to our expert immediately, sir, before we can be sure. It's little more than guess-work as yet. And I wonder whether it's already been in the hands of an expert?" he added pensively. "I should say it had—though not our chap."

Harbottle, who had glanced at his watch, said: "Let me take

it, Chief! I can catch the 6.35 train, and come back first thing in the morning. I've just time to put a call through to Headquarters, and warn them to stand by."

Hemingway nodded, and gave him the letter. As he left the room, with his long stride, Sergeant Carsethorn said in a shocked voice: "But—but are you telling us, sir, that it wasn't a case of suicide at all?"

"I won't put it as high as that till I get a verdict on that letter," replied Hemingway. "But, assuming for the moment that the letter *was* written on the 5th May, and not the 25th, the suicide doesn't look anything like as good. If you hadn't been given that letter, you'd have looked a deal more closely into it than you did, wouldn't you? Let's take a look at it now! First, we have this Mrs. Bromwich deposing that her master had been in one of his bad moods that day. What put him in a bad mood? Migraine, or his brother Gavin, carefully working him up? We shall never know the answer, of course, so we'll leave that. At 10.0, Mrs. Bromwich goes up to bed. Her room's over the kitchen, and there's a door that shuts the servants' quarters off from the main bedrooms. I expect it corresponds with the one downstairs, which I've seen. The gardener, we find, sleeps over the stables. Half an hour later, Gavin goes to bed—or so he states. The Coroner put a question to him about that. I wonder if he had his suspicions as early as that?" Hemingway hunted through the transcript. "Yes, here we are. Asked him if he usually went to bed so early. Answer: No, very rarely. Had you any reason for changing your custom? Answer: My presence appeared to exacerbate my brother, so I thought it wise to remove myself. Quite neat. Gives the picture of Walter beside himself, and leaves us to suppose that Gavin may have been asleep when the gas fumes began to creep out of Walter's room. I should say he took his own measures to keep them out of his own room. We have nothing after that until we come to Mrs. Bromwich taking Walter's early tea to his room. She said there was a funny smell, which made her cough, and she couldn't get into Walter's room. So she goes across the upper hall to wake Gavin. Finds him asleep, tells him there's something wrong. He smells the gas at once, and gets up quickly, and goes with her to Walter's room, first putting on his dressing-gown and slippers. All very natural—and I daresay the dressing-gown had a pocket. He tries the door, finds it's locked, and sets his shoulder to it, breaking the lock. Gas fumes make them both reel back. Then we come to the handsome tribute Mrs. Bromwich paid to 'Mr. Gavin'. He didn't hesitate. He dashed into the room, flung back the curtains, and opened all three casements. The wind was blowing in at that side of the house; it seemed to blow the gas right down Mrs. Bromwich's throat; and fair made her choke. And considering how much gas there must have been in the room, I'm sure I'm not surprised. Mr. Gavin then makes another dash for the gas-stove, and turns off the tap, and gasps out an order to Mrs. Bromwich: she was to go downstairs at once, and ring up the doctor. So that gets Mrs. Bromwich nicely out of the way. By the time she gets back, Mr. Gavin is standing at the head of the staircase, looking dreadfully bad, and coughing fit to break a blood-vessel. Very likely, I should think: there were quite a few things he had to do in the room before she came back. If I'm right, he had to slip the door-key under Walter's pillow, for Dr. Warcop to find in due course; he had to stuff a bit of rag into the keyhole; he had to finish off the job of fixing adhesive tape round the door. I should think he put most of it on when he went in the night before: it was bound to get broken as soon as the door was opened, so he was safe to stick it on everywhere but on the side where the door opens. As for that towel, which we hear got thrust back when the door was burst open, and had obviously been stuffed between the bottom of the door and the floor, my guess is that it was carefully arranged a little way away from the door, to present just that appearance. Well, back comes Mrs. Bromwich, saying the doctor's coming at once. Gavin then tells her it's too late: Walter must have been dead for hours, and it's a case for the police. Well, we know Dr. Warcop isn't what you might call good at fixing times, but he doesn't seem to have much doubt about this. Walter was cold. When he turned up, Gavin told him it was too late for him to do anything, and he let Mrs. Bromwich go with him into the room. Which is when Mrs. Bromwich sees that letter, and gives it to him, and Dr. Warcop finds the key of the room. So there it is: an open-and-shut case, with everyone behaving very properly all round. Later, Gavin gives evidence at the inquest, and the result of that is that all the people who'd been thinking he'd behaved pretty badly to his brother start thinking that, after all, it's a bit rough on him to have to sit there listening to Walter's letter being read aloud in court, and very noble it was of him not to have destroyed it. I'll bet he enjoyed that day!"

There was a pause. The Sergeant, who had been listening, fascinated, to this exposition, said: "You've got me believing that's how it happened!"

"I've got myself believing it," returned Hemingway.

"If it's true," said the Colonel, "if we find that you're right about the letter, you've got a strong case against Gavin, without any further evidence."

"I want a stronger," said Hemingway. "I want that Colt Woodsman pistol."

"Ah!" said the Sergeant heavily. "And he's had plenty of time to get rid of it."

"If he has got rid of it," agreed Hemingway.

"Good lord, sir, you don't think he'd keep it, do you?"

"I don't know. You've got to bear in mind that he thinks we're searching for a rifle. What's more, it isn't all that easy to dispose of a pistol, particularly when you haven't got a car to get you well away from your own district, to some likely pond, or something of that nature. The thing I'm afraid of is that he may have thrown it into this river I've heard so much about."

"You needn't be afraid of that," said the Colonel. "It's quite shallow, and at the moment there's hardly any water in it at all. I've never known such a season: we haven't had a spate since the beginning of March. He's more likely to have thrust it down a rabbit-hole, or to have buried it."

"Not anywhere near Fox Lane, or Wood Lane, or the footpath, sir!" struck in the Sergeant. "If you happened to be thinking he might have done it straight away! We fair combed the ground there, that I'll swear to! I had five chaps out there all Sunday morning."

"I don't see this bird burying it," intervened Hemingway. "Nor yet pushing it down a rabbit-hole, with all respect to you, sir! If he buried it, he'd have run the risk of the new-turned earth's being spotted. There's his own garden, of course, but that seems to me even more risky, with that gardener-groom of his on the premises. As for shoving it down a rabbit-hole, I don't see him doing that. Setting aside, rabbit-holes are places we'd be bound to suspect, you never know when some dog won't sneak off hunting and start excavating the very hole you've chosen. What's more, unless he's found some place where it can stay safely for ever, it's got to be where he can retrieve it as soon as the hunt's been called off. So he wouldn't have poked it into a midden, or a haystack, or anything like that. It wouldn't altogether surprise me if he's got it hidden away somewhere in his house."

"Well, it would me!" said the Sergeant suddenly. "Not when he knew you were on the case, sir! He wouldn't have taken any chances once he'd seen you."

Hemingway regarded him in some amusement. "Now, come on, my lad, what do *you* want to borrow?" he demanded.

The Sergeant grinned, but stuck to his guns. "Look here, sir, I was with you on Sunday evening, when you met him for the first time, in the Red Lion! Do you remember I didn't have to tell him who you were, because he recognised you straight off? Talked about a case you'd been on. Well, it was plain enough that he had a pretty fair idea of what he was up against! I could tell from the way he spoke that he knew the Yard had sent down one of their best men."

"What do you mean, *one* of their best men?" interrupted Hemingway.

The Colonel laughed. "Spare the Chief Inspector's blushes,

Carsethorn! But he may easily be right, Hemingway. Since Plenmeller hadn't an alibi, he must have faced the possiblity of having his house searched. But if you don't think he buried the gun, what do you imagine he could have done with it?"

"Well, looking at it from the psychological angle, sir, I should say he'd go in for something a bit more classy."

"Railway cloakroom?"

Hemingway shook his head. "Too hackneyed for him. Besides, he might expect it to be one of the first places I'd check up on, if ever I got on to the real weapon. If this were London, I should want to know if he rented a safe deposit, but I don't suppose you've got any here, have you?"

"I'm afraid not."

"Ah, well! I daresay it would have been a bit too obvious anyway," said Hemingway philosophically. "He's probably put it somewhere I should never think of looking for it, which means that I shall have to rely more than I like on circumstantial evidence, or read all the books he's written, on the chance that he's used the idea before."

The Sergeant, who had been thinking profoundly, said abruptly: "You know what, sir? Mr. Plenmeller ought to have handed in his brother's guns as soon as he was dead. It's illegal for him to keep them. I don't mean it's a thing we should make a fuss about, in the circumstances, because very likely he isn't well-up in the regulations, and he may think that if the licence for them hasn't run out, which it hasn't, it's all right for him to hang on to them. How would it be if I was to send one of our chaps out to call on him, like it was a routine-job? Just a uniformed constable, sent to explain that all this business has brought it to the attention of the police that the late Mr. Plenmeller's guns were never handed in, and that they must be. He can have a list of them, and check it over with Mr. Gavin Plenmeller. What's Mr. Plenmeller going to do then?"

"Hand over the guns in the cabinet, and deny all knowledge of the Colt," answered Hemingway promptly.

"If he did that, it would look pretty suspicious, wouldn't it, sir?"

"It would, but you'd never prove he was lying. From what I've seen of Mr. Gavin Plenmeller, I wouldn't envy your uniformed constable his job, either. He'd find Gavin all readiness to oblige, and he could think himself lucky if he got away without having had to help turn out every chest and cupboard trunk in the house in an attempt to find the gun. And all he'd have achieved at the end would be to have put Plenmeller wise to what I'm up to. No, thanks! I'd as soon that gentleman went on thinking he's fooled me until I'm ready to put handcuffs on him. You never know: he might take it into his head I'd look well on a mortuary-slab."

"He wouldn't dare do that!" said the Sergeant, grinning broadly.

"Oh, wouldn't he? Seems to me that if he thinks I'm the original Sherlock Holmes it's about the best thing he could do! It's a pity I'm not, because if I were I daresay I should have deduced by this time where I ought to look for that Colt. As it is, I shall have to work on the evidence I've got."

"Look here!" said the Colonel, a little uneasily. "What you've been saying is extraordinarily plausible, but aren't we going too fast? We're all three of us talking as though there were no doubt Gavin murdered Warrenby!"

"There isn't, sir," said Hemingway calmly.

CHAPTER NINETEEN

THIS pronouncement made the Colonel look searchingly at him. "What makes you so confident?" he asked.

"Flair," replied Hemingway, without a moment's hesitation.

"Eh?" said the Sergeant.

"The Chief Inspector means—er—intuition," explained the Colonel. "Well, Hemingway, you know your own business best. What's the next move?"

"I want Sergeant Carsethorn to do a bit of investigation for me, if you don't mind, sir."

"Very happy to, I'm sure!" said the gratified Sergeant.

"It'll be better if you do it," exclaimed Hemingway. "You know the party concerned, and you've already questioned him once. You can say you forgot to make a note of what he said, or any other lie you fancy: we don't want him to spread it all over the village that you've been asking searching questions about Gavin Plenmeller."

"You can trust me, sir!" the Sergeant assured him. "But who is it?"

"I don't think you ever told me his name. But I seem to remember that when you were describing the dramatis personæ to me, in this very room, when I first came down here, you spoke of some old boy who's got a cottage opposite the entrance to Wood Lane."

"That's right, sir: George Rugby."

"Rugby! Then you did mention the name, because that's brought it back to me. My memory's not as good as it used to be," said Hemingway, shaking his head over this lapse.

"Too bad, sir!" said the Sergeant, once more on the broad grin. "Still, it's good enough to be going on with! What do you want me to find out from Rugby?"

"Didn't you tell me he'd seen Mrs. Cliburn and Plenmeller coming away from The Cedars on Saturday evening? You were trying to find out if either of them did anything suspicious, but neither of them did, and neither of them was carrying anything that might have contained a rifle, which were the two points we happened to be concentrating at the time. The really important point escaped you. Now, don't take on about it! It escaped me too—which was probably because you were talking so much I never got time to think," he added, as the Sergeant's face brightened again. "What I want to know now is, which came down the lane first? Mrs. Cliburn, or Mr. Plenmeller?"

"My Gawd!" exclaimed the Sergeant involuntarily. He cast

a deprecating look at the Chief Constable, and said: "Beg your pardon, sir! But he's quite right: I did miss that, and I oughtn't to have. By the time I got round to making enquiries in the village, I'd interviewed so many people—still, it's no excuse! I didn't suspect anyone in particular, and what with old Rugby being one of those who take half an hour to tell you a simple story, and me taking it for granted he'd seen Mr. Plenmeller before he saw Mrs. Cliburn, I properly slipped up." He glanced at his watch. "I'd like to go out to Thornden right now, sir, if you've no objection. The police-station is only two doors off Rugby's cottage, so I can pretend I've got business with Hobkirk; and if Rugby's sitting outside, which he probably will be on an evening like this, it'll be natural enough for me to stop and pass the time of day with him—supposing anyone should happen to be watching what I'm up to."

"All right," said the Colonel. "But you'll have to be careful not to let Rugby smell a rat, Carsethorn!"

"Yes, sir," said the Sergeant. "I shall tell him the Chief Inspector properly tore me off the strip for not giving him a written report of what he said."

"Of course, I *would*!" remarked Hemingway, as the door shut behind the triumphant Sergeant.

"You're having a thoroughly demoralizing effect upon my officers," said the Colonel severely. "By the way, have you done anything more about that other affair? Ainstable's business?"

"I asked my Chief to make discreet enquiries, sir. Which reminds me that I may as well tell him to forget it," said Hemingway, getting up, and gathering his various papers together.

"I won't pretend I'm not glad you're dropping that," said the Colonel frankly.

"Nothing to do with me, sir," said Hemingway, tucking the papers under his arm. "Unless there's anything more you want to discuss with me, I'll be getting along. Precious little more I can do till Harbottle gets back, except get Warrenby's clerk to go through the documents I took away from Fox House, and that can wait till I've had my supper."

"Do you know where he lives?"

"I'll find out, sir."

The Colonel got up, and held out his hand, saying, with a faint smile: "You do find things out, don't you? Goodnight, then—and good luck!"

Upon the following morning, the Chief Inspector consumed a leisurely and a somewhat belated breakfast. He liked to be left in piece at this meal, and since he did not expect Harbottle to arrive in Bellingham until twenty-seven minutes past ten, when the fast train from London made Bellingham its first stop, and knew very well that his identity had been disclosed by the landlord to the three Commercials who had arrived at the Sun on the previous day, it seemed desirable to him not to emerge from his bedroom until these fellow-guests had departed on their several errands. He timed his appearance in the coffee-room well, but he had reckoned without his host, Mr. Wick, proprietor of the Sun, and also its chef, not only fried for him four rashers of bacon, two eggs, two sausages, and a tomato, with his own far from fair hands, but elected to carry this slight repast in to the coffee-room as well, and to stand over the Chief Inspector while he ate it. Simply clad in a stained pair of gray slacks and a dirty vest, he leaned his hairy arms on the back of a chair, and entertained Hemingway with an account of his own career, inviting, at the same time, any interesting confidences Hemingway might feel encouraged to repose in him. But as the Chief Inspector's only contribution to the conversation took the form of an earnestly worded piece of advice, to the effect that he should never show himself to his clients for fear of putting them off their food, he took himself off at last, leaving Hemingway to drink a third cup of well-sweetened tea, and to peruse the columns of his chosen newspaper.

He left the inn a little while before the London train was due, and walked through the town towards the station. He found South Street extremely congested, with various persons trying to park their cars against the kerb, and holding up all the traffic while they performed their complicated evolutions; and when he reached the market-place he discovered the reason for all this activity. Wednesday was Bellingham's market-day, and the wide square was crowded with omnibuses, stalls, vociferous merchants, and keen shoppers. Every branch of trade seemed to be represented, from a stall displaying bric-à-brac to one presided over by a stout individual who invitingly slapped a large and bright yellow object, stentoriously proclaiming: 'HaddOCKS, haddOCKS, haddOCKS!"

Hemingway, threading his way through the crowd, came upon Abby Dearham, who was carrying a basket already over-flowing and who seemed to be in attendance on her aunt. She greeted him with her unaffected friendliness. "Hallo! Whatever are you doing here? Are you marketing?"

"No, but I can see I ought to be," he replied.

"Well, you really do pick up the most marvellous bargains sometimes. Everyone always comes in on market-day: it's one of the done things. If you happen to like goats' milk cheese, the Women's Institute, over there, beside the fruit-and-vegetables, have got some, which my aunt brought in and——"

Hemingway waited expectantly, but it was rapidly borne in upon him that Miss Dearham had suddenly lost interest in him. She appeared to have caught sight of a heavenly vision, and was staring beyond the Chief Inspector, an expression of fond idiocy upon her countenance. Turning his head, he perceived young Mr. Haswell was bearing down upon them, looking quite as foolish as Miss Dearham, and even more oblivious of his surroundings. "I thought you'd be here!" he said.

"Charles, you are dreadful!" said Miss Dearham, in a besotted voice. "You ought to be working!"

The Chief Inspector, realizing that he was intruding into an idyll, and that two at least of Thornden's detectives had abandoned the search for truth, withdrew without excuse or leave-taking, and proceeded on his way to the station.

The train was just pulling out of it when he reached it, and he met Inspector Harbottle in the station-yard. The Inspector came striding briskly towards him. "You win, Chief!" he said.

"Well, I hope I shall, but I'm not liking it much at the moment," replied Hemingway, disappointingly unenthusiastic. "Was it the date?"

"It was. The Superintendent had Acton stay on. He says you're a wonder, sir."

"He's mistaken. However, I'm glad there's something I've managed to spot."

"Anything gone wrong?" asked the Inspector anxiously.

"No, but I'm getting to be annoyed with myself. I don't deny that that letter strengthens my case a lot, but the one thing I want I'm damned if I know where to look for!"

"The gun," said Harbottle. "I've been wondering about that all the way down from town. I don't see that we've a hope of finding it, but I think you've got enough on Plenmeller to justify you making an arrest. What did the doctor say about the stains on the carpet?"

"Oh, they're blood all right! Same group as Warrenby's, too. The doctor got hold of the collar he was wearing when he was shot: that was bloodstained, of course. And I took those papers round to Coupland last night, and he was quite sure two letters at least were missing. That's all right, as far as it goes, but neither the bloodstains nor the missing letters incriminates Plenmeller. I rather hoped I might be able to establish that he came down Wood Lane *after* the Vicar's wife did. Do you remember Carsethorn saying that one of the villagers had seen them both coming away from The Cedars on Saturday? Well, I sent Carsethorn out to Thornden after you left yesterday, to talk to this character."

"No good?"

"I wouldn't go so far as to say that exactly. I should say, from what Carsethorn told me about a highly exasperating interview, that Plenmeller did come into the High Street later than Mrs. Cliburn, but as the old man contradicted himself

219

three times, not to mention remembering what happened, because of its having been at that exact moment that something else happened, only, when he came to think it over, that wasn't on *Saturday*, but on *Thursday*—well, you know the sort of thing!—he isn't the kind of witness anyone would want to call."

"We'll do without him, then," said the Inspector, in a heartening tone. "Hallo! Market-day?"

"Yes. I ran into Miss Dearham and young Haswell on my way to the station—very far gone, both of them!—and I gather the better part of Thornden's in the town. We'll skirt round the side, or I may be made to buy a goats' milk cheese."

The Inspector had no idea why his chief should be made to buy cheese of any kind, but he forbore to enquire into the matter, suspecting him of ill-timed levity. Together they circumvented the market-place, and began to make their way down South Street.

"What does the Colonel feel about it?" asked Harbottle.

"Oh, he thinks it's doubtful! That isn't worrying me. I know Plenmeller did it, but I don't like a case that rests only on circumstantial evidence."

"A lot of murder-cases do," Harbottle ventured to point out.

"Well, if this one does, I can see myself getting unpopular with the D.P.P. over this. I wouldn't mind so much with the ordinary run of criminals, but we're not dealing with that kind. Our interesting friend is too clever to take any chances with."

"Well, what do you—— Hallo, there he is!"

"Where?"

"Just gone into that bank," replied the Inspector, nodding towards a building a few yards farther down the street. "He didn't look as if he was worrying much, I must say. It beats me how a chap can——" He broke off, for he perceived that his Chief was not attending to him.

Hemingway had, in fact, stopped in front of a linen-draper's shop, a most peculiar look on his face, his eyes a little narrowed. Surprised, the Inspector said: "What's the matter, sir?"

His attention recalled, Hemingway looked at him. "Horace, I've got it!" he said. "Come on!"

Wholly at sea, the Inspector followed him down the street, and into the bank.

The bank was as crowded as the rest of Bellingham, most of those waiting in queues before the various cashier's guichets being housewives, much encumbered by baskets and parcels. Gavin Plenmeller had not joined any of the queues, but was writing a cheque at one of the tables provided for that purpose. His back was turned to the door, and, after a quick glance at him, the Chief Inspector stepped up to the broad counter, and ruthlessly interrupted a cashier who was engaged in counting thick wads of dirty-looking notes, behind a notice which gave customers to understand that he was in balk, and must not be disturbed. Upon being accosted, he began, in repressive accents, to request the Chief Inspector to go to the next desk. However, Hemingway had thrust his card under the grille, and the inscription it bore worked like a charm. The cashier abandoned his calculations, and looked a startled enquiry.

"Any one with the manager?" asked Hemingway.

"No, I don't think—— That is to say, I'll go and——"

"That's all right," said Hemingway cheerfully. He nodded towards a frosted glass-door. "That his office?"

"Yes, but——"

"Thanks!" said Hemingway, and turned, just as Plenmeller got up from the writing-table, and came towards the counter.

The Inspector, bewildered, but very much on the alert, thought that there was something more than natural surprise in Plenmeller's face. He gave no melodramatic start, but he seemed to stiffen, like an animal freezing, and the Inspector saw a muscle twitch in his cheek. The next moment the faintly sneering smile had curled his mouth, and he said coolly: "If it isn't Scotland Yard again! Good-morning, gentlemen! Is there anything I can do for you?"

"Yes, there's something I want to ask you," responded Hemingway affably. "It's a lucky thing I caught sight of you. Not but what it's a bit too crowded here for my taste. Let's go into the manager's office!"

"I'm entirely at your disposal, but may I suggest that the King's Head is just across the street? I can't help feeling that the manager might not view with favour an invasion of his sanctum. If you don't mind waiting until I've cashed this cheque——"

"From the look of things, that'll be twenty minutes at least, and I'm in a hurry. I daresay the manager won't object," said Hemingway, edging him towards the glass door.

Plenmeller checked, found the Inspector immediately behind him, and shot a quick, searching glance at Hemingway. His brows went up. "Is it so urgent?" he asked lightly.

"Just a point I've an idea you may be able to clear up for me," replied Hemingway, opening the glass door, and pushing him into the room beyond it.

The manager was seated at a large knee-hole desk, the cashier to whom Hemingway had spoken at his elbow. He looked up over the top of his spectacles, by no means pleased by the unceremonious entrance of three uninvited persons. "Mr. Plenmeller?" he said, surprised. He glanced from Harbottle to Hemingway, and then at the card in his hand. "Chief Inspector—er—Hemingway? You wish to see me?"

"Properly speaking, it's Mr. Plenmeller who wishes to see you," said Hemingway. "He deposited a package with you on

Monday, for safe-keeping, and now he wants to show me what's in it.—*Take him*, Harbottle!"

* * * * *

"But how did you *know*, Chief?" Harbottle demanded, when at last he found himself alone with the Chief Inspector.

"I didn't," replied Hemingway calmly. "I took a chance on it."

"Took—— You never!" said Harbottle, with conviction. A look of foreboding crept into his face. "You aren't going to tell me it was this flair of yours?" he said imploringly.

"I oughtn't to have to tell you!" retorted Hemingway. "Not but what there was a bit more to it than that," he added truthfully. "In fact, I ought to have tumbled to it before I actually did. I told the Chief Constable yesterday that if this were London I should be nosing round the safe-deposits, and why I didn't carry straight on from there, and think of bank-strong-rooms, I can't tell you."

"Everyone was talking you silly," suggested the Inspector helpfully.

"Very likely! And if I have any lip from you, my lad, you'll be sorry!"

"I get into the way of repeating the things you say, sir," explained the Inspector. "But do you mean that just because I told you Plenmeller had gone into the bank you guessed he'd deposited that Colt there?"

"Well, no, not quite," confessed Hemingway. "When you told me that, it came to me in a flash that he was just coming *out* of a bank when I happened to run into him here on Monday morning. Putting two and two together, and taking into account the psychology of Mr. Gavin Plenmeller, it seemed fairly safe to trust my instinct."

"Good lord!" ejaculated the Inspector. "And where would you have been if he hadn't deposited the Colt in the bank?"

"Exactly where I am now. I should have arrested him anyhow. But the instant he set eyes on me I knew I was right. He's a good actor, but seeing me in the bank gave him the nastiest shock he's had—so far."

"But to rush it like that——!" said Harbottle, his respect for forms and ceremonies considerably shocked. "Pushing into the manager's office without a by your leave, and telling him lies about Plenmeller's wanting to show you the contents of a package you'd no proof was in the bank at all! You ought to have had a warrant!"

"Yes, that's where I think quicker than you do, Horace. You try getting a warrant to search a bank! First, you've got to put up a strong case, then you've got to get authority to make the manager disclose that he has received a package from your suspect, and after that you've got to apply for a special warrant, and lastly, just to round things off, you've got to wait for three days after you've presented it before you can execute the warrant! Thanks, I've had some! Meanwhile, Mr. Gavin Plenmeller gets wind of what you're up to, and thinks up an ingenious stalemate. No, the proper thing to do was to rock him right off his balance."

"He couldn't have done anything," argued the Inspector. "We could have had him watched, and the bank too."

"We could, of course, but there's something you're forgetting, Horace. Two things, in fact."

"What are they?" asked the Inspector, frowning.

"All that hanging about would have been a bad curtain. If you hadn't got a silly prejudice against the theatre, you'd know that. And on top of that," said the Chief Inspector comfortably, "I've got a fortnight's leave due to me on Saturday. I *had* to force the pace!"

THE END